THE SEVENTH KING

Maggie Forbush

D1738586

CONTENTS

PART 1: THE LAKES

CHAPTER 1

The old man sat leaning against his usual wall. His torn dirty clothes were the same ones he had on yesterday and every day that I had seen him. No one was on this street by the river. If he wanted to get coins, he was in a painfully bad spot.

I tried not to breathe too deeply as I sat on the cold ground next to him and pressed half a loaf of bread into his dirty hands. He smelled of rot and filth, yet I could not help myself from stopping by to see him. No one deserved to be alone like this.

"You should not risk coming here every day, my dear." The beggar said. His voice was rough and weak.

"I quite like your company." I responded with a smile. I had seen him for months now and had made it a habit to share some of the food I pulled from the garbage left behind the stores. My heart had broken for him as I watched his mind slowly leaving him over time. The first indication that something was wrong was when he started constantly repeating the numbers two and twenty-seven over and over to himself. Then one day he told me 'The gates are not meant to be opened.' There were no gates around us and I had no idea what he was talking about.

I really knew he was losing his mind when he told me, 'He will give up his death freely and yours will follow.' Then came my personal favorite, 'There will be nothing and everything, the beginning and the end, and only the two of you.' It sounded so dark and oddly romantic. I let him ramble these odd things to me as I would sit with him for as long as I felt it was safe. He was the only person I could sit and talk with anyway.

I could tell by the way his eyes were glazed that today was not a good day for his mind. "Trust the Mountain King." He finally said. His words had become even more crazy and more frequently crazy over the last month.

I squeezed his hand gently, "If you say so, I will do it."

"He needs you. You must save the True King." Wherever his mind was today must be very very far away. "You will run through worlds with the five warriors of the west, as swift as wolves, for the king needs you. Do not be afraid."

I looked at his face. Wrinkled and dirty. His ramblings had never sounded this crazy. "Is there somewhere I can take you for the night? It is going to be cold."

"No, no. I have somewhere else I need to be. Watch over yourself." A moment of clarity in his breaking mind. The beggar had not ever asked my name, but it was clear he knew who I was. My face had been plastered all over storefronts for nearly a year. Wanted. A reward offered. I was only still breathing because none of the locals cared to turn me in. Then he looked back at me, eyes cloudy, "Do not be afraid. Go now. He is waiting."

I pressed the other half of the bread into his hands, "Take care of yourself. I will see you tomorrow." I stood and made my way across the river and into the forest where I would stay for the night.

I could tell he was dead from across the street. Some of the bread was still in his hand from the night before. His shabby cloak was crusted in frost. The gods had left us many years ago, but I said a silent prayer anyway. Then I slipped down an alley aiming for the bridge. It was time to leave this town and I knew where I was going.

CHAPTER 2

I opened the lid on the worn wooden podium. *Who had been out here last?* I had guessed right—people did not come hiking in the wilderness while the world was ending. The log book was dirty and the last name written was dated years ago. Name, date, activity, days—*how many days was I expecting to be out here?* Well I was not planning on coming back. I pressed the pen to the paper but no ink showed on the page. I scribbled along the edge of the paper. Nothing. The pen was dead. It was not likely anyone would see the log book anyway. I dropped it back into the box and closed the lid. What was meant to track use of the area—and help rangers know if outdoor enthusiasts who had missed their return dates needed help—was now just a memorial marker.

I adjusted my pack as I looked up the path winding next to the river. This was it. The place I had come to heal those years ago. I had hiked this trail alone under the beating June sun. Stood on the stones in the cold river water. Journaled, cried, and searched my soul for forgiveness on the rock beach. I had found peace within myself that day. Released and accepted my history. Found a reason to accept happiness in my life.

This place was a fitting place for what I was doing now. A small box with my family's ashes was tucked safely in my bag. Why I had slung bear spray on my belt this trip I did not know. I was not planning to leave this mountain alive anyway.

It had not taken me long to reach the campsite situated on a rocky beach next to the river. I spotted an eagle on the way up the canyon, but otherwise the hike had been eerily quiet and lacking in wildlife. I had not wasted time sprinkling my family's ashes and saying a prayer for them. I had thought about this moment for two years, but now I sat staring at the cold black metal in my hands. This part was final. The end. I was not scared, I was at peace with it.

I slowly came back to awareness. The light was changing, the sky turning reddish and the air hazy. I had only seen weather like this with wildfires. I was in wildfire country, but I could smell no smoke beyond my nearly dead fire cracking in the fire pit. I scanned the sky above the mountain tops. No smoke columns either. The fire must be further away. *Would the sky shift so quickly?* Physical pain ached through my chest as I pressed a hand over my heart. I missed him so much I did not know how my heart was still beating. He had taught me all of this—how to build a fire, the weather patterns, the joy, freedom, and calm of being out in the wilderness.

Noises in the brush jerked me from my thoughts. Something was crashing through the forest. And it was not trying to be quiet. No ... there was more than one thing coming.

I jumped up slinging my pack over my shoulders. I learned it early on: keep your pack on, it might protect your back in the event you are attacked by a predator. I clipped the chest strap and realized I was committed to using the gun as the bear spray was still in the pack pocket where I had tucked it when I arrived at the campsite.

A female came bursting through the brush and I nearly fell on my ass as I stumbled back, my fear getting the best of me. *Breathe.* Breathe.

Her eyes got wide with surprise as she crashed to a stop, hitting the ground a few paces in front of me. An arrow was straight through her thigh. A fucking arrow. Blood and dirt covered her hands, face, and clothes. Before either of us could speak a cackling male laugh sounded from the tree line.

"We didn't want to kill you, Sarla, but this is getting rather tedious." The male stepped into the campsite. He had raven black hair and wore black pants with a black short sleeved shirt. He was honed with muscle and held a bow casually in his hand.

"And who might this be? A new friend?" A second male stepped out. He also wore black on black, but his long hair was braided and hung below his shoulders. His face was covered in a neatly groomed beard and his muscles were even larger than the first male's. In his hand was an axe. A fucking axe.

"Like I said. This is getting rather tedious. He has given us permission to just kill you and be done with the games." The first male with the raven black hair drawled as he started to lift his bow. An arrow was already notched into place.

Move. I had to move.

Muscle memory sent my feet sidestepping, my arms raising the gun as I moved. I barely saw the red laser hit the male's chest and I squeezed the trigger. My arms bucked at the force, but I kept moving and turned towards the male with an axe. For a moment our eyes met—time stopped for an instant. My finger relaxed on the trigger. Then male took a step, then another. He was rushing towards me—fast. Unnaturally fast. *When you hesitate, people die.* The thought shook me from my hesitation. Squeeze. Squeeze. Two bullets flew. One hit him in the shoulder. I felt a shock, like static electricity, pulse through my body, but I did not stop. My head was roaring. Squeeze. One more bullet found its mark. The male was only feet from me and I braced as his body crashed into mine. I threw out my hands as I hit the rocks, the gun went flying. As I rolled I saw the male did not move. My chest heaved with a panting breath.

Pain ripped through my scalp as a rough hand grabbed me by my hair. "Fucking bitch!" The male with raven black hair growled.

I was on my back now staring into his black eyes. Evil. That was what I saw. Evil. Hate. Death. Hands wrapped my throat and squeezed. I swung my hands towards his face, but he was too big. Too strong. I saw orange out of the corner of my eye. Bear spray. I stretched my hand for it, but it was just out of reach. I could not breathe. Black spots were already circling my vision.

Use your knife.

It was his voice—my husband's voice—urging me to fight. To live.

I grabbed the chest strap of my pack where my knife was sheathed. Get the knife. *Get the knife.*

Blood spattered my face and the male's body fell on me. I still could not breathe.

"I've got you. I've got you!" A female voice shouted. And the male's weight rolled off of me.

Air rushed back into my lungs and I was coughing. Strong female hands grabbed me. "You have to get up. We have to go!"

A deadly laugh split the air and the red sky turned dark.

"Sarla. Sarla. Sarla. I guess I will have to kill you myself." The voice was nothing but pure darkness and horror. My entire body went cold.

"Die here or come with me now!" The female hissed.

I grabbed her arm and she pulled me up. How she was standing I did not know. Somehow she had more blood covering her … a gash down the side of her face dripping blood.

She raised a hand and splayed her fingers towards the fire pit a few feet away. The embers turned blue as blue and green flames erupted. She was pulling us towards the fire. I turned my head in time to see an arrow burst through her shoulder. Her hand held me tightly as she lurched forward. We were now falling. An angry yell—a growl—bellowed behind us. I could not stop our momentum as we fell straight into the blue green flames.

And we kept falling.

Before fear could even hit my body my breath was punched out of me as I collided face first with glass. Not glass. Snow. The ice crystals had burned tiny cuts into my cheek and hands and knees. I sucked in air. It was cold. It was also quiet. A bird chirped in a tree nearby and I could hear the gentle babbling of a river. Sounds at odds with the adrenaline pounding in my ears.

I peeled myself up from the snow and looked around. It was the same campsite—covered in snow.

I mentally scanned my body. Everything hurt, but I could still move my limbs.

The female … Sarla groaned in the snow next to me and sat up. An arrow through her thigh and one through her shoulder.

"What the fuck?" I had so many questions, but my mouth got the best of me and it was the only thing I could manage to get out. We had just fallen through flames and it was like we had time traveled to winter. My heart was pounding as my mind tried to make sense of what had just happened.

"I am guessing that is not how you thought your day would go?" Sarla laughed then cringed, pressing a hand to her shoulder beneath the arrow protruding from it.

"No." I breathed. "Who—Why were they trying to kill you? Where are we?"

"That. I will answer all of that. But first I need you to help me get these arrows out." She was already tearing back her pant leg around the arrow protruding through her thigh. Black spidered out from the wound like ink. I vomited into the snow.

"Shit. Hey, it's okay. Breathe. This is nasty, but you can do it." Her voice was direct, but warm and encouraging. "I need you to do it or I am going to die out here."

I spat bile from my mouth. I had to pull myself together. I had seen way worse wounds than this, but it had been a few years. I could do this. My chest was pounding. Adrenaline. Massive amounts of adrenaline. I knew I had to ride the wave before I crashed. *I had to survive.* The thought hit me like a ton of bricks. I had not been planning on surviving, but when it came to it, I fought to live.

"Let's do the shoulder first." Sarla continued. I shook my head to clear the thoughts and moved over to Sarla as she spoke. "Break it and then pull it out."

"How am I supposed to break this? It's … metal." I examined the arrow. The entire shaft was metal and dripping a thick black liquid. The point had four jagged prongs, the butt had feathers. I looked at her leg, that arrow was already broken off.

"Fuck. Metal or feathers on the end?" Sarla almost sounded annoyed. Like getting shot with arrows was a normal Tuesday activity.

"Feathers."

"Okay … use your knife. Cut them off and we will pull it all the way out." She said calmly. She was way too calm about this.

My knife. The knife I had fought to grab. The knife that could have helped me live had Sarla not stepped in. Muscle memory seemed to click into place.

I slung my pack off my back and pulled the knife off the chest strap. I set it on the ground next to Sarla and opened my bag. I had a first aid kit in here somewhere. I pulled out tape and a small zip pouch. Pathetic. This first aid kit was not made for wounds like this, but it had to have something to help. Gauze and a few bandaids the size of my hand. That would have to do.

"I am Sarla by the way." At least the males were calling her the right name.

"Genevieve." I replied as I unsheathed the knife. "Here we go."

It was an effort not to vomit again as I pressed bandages to Sarla's shoulder, taping them in place. She had merely clenched her teeth and grunted when I had slid the arrow out. The bandages were in place and thankfully there was not too much blood.

Sarla shifted and winced as she tried to adjust her leg, "Now the leg. Just pull it quick."

I grabbed the end and looked at Sarla. "One. Two." I pulled it out quickly covering the wound with gauze.

"Shit." Sarla gasped.

Shit. The gauze was already soaked through with blood. Tourniquet. I needed a tourniquet. "Put pressure on it!" I instructed as I grabbed Sarla's hand forcing it in place where mine had been as I fumbled with my knife. The handle was wrapped in cording for exactly this use. I quickly freed the cord and wrapped it around her leg, cinching it down.

"How did you know to do that?" Sarla breathed. The bleeding already slowing.

"I took a class a while ago." A class. By class I meant multiple briefings and field training on battlefield patches followed by time in an actual war zone. The lie was easy, she did not need to know everything about me. My hands worked to bandage her leg. "We need help. I don't know much more than this."

"We will go to Beck's. It is a few days from here." Sarla gritted. "He's … He probably won't kill us."

I started shaking. The cold was getting to me. Or the

adrenaline was wearing off. I dug in my bag and pulled out a wool top and leggings.

"Oh I like you. You are prepared." Sarla laughed. A quick change in tone from her brooding last statement. She already was in pants and a leather jacket. She held out the gun to me, "This is yours." I had no idea she had it. "We do not have bullets here so whatever is left is what you've got."

I reached up and grasped the cold metal. I was not sure I wanted it back. "Thank you."

Her hand extended again. A faint light sprung from her fingers and I heard a crackle beside us. The hair on the back of my neck stood up and I felt a knot in my stomach as I slowly turned towards the fire pit. It was now lit with a warm rolling fire. *Where the fuck was I?* "Welcome to Savengard. We don't have guns, but we do have magic."

CHAPTER 3

I watched in awe as warm light oozed from Sarla's hands into her leg. Her face scrunched in concentration or maybe it was pain. The light stopped and she took a deep breath. "Did it work?" I managed to ask.

"I think so. I am going to untie this cord and hopefully I don't bleed out." She winked at me. How she was so calm about the arrows, about the bleeding wound in her leg, I had no idea. She slowly untied the tourniquet and unwound it. "Good. It worked!"

I did not know I had been holding my breath until I let it whoosh out from my mouth. Sarla had used *magic* to stop the bleeding. It was the best case scenario she had explained. The arrows had clearly been poisoned and there was nothing

Sarla herself could do about it. We could watch the poison's progression as black spidered out from each of her wounds. She would need a skilled healer if she was going to live. However, if she was going to move from this campsite, we needed to stop her leg from bleeding so that she might be able to walk.

Her magic had worked to stop the bleeding, but she looked absolutely spent. She lay back into the snow, "I hope you are ready for a hike, because that is the only way we are getting out of here."

"To Beck's? Who is he?" I asked and pulled a small blanket from my pack, offering it to Sarla. How Sarla had not gone into shock I was not sure, but if she did, it would make a hike out of here even more challenging.

"The King of the Lakes. Thanks." Sarla responded as she unfolded the blanket and pulled it over her body as she continued laying in the snow. "He probably won't kill us, but he most definitely won't be pleased to see us either."

"Why's that?" I glanced down the canyon where the trail I hiked in on should have been. It was not there, but there was a different trail closer to the river. It was the only trail I could see and it was mostly covered in snow. Sarla had said it would be a few days hike, but I did not know if that was accounting for the snow and her injuries or if it was a few days without injuries and snow.

"We are not on great terms." I could tell Sarla was being vague on purpose. It didn't matter to me, I was a stranger.

17

"Regardless, we need to get moving."

I did not know how long we had been hiking, but thankfully the sun was still overhead keeping the day cool but not too cold. Sarla had assured me that for the time being we were safe from the males we had just faced. She explained that the portal we had come through would not allow anyone else through it for some unknown amount of time, but it would not be any time soon.

Our option was to start hiking towards help. If we were lucky, friends—or at least not enemies or beasts—would find us sooner rather than later. Both of us knew it was unlikely Sarla would survive hiking several days, and maybe not even one day. But without any supplies, we would not survive if we stayed where we were. Hiking out was our only option.

As we had moved away from the campsite I realized that although the campsite was exactly the same, the landscape became more and more different. The first thing I noticed was the skies were not clouded with gray and brown smog. Not only was the air cleaner here, but everything seemed more vibrant. The trail I hiked in on was surrounded by mostly sage and other brush and grasses with a few trees. The further we hiked on this trail, the more trees there were. Even with the snow I could tell this landscape was more lush and green than where I had come from.

I no longer knew where we were or what time it was. I pushed out thoughts of night time. How cold it could get— or the fact that there was lots and lots of snow when it was supposed to be the beginning of fall. My head was already spinning with what Sarla was telling me.

The two males we fought were assassins under one of the seven kings of Savengard. Kieron, the one with an axe that I put two bullets in, and Rook, the one with a bow who had choked me, were likely still alive despite the bullets we had put in them. Dark magic healing powers or something. The voice of darkness and horror I heard was the king. A king who was known for his dark magic, killing and destruction, and his general desire to rule all of Savengard, as what Sarla referred to, as the "True King."

"Your world, I am sorry, but it is likely gone. Vossarian is known to destroy worlds and he seemed to be tearing yours apart as he chased me through it. I am so sorry." She had been hobbling in front of me down the slick snow covered trail.

"Gone? My ... world? So Savengard is not just a different place, it is a different world?" I asked. *What was I hearing?*

"That is correct. Savengard is a whole different world. Some believe there were once twenty-six worlds that overlapped. Some say there were twenty-seven worlds. The worlds do not overlap exactly, but there are places between worlds that are the same. Like the campsite you were at. I am sure you have noticed that this trail is not exactly like the one you hiked in on. So the further you get from these overlaps the worlds … develop differently. The overlaps allow for portals between the worlds where people can travel between them. Some of us can move between these worlds even without the portals. We are called World Walkers." I could tell Sarla was trying to simplify it for me.

"You are a World Walker? But we came through a portal?" I didn't even know what questions to ask. *Did I hit my head? Am I in a coma?* Dreaming maybe. Before I could figure it out Sarla stumbled on a rock and smacked into the ground. I rushed to her and helped her roll to a sitting position.

"That did not feel great." She gritted out. She had been in front of me and I had not noticed how pale and gray her skin had turned. Sweat was beading on her forehead. She pulled back the collar of her jacket to look at her shoulder wound. Black inked and spidered its way towards her neck.

"Fuck." She breathed, "The poison is spreading too fast. We are at least two days from Beck's." She lurched to her side and vomited on the trail. There was black in her vomit too. "I am not going to make it if I keep walking. You might have to go ahead and try to convince them to come get me."

I dropped my pack to the ground, unzipped it and pulled out a red nylon bag. "How about I try to carry you?" I unfolded the sling. It was a carrying sling made for dogs. We hiked with dogs and if they were injured we would need a way to carry them out. There were holes for their legs and straps to carry between two people or over your shoulders like a pack. I don't know why I had not taken it out of my pack, unnecessary weight since … the accident.

"You really are prepared." Sarla laughed, then coughed, spitting up more black.

"It's for large dogs, but I think we can sling you up and I will carry you." Thankfully Sarla was a full head shorter than me and petite. She clearly could hold her own, but maybe she would be light enough for me to carry her some of the distance. "You just have to navigate."

I let Sarla drink from the water bladder in my pack before she lay in the sling. After a few tries we found a position that did not hurt her and allowed me to carry her across my back.

"Tell me why you aren't on good terms with Beck." I knew if she was talking she was conscious. I had to keep her talking.

"We used to be friends, but a lot has happened over the years and now he thinks we are not fighting for the same things. That we are not on the same side." Sarla said.

"He thinks you are not on the same side, but are you?" The way she had said it was as if there was a big misunderstanding.

She sighed, "We are, but he does not know that and we did not want him to know that."

"What is that supposed to mean? We have a long walk, Sarla, fill me in." My boots crunched in the snow and it was an effort to keep my balance.

"I want to. I do, but I can't tell you. Not yet. It might

jeopardize my kingdom, my people." Her voice was strained. "I am sorry. You saved me and now are carrying me to get me help. I wish I could tell you, but it is not my place."

I understood. I really did. There was a time in my life where secrets were the only things keeping us alive. "It's okay. I understand. You can tell me when you can tell me. But I do need to know what to expect of Beck. If we make it, how do I make sure we both don't get killed."

My legs ached. My back ached. And most of all my shoulders ached. I think everything ached. I did not know why I had thought carrying Sarla was a good idea other than I saw no other option. She was poisoned and my only guide in this new world. The sun had set hours ago. My headlamp batteries had died embarrassingly quickly and I had run out of water. We would have to stop to refill in the river at some point, but if I set Sarla down, I was not sure I would be able to pick her up again. I would go as long as I could. Or until we found a really good spot to make camp. Sarla had stopped talking at some point. Her breath was ragged. The sling was awkward, but it was working. My pack was slung on the front of my body. The adrenaline must still be pushing me. I did not think I would have been able to hike this long. Maybe this was a dream.

If all else fails, stay on this trail near the river. When it splits stay on the one near the river. If we are lucky Beck will find us first.

The directions Sarla had given me were simple. The river must run into a lake. We were going to The King of the Lakes afterall. I blew out a slow breath. *I must be going mad. Keep hiking. Figure it out later. When you are safe.*

Sarla had said we had at least a two day hike. *Did this count as one of those days?* It didn't matter. *Keep going until you make it or someone finds us.* The moon and the stars lit the trail. I stuffed my fear down. Nighttime and darkness could bring out all types of animals and this was a different world. *What animals lived here?* Sarla had referred to them as beasts, not animals. I shuddered and forced it out of my mind. Fear of the dark would not help me right now.

The river sparkled to my left, it was beautiful. Completely serene and beautiful. To my right the mountainside loomed. We were hiking down a canyon of sorts and it *felt* magical. It was as if everything hummed with *life.* Even in the dark each rock, tree, and pile of snow looked vibrant.

A wide flat spot stretched from the trail to my right. Nestled between boulders and a few trees there was a fire pit with plenty of wood against one rock. This would have to do. I had to stop. I had to rest. I crunched my way through the deeper snow and dropped my pack. Then, bending awkwardly, slowly lowered Sarla to the ground. She stirred then jolted upright, "Where are we?"

"A campsite by the river. I need to rest. We need water. It's nighttime." I responded concisely. I looked her over in the light from the stars. "Are you okay? You slept." I was already rummaging in my pack and pulling out a bag of old sugar cubes I had stashed away at some point in time. Blocks of sugar were not much, but we needed something. I tossed them to her, "Try one of these. Don't break a tooth."

Her hand reached up and the fire sprang to life. "Thank you. You did not have to carry me. Or help me. But you did. Why?"

I shrugged, "It was the right thing to do. All of it. I'll get us some water." Before Sarla could respond I stood and walked away towards the river. I made my way down the snow crusted river bank watching my steps carefully. I was exhausted and one wrong step could send me into the river. I took a moment to take a deep breath of the cold crisp air. The night was beautiful. Stars twinkled brightly—brighter than I had ever seen—and I recognized some of the constellations. The water bubbling by was wild and dangerous and yet, it calmed me.

I extracted the water bladder from my pack and now dipped it into the almost frozen water. I had a filter with me, I should filter the water, but it would take too long. I would ask Sarla. I quickly finished up and made my way back up the bank. I knelt in the snow across the fire from her, reopening my pack to find the filter and extra bottle I carried. Before I could ask her about the water, Sarla spoke.

"When we get there, to Beck's, don't tell anyone where you are from." She said carefully, "Not everyone will be okay with the fact that I brought you with me and we need to be—" A crack broke through the air and bright light blinded me as I was flung into the snow. Rough hands pawed at me as I fought to move my arms and kick my legs. But I was pinned. A wet cloth pressed over my nose and mouth. I gagged on the tang of chemicals. Consciousness was slipping away.

"It's Sarla of the Mountains." I heard a male's voice say. It sounded far away as the world turned black.

CHAPTER 4

I was warm and comfortable under soft sheets and blankets. I blinked my eyes and tried to swallow. My mouth was dry. So dry my throat burned. "There is water next to the bed." A warm male voice said. "Drink. It will help." My eyes finally focused. A handsome male was sprawled casually in an armchair next to a fireplace across the room.

I sat up slowly, looking for the water, and found a glass on a small table next to the giant bed I was in. *When was the last time I slept in a bed?* The water soothed my dry throat and mouth. "I'm Beck. This is my ... house." The male sounded bored as he gestured to the room. The room was magnificent. Soft white walls with warm wood trim and floors. Double doors marked the rooms entrance and giant windows with flowing drapes led me to believe the view would be more beautiful than the room.

"King of the Lakes." I whispered.

"So you know me. Mind telling me who you are?" He had deep dark blue eyes that I could see from all the way across the room. His stupid perfect hair was light brown and highlighted by what I could only imagine were days under a warm sun.

"Genevieve."

"Genevieve from where?" The authority in his voice made my shoulders stiffen.

"Far from here."

"Sarla would not tell me either." He sat back in his chair again.

"Is she okay?"

"She will live, yes. Nasty wounds." Beck was examining his tanned hands. "I was surprised to see her wounded and you, her companion, with only bruises. Perhaps it was because you had a gun."

We don't have guns here. Sarla's voice echoed in my mind. I kept my mouth closed, willing my face to be neutral as my heart pounded. "Where is she?"

"She is being tended to by the healers. She was not able to tell me much before she passed out." Beck paused and raked his eyes over me, "You do not have to tell me today, Genevieve," he said my name like you would say a lover's name. Slowly. Letting it roll off of his tongue. He stood gracefully, "But you will tell me what happened. You are safe here. Rest. Clean up. Wander

27

out of your room when you are ready and someone will point you towards the dining room." He was across the room to the double doors before he finished speaking. "Take all the time you need." And he slipped out the door.

I carefully swung my feet to the side of the bed. Everything hurt. My muscles were excruciatingly tired. I pulled aside the bedding and saw I was wearing a long shirt that went down to my knees. I pushed out any thought of how my clothes had been changed. My hands were still dirty and I did not smell fresh. They must have changed me, but not cleaned me. I pushed to my feet and moved towards a door that opened to a room with white tiled floors. The bathroom.

The room was serene. There were white tile floors and white marble counters, the fixtures were gold, and the towels were the softest towels I had ever felt. The shower itself was the size of a small room. A bathtub big enough for two sat inside the shower room. And the ceiling—made of glass. The entire ceiling put the sky on display. Pink tinted fluffy clouds floated across the clear blue sky. It was dusk. The sun must be setting.

I turned to face the mirror. I looked like I had crawled out of a gutter. My neck was covered in bruises. My hair was matted and greasy and only half of it remained in the elastic band that used to hold my hair up and out of my face. Blood and dirt crusted my hairline.

I turned the shower on—the water was instantly warm. I could not remember when I had last taken a shower, let alone a warm shower. I stepped into the waterfall of water, watching blood and mud swirl off of me at my feet. Bottles set on a wooden bench revealed mint and rosemary scented soaps that pleasantly tingled on my scalp and skin. The aches in my body relaxed under the warm water.

Just as the dirt washed away, questions and thoughts poured into my mind. I stuffed them all down. I did not have the capacity or energy to address any of them right now. Beck told me I was safe, but everyone here was a stranger. *Get clean. Get food. Then figure it out.* They would have killed me or locked me up already if they thought I was a threat.

I wrapped myself in a fluffy white robe and found a hairbrush in the drawer. I spent extra time brushing out my long brown hair. It felt good to be clean. I even indulged in the mint and rosemary lotion that was set on the counter. As I walked back to the bedroom I realized I did not have clothes. I nearly jumped at the soft knock in the door. "I have some clothes for you." A gentle female voice called, "May I come in?"

"Yes." I replied tentatively. A stout older female wearing a plain blue gray dress came bustling in. Her arms were full of folded clothes.

"I brought a few sizes and styles. I hope something will be to your liking. It is all casual for this evening. No need to not be comfortable." She began laying out the clothes on the bed.

I selected a pair of blue high waisted pants that looked crisp and a step above casual, but they were made of flowing soft fabric. I paired the pants with a soft gray turtleneck made from a thin knit. "Thank you. This will be fine."

"Here are some underthings and try these on too." She set a pile of light colored lace on the bed and handed me a pair of wool slippers with a leather sole. The slippers fit. "My name is June. If you need anything else just let me know."

"Sarla?" I questioned. I had to know if she was okay. Where she was.

June shook her head, "The healers are keeping her unconscious while they work the poison out. I'll have someone fetch you when she is awake." She turned to the door.

"Where can I get some food?" I was almost too nervous to ask, but June only smiled kindly at me.

"I'll take you. I will wait in the hall for you to get dressed. Take your time."

I tucked the turtleneck into the top of the pants and fastened the side clasps. I did not look half bad. The flowing pants hid how skinny I had become in the last few years. Hiding in tunnels and forests and back alleyways had not been a lifestyle that included eating reliable meals. My skin somehow looked better than I expected. It was clear and soft, even if my eyes and cheeks were sunken from near starvation. I paused as I looked at my eyes—they had once been deep brown, but over the years they had continued to lighten and the ring around the irises were now a darker gray. My shoulders and arms were boney and you could nearly see my ribs through the knit shirt, but the high neck covered the bruises that painted my neck. I sighed and turned to the door to find June.

House? Beck had said this was his house. Gigantic castle might have been a better descriptor. The wide wooden planked hallway had to be ten feet wide with fifteen foot ceilings. It was clean and huge, but the warmth of the decor allowed it to still feel cozy. Plants and benches with knit blankets and pillows dotted the hallway. As June led me down the hall, old habits had me counting the doors. We descended a massive staircase into what looked like an entryway. Seats and couches scattered the massive room along the walls. "Down that hall, you can't miss it." June pointed down an equally grand hallway before turning and walking down a hallway past the stairs.

I heard males arguing as I approached open double glass doors. "We wait. I need to know what happened before he comes swooping in to take her back to the Mountains."

"He will be pissed, Beck. If you truly want to make him an ally it is better to tell him soon. It will be bad if he finds out she has been here a while." A second male voice urged. It sounded vaguely familiar.

I turned into the room. Beck shot to his feet, nearly knocking over his chair. His clothes were clearly expertly tailored. His pants were fitted, but casual, and he wore a perfectly fitted three button long sleeve shirt. I could see the muscles of his chest and arms bulging beneath it. This was a male who spent hours working on his body. "You are clean." He blurted. It was far different from the lethal composure he had when I had first woken.

"What Beck is trying to say is that you clean up nicely, Genevieve." The second male said lazily. His clothes had a similar style, but huge muscled and tattooed arms were on display from his sleeves that had been scrunched up to his elbows. "You are probably starving. Come sit and we will get you some food."

Both males had glasses of amber liquid in front of them. The second male sipped from his glass as I approached the table. I did not know where to look. The room was almost all floor to ceiling windows. The darkness of the night swallowed up any view there might have been, but snow touched and gathered in the corners of the glass. There was a grand fireplace at the far end and a massive table took up much of the space.

Then there were the two males. Both extremely muscular and stupidly handsome. The second male had darker blue eyes than Beck—if that was even possible—and dark brown hair. The shadow of a beard covered his angular jawline.

Beck waved a hand and a plate of food appeared at the place across from the second male, "Genevieve, meet Devron, my general." A general. I was to sit and eat in front of a king and his general.

I sat. The food looked and smelled delicious. Chicken on rice

32

with asparagus. It was simple, but I had not had a full meal in years. To me it was a feast. A glass of water and one of wine also appeared. "Thank you." I managed to whisper. It was clear that the males had already eaten and had moved on to drinking. I glanced at both of them before I picked up a fork and began eating. The food tasted even better than it had looked.

Devron broke the silence first, "Apologies for our ... aggressive first meeting." That was how I knew his voice. He had been there when we were taken. "Where are you from, Genevieve?" Devron asked. He was swirling his drink and leaning back in his chair. His body was casual, but those dark blue eyes were piercing—threatening. "How long have you known Sarla?"

I swallowed my mouthful, racking my brain on what to say. *Don't tell anyone where you are from.* Sarla's warning before we were taken. "You took us from the site along the river." I did not answer his questions.

"We would have been more welcoming, but we err on the side of caution these days." Amusement twinkled in his eyes, "What are you doing in our lands anyway?"

"Sarla needed help. She said you were the closest." I said carefully.

"Are you going to tell us what happened?" The amusement was fading from Devron's eyes, his voice almost threatening.

"Devron, let Genevieve be our guest tonight." My shoulders relaxed at Beck's reprimand. "Tomorrow though, tomorrow you need to tell us what happened." He slammed back the contents of his glass before reaching for the crystal decanter to refill it, pouring Devron another two fingered pour as well. It was a threat. I had until tomorrow to figure out my story and if I did not—the hospitality would run out.

I was halfway through my plate of food before I realized I should have been worried about poison or drugs in the food. Rule one of being captured was to not tell them anything. Rule two was to be wary of the food. It had been so long, I was forgetting my training. But they had given me clothes and a room to stay in. They would not have bothered with poison. If they had wanted to kill me I would already be dead. I finished the whole plate.

Beck and Devron discussed the coming storms clearly trying to find something to talk about that did not matter if I overheard. I could see Beck watching me from the corner of my eye. I kept my head down, trying not to invite conversation from either the king or the general. From what they said, there would be a lot more snow in the coming days. Storms were good to escape in. Especially storms with enough snow to cover your tracks.

"Thank you for dinner, I think I better get some sleep." It felt stupid to say, but I could tell the two males were growing tired of avoiding real conversation. I did not need them circling back to asking me questions. I pushed back from the table.

"We will see you tomorrow ... Genevieve." Damn Beck and

the way he said my name. The way it rolled off his tongue. Like he was tasting each syllable. My body heated as his eyes burned into me. I could only swallow, nod, and will myself to be casual as I walked from the room. The door felt too far away.

As I exited a laugh broke out behind me, "Shit Beck, keep your pants on," It was Devron, "You already want to fuck her and you know nothing—"

"Don't." Beck's command was icy.

I hurried away down the hall to the stairs before I could hear more. Lusted after was better than dead. I just needed to play the game until Sarla woke up.

CHAPTER 5

Waking was like rising from the dead. I do not think I stirred at all in the night. No dreams … or nightmares. But here I was, in the beautiful bedroom, warm and tucked between luxuriously soft bedding. A cozy fire crackled in the fireplace and a tray of food was on the low table between the two armchairs. Beck thankfully was not sitting in one.

The floor was warm on my feet as I padded over to the tray— coffee. I ignored the cream and sugar in the cute little jars next to it. I sat and sipped from the steaming mug. It was so good to sip coffee again. If they were trying to win my trust through food and drink it was working.

Beck had said he wanted answers today. I had been treated well, nothing to indicate we were in any danger. Sarla—I needed to see for myself that she was being treated well too, even if she wasn't awake. But first, food. I lifted the lid on the plate to find scrambled eggs and toast. I was nearly done eating when I noticed a folded paper tucked under the plate.

Come find me after breakfast. Beck

His handwriting was neat and precise. I tossed the note onto the empty plate and sat back sipping more coffee. *How long could I wait before he came looking for me?* Perhaps I did not want to find out. Go on the offensive. Demand to see Sarla. Wing it from there. I rolled my eyes at myself. Winging it was not a plan, even if I was typically good at it. I threw back the remaining coffee and headed to the bathroom to freshen up.

When I emerged clothes had been laid out on the bed. I ran my fingers across the thick knit sweater and gray v-neck shirt. The pants that were folded next to them looked almost tactical —pockets on the side of each leg, a tear resistant fabric in the front and the back consisted of a stretchy soft material. Brown leather boots were neatly placed on the floor nearby. I guess this was what I was wearing.

The clothes fit surprisingly well. I always had a hard time finding clothes with my height, but these fit and were comfortable. I took a deep breath before opening the door to my room. *Come find me. Where the hell was I supposed to look?* I had only been to the dining room. I guess I would start there.

◆ ◆ ◆

Snow swirled outside of the giant windows, so thick I could not see more than twenty yards. There must be a view with windows like these all throughout the residence. I had no idea what time it was, but it still felt early. The dining room was empty. I cursed under my breath, I would have to go poking around. I turned and nearly collided with a broad chest, my hands flew up on instinct to protect myself.

Beck. It was Beck. He had found me first. His strong hands gently grasped my forearms to stabilize me—or keep me from punching him. His voice had a hint of a chuckle in it, "I am sorry I startled you. Are you alright?"

My chest heaved as I took a deep breath to calm my body, "Shit. Yea. Sorry." He gently let go of me and I forced myself to look at his face. His brow had raised at the curse word, but his eyes were scanning me, concerned. I could get lost in those eyes.

"How about a tour?" I nodded slowly—completely distracted by his perfect and symmetrical features. People should not look like this. "I will show you around and you tell me what happened with Sarla."

Sarla. Her name snapped me back. "I want to see her first." The words came out more demanding than I had planned.

"It is not pretty." Beck said cautiously. "You should wait another day."

"No. I need to see her. I need to know she is okay." Firm. Strong. I sounded more confident than I felt.

"Okay. Come with me." Beck turned slowly, as if he was not sure he should actually show me. I followed. It was too easy. If he was not to be trusted then all of this was too easy. We made our way back towards the room I had been staying in. We passed my room and continued a few more doors before stopping in front of another double door on the opposite side of the hallway. "It is not pretty. Are you sure?"

"Yes." I didn't wait for him to open the door. I turned the handle and pushed the heavy door inward. The room was dark and swirling. The air was swirling. It was thick. The room was dimly lit. Two females were near the bed—black inky darkness seemed to be leaking from the sheets. And there was Sarla. Her eyes closed and pain across her face. She was unconscious. The black inky darkness was seeping from her. Her arm was nearly all black, but the spidery black no longer reached up her neck. Nausea hit me, the dim room seemed to grow darker, and I felt the room tilt.

"Genevieve!" I heard my name as if it was being called from far away. I blinked and blinked. We were back in the brightly lit hallway. Strong arms were wrapped around me. I was sitting on the floor. I pushed away on to my hands and knees, nausea still rolling in me. A hand rubbed my back, "Breathe. Take a deep breath." I did. After another breath, the nausea slowly subsided. His hand kept rubbing. I sat back, shaking off his hand, and scooted my back to the wall. Beck was kneeling on the floor with me. "You passed out." His eyes were full of concern. "You are not used to magic are you?"

I leaned my head back against the wall and rubbed my face, "I am okay. That was ... a lot." My body shivered. I was trying to shake off the swirling heaviness the air held. It was a thing of nightmares. "Will she be okay?"

"Yes, it may take some time, but she is making great progress." Beck was reaching for me. I jerked away from his touch and he pulled his hand back slowly. "Let's get you some tea." He stood and offered his hand this time. *You want to fuck her.* Devron's words from last night still echoed in my ears. I ignored his hand and pushed myself to my feet.

I followed him down the hall and into a small library. Cozy couches and chairs were tucked throughout and floor to ceiling bookshelves covered every wall. Beck gestured for me to sit in an armchair. I sat, my knees still felt weak and there was not enough air in my lungs.

Two steaming mugs appeared on the low table between our chairs. I cupped one under my nose and breathed in deeply—lavender and honey. Neither of us spoke for a long while.

"Are you from Savengard?" Beck broke the silence.

"Yes." A complete lie.

"How many kingdoms make up Savengard?"

I just stared at him and swallowed, my mouth going dry. He waited as I racked my brain. Seven. Vossarian was one of seven kings. "Seven."

He laughed, then his eyes turned lethal, "Let me spare you from lying again. You are not from Savengard. I know you came through a portal with Sarla. The two of you hiked about six miles before you carried her another fourteen." My face must have shown my shock. His eyes turned from lethal to amused, "You also carried a weapon we do not have in Savengard. So the questions remain: Where are you from and how do you know Sarla?"

Fourteen miles. *How was that possible?* I had not carried another adult for over a decade and never anywhere close to that distance. It didn't matter. What mattered was that he knew—he knew almost all of it. "I do not know where I am from, but it is not here." He stared at me waiting. "I met Sarla moments before we came through the portal," his eyebrows raised. "Wrong place and time I guess. I was ... hiking and she came upon me. She was injured and chased. I helped her fight the males that were chasing her and she took me through the portal to escape them." This could be a mistake, but he had given no reason to not trust him.

"Were you from the world you just left?"

"Yes."

His eyes scanned me as if he was considering something. "Who was pursuing Sarla?" He finally asked.

"Two assassins and Vossarian." I was eyeing him carefully back, hoping to catch his reaction. Hoping to see if I had just put us in danger.

"Do you know the assassins' names?" He asked.

I racked my brain. Sarla had told me their names, "Rook and Kieron."

His face was infuriatingly neutral, but his eyes had flashed a hint of surprise when I said the assassins' names, "And what do you know about Sarla?"

"That she isn't trying to kill me." I left it at that. I did not know much about her, but my gut said she was trustworthy. I was not going to offer more.

He blew out a breath, "Well, you are both lucky to be alive. Kieron is not known for losing fights. You are safe here, you can stay in my residence for the time being ... Thank you for telling me." The thank you was tight, as if he forced himself to say the words. I could only nod. "How about we postpone our tour until after lunch?" It wasn't a question.

Lunch had found me in my room. When I finished eating I wandered back out into the hallway. June found me moments later, "He went out and asked that I show you the residence." She was warm and kind and her silver hair neatly braided down her back made her seem ... motherly. Safe. "Shall we?"

June explained we were in the guest wing, down the stairs

across the hall was the informal dining room, a lounge, and an office. The formal ballroom was down another wing, near the kitchen, and had an attached deck, patio, and lawn—perfect for parties June had assured me—like it was something I would care about.

There was another wing for staff and one for the permanent residents—Beck and a room for Devron when he needed it, but she did not tell me who else might live here. The home was ginormous. There were many hallways she did not take me down. Eventually, we were walking down a long glass corridor, "The training facilities are down here." Doors opened to a large room. Weights, multiple open training rings, and a strip of turf at least fifty yards long stretched before me. "You are welcome to use it whenever you like."

"Thank you," I knew I would be coming back. June deposited me back in the small library Beck and I had sat in earlier. I looked for a book or something to keep me busy. The weather outside was still showing no signs the snow would stop. If I was going to make a run for it, tonight was a good night to do so, but I could not just leave Sarla. I had a warm bed and food, luxuries I had not had for a long while. I could wait a few more days.

I wandered the stack of books looking for something to read. My fingers lightly trailed along the leather spines of the books. *The Beasts of the Wastes*. The title jumped out at me. I pulled the book from the shelf. As I flipped through the pages, I realized this was not a novel, but a catalog of sorts. Ink drawn beasts covered the pages, with descriptions and histories. I slipped the book back on the shelf. I had enough nightmares, I did not need to read about magical beasts that looked ready to tear anything and everyone to pieces.

I ate dinner alone and after a few hours found myself wandering to the training wing. I needed to escape my thoughts and working out might do the trick. When I arrived I realized I was wearing slippers and had no appropriate workout clothes. I folded my sweater and set my slippers next to it on the turf. I would run. I would run as many ladders as I could. Until I collapsed. I had a warm bed to sleep in anyway.

My legs felt stronger, I moved faster. I guess a few real meals of food would do that for a person. Up and back, up and back I ran. I began sweating and removed my shirt. No one else was here anyway and the lacy bra was surprisingly supportive. I almost felt bad about the sweat soaking the beautiful creamy white fabric, but it was too late now. Up and back. My feet carried me swiftly. The rhythm of my stride pounding out the thoughts from my head.

When my lungs started burning I kept pressing. Up and back. One final push and I found myself dropping to my hands and knees, chest heaving. I rocked back on my heels pressing my forehead into the turf and breathing heavily.

"I did not expect to find you here." Beck's voice broke the silence roaring in my ears. I would have jumped with surprise had I not been utterly exhausted. I looked up at him from under my arms. He was leaning on the door. The same style clothes as the first night, arms crossed, and a smirk plastered on his perfect mouth. "Needed to work some shit out?" He asked.

"Something like that." I pushed myself to a sitting position, still trying to catch my breath. I should have been embarrassed to be in my pants and nothing but a lacy bra, but I could not find a fuck to give. I didn't even know what I was doing here. What I was doing *alive.* Those had been the thoughts I had been running from. They all came rushing back. Thoughts reminding me that everything I cared about was gone. That I was tired of running. Tired of surviving. That I had nothing left to live for.

"Do not think that." Beck said, concern flashing in his eyes, "Your thoughts are plastered on your face … and I know that look."

"You know nothing about me." I quickly gathered my shirts and slippers from the turf beside me.

"I know you are not from here, you seem to have a wide variety of survival skills, you are a fighter," he crossed the space between us in a few strides and now stood unnervingly close. "You are smart and beautiful and something haunts you. Haunts you so much you have thought about not living anymore." His fingers brushed a sweaty strand of hair off of

45

my forehead before gently tilting my chin up and forcing me to look into his eyes. "Did I get that right?"

My heart was about to pound out of my chest with him standing so close. Touching me. *When was the last time I had been touched?* I forced myself to side step out of his touch and body heat. "See, you know nothing about me." I winked at him and slipped out the door.

I swung the bedroom door closed and pressed my back to it. I had practically jogged my way back to my room, shirts and slippers bundled in my arms. I could still feel his fingers brushing my face. My blood was still heated—not from running—from desire. It had been over two years since I had been with someone.

Get your shit together. I muttered to myself as I tossed the clothes on the bed. I had to live here until Sarla was healed at least. I did not need to go complicating things by sleeping with anyone.

I stalked into the bathroom and turned the shower cold.

Two days passed and I did not see Beck or Devron. If anyone besides them lived in the residence I did not see them either. June was the only face I saw. Appearing with impeccable timing for meals or if I was snooping too deep in the residence.

Old habits had me mentally mapping most of the building, noting the exits, marking hiding places.

On the third day she informed me that Beck would be returning and requested my presence at dinner. I could not refuse. He had let me stay, fed me, and given me clothes. I could not stop thinking about the way he had touched me. His hands on my arms when I ran into him. His arms wrapped around me when I woke from unconsciousness. When he brushed hair out of my face and lifted my chin. It had been too long since I had been touched.

You want to fuck her. Devron had said it the first day. I could not unhear it. I did not know what I would do if Beck tried.

CHAPTER 6

I was staring at a knit dress on the bed. Clothes seemed to appear here as if to order me what to wear. It made me want to cringe, but it did not seem like I had a choice. June had come by earlier and fixed up my hair and applied light make up to my face. My plain straight brown hair now had some shape to it after years of simply hacking off the ends with a knife. June had trimmed layers that flattered my face and gave my hair new life. She had simply darkened my eyelashes, applied a soft pink lip color, and added a blush to my cheeks to match. My eyes looked bigger with my lashes darkened. I actually felt ... *pretty*.

I picked up the dress, it was soft and beautiful. *But a dress? Really?* It was not even some fancy gown. *That* I might be able to get behind. But this. This felt weird. All of it was weird. I was in a different *world.* I guess I was wearing the dress.

The dress had long sleeves and the hem hung down to the middle of my shins. From the front it was simple, but the back dipped dangerously low. It was form fitting and hugged what little curves I still had, leaving not much to be imagined. I pressed up on my breasts and let them drop back into place, they were not as perky as they had been when I was younger, but they looked fine. At least the dress was still relatively comfortable. I slipped into the open back leather block heels that had been set out next to the dress.

I would have picked this outfit for a night out with … friends or my husband. All of them were dead now. I shook the thought from my head. Whoever was choosing these clothes had good taste.

Beck was waiting at the bottom of the stairs. His eyes flashed in approval when he saw me. They wandered over my body and the corner of his mouth curved upward. I guess I was flattered. I had not been looked at like that in a long long time. I reached the bottom of the stairs, "Hey." *Hey? That's it? That was all I could think of to say?*

"I have a surprise for you." Beck smiled and it made my palms sweat. His hand grazed the small of my bare back as he guided me towards a low lit hallway that I had not yet explored. It was smaller than most of the other halls and led us to a set of spiral stairs.

The room that greeted us was—magical. One wall held a

fireplace that extended the length of the wall. The other wall was all glass. And above us was a sloping glass ceiling. Snow lightly fell outside and after days here I could finally see the land around us in the fading light. Forest touched the property and a clear gentle slope reached down to what must be a lake. It was frozen, but there was clearly a dock and grand boat house. It was lit with twinkling lights. Dim twinkling lights flickered through the snow further off—other homes on the lake. Two high backed cushioned chairs were set at a small table for two.

"This is …" Romantic. Intimate. *Was this a date?* "Beautiful." I managed to say. *Keep your pants on.* Devron's laugh rang in my head. In fact I had not been thinking about keeping my pants on at all for the last few days.

I entered the wilderness planning to not be alive anymore, but when my life was ending with an assassin's hands around my throat it was my dead husband's voice that had urged me to fight. To live.

Now I was in a different world. One with *magic*. Living on borrowed time and the goodwill of others. To keep my thoughts in check I had been punishing myself in the training room, working out for hours until my body nearly gave out, and trying to push out thoughts of sex with Beck from my mind. I had barely met the king and all I could think about was crawling into bed with him. I felt pathetic. Lonely. Unfaithful. But I was still alive. My husband was not.

"I thought we could get to know each other better." Beck

was guiding me to a chair as I gaped at the view. "Seeing as I do not know you at all and you do not know anything about Savengard." He teased as he pulled out the chair for me to sit. "Especially if you plan to stay." To stay. *To stay here or in Savengard?* He could be implying either.

After one glass of wine, what I thought might be an awkward and too intimate dinner had quickly turned to easy conversation and laughter. I was *laughing* again. Beck told me stories of growing up playing on the lakes with Devron, wreaking havoc during formal events and courtly gatherings.

"It all feels so long ago now." Beck chuckled. We had been laughing about a particularly spectacular event where he and Devron had set off fireworks from the dock—but some flew into the boat house, setting off their stock of fireworks and burning the boathouse down in explosions of color.

"How long ago was this? Fifteen, twenty years ago?" I wiped the corners of my eyes. I almost had tears streaming down my cheeks from laughing so hard.

"More like three hundred and fifty." Beck got out between laughs.

I choked on my wine. "I am sorry, what?"

"Three hundred and fifty years ago." I just stared at him. Beck's eyes flashed, "How old are you?"

"Thirty-three."

"Ahh." He leaned back in his chair, no more laughter on his face, "That is right. You age differently where you are from." I just stared at him. "In Savengard, once we reach maturity our aging slows down significantly. Some of us can live for thousands of years."

"How old are you?" My eyes were wide with shock.

"Three hundred and seventy-two." He raised his glass in a mocking salute.

"Where I am from, people hardly live past eighty years. And they are gray and wrinkled and decrepit by then." It was sobering. Thinking about my mortality—and the fact that my world might not even exist anymore.

"You might not age that way in this world." Beck had a far off look in his eyes. "Not many people world walk and fewer stay once they have crossed. If you are open to it, we can have a healer examine you. See if they can give you some answers."

"I might take you up on that, but for tonight, we need more wine." I grabbed the bottle and filled his glass, then mine. I could not open that box right now. Emotion and fear and hurt threatened to burst out of me. So I shoved it back down. Wine would help. It would take the edge off, just like the punishing workouts did as well.

"Do you have a family?" Beck's question hit me like a ton of bricks. "You have not talked much about where you are from or your life there."

My throat burned and tightened. There was not enough

wine in the world to stifle this pain. I had gone looking to solve that problem before I ended up here. "I did. They were all gone before ... they have been gone for years." I looked out across the lake. Tears threatened to slide out of my eyes.

"I am sorry. I lost my family too. A long time ago." He lay his hand on top of mine. "We do not have to talk about this. Not tonight." I gave him a small smile. His face lit up, "Come! Finish your wine, throw it back. I have an idea."

He practically dragged me down the stairs to a room with a bench and wooden lockers. He pushed a large puffy coat into my arms and dropped snow boots at my feet. Then frowned at me. "A dress is not the best choice of clothes for this, but we can come back in whenever you like."

Fuck it. I put on the coat and boots and followed him outside. The wine kept me warm enough anyway. The air was crisp and calm. Snow fell lightly around us. I burst out laughing when Beck pulled two sleds from beside the door. The king's grand idea was sledding. I snatched one from him, "If we are racing I will definitely win!"

"Oh I don't think so." His voice was light and fun and full of challenge. He pointed down towards the lake. "First one to the boat house wins. You count us off." He was positioning his sled at the edge of the rolling slope.

I set mine next to his. I was definitely losing this race. I had done enough sledding in my life to know that his weight would carry him faster than me. "Get ready." We both stood back a couple paces. We would take a running leap onto our sleds. "Get set—"

He playfully pushed my arm and yelled, "Go!"

I could not stop my laughter as we both stumbled through the deep snow in our boots and dove into the sleds.

We made it all of fifteen feet before crashing into each other and falling off. The sleds zoomed away from us down the hill as we tumbled. Beck roared with laughter and I found myself giggling uncontrollably.

I was laying on my back, head down hill, trying to catch my breath. Snowflakes lightly fell on my face, catching on my eyelashes. *When was the last time I had laughed?* "This is the most fun I have had in a long time." I breathed. It was true. I had not had fun in years, I had been too consumed with revenge and survival to bother with having fun. I turned to look at Beck.

"We are pretty fun around here." He was grinning like a kid and there was light in his eyes. He stood and offered his hands to pull me up. "Again?"

I looked down at my dress, it was crusted in snow, my legs were red with cold. "I think I need pants for our next sledding adventure. Rematch another day? I was winning, you know." I gave him a smirk that said I knew I would lose, but would talk shit anyway.

He laughed. He had such a deep, booming laugh. "Rematch another day. Let's get you warmed up." He did not let go of my hand as we trudged back to the door.

He took my coat and held out his arm for me to balance as I slipped out of the boots. The floor was warm on my bare feet, "How are all the floors warm?"

"Magic." He winked.

"So you warm the floors, start fires, summon food … heal people. What else does your magic do?" I had seen no other signs of magic, but I also had not seen them much. I had been alone most days.

"A lot. Each person's magic is different and is based on where they are from and their bloodline. Some people are more powerful than others, but no one has limitless power. Imagine each person is like a glass of water—some people have bigger glasses of water than others, so more magic, but as you use that magic, the water pours out. Each glass—or person—has a stream of water refilling their glass. Again, some streams flow faster than others. If you pour out all your magic at once, you die. Does that make sense?"

I nodded and Beck smiled a fiercely handsome grin back at me. Then he continued, "You experienced the opening of a portal and traveling through it. Some of us can travel long distances almost instantly. Some people have magical gifts that are more useful than others and some have more lethal magical gifts. Nightcap?" He was so casual about it. What was unbelievable for me was everyday life for him—life that lasted centuries.

"Sure." I breathed. My head was spinning, but I was not ready for bed. I dreaded the quiet of my room. No distractions. That was when my emotions and thoughts threatened to consume me.

We returned to the glass room we had eaten dinner in, but Beck plopped onto a couch near the long fire, patting the cushion next to him. I sat and he offered me a soft knit blanket and a glass of wine—both seeming to appear out of thin air.

"What is it like to be alive for hundreds of years?" I asked.

It was late—really late—when I finally had to admit my yawning was getting ridiculous. Ever the gentleman, Beck walked me back to my room. He walked close enough that I could feel his body heat. As we got closer to my room I realized I would have to say goodnight—*Do I give him a hug? A nod?* I suddenly was not tired, but nervous.

Then we were there, in front of the room he was letting me stay in. "Thank you for letting me get to know you, Genevieve." His voice was tender—and the way he said my damn name. I shifted on my feet. "I am happy you stumbled into my lands."

"Thank you for letting me stay here. And … tonight was fun." *Had he stepped closer to me?* We were nearly sharing breath. My eyes were on his lips. A strong hand tenderly touched my chin lifting my gaze. I would drown in those blue eyes of his. "Beck—" I started, but I did not know what I was going to say.

His other hand pulled my hips to him. Our bodies were now touching. His hand slid into my hair and he pressed his lips to mine. I would melt right here. Into a pool on the floor. I craved touch. The feel of his hands and his strong chest against me—

I found my hands pushing him away. This was dangerous territory. Dangerous to refuse. Dangerous to accept. I would lose either way. Refusal meant I might not be welcome here. Acceptance might only delay it. I could not even consider it being more. A relationship. Things had been easy. But I did not know him. I did not know if I wanted *him*. I wanted to not be alone anymore. But I was practically forced to be here. No where else to go.

He let me inch back, but did not let go. Desire burned in his eyes as they searched my face. "Genevieve?" *The way he said my damn name.* I stopped resisting and he pressed his body back into mine. Pressing me against the door. His kiss was desperate, like he wanted to taste my lips, my mouth. My body opened for him. His hand fumbled for the handle and we were half stumbling into the room.

He tugged my dress up, his hand grabbing my ass over the lace underthings that had been picked out for me to wear. I pulled his shirt up and he helped me tug it over his head. His muscles were cut and huge. A patterned tattoo covered his left pectoral. I ran my hand over the inked skin before helping him lift my dress over my head. The fire in his eyes as he looked over my body told me that *he* had picked my underthings.

He was guiding me backwards in the dark to the bed. One hand tangled in my hair, holding the back of my head as he kissed me, the other hand undoing his pants.

As we bumped into the bed he pressed against me. I felt the length of his hard cock through his pants. I could not help the moan that escaped my lips. The moan was his undoing. He turned ravenous as he pushed me onto the bed. He removed his pants and I sucked in a breath as his cock freed from them. His muscles rippled and flexed as he lifted my hips to pull my lace underthings off.

The evening had been the foreplay. There would be no fingers or tongues. We would not go to second base then wait for sex after we knew each other better. No. He wanted to be buried inside of me. And I was going to let him.

He knelt on the bed between my legs, spitting in his hand before rubbing it on his tip. He pulled my legs up and slid to my entrance. He looked into my eyes as he pushed himself in only a few inches. I gasped at his size. He stretched me to the point it burned. A guttural sound escaped his lips in approval as he pulled out to the tip and slid back in further. His body pressed me into the bed as he kissed me. His tongue slipped into my mouth. I moaned again as his cock thrust to the hilt. My body was shaking in pleasure as he thrust deep in me again and again. My fingers dug into his back.

Then he was flipping me on my stomach. One hand sliding

under my chest and firmly settling around my throat. The other hand lifted my hips. He slammed to my core. *You want to fuck her.* He pulled out to tip and slammed back in. This was fucking. Lust. Pure physical desire and need. I did not care. I could not even think of words. Of any word.

I was moaning. Screaming. Gasping through the firm grasp on my neck as he pounded me harder and harder. My climax broke over me like a wave. Then another. And another. Beck groaned, his body shuddering as he came. His seed spilled into me. Sending another climax washing through me.

Beck's breath was warm on my neck. He was breathing heavily. His body sweaty against mine as he leaned over me. He pressed a kiss to my shoulder blade and slid himself out. Wetness dripped out with him. I whimpered at the feeling of the slow pull. What was just so full now felt empty and aching.

He lay on the bed facing me. I could not move. I was utterly spent. Still quivering. His hand gently pushed my hair out of my face. Then he gathered me in his arms, my head resting in the crook of his shoulder. His hand idly stroked my back.

CHAPTER 7

I woke to Beck siding his arm from under my head. He pressed a kiss to my forehead. "I am late. Stay in bed. I will send up breakfast." He was slipping on his clothes and I snuggled back into the pillows. "I will find you later today." He licked his lip as he gazed at me. His eyes still burned with want and desire.

"Okay. I'll see you later." I mumbled as I snuggled back into the cozy bed. He did not have to tell me twice to stay in bed. I was still exhausted from the late night and too much wine.

The click of the door closing had reality slapping me awake. Beck had spilled himself into me. *Fuck. Fuck. Fuck.* I was not on a contraceptive. Had not even thought about it and Beck had filled me so full I could still feel it leaking out. I had been stupid.

I knew better. Had better self control than to risk a pregnancy, especially with a male I hardly knew. I rubbed my hand down my face. I would either have to talk to him about it or ask June what to do. Both options made me want to vomit.

It was early, but I was not going back to sleep now. I hauled myself out of bed. I was tender between my legs where Beck had pounded into me. Still sticky from our climaxes. Shower first. Then to the training facilities. It was my crutch. Punishing workouts to chase away thoughts and emotions I could not face.

I did not bother to soap knowing I would be dripping in sweat soon. My shower was quick. I selected clothes from the tall wardrobe in the corner—after Beck found me in the training facilities the other night, workout clothes had appeared in the wardrobe. They were ... revealing—tight shorts and cropped tight tops with built-in support. Beck had clearly been the one to select them. I chose a pair of pink shorts and a simple matching pink racerback crop. I threw on a loose fitting shirt over it—just because Beck had selected it did not mean I could not adjust. I tied the laces on the white mesh shoes that had also appeared with the other clothing. They felt like they weighed nothing at all.

Breakfast had not appeared yet, but it did not matter. I would eat when I was back.

My legs burned as I pushed them faster. I had never run so fast. Fifteen more yards. Ten. Devron entered the facility. Five yards. I did not slow until I crossed the final line.

"You are fast, but you are holding back." Devron was smiling.

I laughed and shook my head in disagreement. We might have gotten off on the wrong foot, but everything about Devron today was different. "I have never felt this fast." I panted. My chest was heaving. My arms rested on the top of my head as I tried to catch my breath.

"Sarla's awake." Devron jerked his chin towards the door. I was moving towards it in a heartbeat. It had been over a week. She was awake. I had to talk to her. Devron grabbed my arm as I passed. "I know he slept with you." My body went completely still. There was warning in his voice. The relaxed male from seconds ago was gone. "He was late. He is never late. Plus he did not stay in his room last night."

"We are both adults." I tried to sound calm. Casual.

"And after fighting Vossarian's assassins, carrying Sarla fourteen miles, and seeing how you train," his head nodded toward where I had been sprinting, "I know you can take care of yourself. But Beck, he is used to always getting what he wants and he is ... he has his demons." Devron was choosing his words carefully. Warning me. Not reprimanding me. "Just be careful."

The general was *warning me*. I knew his allegiance was sworn to Beck. They had grown up together. He was Beck's general. His right hand. But he felt the need to *warn me*.

"I need to see Sarla." I did not know what else to say. He let go of my arm and I hurried towards the room Sarla was in.

Sarla was more than awake. She was out of bed and sitting in a chair, sipping from a mug, looking like nothing ever happened. She was beautiful. I had not had time to notice when we met or trekked through the snow. Plus we were both covered in blood and dirt. Her hair was somewhere between blonde and brunette and barely there freckles dotted across her nose. Her hazel eyes leaned towards green. She did not need makeup or fancy clothes, her features were stunning.

"Beck said you were here and fine! I am glad he decided not to kill us." Her smile turned to a laugh, "You slept with him didn't you?"

"How does everybody know this?" My cheeks heated and I sunk into the chair across from her.

"Well he sure looked smug this morning. And he seemed to think you might choose to stay here when I leave ... And it looks like you had a long night." There was amusement in her voice.

I stuffed down my embarrassment. "Enough about me. How are you?"

"Oh I am fine." Sarla waved her hand as if to shoo away any concerns. "Beck told me you carried me fourteen miles before Devron found us."

"I have no idea how I did that."

"Thank you." There was thick sincerity in her voice. "I will be

63

leaving at some point. I am not strong enough to jump myself, or even jump with someone yet. Maybe I will stay for The Melt, it is always a good party and I have not been in years. Either way, you can come with me when I am able to go. Explore the kingdoms, find where you would like to live. Stay with me for as long as you want."

"Jump?" I asked.

"It is like what we did through the portal, but within our world. Some of us can jump. Some can jump farther than others. We call it 'walking between worlds' when we move between worlds. The healers say I will need to wait to make sure my strength is back before I do it again. Then like I said, you can come with me if you like."

"I … I don't know what to do with myself now." I had not thought about what happened after Sarla was healed.

"You do not have to. You are starting a new life. Take it day by day. Stay here for now, come travel with me later. The choice is yours. My offer for you to stay with me stands. Always." She gave me a genuine smile.

"Thank you. I will think about it." Before all of this I did not have plans. Everything was over. Hopeless. But I had fought for another chance. I just had to figure out what I wanted to do with it. I looked down at my clothes and remembered I had come from training. "Well I should probably get cleaned up."

"I will see you at dinner then. I have some things to take care of anyway." Sarla said with a smile. I took it as my queue to let her have her space. I had a conversation I needed to take care of anyway.

I found Beck in his office by the dining room. He crossed the room in a few strides to kiss me. It was a kiss as if we had kissed one hundred times before. As if we alway greeted each other with a kiss and forever would. "How are you?" He asked.

"Good. I … I need to talk to you about something." I refused to let this be weird. We were both old enough to have this conversation without it being weird.

"Anything. What is it?" He was already back at his desk shuffling papers as he sat down.

"I am not on a contraceptive and I … is there something I can take after last night?" I held my chin high trying to keep my confidence.

He did not stop looking through his papers. "You won't get pregnant if that is what you are worried about."

"I am worried about it."

"Don't be."

"I'm just supposed to take your word for it." My words had a bite to them. He was not taking me seriously. Hardly even paying attention.

He was standing in an instant. Hands pressed into the desk, muscles tense. "Yes." The air around him seemed to pulse and shimmer.

I willed myself not to step backwards. His eyes burned into me. His chest heaved as he blew breath out his nose—like he was trying to calm himself. Fuck him if he was offended. This was my body and I would advocate for myself.

"I need more of an explanation." I set my jaw and stared back at him.

"It is not enough that I let you stay here? That I have given you every benefit of the doubt when you appeared in my lands?" He was fuming. His eyes darkened with rage. "I have fed you. Clothed you. And you still do not trust me?"

My body was screaming at me to run. That I was in danger. *Just be careful.* Devron's warning from this morning. I held my ground. "I am the one who would have to carry a child, birth it, care for it. You could just walk away. So no, I do not just trust you on this." My voice was venomous.

His eyes changed. "I can't have kids until I am in a joined union." It was nearly a whisper. The air stopped pulsing and he slumped back into his chair.

"I'm sorry, what?"

Beck rubbed his face. "When I was younger, I was dumb and promiscuous, and my parents feared someone would take advantage of me—try to gain status with a baby. I got a girl pregnant. My parents did not approve—she did not come from a noble family. So they put a spell in place. I would not be able to get anyone else pregnant until I was an official union."

"What happened to the girl and her baby?" I nearly

whispered it. He did not have to tell me all of this, but he had.

"I have a daughter. She is grown now and off, living her own life. She wants nothing to do with me. Things didn't work out between me and her mother." I did not know what to say so I kept my mouth closed. "I will have the healer come this afternoon. She will get you whatever you need to feel comfortable."

"Thank you." I said and I turned to leave.

"Was it a mistake? Last night?" His voice was gruff.

"No." Maybe. The sex was not a mistake, I had wanted it. But maybe I had complicated things too much.

"It wasn't a mistake for me either, Genevieve." My body heated at the sound of my name.

"Good." I did not let him speak again as I slipped out the door. Had I stayed I would probably have let him take me on his desk.

True to his word the healer arrived at my room a few hours later. "You sure look better than the last time I saw you." The healer was a female around my own age—or looked my age. Who knows how many centuries she had been alive. Her hair was blonde and pulled into a smart ponytail. Her clothes were crisp yet casual. "You were unconscious, but I am glad to see you well. My name is Esmay. It is nice to meet you."

"Nice to meet you, too."

"Beck asked me to give you a quick check to make sure

you have healed. He also told me about the ... aging concerns. And said to help you with anything else you might need." She gestured for me to take a seat in one of the chairs.

"Yes, that sounds good." I said as I sat.

She briefly explained what she would be doing, waiting for my consent before touching me or examining me each time. "Well you are completely healed. Go easy on the training. Maybe take a rest day here and there." I had not even told her I had been to the training facilities. "Now when it comes to aging —there is not a definitive answer. Some believe aging responds to the world you are in currently, not the body or world you were born in. I have seen nothing in your exam to indicate otherwise."

"So I will age like you?"

"Most likely, but we might have to wait and see." I could not think about that right now. When I did not respond, Esmay continued, "What other questions do you have?" She was so kind. So unassuming.

"I need a contraceptive."

There was no judgment. No hint of a smirk or wink of knowing. Only pure professionalism as she responded. "Of course." She dug in her bag and pulled a small vial with a dropper top. "One drop under your tongue within twenty-four hours after having sex."

"Not everyday?"

"Only if you are having sex everyday. Otherwise just after

you have had sex."

"Are there side effects?" Contraceptives were notoriously dangerous in my world. They could drive you mad. Make you ill. Kill you.

"None. This was developed by the brightest female healers across multiple kingdoms. They use a combination of herbs and magic to ensure efficacy and safety. And we should discuss your cycle. That really will be the first indication of your aging. Here females have their cycle every five to six months. I am assuming you are used to it more frequently?" I nodded. "Right, if that remains then you are aging the same. If it lengthens to five or six months then you will likely be aging like the rest of us."

I only nodded, "Thank you ... For everything."

"You are welcome. If you need anything else, just have Beck give me a call." She packed her things and left me staring at the small bottle. I dropped a drop under my tongue as soon as she closed the door behind her.

CHAPTER 8

Dinner was *fun*. Devron had brought his partner, Aada, who I instantly knew I would like. Beck and Sarla, it was revealed, knew each other from being two of the few remaining World Walkers. They had trained together when they were younger, before Beck took the throne in his kingdom.

We laughed and drank and bantered as if I had known all of them my whole life. I fit in with them somehow. They ruled kingdoms and lived for centuries and I somehow did not feel out of place. I did, however, notice the side eye Devron gave Beck whenever he rested his hand on my leg or kissed my temple or stroked idle circles on my back. The touches were not unwelcomed, but they were almost *too* familiar. We slept together once and he was acting as if we had been together for years. I tried to ignore it. I just wanted to feel *normal.* So, like usual, I stuffed down my feelings of wariness and guilt and convinced myself I was reading too much into Devron's glances.

We were all nursing dessert wine when Beck suddenly pushed back from his chair. "Sarla, I have a surprise for you!"

A moment later a male with dirty blonde hair pulled into a ponytail and a long beard strode into the room. "I hope you all saved me some wine." His voice was deep and cheerful. His eyes sparkled and lit up in a smile as he looked at Sarla.

"Alias!" Sarla was across the room in an instant. The two of them kissing and Alias wrapping her in an embrace.

Beck sat back down with a big grin on his face, "I thought you two would like to see each other. I told Alias he is welcome to stay here with you through The Melt if your king can spare him."

"I would say this is a good start to becoming allies again, Beck." Sarla was beaming as they returned to the table. *Allies again.* So that was why Sarla was worried Beck might have chosen to kill us. Something must have happened that ruined their alliance.

A chair for Alias had appeared from nowhere and Aada and Devron welcomed him, Devron eyeing him carefully. Sarla introduced me and Alias took my hand in both of his, "Genevieve, I owe you many thanks for dealing with this one here." Alias said as he nodded to me, sincerity in his eyes. Alias,

Sarla explained, was her partner and the general under The King of the Mountains.

They offered no further explanation and I was suddenly aware of how our dinner conversation had stayed firmly planted around times long in the past. It had revealed nothing regarding the current state of the kingdoms. I had a sinking feeling it was because they—or one of them—did not want me to know.

Sarla was the first to excuse herself and Alias. Claiming that although she looked fabulous, she was still exhausted and healing—we all knew they had other things to catch up on too. Devron and Aada left next. They wished us a good night and Aada promised to take me to her favorite little wine spot in town.

Beck walked me back to my room. Not my room—I realized we were in a completely different wing of the house. We stopped outside a door, "I thought you might like to see my room tonight." He paused, his eyes searching me for approval of his offer, "I am sorry about earlier. You were right and I was an ass."

"It's fine." I brushed his apology off. It was not fine. Something felt *off*. I stuffed the feeling down. No, I was just in my head. Being paranoid after years on the run. It *had* been a fun evening. Maybe I just had too much wine to care, "Let's see this room."

His eyes twinkled and he opened the door.

It was massive. A grand entry with a living room beyond. He pointed to a private office and half-bathroom on one side of the living room. Large double doors led to a bedroom on the opposite wall and huge floor to ceiling windows framed a magnificent view of the lake.

He hugged me from behind. Hands teasingly close to my breasts and my waistband. "Do you like it?" His whisper in my ear was followed by a quick nip of his teeth. My skin pebbled, between my legs growing warm.

"I do." I did. It was a handsome room. Excessively large, but it still felt cozy and welcoming.

"Good." His hand slipped down the front of my pants and he made a noise of desire as his fingers stroked between my legs. I could not help my back arching, my ass pressing into him, my head dropping back.

He turned me around, taking my face in his hands and kissing me gently. Eyes staring deep into mine between kisses. If last night had been fast and full of pure physical need, his kisses promised that tonight he was going to take his time.

His hand slid into my pants again. Rubbing me on top of the lacy underthings I suspected he had selected for me. His fingers curled under pressing the lace against my entrance. I could feel my wetness and knew he could feel it on his fingers too.

His kisses pressed harder, his tongue stroked the inside of my mouth greedily trying to taste me. I met him stroke for

73

stroke as my hands gathered his shirt to lift it over his head.

He returned the favor. My shirt dropped to the floor as he cupped and squeezed my breasts. I stepped out of my pants. Somehow we had moved across the room. He was pressing me against the wall as he dropped to his knees lifting one of my legs over his shoulder as he sunk his mouth between my legs. This lace had to go. I needed to feel his tongue on my skin. I tried to tug the sides of my underthings down. He hooked one finger into them pulling the lace to the side then plunged a finger into me in one slow stroke.

I could not control the moan that came out of my mouth. Had my leg not been over his shoulder I might have melted to the floor. He stroked his finger in and out, adding a second and staring up at me with eyes full of approval and fire when I gasped as he stretched me.

He pulled my soaked underthings down, then froze. His finger traced horizontally across my lower abdomen. "What happened?" He sounded as if he was willing to kill.

The five inch scar. The scar left from where doctors had swiftly and expertly cut my infant son from my belly to save both our lives.

"Who hurt you like this?" He growled. The sex had left his voice.

"No one hurt me. It was … medical." He gently touched the scar again. "My son … we would have died … it was the only option."

"You have a son?"

"Had." I whispered. I saw pain and understanding flash in his eyes.

He stood and kissed me. "I would love to hear about him. If you ever wish to tell me." I could only nod. My throat was tight and burning. "Come." He led us to his bedroom where he gently removed my bra and slid out of his pants.

He laid me on the bed and slid into me slow and deep. Our sweat mixed. Our mouths tasted each other. Our bodies moved together. His throbbing cock thrusted every thought and memory out of my head.

And when we were laying next to each other both breathing heavily, Beck turned my face towards his, "I want to know everything about you, Genevieve. Everything. You can tell me whatever you want, but I do want to know you. All of you … and I want you to stay here."

CHAPTER 9

The small library in the guest wing had a wide variety of books. I ran my fingers along the leather bindings as I read down the single shelf that seemed to contain books on the history of Savengard. *The Twenty-Seventh Realm.* I read the title again. Sarla had told me that some believed there were twenty-six worlds, but some believed there was a twenty-seventh world. I pulled the book from the shelf and turned the faded red leather over in my hand as I walked back to the chair I had been curled up in.

The book read like a novel, not a history. Something deep in my core flickered as I read tales of a world made of black obsidian glass that reflected the truth back to the viewer. Some of the stories talked about beings that bestowed gifts to the visitors—gifts of unyielding power, destruction, death, or endless near immortal life. All one had to do was ask.

There was no bargain. No payment. No selling of your soul. These beings gave these gifts because they *liked* watching the destruction and pain, they *fed* on it. The stories detailed many a king and conqueror who had tried to reach the twenty-seventh realm to receive these gifts and just as many stories of the endless horrors that trickled through the worlds in response to these given gifts.

I closed the book. It sounded so real, but it could also just be a myth. I brought the book back to the shelf. As I slid it back into place I had a deep feeling that this was a book I should not have opened. I grabbed another book and hurried back to my chair.

I found myself drawn back to the library again and again. I never found *The Twenty-Seventh Realm* again. There was not even a gap on the shelf where the book had been. Good. I shook off the shiver that ran through my body and selected a book with a title that promised it would be about using magic.

I closed my eyes and turned my thoughts inward just as the book had instructed. This was stupid. There was no magic in my world. I took in a deep breath, counting to five. As I blew the breath out of my mouth my mind wandered—it *ran*. Memories spilled into my head and not memories I wanted to relive. My eyes flew open and I stood. See. No magic.

I set the book on the table and left the library. I did not know where I was going, I just wanted to get far away from the quiet. Far away from my thoughts. I walked the corridors noticing more and more guards seemed to be placed around the estate and residence each day. There had been none when I had first woken here. As I rounded the corner I nearly ran into Aada.

"Genevieve! I was coming to find you." Aada and her long flowing hair moved with unearthly grace. "Come out to dinner with me. Beck and Devron are so caught up in whatever it is they are doing, I was hoping we could have some time just us girls."

This was perfect. I needed to get out of this huge house. "Of course! I would love to."

Aada linked her elbow in mine and turned, heading back towards my room, "Perfect, let's get dressed up and we will head out of here. I know the perfect place to get dinner."

Aada flipped through the clothes in the wardrobe. I watched her chew her lip in concentration before pulling out a pair of tight fitting pants, the backless block heeled shoes, and a lacy bra. She gave me a wink and summoned from thin air a beautiful cream colored sweater with a plunging neckline. "This will be perfect for you." She pressed the clothes into my hands and summoned an armful of clothes for herself, which she promptly tossed on the bed. A bottle of sparkling wine and two glasses appeared next.

I asked Aada all about how she and Devron met as we changed our clothes and sipped the wine. The sweater dipped so low my lacy underthings peaked out. The pants were made of material similar to leather, but thinner. I looked over myself in the mirror, I had at least put on some muscle since I arrived. It had not been that long, but clearly regular meals and training was doing me good. There was a quiet knock on the door and Sarla poked her head in, "I thought I heard you two giggling in here!"

She slipped in and plopped herself down on the bed. "You are coming out with us tonight, Sarla!" Aada announced as she summoned another glass of wine for Sarla along with an outfit for her to wear. Sarla only laughed and changed her clothes without even questioning.

I felt like a young girl again as we picked through the makeup June had left on the dressing table. I darkened my eyelids and eyelashes before painting my lips a beautiful red.

"Oh you look wonderful!" Aada said as I turned to show her. She had a tight short dress on with boots that came up nearly to the high hem of her skirt. I could not help the smile that was plastered on my face. I had not been out with female friends in a long time.

We were nearly giggling as the three of us pranced down

the hall to the front of the residence. Aada had arranged for a carriage to take us to town. Beck and Devron were crossing the entry hall as we made our way down the stairs. "We are going out!" Aada proclaimed gleefully, "Hope you boys have a fun evening, because we sure are going to."

She planted a kiss on Devron's cheek as he just smiled at her and jokingly told her to not get into too much trouble.

"Can I talk to you for a moment?" Beck's question was not as much a question as a command. I stepped aside with him. His eyes raked over my clothes, "I do not want you going out."

I could barely contain my laugh as it cackled out of me, "Beck, it is a girl's night out." His jaw muscles worked and I cut him off before he could say more, "You and Devron have a good night, we are going to go enjoy a wonderful dinner and I will see you when we get back."

I turned away from him before he could respond. Alias was sauntering down the stairs, a bottle of amber liquor in his hand, "I heard the girls are going out so I thought I would bring down some of the Mountain's finest for us to enjoy." He said to Devron and Beck cheerfully.

"We are going to LuLu's and Maurice knows we are coming. We will be well looked after." Aada informed Beck with a forced smile as she gestured to the two guards flanking the carriage. Both were heavily armed.

I said goodbye and joined Aada and Sarla at the door. I looked back at Beck before we walked out. He was ignoring Devron and Alias and staring daggers into me. I felt Sarla's arm link into mine as she pulled me out the door.

"Mmm this fish is probably the best fish I have ever had!" I nearly moaned at the flavor. Aada and Sarla just laughed.

"It is quite good isn't it." Sarla agreed.

LuLu's was a cozy place. The restaurant was long and narrow, the walls an old and nearly crumbling brick. The kitchen was open to the restaurant and a bar with tall stools ran the length of it. Maurice, the short and slightly round older male who owned the place, had tucked us into a back corner table that was cozy and had a good view of the entire room. Patrons were loud and laughing, everyone minding their own business and having a good time.

Aada refilled our wine glasses from the bottle that had been tucked into an ice filled metal bucket. "Okay Genevieve, I need the juicy details. How are things going with Beck?"

I felt my cheeks heat as I blushed, "Things are going well. He is obviously very busy, but it's going well."

She just stared at me, waiting for me to go on. I sipped my wine. "Just 'it's been going well'? I think it has been going better than well! I offered to be your plus one for The Melt and he brushed me off saying that you would be accompanying *him*." She said with an eyebrow raised, "It is a big deal to be his date for The Melt."

"I guess we have not talked about it ..." My voice trailed off. *Shit.* I had not even thought about it. It would send a message if I was with Beck at The Melt. "I am not sure I'm ready for that." I conceded.

Sarla spoke carefully, "I know things are probably feeling a little complicated, but it seems like you two get along quite well."

"I think he is making some big plans, Genevieve." Aada cut in as she leaned forward resting her elbows on the table.

"What is that supposed to mean?" I laughed nervously.

Aada smiled, "Genevieve, he has not been this attached to someone in a long time. I think he is trying to make his intentions clear to you that he wants you here long term."

"He did ask me to stay here ..." I offered.

"Longer term than that." Aada responded with a teasing smirk.

"Are you suggesting he wants a union?" Sarla asked, her eyes wide. I looked between the two. *Marriage?* This was not good.

"No. I think he is great, but it's only been a few weeks. I am *not* there yet." I protested. I hoped Aada was wrong.

We all sipped on our wine, both of them staring at me intently. I averted my eyes. "Well I sure would love to have you here!" Aada finally said.

I gave her a small smile. She was great. Being out with the two of them was great. I was lost in thought as Sarla guided the conversation back to Aada and away from Beck's intentions. I knew it had been dangerous to get involved with Beck, but I had let my physical needs overshadow my good sense. He was great. I just was not sure I was ready for any of this.

As we left the restaurant I had the strange sensation that someone was watching us. I stole a quick glance around the streets and only saw shadows. "Miss." One of the guard's voices broke me from my moment of panic. He held out his hand to help me into the carriage. I glanced over my shoulder again, down one of the dark side streets—the shadows were different. I shook my head. *You are just paranoid and drunk. You are safe here.* I reminded myself. No one was hunting me in this world. I took the guard's hand and stepped up into the carriage.

CHAPTER 10

Sarla would be leaving eventually, but first, The King of the Mountains was coming. As far as I could tell, Beck was using this as an opportunity to build his diplomatic relationship with the other king. Just as his invitation to Alias was also used to start building that relationship. Sarla's unplanned arrival was fortuitous as she was a member of The King of the Mountains' court and she had ties to Beck and his court.

I would have to choose. Stay with Beck or go with Sarla. The conversation with Aada from our night out a few days ago was still on my mind, but I could not stop the momentum with Beck.

I slept with Beck every night. He fucked me in every part of his room—the couch, the table, across his desk, against the floor to ceiling windows—and it had gotten rougher and rougher each night. It was always whatever he wanted—whatever he needed—and I obliged. He had even held my head, fingers tangled in my hair as he pounded into my mouth. Shoving my head down as I struggled against choking and gagging while his seed erupted into my throat and spilled out my lips. It did not matter if it was good for me, what mattered was that when he was inside of me, I stopped thinking. And the small bruises and aches from sex with him made me at least feel something.

Outside of sex he was tender and playful. He made sure I had every comfort. He even moved my clothes to a second closet in his room—"There is no reason to trek halfway across the estate to change clothes." He had reasoned, but assured me the other room was still mine whenever I needed it. My pack with my old clothes, knife, and gun was still tucked in the bottom of the wardrobe.

I was starting to get restless. The blowing snow seemed endless. I needed to get out. Or *do* something—even cooking myself food was not an option, the cooks had shooed me from the kitchen when I had asked.

Aada was caught up in court matters, but would be available again soon. I had not seen her since our night out, but Devron had assured me she was just busy before The Melt. Sarla and Alias did their best to spend time with me, but they were equally busy in meetings with Beck, Devron, and others I never met. I was not delusional enough to think they would include me in their discussions.

So I found myself splitting time between the training facility and the small guest library. Usually, loitering in the latter late into the evenings until Beck found me and whisked me to his bed. A fist of guilt was growing in my chest. I was not ready for a commitment and what started as a distraction from my problems now was turning into my biggest problem—Beck had quickly become comfortable with my presence in his life whenever he wanted me.

"I need something to do. You have offered me time to rest and be taken care of … and I am so grateful … but I'm getting restless." We were in Beck's shower late one night.

"Hmmm," his only response as he slid slick soapy hands down my back and squeezed my ass.

"You are not even listening," I grumbled as I pulled away.

"I am sorry I am so busy right now." His hands found new skin to soap. His eyes wandered with his hands along my body, "I promise to spend more time with you, show you around more, help you find a … purpose." He squeezed my breasts with the last word, biting his lip.

I was having none of it, "My purpose is not to warm your bed. I need … a life."

"This isn't a life? Doing whatever you like. Being cared for." That lethal authority bit into his tone.

"I said this has been wonderful, but I *want* to do something more." I countered as I rubbed my hand across his chest to calm his temper.

"Okay. Consider it done. We'll start after The Melt." It was dismissive at best. He plunged his finger into me and I gasped. End of conversation. But this was what we did. Sex. It numbed my mind and made my body feel. *Was it the same drug for him? The same escape from reality?*

The next day I found Devron in the training facility. I went about my business, letting him go about his. Then I saw him watching me. He was smiling broadly. I stopped and he finally spoke, "I am impressed, but you are holding back."

"What do you mean holding back?" It was not the first time he had told me I was holding back. I was breathing heavily, completely spent.

"Don't you feel that thrumming in your blood?" He tapped his chest, "You might not want to admit it, but you have powers. Magic."

"That is not possible. There is no magic where I am from." I swallowed down the fear that rose in me as I thought about how I had tried to reach inside and find my magic. All I had found was memories that were better not remembered.

"It is possible. You are already stronger ... faster. That is your magic. You have to learn to release it. To use it." He was completely serious.

"It's not possible." I would not accept it.

Devron just shook his head, "Not with that attitude. But either way, after The Melt I hear that we get to dive into combat training." Beck must have already talked with him. I was pleasantly surprised he had listened.

"You must have more important things to do." I replied. I liked Devron. I could tell he was lethal, obviously he had to be to be Beck's general, but he had that look that he *respected* death and had mastered it.

"I am happy to do it. This world is full of monsters and if you want to survive it you need to know how to fight. Who knows, we might all find out that this was the most important thing for me to do. Time will tell." He was hiding something. I did not press him. I had my secrets, he could have his.

When I wandered into the small library after lunch I was surprised to see Beck there with a stack of books arranged on the desk. "Hey you." He kissed me and gave my ass a squeeze.

"I wasn't expecting to see you here." I laughed as I batted his hand away.

"I have selected some books for you, so you can start to learn about Savengard. After The Melt I will teach you all you need to know, but in the meantime, if you want to read them you can." He guided me away from the desk and plopped us onto a couch. "I thought today I might tell you the overview. The stories we learn as children."

"Okay!" I smiled at him. He really had been listening to me in the shower. I snuggled under a fuzzy blanket, my feet in Beck's lap.

Before he could begin, June poked her head into the library. "Your Grace, I am sorry to interrupt. You are needed for the final walk through before The Melt."

"Thank you, June. Yes, I will be right there." He kissed my forehead, "I am sorry, we will do this another day. I will see you for dinner."

I only nodded as he left. He was the king, what did I expect? I sorted through the books Beck had left on the desk and selected one. Snuggling back under the blanket I started reading.

Beck found me in the same spot he had left me in. "You are still in here? That must be a *very* good book."

How late was it? I closed the book I had been reading and pulled the blanket out from where it was tangled in my legs.

The book had started with a detailed map of Savengard. On the western coast was The Land of the Coasts. Further west from it all appeared to be sea. To the northeast of the Coasts was The Land of the Cliffs. Moving further east was The Land of the Mountains. Moving southeast from the Coasts was The Land of the Lakes. Then moving east from there was The Land of the Giants and The Land of the Plains. The entire eastern side of the map, spanning from The Land of the Mountains to the Land of the Plains was The Land of the Deserts. The Land of the Deserts appeared to continue to the most eastern part of Savengard that the map showed. Coasts, Cliffs, Mountains, Deserts, Plains, Giants, Lakes. The Seven Kingdoms of Savengard.

In the center between all of the kingdoms, and in small fingers that sometimes stretched up between the kingdoms' borders, was a shaded area labeled Wastelands. In the center of the Wastelands was another irregularly shaped area labeled The Lands of the Mother.

The book had sections on each of the seven kingdoms, as well as a section on The Lands of the Mother, which was apparently not a kingdom. There was only a brief mention of the Wastelands stating that it separated The Lands of the Mother from the other kingdoms. I remembered the first book I opened here, *The Beasts of the Wastes*. It was a thing of nightmares and I still could not grasp how this world was so *different* and yet so similar as the world I had lived in.

I had been caught up in reading the history of The Land of the Lakes and had just started the section on The Land of the Mountains when Beck had returned. He smiled at me, "Do you want some dinner? Or should I leave you with the books."

"Definitely dinner." I had not realized how hungry I had gotten. I was not just reading. I was hoping to find information that would tell me more about why the Lakes and the

Mountains were not allies, but I wasn't going to tell Beck that.

CHAPTER 11

I sat in a silky robe, staring at the deep blue gown hanging in front of me. It was the color of Beck's eyes. The welcome ball for The Melt would be starting soon—everyone would be on their best courtly and modest behavior tonight and as the days of parties continued, things would get ... rowdy. Beck had given me a brief rundown of what to expect. Including that he intended to introduce me to his courtiers.

"You don't like it?" Beck stepped out of his dressing room. He was wearing a perfectly tailored deep blue suit. It coordinated perfectly with the gown. Atop his perfect hair sat a golden crown with blue sapphires. How strange it was to see him wearing a crown. But he was a king.

"I love it. I am just nervous." I was nervous. I had not been to a social event in years and never a royal party. Never as the guest of a king. This would send a message I was not sure I was ready to send, but I was not sure I didn't want to send it either.

"There is nothing to be nervous about. This is supposed to be a good time. A celebration. Nothing official about it." He was removing the gown from the hanger. "But I do request that you wear clothes … at least to start the evening." He winked.

I huffed a laugh and let him help me slip off the silk robe. Light blue floral lace underthings had been selected for me to wear under the gown and as I looked down at myself I almost wanted to laugh. Pastel and floral anything was just so at odds with … *me*. June had arranged my hair half up and applied tasteful but conservative makeup to my face. Beck held the gown for me as I stepped into it. Then he fastened the back buttons for me. When I stepped in front of the full length mirror my breath caught. The thin barely there straps held up the layers of beautiful fabric. The top of the gown hugged my breasts and came together at the bottom of my breast bone where a band separated the top from the billowing skirts. I had not worn a gown in a long time and nothing like this. I hardly recognized myself.

"You *do* clean up nicely." Beck whispered as he kissed my neck. "Let's go before you decide to hide in the closet all night."

Crisply dressed servers offered us crystal glasses of sparkling wine as we entered the formal ballroom. It had been transformed into a grand space with twinkly lights that hung

... no they just floated in the air between our heads and the tall ceilings. Guests filled the room hugging, chatting, and laughing. Many turned towards us as we walked through the room, bowing their heads to Beck and saying, "Happy Melt, Your Grace." He returned their greetings as we crossed the room.

A waltz was playing, but no one was dancing on the dance floor in the middle of the room. Beck stopped and faced me, taking the crystal glass from my hand. A server appeared at his side and Beck placed our glasses on the tray for the server to whisk away. "Dance with me." He said as a smile crossed his face and he extended a hand. It wasn't a question.

I took his hand. It had been over ten years since I danced like this. *Please do not look like a fool.* I silently prayed to myself. Beck's other hand wrapped my lower back and pulled me close to him. A moment later he swept me across the floor to the music of the waltz. My feet moved from memory. I hadn't forgotten. His smile grew as we moved around the dance floor. "Why am I not surprised that you are an excellent dancer?" He whispered in my ear.

I forced a smile. I could only dance because it was one of the "skills" all the females were forced to learn during our years of service. To dance. To cook. To clean. And all of the other nonsense they thought was necessary to make the males happy and make us good for breeding. I forced the thoughts out of my mind and let the music from the waltz sweep me away.

The music stopped and guests clapped. Beck gave my cheek a kiss and guided us from the dance floor aiming towards Devron, Aada, and Sarla who were laughing together at a tall table.

They met us with kisses on the cheeks and compliments to our attire. They were equally well dressed. Both females wore stunning, long gowns. Aada's dress was delicate and form fitting with a light blue shimmering lace overlaying an ivory silk. Sarla's dress was an emerald green satin with sleeves that hung off her shoulders and a slit that reached high up her left thigh. Devron wore an expertly tailored deep blue suit with a tie and pocket square that coordinated with Aada's beautiful dress. I knew nothing of fashion, but I could tell the fabrics must have been expensive and everyone looked amazing. "I will leave you here while Devron and I make the obligatory rounds. Take care of her, you two." Beck said it as if *taking care of her* really meant, *show her a good time, but don't break anything.*

They all laughed and Aada and Sarla waved him and Devron off as the males sauntered into the crowd. Soon Aada was pointing out members of the court and introducing me to old friends. Everyone was polite and welcoming. If a too personal question was asked of me, Sarla or Aada expertly diverted the conversation. I was grateful for their expert social skills and found myself actually having a good time, letting my guard down, blending into the crowd, and soaking in the joy from the festivities.

I watched Beck float around the room, laughing and chatting with the guests. Females seemed to fawn over him. Laying their hands on his arm as they laughed at everything he said. Every male acted like they were the best of friends. It was clear everyone loved him. That they all wanted to say hello and shake hands and take whatever time he was willing to give to speak with him. He seemed to entertain it all, basking in the attention. I was glad he left me with Sarla and Aada.

The three of us found a table near the roaring fireplace and close to the tables covered in food. I was trying to keep my laughter quiet as Aada whispered to us made up backstories for the courtiers picking their way across the tables of food —a game that was becoming more ridiculous and scandalous as the night went on. I turned away in an effort not to spit wine out my nose. I had barely composed myself when an immaculately dressed male entered the ballroom with Alias at his side. Something inside of me hummed. I could not tear my eyes away. Guests stepped back from the males and a few males seemed to position themselves between their partners and the new arrivals.

I watched his face as people shrunk back from him—it was calm and neutral. If people shrinking from him bothered him, he did not show it. His black suit seemed to draw darkness into him and his crisp white shirt was unbuttoned at the collar—a stark contrast to the bowties most of the guests were wearing.

An emerald green pocket square was tucked neatly in his jacket pocket. Ink on his skin peeked out of the open collar and onto his neck. A dark crown with white gold tips sat on his head. The sides of his head were shaved, leaving a strip of long hair down the center of his head that was tied neatly into place. They were walking right towards us.

"For someone who was nearly dead, you sure look good." The new male said in greeting to Sarla.

Sarla's face burst into a huge grin as she threw her arms around the male in an embrace. She pulled back then straightened his jacket. "I did not expect you until tomorrow! Getting fancied up isn't really your style, Ryett."

A small smile twitched the corners of his mouth upwards, "I thought I would make an exception. You look well Aada. It has been a long time." He said as he turned to Aada. She nodded to him, her face neutral. Then he turned to me. Our eyes met and the room vanished.

Visions of jagged mountains, bubbling streams, glaciers, and forest fires flashed through my eyes. A wave erupted from my heart, rippling out through my body. It crashed against my skin as if barely contained.

In an instant the room was back and I was staring into ice blue eyes. A flash of shock crossed them before returning to cool neutrality.

"Genevieve, meet Ryett, King of the Mountains. Ryett, meet Genevieve, the friend who kept me from death during my last trip." I barely registered that Sarla introduced us.

"It's a pleasure." Whatever had just happened, Ryett was not going to acknowledge it.

"Likewise." I replied, trying to gather my composure.

Sarla was giving us a questioning look, but gracefully proclaimed that we all needed more wine. Devron arrived at that moment, the two males grasping forearms in greeting. Devron pulled Ryett's attention away to what was obviously official business. Our group floated towards a tower of crystal glasses filled with sparkling wine. Guests seemed to shrink away from us as we moved across the room. I excused myself, claiming to need some air and slipped out one of the tall glass doors onto the balcony.

The night was cold, but the balcony was wrapped in warmth, presumably by the same magic that decorated the estate, keeping everything comfortable for guests. Thankfully no one else was outside. I leaned my hands on the railing and closed my eyes. Breathing through my nose.

The images of what I had seen lingered in my mind. *What was that?* Ryett seemed equally shocked. I shook off the feeling as I scanned the night sky looking for the familiar constellation that always grounded me. The three stars flickered brightly and I stared up at them. Finally, I felt that I could breathe again. That I wasn't being suffocated by this dress. By the party.

"I came to see Sarla, but I am pleasantly surprised to find her new friend here." A cold voice broke me from my thoughts. I spun around and found a male leisurely walking towards me. Like the other guests, he was dressed in the finest clothes. His black suit and black shirt were immaculately tailored. His clothes did nothing to hide his muscles. *How were all these males so muscular?* "You sure are beautiful." He continued. I was frozen. His voice. It was Vossarian. Vossarian was here. My choice was to face him or fling myself off the balcony. I could not move as he approached me. He stopped mere inches from me. His eyes were blacker than his suit. Soulless. His hand reached up to my face.

Instinct kicked in and I smacked it away. "Don't touch me." I snapped. He grabbed my wrist, a cruel smile started to turn up the corners of his mouth. "Let go—" My voice was barely a whisper.

"When someone says no, it means no, Vossy. Didn't you learn that as a child." Ryett. He was leaning against the glass door inspecting his nails.

"Ah, how is my dear Sarla? We sure had fun the last time we saw each other." Vossarian let go of my wrist and stepped back from me. I slowly slid further away.

"Did you think you would be able to kill my cousin? Sending your pets was a poor choice. I am disappointed in you, if you had a disagreement you should have returned her to me to deal with it. Based on what she has told me, you broke our agreement." Sarla was Ryett's cousin. She had not mentioned it. "Regardless, what are you doing here Vossy? I don't think you

RSVP'd."

I jumped as a strong hand slid around my waist pulling me close. Beck. Relief washed over me and I sunk into him. "No invitation was sent." His voice was lethal.

"I do love a good party and wanted to wish you all a happy Melt. I did not know you two were friends again," Vossarian straightened his jacket sleeves. It was all lies. Fake pleasantries. "I also wanted to hear your answer to my proposal, Beck."

"It's a fuck no. Now leave." Power was rippling off the air around Beck. When I glanced at Ryett the air was also moving, a faint dark light glowing from him. He was still leaning against the glass.

"Calm down you two. Do you really think I would expose myself to you with your best warriors in attendance. No. Your spell of peace for the party is quite convenient." Vossarian chuckled.

Spell of Peace. Beck had mentioned a spell to keep the young warriors from getting too rowdy and fighting. "No one needed to lose their life over some drinks." Beck had explained. That same spell must be keeping the three kings in check.

"You have your answer. Leave." Ryett's voice was bored, but laced with authority.

"I think I will change my offer." His dark eyes raked over me and Beck's hand tightened on my waist. "She comes with me and I will leave your people alive when I take your kingdom, Beck. Seems like a fair trade." Vossarian was talking about me. I was the "she."

Beck moved me behind him as if to shield me. "Get. Out." Had there been no spell of peace, the tone in his voice indicated he would have spattered Vossarian all over the windows.

Vossarian only laughed darkly. "Very well. You two have fun with whatever you are up to. I promise not to interrupt the rest of your party. The offer stands ... for now." And he was gone. The air seemed to fold in on itself, swallowing him.

Beck whirled to me looking me over, his hands on my shoulders, "Are you okay?"

"I'm fine." I replied, but I could not stop my hands from shaking. I looked over his shoulder as Ryett slipped back inside without a word.

We did not return to the party. Beck deposited me in his room and told me not to wait up. He would be with Devron and his commanders discussing what to do about Vossarian. I nearly begged him to let me go back to the party or at least go with him, anything other than being left alone. The no he gave me did not leave room for questioning.

CHAPTER 12

I lay awake in bed. The music and laughter from the party had long faded away. It was late when Beck stumbled in—he was piss drunk. I rolled facing away from him and pretended to be asleep. His clothes made soft thumps as he dropped them to the floor. The bed shook as he climbed in and he made his way across to me.

Rough fingers brushed my hair off of my neck and he started kissing my shoulder. Working his way up towards my ear. "I will kill him for touching you." He whispered, his words slightly slurred.

"I'm fine. Let's just go to sleep." I tried to shrug him off. Teeth bit into my neck. Hard. I yelped in pain.

"I don't want to sleep." Beck pressed his steel hard cock

against my backside. "I want to be in you."

"I want to sleep." I squirmed away only to find his rough hands pulling me onto my back. Beck positioned himself between my legs, knees pushing my thighs apart. "Beck!" His drunk eyes were glazed and did not even react to me snapping his name. I tried to shove him. He pinned my hands to the bed, my wrist bones creaking under his grip.

His mouth sloppily pressed to mine, tongue sliding in to taste my mouth. He moved lower, licking my neck and biting my shoulder. I cried out as his teeth dug into my skin. "Don't you like it like this, Genevieve? Don't you like when I fuck you?" He pulled my arms above my head, pinning both wrists with one hand. The other hand dropping to guide himself to my entrance.

"Beck. Stop!" I bucked my hips to get away, but his strong hand pinned them down. He thrust himself in deep with one stroke. I cried out at the pain of it. We had rough sex all over his room, but he had never done this. Never forced himself on me.

"Do you want someone else to fuck you?" His eyes were now lethal. *What the fuck was he talking about?* "Tell me you only want me to fuck you." He pulled out to his tip and pounded another hard thrust into me, "Say it!" Rage. There was rage in his voice.

"I only want you to fuck me." I whispered. I stopped resisting. Felt my body and mind numb to what was happening. I had been here before. At the mercy of a male. I

103

trusted Beck and now that trust was all gone. Vanished.

"Again." He demanded. Pins and needles seemed to be biting into my wrists and hands where he held them down.

"I only want you to fuck me." I said it louder. I was not going to fight my way out of this. I would give him what he wanted for now. It was better than the alternative—and it was not as if we hadn't been together plenty of times before.

He grunted as he pounded into me. I could see sweat beading on his body and shimmering in the starlight that trickled in through the windows. It was as if Beck wasn't even there. His eyes were lethal and demanding and there was no Beck behind them.

"Tell me you only want my cock in you." Beck lifted one of my legs across his front, twisting my lower body. My legs rested on top of each other, one hip pressed into the bed. His hands grasped my shoulders with a strength I knew would bruise. My collarbones creaked. "Say it!" There was a low gravely demand in his voice. He continued pounding into me, his crushing grip on my shoulders keeping me from sliding up the bed.

It was pain. Pain and numbness. My body betrayed me as a small cry exited my mouth. "That's it Genevieve, come on my cock." A hand moved to my throat and pressed. "Tell me you only want my cock."

I was gasping for air. Both of my hands grabbed his forearm trying to move it. There was sexual choking and there was being choked. I was being choked. "I only want your cock." I rasped out.

He pounded into me harder. "Yes!" He growled. My vision was getting splotchy. He slammed in so hard I thought his cock would split me in two. A groan of pleasure released from him as he pressed deeper into me. I could feel his cock twitching and spirting in me as he pressed and pressed.

He let go of my throat and collapsed across me. I gulped in air, coughing. He lay on top of me breathing heavily. I didn't dare move. *Did this really just happen?* I wanted to scream. To cry. To do anything. But I just laid there. Completely still. Finally, he kissed my neck and rolled off of me. He slid his still hard cock out slowly with a satisfied groan. The ache and burn between my legs told me I might have torn.

He planted a sloppy kiss on my shoulder and was asleep moments later.

I laid still for minutes, counting his breaths. Then silently, I slipped out of bed. I stood naked next to the bed and looked down at him. I could cut his throat right here. Be done with it. But instead, I threw on my lounge clothes and a big cozy sweater. I closed the door quietly behind me as I left the room.

An hour later I found myself on a large balcony, curled under a blanket and staring blankly into a flickering fire pit. The stars still twinkled brightly, the sun would not be up for a while longer. I had every excuse for Beck. But I knew it was done.

Over. The excuses did not matter, I was not young and dumb anymore. Good males did not do this shit. I did not have to stay.

I was preparing myself for what I had to say to him. How I was going to tell him I was leaving. How I would not give in to his apologies or explanations. I knew he would have them. He had treated me like a play thing. Besides the night we went sledding, had he even tried to get to know me more? Just because he said he wanted to, didn't mean he did. I was stupid. Just waiting for him each night. Like I did not have anything else to do. Like I could just be summoned when he wanted me.

"How about a coffee?" A small noise burst from my lips as I startled. Ryett. Ryett just smiled kindly at me, two steaming mugs in his tattooed hands. "They are both black, but I can scrounge up some milk and sugar if you like."

"Black is perfect." My throat ached, it hurt to talk. I extended a hand to accept the mug and my sweater slid up my arm revealing bruises already purpling my wrist. Ryett's eyes snagged on the spot as he handed the mug to me.

"May I join you?" His eyes lingered on my partially exposed shoulder. If my wrists were already bruised, bruises were probably showing on my shoulders and neck too. I tugged my sweater tighter around myself.

"You brought coffee. How could I refuse?" I tried to flash a small smile. Ryett sat in the seat across the fire from me. He had ditched his fancy suit jacket and his shirt was unbuttoned further at the collar, the skin showing beneath was covered in tattoos. "Why are you up?" I asked him.

"Sometimes I can't sleep when a lot is on my mind. A fire and some fresh air calms me." He sipped from his mug. "Why are you out here?"

"Same as you." I had not consciously picked it, I just found myself here. I could not stay in that room with Beck, but I was not going to say that outloud. I looked into the blackness of the coffee grasped in my hands.

"Are you alright?" There was genuine concern in his voice.

"I'm fine … what …" I didn't even know how to say it, "What was that when we met? I saw things and …" my voice trailed off.

I felt my cheeks heat, I should not have asked him. He must think I am crazy. Ryett stared at me. Considering. *Was I losing my mind?* It was just a flash, but I thought he had felt something too.

"Our magic … responded to each other." He said carefully.

"I don't have magic." I blurted out.

The corner of his mouth twitched upward, "You do. And it is awakening."

"I don't." I could not address having magic. That both he and Devron had said it. That I had utterly failed at summoning it. I changed the subject. "Thank you for stepping in with Vossarian."

"You are welcome." His eyes were caught on mine. It was as if we could not look away. The ice in his eyes captivated me.

"Where did you get those bruises?" Did I detect a hint of anger in his voice? I did not respond. I couldn't even lie. So I kept my mouth closed. It wasn't his business. I swallowed. Our eyes were still locked. "I know we have just met, but you saved Sarla. I am in your debt and ... here if you need anything." His voice was strong, yet painfully gentle.

"There is no debt. She saved me too." I broke away my eyes from him, sipping the coffee and staring into the fire.

Ryett simply pulled a blanket over his legs and sipped his coffee. I could feel his eyes on me. Finally, I looked back up at him and he spoke, "You should come to the Mountains. I think you would like it."

"Oh?" It was a bold statement coming from someone who had just met me, "What do you think I would like about it?"

"We have beautiful towns that are nestled among the mountains, the air is fresh and clean, and the views are unparalleled. If you are out here finding comfort in the fire, then I feel bold enough to assume you would also find comfort in the quiet of the mountain forests." His voice was deep and smooth. He was confident, but there was no arrogance in his assessment.

I let heartbeats pass before responding, "I think you are right." I held his gaze a few heartbeats more before looking back to the fire. I *had* always found comfort in the mountain forests back home.

We sat in silence for a long while staring into the fire. As the sun began to rise we both extracted ourselves from our blankets. I set my blanket back on the chair and turned only to find myself inches from Ryett. My breath caught. I could feel his body heat, smell his skin. The hint of smoke and cedar and pine. I swallowed and restrained myself from reaching out to touch him. Restrained myself from looking up to his mouth. To those ice colored eyes.

"Anything you need … just let me know." I could tell Ryett was restraining himself from touching me as he said it. I only nodded a thank you and stepped around him, aiming towards the training facility. I had some shit I needed to work out.

CHAPTER 13

I found Beck still in his room nursing a coffee. Pastries were arranged neatly on a tray set on a low table. "You were gone when I woke up." He said stiffly.

"I went to workout." I mumbled as I aimed for the bathroom.

But Beck blocked my way. "What's wrong?"

"What's wrong?" I seethed. "This. And this is wrong." I pulled up my sleeves and tossed my hair back revealing the bruises and bite marks that covered me.

Beck sucked in a breath. "That happened last night?" He asked quietly.

"You don't remember? Don't remember how you held me down?" I spat venom in my words.

Beck rubbed hands down his face. "I am so sorry, Genevieve.

I was furious with the stuff with Vossarian and ... I drank too much. I clearly did not realize how rough I was being. I am sorry."

"That is not an excuse! I asked you to stop and you didn't!" I shoved my way past him.

"I'm sorry! I'm sorry! I'm sorry!" He followed me into the bathroom. "It's not like we don't have sex all the time."

His words made me livid, "Are you kidding me? It is not the same!" My voice was shaking. I was crying. I did not care. "I am done with whatever this is between us. I will move back to my old room today and start making arrangements to leave."

"No. Please stay. I will make it up to you." He looked devastated. "I will do anything. Tell me what I can do."

"I am going to shower. Please move my things to my old room. Then give me space." I stepped into the shower, turning my back on the king.

Beck lingered for a moment, then closed the bathroom door behind himself as he left.

I hid in my room the rest of the morning. I was able to get some sleep, but woke up as June delivered lunch to me along with a white dress and white heels for that evening. Tonight every guest would wear black or white. I guess I was to wear white. I hated wearing white. It was a color I had only ever worn for my wedding and even then I opted for a softer ivory.

The rest of the time I always found a way to spill on or stain white clothes and avoided them. The dress was short, but had long sleeves and a high neckline—it would cover the bruises Beck had given me. I turned the dress to see the back, it was backless.

June returned later to sweep my hair into an elegant twist at the back of my head. Pulling out a few strands to cascade down. "Why does everyone seem so frightened of The King of the Mountains? He seems pleasant enough ..." My voice trailed off.

June's fingers paused, then she smiled at me in the mirror, "He has done a good job building a reputation to be afraid of."

"And what do you think?" I pressed.

She stepped to the dressing table and started sorting the makeup, "I think you should not always believe what people tell you."

She turned back to me, a palette of pink eye shadow in her hand. "Can you do something dark and smokey instead?" I was so tired of the soft pink and pastel blue and creamy white ... *everything*. I was done with it just like I was done with Beck.

She hesitated, "Beck may prefer your makeup softer."

"Beck can go fuck himself." I bit out.

June choked on a surprised laugh, "Dark smokey eyes it is."

We settled on a nude lipstick and June surprised me when she summoned a little glass jar filled with a black powder.

"For your nails," she gave me a mischievous smile. "Might as well go all out." June showed me how to dip my fingers and toes into the jar. My nails emerged colored black with the faintest purple undertone. I loved them.

"I know this is a crazy question, but can you … is it possible to make the dress black?" It was crazy. How I thought June could just change the dress I did not know, but she had magic, maybe she could.

June gave me a wink and snapped her fingers. The dress turned ink black and so did the shoes. "This look suits you, Genevieve." She said with a smile and left me to dress.

I slid into the black dress and stepped into the pair of black heels that had a single strap across the toes and one around the ankle. When I faced the mirror I smiled. I could not remember the last time I looked this good. This look did suit me.

There was a knock at the door. "Come in." I called.

Beck froze mid stride into the room. His white suit jacket was edged in black and like all his clothes, tailored perfectly to his muscular body. His jaw dropped before he quickly composed himself and snapped his mouth closed. "You look exquisite." He managed to breathe.

"Thank you." I held my head high and my back straight. I watched his eyes scan my body, the shoes, the dress, the tips of my fingers. He kept his mouth closed. If changing the dress bothered him, he was smart enough not to mention it.

"I brought you something." Beck fumbled with a small bag he carried. "This will help your bruises. It smells strong, but if you put it on before bed you should be healed by tomorrow." He set a small jar on a table. "And this … this is another apology. I know it does not fix things." He opened a small velvet box. The most beautiful diamond earrings sparkled up at me.

It did not fix things. But my anger softened. "They are beautiful. You didn't—"

"I did have to," Beck interrupted. "I can't say I am sorry enough. Will you wear them tonight?"

"Yes. Yes, I will wear them." My hands shook as I put the earrings on. They were magnificent.

"Genevieve—"

"I won't embarrass you. I will do what you need me to do through The Melt, but I think I really should leave after." I was not going to let him hook me back in with presents and apologies.

Beck's eyes were searching my face. "Just … Please don't think about where you will go or about leaving for a few days. And I promise, when The Melt is over, I will let you do whatever you wish. I will take you wherever you want to go if you still want to go."

"Okay." I breathed. Beck had stepped close to me. I was drowning in his scent, in his damn deep blue eyes. My body betrayed me and started warming between my legs, "Okay."

He pressed a kiss to my forehead, "Lets go try to have fun tonight." He offered his arm.

It was not hard to have fun. We enjoyed a ridiculously fancy meal at a long table filled with guests. Beck was mostly back to his usual self—resting his hand on my leg or drawing shapes idly on my bare back with his fingers. He kept me close, a hand on my waist or fingers laced through mine as he made the rounds with his court. I kept my promise. I smiled and made light conversation. I leaned into his kisses when he pressed them to my temple.

Eventually, the party moved outside to the deck and patio below. Magic kept us in a bubble of warmth. Twinkling lights and sparkling wine left everyone in good spirits. Finally, Beck was pulled away with some of the business owners from the town. I waved him off with a smile and barely noticed the flash in his eyes that seemed to say, "Stay put." Maybe it wasn't possessiveness, maybe he was truly worried about how Vossarian had shown up the night before. I convinced myself it was the latter. Maybe last night had been a fluke. I shook the thought out of my head, I knew better. I still had to leave regardless of the apology diamonds.

I stayed put—pretending to be enjoying myself as courtiers flitted by. I clutched my sparkling wine in one hand and grasped the railing with the other as I looked out into the night sky. *Where was Sarla or Aada?* I had not seen either of them in the crowd for hours and I hated just standing here by myself. As the night wore on, I noticed more and more people pointing out to the lake. I finally realized they were looking at something. The lake was melting before our eyes. Water was now visible. Thin slicks of ice floated across the surface as they slowly disappeared. *The Melt.*

Clinking glass brought my attention back. Beck was standing on the steps. Everyone hushed. "Thank you all for joining me at this Melt! I hope you all are enjoying yourselves … and continue to enjoy yourselves." Some voices in the crowd let out wild whoops. Beck laughed, "Do try to contain yourselves … which is an ironic request coming from me." People cheered again and Beck slammed back the contents of his drink before yelling, "Happy Melt!"

"Happy Melt!" The crowd echoed back.

Music started and what was once a reserved dinner quickly turned into a wild party. Some of the males whooped and ran down to the dock, dropping their clothes as they went, and plunging into the frigid water.

"Happy Melt." Ryett was suddenly standing beside me holding up a crystal glass of sparkling wine to clink with mine.

"Happy Melt." I clinked his glass with my own. My blood was thrumming in me. Electricity seemed to crash against my skin, begging to get out. Ryett captivated me. I could not tear my face away from the ice in his eyes. "No plunge in the lake for you?" I managed to ask.

Ryett snorted, "I have taken plenty of plunges, but I will leave it to the younger males tonight."

"I do not blame you. It must be freezing."

"I really just don't want to mess up my hair." I choked on my wine laughing at Ryett's response. "What? I spent a lot of time on it. Do you know how much shit you have to put in your hair to keep a crown up there?" Ryett was laughing with me.

"I wouldn't want you messing it up then!" I loved his laugh. It was full of joy and unrestrained. I scanned his face. I had been so caught up in his eyes, I had not noticed his jaw line, the point of his nose, the neatly trimmed stubble on his face that was rugged and refined—

"You two planning your jump into the lake?" Sarla gracefully joined us, clinking her glass with ours before finishing its contents.

"Someone is worried about messing up their hair." Ryett replied, sarcasm dripping in his voice.

Sarla chuckled, "And by someone you mean *you* do not want to mess up your hair, Ryett. You are getting rather self absorbed in your old age." She gracefully turned and made eyes at me urging me to look across the patio. When I glanced, I saw Beck in a group of males. His gaze was fiery and locked on me.

"Excuse me. I hope you both have fun tonight." I said and nodded to them both. Then I casually walked to Beck. "There you are!" A warm smile plastered my face. I allowed him to wrap an arm around my waist and pull me close as I leaned into the kiss he brushed to my temple. He introduced me to the other males he was with. I immediately forgot their names, but surprised myself by expertly guiding the conversation to

117

something light and casual—and one I did not have to do more than nod, smile, or laugh when appropriate.

Beck stayed glued to me as we spent hours making pleasantries with the people who wanted to have face time with him. The music had gotten loud and sparkling wine and amber liquor was flowing freely from the bar. I kept sipping the wine as Beck switched to the amber liquor. He could really throw them back, and servers glided by with a tray topped with a new drink for him whenever his was near empty.

Eventually, my feet started aching and I whispered to Beck that I needed to excuse myself to freshen up—really I planned to sneak away to bed, "Please excuse us. Enjoy the party." Beck nodded to the two couples he had been chatting with. They had been introduced, and although their titles meant nothing to me, their fine clothes and jewelry told me they were important. They nodded back graciously to both of us and Beck steered me away towards the glass doors into the residence. I guess Beck was coming with me.

I did not have anything to say to Beck as we made our way down a quiet hallway. I had kept my promise to him, playing nice and sticking to his side this evening. I was still planning to leave as soon as I could. I was not going to make excuses for Beck and no amount of wine or diamonds would change my mind.

Beck suddenly gripped my arm above my elbow—his grip was crushing as he turned me towards him. The hallway seemed to fold in on itself around us. I gasped and let Beck pull me close. Then we were standing in his private living room. "What was … you just transported us here?" It felt different from going through the portal with Sarla, less falling, more like the world folding in on itself and unfolding into a new place.

"Yes." Beck stalked to the wet bar and poured himself a tall drink. He threw back half of it before turning to me. "Ryett, huh? Is he why you want to leave? You don't know what he is, do you?" His voice was calm—too calm.

"What are you talking about?" I had not seen Ryett since he joked about jumping into the lake. That had been hours ago.

"I saw the way you looked at him. The way you *laughed*." He slammed back the rest of his drink. Then poured another.

Jealous. Beck was jealous that I had been talking with Ryett. "I was having a good time and he was making a joke! Am I not supposed to entertain and keep your ally happy?" I snapped more than I should have, but the thought that Beck was pissed about me enjoying the party—that he thought I was flirting—I was furious.

"He is not my ally." Beck bit out.

"Aren't you trying to be allies?" I knew I was playing with fire. I should be deescalating this conversation, not throwing on fuel. I had already seen what Beck could do. I still could not stop the anger in me. "What was I supposed to do? Ignore him? Should I not ensure he is having a good time?"

"*Not like that*." The glass shattered against the wall. The calm was gone from Beck's voice."Definitely not with *him*."

I braced myself. I should back down. Apologize. I couldn't. I was furious and I knew what came next. I knew what was coming if I didn't. I did not care. "There was *nothing* more to it. Don't you dare—"

Beck was suddenly inches from me, "Don't I dare what, Genevieve?"

"Don't you dare treat me like your property." I could not keep my voice from shaking, but I continued to glare back at him.

Some males could take the verbal sparring. Some males resorted to other forms of control. As soon as Beck had shattered his glass against the wall I knew which kind of male I was standing in front of. My head snapped to the side before I felt the pain. I tasted blood in my mouth and the side of my face stung.

Beck had hit me. I spit blood on the floor and turned my face slowly back to him. There was no remorse in his eyes. Pure fire and rage. I met his stare. I would not back down. And it might kill me.

"A black eye and split lip is harder to hide than bruised wrists, *Beck*." I spat his name. Let him know how disgusted I was. "What next?" Stupid. I must have a death wish. What a stupid thing to say. The room folded in again and reappeared an instant later as my back smashed into the wall. Beck's hand gripping my jaw.

"What *next*? What's next is that I remind you of your place here. You seem to have forgotten that I took you in, protected you, when you should not even *be* here." His breath was warm on my face and it reeked of alcohol. He twisted my chin to the side and pressed his face against mine, his lips grazing my neck.

"That does not make me *yours*." I threw as much venom as I could into the words. It would be the final nail in my coffin. I did not care. He was right—I should not even be here. Should not even be alive.

The back of my head cracked into the wall. I saw stars. *Fight back. Fight!* A small voice inside me urged. I couldn't even see the room. I blinked and blinked trying to regain some sense of my surroundings. I felt Beck yanking my dress up and I threw all my weight into shoving him off of me. "Get off of me! I told you things between us were *over*."

He stumbled back, then the air rippled around him. His hands were glowing, his voice pure taunting rage, "You think you can say no? You think you can fight me?" I slammed into the wall again—he wasn't even touching me. The air was holding me. He stepped back to me slowly. The back of his hand connected with my cheek again. The wind held me. I could not bring my hands up. I could not move my legs. I was completely pinned against the wall. Then his hand tangled in my hair and pulled my head back. His body pressed against mine. His lips grazed my ear as he whispered, "You are mine. You won't win, I will fucking—"

"BECK!" A male voice boomed across the room. Beck's hand was suddenly freed from my hair, his body no longer pressed against me. I sunk to the floor, "I should beat the shit out of you!" The male was yelling. I heard the crash of furniture breaking.

"Stay the fuck out of it!" They were fighting. The air was heavy and swirling.

I forced myself to look. My head was foggy. Both males were bloodied and swinging. Beck's living room was a disaster —furniture overturned or shattered. Devron took Beck to the floor and in a sweeping move had Beck's legs pinned and an arm around his neck. Beck roared and a silver mist bulged around them. Devron was containing their powers, shielding them in.

"Get out of here, Genevieve!" Devron yelled as he struggled against Beck in his arms.

I pushed to my feet. The room swayed—I must have a concussion—but I willed my feet to move. To run. I pulled my dress back into place as I hurled into the hallway, I ran for my room—I would get my bag and head to the woods. I was not just going to put space between us, I was leaving.

Thankfully no guests were in the halls. Just as I saw my door, twenty more yards to go, the floor moved. Everything rippled and swayed. *Earthquake?* I slammed into the wall using one hand to balance myself as I ran. It was not an earthquake, it was magic. The whole building was thrumming and vibrating with magic. The floors stopped moving seconds later and I pushed into my room. *Beck wouldn't kill Devron would he?* No. They had been friends their whole lives. I pushed the thought out of my head. I had to worry about myself.

My pack was still there, tucked in the back of the wardrobe with my boots. I threw on a thick cardigan, slung the pack over my shoulders and slipped into my boots. There was no time to find socks or warmer clothes. I hopefully still had a layer in my pack, but it was a risk I had to take. I had to go *now*.

I hurled down the hallway as Sarla burst from her room. She had a sheet wrapped around her otherwise naked body and Alias had his pants barely pulled on behind her. "Shit! Are you okay? What's happening? Where are you going?"

"I have to get out of here!" I gasped as I ran past. I exited a side door that I knew led to a deck and stairs on the back side of the estate. The opposite side of the building from the party and the lake. No one would see me leaving.

I crunched through the snow moving as quickly as I could. Every few steps I would break through up to my knee. I kept going, the lights from the estate disappearing behind me as I pushed through the woods. I had no way to cover my tracks but hopefully no one would think to look outside of the estate until I was long gone.

Music and the sounds of voices from the party slowly faded as I ran. The forest was quiet except for my crunching steps and heavy breathing. I chanced a final look behind me and collided with a broad chest. "You are too easy to catch." A cold voice said. Hands grabbed me and a strong smelling rag was pressed to my face.

CHAPTER 14

The room I woke up in was cold. The floor was all dirt. I sat up slowly and wrapped my arms around my legs, trying not to shiver. I took inventory. My boots were gone. There was nothing in the room. No sign of my pack. I felt my ears, the diamonds were gone too. Somehow my head did not hurt. Maybe I didn't have a concussion. I did not feel dizzy or sick. My eyes seemed to focus just fine. I sat quietly in the dim light, trying to make sense of what had happened.

Then the wooden door banged open and Vossarian strolled in. "You are too easy to catch, Genevieve. Want to tell me why you were in the woods, bruised and bleeding?"

"Not particularly." The walls were smooth stone and a narrow window not more than a foot high was tucked up to the ceiling across from the door. *Where the fuck was I?*

"Hmmm, I guess it doesn't matter. I have a proposal for you." He said. I just stared at him, "Become my queen."

"What's in it for me?" I bit out.

He laughed, "Don't you want to rule? That is what you had with Beck, the chance to become a queen. I thought I would extend the same opportunity. I need someone like you by my side."

"It's a no from me." I responded. I did not want any of that—especially not with him.

"That's too bad. Your other option is not going to be as enjoyable for you. Beck's going to bend over backwards for me when he finds out I took you, that I made you my pet." He walked across the dirt floor and squatted down in front of me. "I am going to take my time though." His hands shot forward, prying my mouth open and shoving in a small pill before holding my jaw closed. I struggled in his grip. The pill dissolved quickly and he released me with a smirk. "I am going to break you." He whispered.

I could not do anything but glare at him. Terror was filling me. *What was that pill?*

Two females entered the cell. They both wore skin tight full body suits that covered from their necks to their wrists and ankles and shimmered in whatever light was leaking into the cell. "Get her ready." Vossarian snapped and stalked out.

Get her ready meant leading me out of the dungeons and to

a small room. The females bathed me and dressed me in what I could only describe as straps. Bands of black fabric crossed tightly over my torso, pieces of the fabric barely covered my crotch and nipples, and a single band wrapped my neck. They rubbed oil on my body that had a shimmer to it and painted black sweeping eyeliner on my lids. My hair was slicked back and tied at the top of my head.

By the time they were finished I noticed my heart rate had risen. The room was not as clear as it had been. Any sounds sounded further away. The door opened and a huge male pushed in a tall narrow cage. I recognized his long hair, the beard—Kieron. It was the assassin I had put bullets in. He had lived. The females were helping me stand and guiding me to the cage. My legs were not my own anymore.

The pill. Fuck.

Kieron lifted me easily into the cage. Each touch of his hands sent electric pleasure tingling through my body. *Was this some sex drug?*

Stay conscious. I needed to remember what happened. My body was not my own anymore, but I had to keep my head.

Kieron pushed me down a long hallway. My legs felt weak and I had to clutch the bars of the cage to stay standing. There was music getting louder and louder. Doors opened and flashing lights and music met us. There were people dancing. Grinding on each other. All of them nearly naked. Many were smeared in paint that was glowing or their skin shimmered

127

like mine did in the flashing black lights.

My heart raced and I tried to get a look at my surroundings. Kieron left the cage—me—in the middle of the room. Lights flashing all around and bodies closed the gap of the path he had pushed me in on. Hands reached into the cage to touch me. Rubbing my legs. Sliding fingers along the straps that covered me. Each touch sent uncontrollable pleasure through my body. My body wreathed.

"Let's make sure our guest has a good time tonight!" Vossarian's voice boomed.

Where is he? I scanned the room and saw him lounging in a chair—on a throne. His black pants and unbuttoned black shirt were free of any glowing paint. Females danced around him.

I locked eyes with him. The corners of his mouth turned up. I was breathing heavily, my heart pounding. I could hardly keep my eyes open. *Stay in your head. Stay in your head.* I let go of everything and held onto the fine thread of consciousness. The drug would make me blackout if I did not fight.

I felt my body sinking down the bars as I sat in the small space at the floor of the cage. I leaned my head back against the bars. I was so tired. The flashing lights were making my head spin. *Look at him.* I forced my eyes back on Vossarian. More and more hands were touching my skin. They felt so good. My blink was too long. The smirk on Vossarian's face was the last thing I saw before everything went dark.

CHAPTER 15

My head pounded and it hurt to open my eyes. I was back in the cell. A thin blanket had been tossed over me. I pulled it tightly around myself as I lay on the cold floor. I took inventory: head hurt, eyes hurt, nothing else hurt. I felt for the thrumming in my blood Devron had said was magic in me, nothing. I curled under the blanket and closed my eyes.

I must have fallen back asleep because I jolted awake to the touch of a hand on my face. Vossarian chuckled. "Did you have a good time last night sweetheart?"

"Fuck you." I gritted out.

He laughed. "You still have fire in you. Tell me, have you ever felt pleasure like that? Wasn't it fun?"

"No, Voss. Being drugged and groped by strangers and

waking up on a cold dirt floor is *not* fun." I pushed myself up to a sitting position and held the blanket so it covered my body.

"Hmmm, I guess we will have to try again." He grabbed my jaw, forcing my mouth open, and shoved in another pill. I tried to stand, tried to hit him, but air laced with magic pushed me back to the ground and held my arms down. "Behave or I will let Kieron keep you for the night, after the bullets you put in him I am sure he would enjoy some alone time with you." I stopped resisting.

If last night had been straps, the poor excuse for clothing the females put me in tonight was mesh. I might as well have been naked even with the black mesh that covered from my wrists to my neck and to my ankles. Just as what had happened the night before, the room started swaying, my heartbeat quickening. All I could feel was the mesh pressed on my skin, the little pin pricks of air it let through. Kieron rolled the cage down the hall and back into the room filled with black lights, loud music, and people dancing. Vossarian was sitting on the same throne in his usual black clothes.

I stayed conscious longer, glaring at Vossarian, trying to ignore the pleasure rippling through my body. But I only woke up on the same cold dirt floor. Head pounding.

What did I know about drugs? I tried to make my brain work despite the pounding. Drugs could be addictive, changing the neuro pathways in your brain. You could build up tolerances to them, eventually needing more and more. If you took too much they could kill you. That was all I knew. I needed to be able to stay conscious long enough to learn how I could escape. So I either needed to figure out how to not take the drug or hope that I would build up a tolerance—or get enough drugs so that I did not wake up.

The room darkened as the sun dropped. I weighed my options. From one corner of the room I could see out the small window and a few stars sparkling in the sky. The stars brought me hope. Hope that I would see the night sky again. That I would find a way out.

Three stars shone bright tonight—The Hunter's Belt. It was the constellation I always recognized first. The three stars marked the hunters belt while nearby stars created the bow and bounty the hunter carried. Legends told that the three stars of The Hunter's Belt represented the three warrior tribes that once ruled the continent. I had spent my whole life in the territory believed to be ruled by the western tribe. The familiar stars gave me comfort. *Were the stars the same in this world? Or like the landscape, were they different?*

I brought my thoughts back. I had to make a plan. My stomachs churned with my options. Winging it was not going to get me out of here. I might only have one chance to get this right. *Play the long game.* I was going to convince Vossarian that he was breaking me, then when they dropped their guard, I would find a way out.

That night, Vossarian returned. It was the same routine—

he shoved the pill in my mouth, I was taken to be cleaned and dressed, then I was rolled to the room with lights and loud music. Vossarian always sat on his throne watching me. At least he did while I was conscious.

The next night was the same, but I did something different. I scanned the crowd. Trying to figure out who was here, dancing. *Was there anyone important?* All that stood out was features on some of the people—mostly the females—and all had paint on their nearly naked bodies. Something was off about them. Pointed ears, or eyes that seemed larger, or limbs that were slightly not normal proportions. It had to be the drugs or the lights.

The following night I scanned the crowd again. I saw the same thing. Many of the painted and nearly naked bodies had features that were not what I was used to seeing. I looked back to Vossarian. He was leaning forward on his throne staring at me. I had been careless, he had seen me paying too much attention. I sunk to a sitting position, letting the hands touch my skin and send electricity through me.

CHAPTER 16

Vossarian entered my cell and leaned against the door. "Having fun, yet?" I just glared at him. "I see. You still think you can escape. What have you been doing each night? Looking for the exits?" I did not respond. He crossed the room and knelt down in front of me. His hand reached up to grab my face, but I was faster this time. I hit his hand out of the way. I saw the pill skittered across the floor before stars flashed in my eyes. My cheek burned where Voss had struck me. "I warned you to behave." He hissed at me. I spit at him in response. Rage filled his eyes, "Have fun with Kieron." He turned and walked to the door.

Kieron's large frame filled the doorway. Voss whispered to him before leaving. Kieron entered my cell and placed a chair in the middle of the floor. I could not help but press myself against the wall. Kieron was huge. He had at least a hundred pounds on me and was a whole head taller.

I watched as he removed his shirt and draped it over the back of the chair. Then he tied back his hair. His muscles rippled and flexed with his movements. Scars covered his skin—including two that looked much like scars left by bullets. He could heal, but he was still scarred. He adjusted the leather cuffs that wrapped his wrists and sat in the chair. Tonight was not going to be fun. "You are lucky Voss gave me very clear instructions on what I can and cannot do to you." He said, his voice sounded almost bored.

"Good to see you, Kieron. Looks like you have at least two reminders of me. Should we add another?" My body screamed at me to keep my mouth shut, to preserve myself, but I knew the con would work better if they thought they had wiped the fire from my blood—to do that I had to show I still had some fire left.

He laughed, "Bullets are nothing compared to what I am going to do to you." His eyes were dark and amused. He knew he had the upper hand. Knew that there was nothing I could do against him here.

I wanted to curl up in a ball, but I forced myself to spit venom instead, "Was it necessary to remove your shirt or is that just because you like to look at yourself?"

Kieron leaned forward, resting his forearms on his thighs.

Rope appeared from nowhere in his hands. He let it sway back and forth between his legs before he rose slowly. "Let's see if you still run your mouth by the end of the night."

There was nowhere for me to go. I could not press myself through the cold walls. I could not side step and keep space between us. I had two choices: fight or follow his instructions. I would lose in a fight, but it might be worth it. I let Kieron walk right up to me—he was standing close, towering over me. His hand reached for my wrist and I struck. Pushing off the wall I threw my body into his and thrust my knee into his groin. He bent over with a grunt and staggered a few steps. I brought my elbow up to drop on the back of his head, but felt my back crunch against the wall instead. Kieron had moved fast. Unnaturally, fast. His forearm pressed against my throat. I could barely suck in a breath before the rope was around my neck and burning my skin as he pulled it tight. My hands were bound together a moment later. The back of Kieron's hand struck my face and I slumped to the floor.

He turned his back on me as he walked back to the chair, the rope trailing behind him. He sat and brushed invisible dust from his leather pants, "Come." He yanked the rope and I had no choice but to scramble to my feet. He slowly pulled the rope, forcing me to walk towards him until I was standing between his spread legs. He slipped the rope beneath one of his boots, "I like a female on her knees." He yanked on the rope again and I was forced to my knees as the rope pulled me down.

His rough hand grabbed my chin and lifted it until I was staring up at him. The corners of his mouth twitched upwards before the back of his hand connected with my cheek bone. I slumped against his thigh as pain seared in my face. A tug of the rope had me back on my knees. I forced myself to glare back at him and threw every bit of venom I had left into my words, "So the muscles *are* just for show." I tasted blood before I felt the pain in my other cheek.

I was pulled back to my knees by my hair. I blinked through the pain and set my eyes back on Kieron's face. "We do this until you beg me for pleasure instead." He said, cruel amusement lit his eyes.

"What's the point, I can't imagine you have ever pleasured a female." I could not keep this up. I braced myself for another blow, but one did not come. Instead I felt cold metal against my breastbone.

I opened my eyes and saw the knife Kieron had pressed to my chest. I gasped as he sliced up between my breasts and arced the knife tip out to my shoulder. He flicked my blood from the tip of the knife before lifting my chin with it.

"Beg me for pleasure and find out." He flicked the tip across my cheek and I felt warm blood drip. "Have you had enough?"

I just glared at him, my breathing was unsteady, the cuts burned and my face throbbed. I tried to think of something awful to say to him. My head snapped to the side as he struck me again. The knife under my chin forced me back to my knees even as my head rang. His hand lifted again and I braced myself for another blow.

He laughed and stroked my hair, "How about now?" I shook my head no. My head jerked back as he pulled my hair. "Ask me for pleasure. You have had enough." It was a command.

"No." I whispered. My inner voice screamed at me. It was not worth it. But Kieron would not be satisfied if I gave in yet. He had to believe he had broken me—that I was an accomplishment—he did not believe it yet. The side of my face felt like it ripped open as his hand struck me and I crashed into his thigh. The blow made me see stars and black splotches clouded my vision.

My bound hands grabbed the rope around my neck as he yanked me up to my knees. Tears streamed down my cheeks as I tried to clear my head from the blackness.

His fingers gripped my chin and turned my face from one side to the other. Then he raised his hand again. A whimper released from my lips. I was done. He would beat me to unconsciousness, but that would not serve me. I needed him to think he had won. At least I had convinced myself it was the best choice. Maybe he had won.

"Beg me." He commanded.

Even blinking hurt. "Please." I whispered.

"Please what?" His eyes lit with amusement.

"Pleasure ... please." He cocked his head, waiting. "Give me pleasure, Kieron." My voice sounded as desperate as I felt. I didn't care. He had won.

"Again." A smirking smile crossed his lips. The bastard was proud of himself.

"Give me pleasure, Kieron." His fingers still held my face forcing me to look at him.

"Sit." He commanded. I slumped against his leg. The smooth leather of his pants against my cheek. "Open your mouth." I did and felt the familiar pill placed on my tongue.

Kieron's hand stroked my hair. His other hand gently rubbed a strong smelling salve on the cuts and bruises he had inflicted. Whatever it was seemed to numb the pain. His touch became so tender it sent warmth into my body. I didn't dare move. His fingers brushed across my lips. Teasing. I watched in horror as he flipped the knife over in his hand and brought it back to my chest. But instead of cutting me, he sliced through the pathetic excuse for clothing that was barely covering me. The delicate fabric fell to the dirt.

The drugs started to take hold of me as his hand rubbed across my shoulder and removed the rope from around my neck. Then he untied the binding on my wrists. I watched his hand loosen the fastening on his pants. Then he lifted me from the floor into his lap with ease. His large hands sent burning pleasure through my body. He guided me to lean back and rest my body against his muscled warm chest. His breath and lips caressed my neck as his hands wandered along my naked body.

I had no control over my body anymore. I didn't even try

to stay in my head as Kieron's hands burned pleasure into my skin. I did not want to remember this.

CHAPTER 17

I woke up alone in my cell. I was naked, but had a thicker blanket wrapped around me. Surprisingly my face did not hurt and thankfully I did not remember what had happened with Kieron after he pulled me onto his lap. I rolled over, pulling the warm blanket tighter and cried until I fell back asleep.

I did not know how long I had been asleep when my cell door banged open again. I didn't move. "It's time to come play." Vossarian. I held still. "I can send Kieron back if you would rather."

No. I rolled over and slowly pushed myself to sitting, keeping the blanket around me.

Voss knelt in front of me, but before he could grab my face I simply opened my mouth. Approval flashed in his eyes, "Good girl." He set the pill in my mouth and stroked my cheek. I jerked away from his touch. He only chuckled and left.

Kieron watched me from the doorway as the two females brought me to be cleaned and changed. There was no mark left from the slice he had slit up my chest and across my shoulder. I assumed my face was also unmarked.

Before Kieron lifted me into the cage he brushed my hair back, running his fingers around my neck. Then he whispered in my ear, "I am disappointed. I thought you would be more fun to play with. Maybe it is just an act. Or maybe it was just that easy to break you." *An act? Easy?* I wanted to gouge his eyes out. But he shut me in the cage and wheeled me out to stare at Vossarian and be groped by strange hands.

I sat in my cell the next day waiting. Tonight was going to be awful. Kieron's statement had made me worry. *What if they did not believe they were breaking me? I had given up too easily. How many times had he hit me before I had begged for pleasure? Did I fight back enough or just allow him to beat on me?*

Tonight I was going to fight. I would lose in the end. But I was going to fight. Best case, I would give Kieron a new scar to remind him of me.

Like clockwork, Vossarian entered my cell. This time I stood up, my back against the wall. He walked towards me, "Time to play."

"No." I said it strongly, more strong than I felt. He reached for my face and I stepped to the side, "I said no!"

Annoyance flashed in Voss's eyes. I felt a strong hand tighten around my throat and force me to my knees—but there was no hand. Magic laced the air, swirling around me. "One more chance, Genevieve." Voss warned.

"No." I bit out. The invisible hand released me and I fell to my hands.

Voss walked back to the door. He spoke loud enough for me to hear him, "You were right, I owe you a hundred coins. I will be back in a few days. I don't care what you do, just leave her in one piece." Then he whispered something else that I could not hear.

Kieron's frame filled the doorway. *Had Voss just said he did not care what Kieron did? That he was not going to be back for days? Fuck.* Terror gripped me. *Get up. Get up and fight!* The voice inside of me was screaming. I pushed myself to my feet—I had invited this fight, time to see it through.

Kieron brought the same chair, placing it in the middle of the room and draping his shirt over the back. He sat and stared at me—his face unreadable. I stood with my back to the wall, glaring at him.

It felt like minutes, the two of us just staring, one of us would break the silence eventually. I was going to make sure it was him.

"You do not seem like a female who would be content with

a life of leisure, fancy clothes, and smiling at parties." He had spoken first, "No. You are too uncut for that. I think Beck turned you into his little pet, fucking you whenever he wanted, dressing you up to show you off, and ignoring you whenever it suited him."

It was a blunt and surprisingly accurate assessment. I had not realized it was that bad. I pressed my lips together and he went on, "I am guessing he got too drunk or you spoke up too loudly or both and he tried to remind you of your place. That is why you were bloodied and running through the forest wasn't it?"

I tried to keep my face neutral. Kieron chuckled, "I thought so. Voss thought you had already broken, but I have been doing this long enough to know better. Our bet won me a small fortune, so thanks for that."

"I'm getting bored. What's your plan? Beat me, drug me, fuck me?" I did not take my eyes off of Kieron as I spoke.

He smirked, "Is that what you think happened last time? No, I like the females I fuck to be conscious." The rope appeared in his hands and he watched it sway back and forth. "Tonight you don't get drugs. Let's see if the withdrawals or the pain get you first." He stood and took a step towards me, "Then I am going to fuck you until you scream for me."

This was going to be a bad night.

I woke naked and sick under the large warm blanket. I rolled over wrapping the blanket around myself—I would not cry today. I spent two days with Kieron, but I had invited the horror I endured and unfortunately I *would* remember all of it. I refused to feel bad for myself.

When Voss came next, I let him place the pill on my tongue and turned my face away from his stroking fingers. The females dressed me in scraps yet again, rubbing the shimmering oil on my body. I walked to the cage where Kieron was waiting, but he stopped me. He grabbed my hair and gently pulled my head back, slowly forcing my neck to open to him. He ran his lips up my neck to my ear. His breath was warm as he whispered, "Good girl. Keep behaving and things will get better for you." I was going to be sick, but I just looked away from him as he closed me into the cage.

That night Kieron pushed the cage closer to Vossarian's throne. It was not the only thing that was different. Important looking males came and chatted with Voss. They all looked me over when Voss gestured in my direction. I could not hear what they said over the music, but everything looked official. I lost consciousness while the males were still there.

It was the first time I felt relieved to wake up on the cold dirt. It was the devil I knew. I didn't even realize I was worried I would find myself somewhere new until I had woken up. *Who*

were those males? Did I even care?

When Voss came that night I opened my mouth for him again. This time I did not pull away from his touch.

CHAPTER 18

I lost count of the days. They barely fed me, I could feel my body was getting weak from laying in a cell all day and sitting in a cage for who knows how long at night. I was behaving and nothing was changing. Vossarian was right, he would break me. I needed a way out of this. It made my stomach churn thinking of what I had to do, but I saw no other option. I had to try to get closer to Voss. It was the only way I could think of to stop spending my time locked up in a cell or a cage.

The cell door opened and two males swaggered in. I could smell the reek of alcohol on them. "I thought I would come see how Voss's new toy is doing. Are they treating you well down here?" One of the males drawled. The dim light from the narrow window shimmered in his black hair. The other male just snickered and leaned against the wall. He had a scar down his cheek and a slightly hooked nose.

I scooted back against the opposite wall and stood. Two drunk males in my cell was not a good sign. This did not seem like a sanctioned visit and if it wasn't, I was in a lot of trouble. The male with the black hair crossed the room and put his hands against the wall on either side of me. His eyes were death and evil and hate. Rook. Rook was in my cell. Piss drunk.

"Remember me?" He sneered as his eyes raked over my nearly naked body. "Maybe this will jog your memory." His hand clasped around my throat and he squeezed cutting off my air. My hands shot up to his arm, trying to pry his hand away. "Sarla's not here to save you this time." He hissed at me.

"*Get out.*" Kieron's deep voice was laced with anger.

Rook let go of my throat and I gasped as I sucked in air. "Come on now, Kieron, Byron and I just wanted to play. Didn't your mommy teach you to share your play things?" He turned away from me slowly, "Or was she cut up into pieces before she could teach you that lesson?"

The other male—Byron—took a threatening step towards Kieron, rolling his shoulders and cracking his knuckles. Kieron moved so fast I could hardly register what was happening. I heard a crunch and Byron slumped to the floor, his head twisted to the side. Kieron had snapped his neck. "*Get the fuck out* and take your dog with you." His voice was low and laced with rage.

147

Rook tensed as he looked at his fallen companion. "You're no fun." He growled, but he slowly moved around Kieron, scooping the dead male up carrying him from the cell. Kieron slammed the door closed behind Rook and leaned his back against it. His chest heaving with his breaths as if he was trying to calm himself.

"That was highly offensive to dogs." I said finally. Light flashed back into his eyes as he looked at me and I swore I could see the corner of his mouth twitch upwards. He did not say anything so I continued, "And if you say you are 'more of a cat person,' I am breaking up with you."

He *chuckled*. A real and warm deep chuckle. Then he left my cell without saying a word.

That night I opened my mouth for Vossarian and his drugs. As he placed them on my tongue I closed my mouth around his finger and sucked it into the back of my throat. My hand grabbed his wrist guiding him to pull out slowly. His soulless black eyes lit with fire at what I had done. *Good. This might be easier than I thought.*

Kieron led me by a leash around my neck through the crowd and to Vossarian at his throne. Voss patted his thigh, "Sit." I sat and he pulled my body back to lean on him. His hands were the only ones touching my body tonight. Electricity and fire sent pleasure through my skin. I let him do whatever he liked and let go of trying to control my body's physical reaction. I breathed deeply and held on to consciousness as long as I could.

More males came that night. They talked of goods and shipments. Nothing indicating what exactly it was they were transporting. But Vossarian had let me get closer to him—it was progress.

The cell door opened and the two females walked in followed by Kieron. *Had the day already passed?* I looked up to the window and saw the light still streaming through it. It was still daytime. One of the females unfolded a dress in her arms and indicated to me that I was to put it on. I looked over her shoulder and saw Kieron leaned against the door frame, watching. I turned my back to him and allowed the females to help me slip out of the tiny pieces of lace I had been dressed in the night before and into the dress.

The red fabric draped closely against my body. The neckline dipped between my breasts and down to my waist. A high slit rose to my right hip. The second female held up two golden bracelets. I lifted my wrists for her and she clasped them around my wrists. A small chain connected them and another, dangling like a leash, remained in her hand—these were the most ridiculous handcuffs I had ever seen. I could easily break the chain. Then I realized that that was the point. They were not functional. They were symbolic.

The female led me to the door and handed the chain to Kieron before the two females disappeared down the hall. I looked anywhere but at Kieron. "Keep your mouth shut and do what I tell you to do." He said. Then he took my arm in his hand, in spite of the leash, and guided me down the hall. We wound our way up and up before ascending a set of wide stairs. Black double doors met us at the top of the stairs. They opened as we approached and light met us as we entered a wide marble hallway flanked by pillars.

Kieron led me down the hall and to another set of double doors. The doors had to be twenty feet tall and they opened on their own. My knees buckled at what I saw before me. Armed males stood in uniform over a row of males and females kneeling on the marble floor, their hands and feet in chains. Their bodies were bruised and bleeding. Most hung their heads. My eyes followed along the row of prisoners and to the opposite side of the large room. Vossarian sat, legs spread upon an iron throne.

"Come." Kieron commanded quietly and I followed him, led by the thin golden leash. We walked down the entire row of prisoners. Kieron placed me at the bottom of the steps leading up to Vossarian's throne and he took his place next to me. Vossarian simply looked me over and nodded his approval to Kieron.

Footsteps echoed through the hall and I turned to see a group of three males, finely dressed, swords hanging from their belts, slowly walking down the row, inspecting each prisoner. As they reached our end of the room, the male in the middle, who seemed to be the one in charge of their group, said, "You said there was trouble with this bunch? They are from the twelfth world?"

The twelfth world? These people were from a different world. Like me. Things clicked into place. The people I saw each night, the ones with features that were different, they must be from different worlds too.

"Yes, the twelfth world. Hard workers, but short lives in their world. There was some trouble, but it has been taken care of. Unfortunately, it means you lost five males, but the remaining lot is ready." Voss answered, his voice bored, as he pointed to the side of the room behind the prisoners. I followed his finger and saw five bodies strung up and bloody against the wall. My legs became weak and I sucked in a breath. Kieron's hand tightened around my upper arm, had it not I would have collapsed to the floor. I looked away, swallowing the sick that threatened to come up my throat.

The male grunted in displeasure and turned back to Vossarian, "Very well. I imagine the price remains the same." He then turned to me and our eyes met for a moment before I dropped mine to the floor. My heart threatened to beat out of my chest. "Where did you find such a fine female, Voss?"

"She is quite nice isn't she." Vossarian laughed, he did not answer the question. "I will have my men escort the lot to your transport."

A whip cracked and some of the females let out small cries of fear. Chains clanked as the prisoners were hauled to their feet and forced to shuffle out the tall doors. The three males nodded to Vossarian, exchanging words with the king, before leaving the hall themselves. I did not hear what was said. I could not hear what was said. My head was roaring with anger. These poor people. *What happened to their world? Why did Vossarian want me to see this?*

Kieron led me back to my cell. Neither of us spoke until he reached to remove the ridiculous golden handcuffs. I couldn't keep my mouth closed any longer, "What was the point of that? Why did you bring me there?"

"To show you that there is always an alternative way to deal with you. Keep behaving and you will be at the king's side in golden bangles instead of on your knees in chains." He closed the door in my face and I was alone.

That night was the same as every other night. Vossarian placed the pill in my mouth. I was washed and dressed and brought to the room with music and lights and hands.

CHAPTER 19

I lay in my cell, my head pounding. The door opened and Kieron entered. I stood leaving the blanket on the floor. He crossed the room slowly, summoning a glass of water from thin air and extending it to me. I carefully took the water and drank, my headache seemed to wash away with each swallow. I handed the glass back to him and it disappeared from his hand. Neither of us had spoken.

He stepped close, towering above me. I averted my eyes and looked at the dirt floor. His finger traced along the silk scraps I was still wearing from the night before. Two pieces tied behind my neck draped down my front, barely covering my breasts and eventually combined into a single piece of smooth fabric below my navel. A thin piece circled the narrowest part of my waist.

His fingers traced down my arm, then my naked waist before walking along my exposed hipbone. The tips of his fingers skimmed underneath the edges of the delicate fabric. I didn't move—I couldn't move—I was hardly breathing. His other hand firmly spread across the middle of my back and his boot nudged my bare feet into a slightly wider stance.

He had broken me. I had no fight left. I was letting him touch me, letting him do whatever he wanted.

"Look at me." He said quietly. His fingers stroked circles on my bare hip. I lifted my chin and looked at him.

I was not a small female, but standing so close to him—feeling his huge hands on me—I was small and weak in his presence. I forced myself to keep looking at his face.

I knew where these encounters always led with him. And I knew it was useless to fight back or resist. I had tried.

His fingers teased their way back up my body and his thumb stroked across my bottom lip. A pulse of warmth flowed through my body and electricity hummed under my skin. *He had broken me.* A breath shuddered out of me.

His lips slowly curled into a small smile. "Good girl." He said and he stepped back from me. A small table appeared with a plate of bread, cheese, and fruit, along with a glass and pitcher of water, "You get the night off. Voss is gone and unfortunately, I need to take care of a few things."

I could cry with relief. No drugs, no loud music, no strange hands touching me, no long night of Kieron. A steaming bath appeared next, along with a folded pile of clothes.

"Enjoy your evening." He said and he closed the door behind himself.

I did enjoy my evening. They had never given me this much food or water. I lingered in the bath and let myself breathe. No one was coming back for me tonight. The clothes actually covered my body and kept me warm. I enjoyed every minute —until I lay shivering and nauseous on the floor hours later. Withdrawals. I was having withdrawals again. I shivered the rest of the night, wishing I was dead. Praying for the music and the hands and the warmth and everything the drugs brought with them. I would even have settled for more of Kieron over this.

Vossarian was back the next day. I greedily took his fingers in my mouth as he fed me the pill. Anything to stop feeling so sick. He lingered, holding my chin in his hand. Just when I thought he might say something he stood and left.

Kieron put me back in the cage that night. I could barely keep my eyes open by the time he rolled me close to the throne. I had not even tried to stand tonight.

When I lifted my eyes to Voss I realized another male sat next to him. His tattooed hands rested casually on his legs and the sides of his head were shaved, leaving a strip of long hair down the center of his head. Ryett. Ryett was lounging in a plush velvet chair watching the room. A male wearing all black with a chest harness full of silver blades stood behind Ryett's shoulder. My head was leaned back against the bars. I forced my eyes to stay open—for a moment they locked with Ryett's. Ryett leaned forward and started speaking to Voss. Everything went dark.

It was light in my cell when Kieron and the females opened the door. The red dress was draped over one of the female's arms. I shook my head no to Kieron. I did not want to see another group of people chained and beaten. "You know the alternative option." Kieron said flatly. I let out a sigh and turned back to the females.

When I was dressed and secured in the ridiculous handcuffs, Kieron led me back up towards the towering double doors. I swallowed and braced myself for whatever I was going to witness today as the doors opened for us.

More prisoners in chains kneeled, beaten and bloody along one side of the large chamber. The same guards stood behind them with their whips and swords. My eyes ran along the row, my stomach sinking. I clenched my jaw shut as Kieron squeezed my arm and nearly dragged me towards the front of the room. Vossarian sat on his throne and to his left two guards stood with two males. Their backs were to us. Voss nodded to

Kieron as we approached. One of the males glanced over his shoulder. Ryett. It was Ryett and the male with him from last night. I stumbled as we passed them and a male, his skin sliced into strips and strung up by his arms, was revealed behind the four males. Kieron guided me firmly into place at the bottom of the steps below Vossarian's throne.

One of the guards cracked his whip across the back of the male and a scream broke the silence in the chamber. "Last chance to tell us." The guard growled at the male. He drew back his whip, but Ryett raised his hand. He then placed his open palm in front of his companion who drew a silver knife from his harness and placed it in Ryett's palm.

I could not help the cry that released from my lips as Ryett took two steps towards the male and slit his throat. Blood sprayed across the floor. "I am getting bored, Voss." Ryett said as he handed the knife back to his companion. "This lot will do and I will deal with any incendiaries on the journey. We are more than equipped to handle some disturbances."

"Very well." Voss waved his hand and the guards yanked the line of prisoners to their feet. Ryett turned, followed by his companion, and strode from the room without another glance in my direction. Chains clanked as the prisoners were led out after them.

I was frozen in place. Guards dragged the dead male's body from the room. It hit me all at once. They were slave traders. Sarla had not mentioned any of this when we first met. *Sarla and Ryett were slave traders.* I had just watched Ryett kill a defenseless male. I wanted to vomit all over the floor. How had I been so blind. Sarla was involved in this. This is why Beck told me to stay away.

My head spun as guards came and went and spoke with Vossarian. I did not hear any of it. I stood there clenching my teeth together, trying to not scream with rage and rake my nails down Vossarian's face. Kieron finally pulled on my arm to leave.

I was numb as Kieron led me back to my cell. I barely heard him as he removed the handcuffs and told me I would not be summoned that night. I did not even care as I lay under the blanket shivering and sweating in the absence of the drugs. Everything I thought I knew about this world and the people in it was cracking into pieces.

CHAPTER 20

My head pounded twice as hard when I woke up. It hurt so bad I did not realize someone was in the cell with me until a hand cupped under my head and a glass was raised to my lips. "Drink." It was not Voss or Kieron. I drank and blinked my eyes trying to get focus. Ryett was kneeling on the dirt floor in front of me.

I slowly pushed myself to a seated position. He held out the glass again. I cautiously took it from him and drank, the pounding starting to subside. "Beck is tearing apart his kingdom trying to find you." I just stared blankly at Ryett. Fuck Beck, at least he was suffering for what he did. *Why was Ryett here?* "I am going to help you."

Not what I was expecting. "What?" It was all I could say.

"I am going to get you out of here, but I need you to trust me." Ryett said. "I am sorry in advance."

Did it matter? Did it even matter if I was being beaten by Beck or drugged by Vossarian or beaten and drugged and fucked by Kieron? It would just be some new nightmare with Ryett. Beck had alluded to Ryett's character, that he was not to be trusted. I witnessed him take nearly fifty slaves and brutally kill a defenseless male without hesitating. But Beck had turned out to not be trustworthy either. "Okay." I heard myself saying.

"Okay." Ryett repeated back. "You are going to get out of here. I promise."

I only leaned back against the wall as Ryett slipped out the door.

Ryett was with Vossarian again that night. Kieron had pushed the cage closer to the throne. After a little while, Voss stood and opened the cage. He took my hand and led me back to his throne where he perched me on his lap. I felt his hands sliding over me as I leaned back into him. "What do you think of my new pet?" Vossarian asked Ryett.

"I think Beck is going to do whatever you want him to in order to get her back." Ryett replied. I forced my heavy eyes to look at him. He was scanning my body. His eyes caught where Vossarian's hands were touching me. "You have not told him you have her?"

Vossarian laughed darkly, "No, I quite like watching him destroy his kingdom as he looks for her." Vossarian's hands ran along my skin.

"I know how you can make up for breaking our deal, Vossy." Ryett's voice sounded further and further away.

"Hmmm, what do you have in mind?" He pulled my head back on his shoulder, baring my neck. I let him brush his lips along my shoulder and up my neck. I could not move if I wanted to. It did not matter how sick his touch made me, the drugs held me captive and I let out a small moan at the sensation of his breath on my skin.

"Give her to me." Ryett had leaned forward in his seat. His companion with the knives tensed behind him.

Vossarian laughed, "You want to buy her? Tell me you aren't just going to hand her back to your new buddy Beck?"

"I said *give*, but I will buy her if that is what it takes. I have my own business with Beck and if it means he will do what I want then maybe I will give her back. But, I like the idea of keeping her for myself." Ryett's eyes raked over me. *Buy me?*

"She is not for sale, Ryett." Voss's fingers wrapped around my neck, claiming me.

I was barely still there—my eyelids barely flicked open. *Hold on just a little longer.* I urged myself. My body arching and grinding into Voss's lap.

"Voss, you tried to sell children behind my back and hunted my cousin for stopping you. That was my one rule

161

—no children—and you broke it. I should be ending our arrangement over this, but here I am." Ryett's voice was lethal. "So yes, let me buy her from you and we will call it even."

Selling children? Vossarian stroked a finger up my thigh. My body arched at his touch. He chuckled, "Okay, Ryett, you might not like the price and I sell whoever I like going forward."

No. Ryett could not agree to that. They were talking about *children.* Ryett's eyes ran over my body again. "Fine. I know there's a good market for them anyway." He sat back in his seat almost looking bored. Voss continued stroking my skin, running his fingers down my center from my throat, between my breasts and dipping them between my legs. I let go of the small thread my mind was holding on to and my consciousness left me.

Ryett was back in my cell the next day, this time Vossarian was with him. Light filtered in through the small window. "We will leave tomorrow. I want all her things as well." They had clearly been here talking before I had woken up. I lay still on the ground even though my eyes were open.

"Why do you want her things?" Voss leaned against the wall.

Ryett's face was not kind today, "Does it matter?"

"I suppose not, Ryett, and for the ridiculous price you were willing to pay I will make it happen." Voss was flicking invisible dust from his sleeve. "Come, we have more to discuss."

Ryett did not even look back as they left the room. I just closed my eyes and tried to go back to sleep.

I woke up to Kieron and the two females, "Ryett wants to play." Kieron said flatly.

No drugs. It was going to be a rough night. They took me to the same room and dressed me in the usual scraps of fabric. A collar was fastened around my neck and Kieron led me down the hall by a rope.

Without the drugs the flashing lights and loud music made me wince. Hands touched me as we made our way through the crowd—no pleasure washed over my skin.

Vossarian and Ryett were seated in their usual spot. Ryett stood and took the rope from Kieron. He walked a slow circle around me. I tried to hold my head high as his eyes burned into me. *Who was this male? What happened to the smiling, joking king I met at Beck's?*

He sat in his velvet chair and pulled on the rope, forcing me to step close between his open thighs. "Get on your knees." I remembered Kieron's hands hitting me. His knife slicing my skin. *Trust me.* The words Ryett said to me in my cell. I didn't, but I did not have a choice. I was damned either way.

His eyes hardened at my delay and I slowly got on both knees. My hands rested on his thighs. He gave me a wicked smile and pulled a pill from his shirt pocket. I was relieved to see it. I would rather black out than know what was about to happen to me.

His hand moved towards my mouth and I opened my lips, staring him in the eyes. He placed the pill on my tongue then stroked my hair. "Good ... Voss I would have paid more had I known you had already broken her."

"I am glad you are happy." Voss laughed. "Enjoy yourself."

"I will." Ryett pulled out another pill and placed it on his own tongue. He tugged on the rope, "Sit on my lap."

I obeyed. His hands guided my hips as I sat. Instead of only feeling the electric pleasure through my skin I felt his touch. The calluses on his hands. The warmth of his skin. His hands roamed my body, but it was not the groping or claiming touches I had felt each night. It was gentler.

I could see Vossarian watching us from the corner of my eye, a smirk of approval on his face. The drugs started to take hold and I focused on Ryett's hands. Pleasure like I had never felt met my skin wherever he touched me. My breathing grew heavy and my body relaxed. I arched in his lap and felt his hardness press against my ass. I could not help but think of him inside of me.

They *had* broken me. I did not care that my body was on display. That I had been *sold*. I just wanted the pleasure. I *needed* the pleasure Ryett was giving me. I would beg him for it. I ground my hips against his hardness again.

Ryett's hand stroked my cheek, his finger parted my lips and plunged into my mouth. I gently sucked it and drug my teeth along his skin as he pulled it out.

I needed more of him in my mouth. My eyes met his as I leaned my face against his palm. I saw a flash of shock cross his face before it returned to cold hungry amusement. "You are going to have to excuse us for the night … it's been a great party." Ryett spoke to Voss, but his eyes were glued on me.

Voss's laugh was far away, whatever he said I did not hear. Ryett stood me up and took my hand as he led me through the crowd. People reached for me as we passed. His hand moved to my waist and he pressed me close to him as if to shield me from the others. I did not know where he was taking me. I did not even care. I just wanted him to keep touching me.

He took me down a hallway I had never seen. My legs were weak and my eyelids would barely stay open. My empty body ached for him. He pulled me through another door into a dimly lit room. The music was gone as soon as he shut the door.

His voice was so far away. I didn't know what he was saying. I felt something soft and firm beneath my thighs as he guided me to sit. I lifted my face to him standing in front of me. I ran my hands across his stomach and could feel his hard muscles beneath his clothes. His hands supported me as he lay me back into the softness. My body opened for him. *Touch me,* my body begged. I tried to speak, tried to lift my eyes to him, but my consciousness left me.

PART 2: THE MOUNTAINS

CHAPTER 21

I retched into a metal bowl cradled between my legs. A strong firm hand held my hair. I did not know where I was or how I had gotten here. I remembered sitting on Ryett's lap, him taking me to a room. I remembered strong arms lowering me into a bath. I remembered holding onto a shoulder as someone helped me step into pants. It was all just pieces.

I saw my hands shaking as they clutched the sides of the bowl. I was sweaty and shivering and I could not stop vomiting. I would rather be dead. I would rather be drugged and my body overwhelmed in sick pleasure. I vomited again.

When I stopped heaving, a cool cloth gently wiped my face and neck. Hands took the bowl away. A warm mug of strong smelling liquid was tipped against my lips. It tasted bitter, but soothed my burning throat. I curled up on my side and blankets were tucked around me. *Blankets.* I was warm. I was not lying on the cold dirt floor. "Sleep, you are safe." A male voice said gently. A strong hand rubbed my back.

I did not feel safe. I felt like I was dying.

When I woke up again I did not feel like I was dying anymore. I was tucked into a massive bed, cozy blankets wrapped around me. Dark curtains hung in front of windows. I slipped out of the bed, my feet landing on a warm rug. I looked around. In the dim light I could see my pack sitting on a chair and my boots in a tray on the floor next to it. The black dress and sweater I had been wearing when I fled Beck's were draped over the arm of the chair.

I looked down at myself. I was wearing male clothing. The pants and short sleeved shirt were large on me, but made of the softest material I had ever felt.

I slowly walked to the door. I felt weak. Empty. But I was somehow still alive. It was proving to be very difficult to die.

I opened the door and peeked into the hallway. Beautiful wooden floors met me as I walked down the short hall past another closed door and into a great room with tall windows. I could see evergreen trees and mountains all around—endless mountains still covered in snow.

"How are you feeling?" I jumped at the voice. Ryett was

sitting at a large worn table in what must be the kitchen.

"Not dead." I replied.

"Detoxing can be nasty. You should take a seat." He had papers in front of him and barely looked up at me.

I didn't sit. My memories came flooding back—Ryett had bought me from Vossarian. They were slave traders. He murdered a male. He had taken me to a room before I blacked out. "You—" I did not know what I was going to say. He had agreed to let Voss traffic *children.*

"Saved you from Vossarian's disgusting sex dungeon? Yes. You're welcome." He now looked at me. I had forgotten the beautiful ice color of his eyes.

"How long have I been here?" I tore my gaze from his and looked around at the cozy home.

"Eight days. You responded well to the detox brew ... I am sorry I did not have any proper clothes for you, you will have to wear mine until we get you something."

Eight days? He bought me eight days ago and I remembered next to nothing and he wanted to talk about *clothes*? Fuck clothes. "You sell slaves. You *bought* me."

Hurt flashed in his beautiful eyes, "It is more complicated than that. Yes, I bought you, but you are free. You are not my slave, Genevieve. I am not the bad guy. I never hurt you—"

"You killed that male. All those people in chains ... You drugged me and brought me to a room ..." There was anger in my voice, but I trailed off as I remembered the way he touched me, how I had wanted him. I was suddenly embarrassed and acutely aware of how the large shirt did nothing to hide the shape of my breasts and my peaked nipples beneath it.

Ryett's hands flattened on the table, "I am sorry. I did not hurt you, I promise. I needed Voss to think—" He didn't finish what he was saying, but instead took a deep breath. "Please, you should not be up, come sit down and let me get you some food before you pass out."

I just stared at him for a few heartbeats, then I slowly walked to the table and pulled out one of the chairs. I had not realized how hungry I was. I watched Ryett heat soup on the stove, he watched me and occasionally stirred it.

"How much?" I asked.

"What?"

"How much did you pay for me?" He had *bought* me and Vossarian had said Ryett would not like the price.

"It doesn't matter." He said, turning his back to me. "I would have paid whatever amount he demanded."

"Why? Because you are trying to be allies with Beck?"

He turned the stove off and faced me again. "Because no one should have to endure torture or slavery."

"And what about the other slaves you bought?" I still could not shake the memory of him slitting the male's throat. Blood spraying across the floor.

"They are being well taken care of until we can move them to their new homes. Where they will live freely." He ladled soup

171

into a bowl.

"And I am just supposed to believe you?"

"You can believe whatever you want. I have told you the truth." He slid the bowl of soup across the table to me.

Neither of us spoke as I ate the soup. He remained standing, leaning against the stove as he watched me. When I finished he took the empty bowl from me and washed it in the sink before setting it on a towel to dry. A king had just cooked me food *and* cleaned up after me. A king who lived with and sold slaves would not have done either of those things. I would choose to believe him. Believe him until he showed me more proof.

"This is one of my private residences. My favorite actually." He finally spoke. "Is there anything I can get for you? Anything you need?"

"No." I shook my head. "Thank you."

"Let me know if that changes or if you feel sick. You seemed to handle the detox well, but sometimes the sickness of it lingers. There is a tea you can drink that will help."

"Thank you." I looked around the cabin. The tall windows that framed the mountains were a dream. It just made me want to cuddle up under a blanket and read for hours as the snow drifted by. I stood and walked to the windows taking in the full expanse of the view.

"I could stare at this view all day." Ryett said from behind me.

"Me too. It's beautiful." I responded.

"Make yourself comfortable. I have a few things to take care of, but holler if you need anything." Ryett disappeared down the hallway and left me standing in the open room. I suddenly felt tired and realized I had not even looked in a mirror before coming out here.

I made my way back to the room I had woken in and found another pair of pants and a shirt folded on the bed. I slipped into the bathroom to wash myself before I knew I would be sliding back into bed. Thankfully when I looked in the mirror I did not look too terrible. I was at least clean and maybe just slightly disheveled.

I washed and pulled on the new set of clothes—which were just as big on me as the first pair, but they were fresh and smelled comforting. I wanted to curl up in that smell and breathe it in. Then it hit me. The clothes smelled like Ryett. Like smoke, cedar, and pine. What I had completely ignored earlier. Ryett had given me *his* clothes to wear. How did I go from struggling to survive on my own to a new *world*—and a world where I was in the company of *kings*? I was wearing a king's clothes. I was too tired to think about this. I pulled the bedding up around myself and closed my eyes, trying not to think about Ryett's soft clothes on my skin.

The house smelled amazing. Whatever was cooking made my stomach growl. I slipped into the bathroom and straightened myself up before leaving my room. I found Ryett at the table again with a plate of food in front of him.

"I didn't want to wake you." He said simply as he stood and pulled another plate out of the oven. He set it on the table in the place across from him. "I hope you are hungry."

"It smells delicious." I sat down and took a bite, "It is delicious."

He gave me a small smile and we both ate in silence. I watched him wash the dishes—he had waved me off when I tried to get up to help.

"Some fresh air will do you good. Come." He said as he crossed the living room and scooped up blankets from the couch. I followed him outside to a large deck with a fire pit that lit as we approached it.

I slid into one of the cushioned couches and Ryett handed me a blanket. It was just like that morning at Beck's. The two of us with the stars and the quiet and the fire.

"If you need or want to talk about any of it, I am here." He said.

I shook my head no. I was not ready to talk about it. I just wanted to forget all of it. To pretend it didn't happen. But I could not forget how I felt sitting on Ryett's lap. As his hands ran along my skin.

"How long was I ... gone? With Vossarian?" I finally asked.

"Around two months." He replied. My stomach dropped and my throat burned. *Two months.* I had endured that hell hole for two months. I started shaking and before I could say anything else, Ryett was on the couch next to me. I looked at him and could not stop the tears from falling down my cheeks. He scooted closer and took my face in his hands. His calloused hands brushed the tears from my face. "You are out. You are free." He said gently.

I wrapped my arms around him and he pulled me close. His hand rubbed my back and he held me until I stopped shaking. "I don't think I can say thank you enough." I finally managed to say.

"You are welcome." He whispered into my hair.

"We should get some sleep." Ryett finally whispered. I had stayed cradled in his warm arms staring into the fire and he had let me. I only nodded, extracting myself from his arms, and followed him into the cabin. I folded the blanket he had given me and draped it over the couch.

I did not want to go to bed alone and it was not because I was lonely. No. I had jumped into bed with Beck because of that. Because I was lonely and craving touch. Any touch. This was different. I was not lonely and I had been touched too much over the last months. I could not explain it—I just wanted to be near Ryett. I was drawn to him. Something deep within me pulled me towards him.

He draped his blanket on the couch, "Is there anything you need?"

"No, I am all set. You can stop fussing." I teased.

He laughed, "Fussing? Me? I am not fussing." His eyes burned into me as he backed away down to the hall. He gave me a wink, "Good night." Then he turned and went into the first room, closing the door behind himself.

The next morning I found Ryett in the kitchen again sitting with a mug of coffee.

"Have you eaten yet?" I asked. He shook his head no. "Let me make you breakfast, then." I said, giving him a smile and opening the icebox to see what food I could whip up.

"You do not have to do that." He said. "I should be taking care of you. You are still recovering."

"No, no. I owe you big time. Probably a lifetime of breakfasts, but we will start with this one." I said over my shoulder. I found eggs and set the bowl of them on the counter. Then I picked up some cheese and sniffed it. I felt Ryett come up close behind me —the warmth of his body—and he pulled the cheese from my hand.

I turned to him. He set the cheese on the counter and reached around to close the ice box behind me. "You do not owe me anything." He said. His hands braced on the counter on either side of me. My backside was pressed against the cabinets. I could see every detail of his skin. His beautiful tattoo that climbed up his neck, each hair of the stubble on his face. I looked up into his beautiful ice colored eyes. "You do not owe me anything." He said again softly.

"Okay." I breathed. My hands raised to his sides and my fingers grasped his shirt, then his waist. I pulled him closer. He dipped his head down, bringing his face close to mine. I wanted every bit of him. To kiss him. To feel him against me. I could feel his chest rise with his shuddering breaths. My heart was pounding. His fingers tangled in my hair as he cupped his hand around the back of my head. His lips grazed my cheek before his nose brushed mine.

A knock interrupted us. We froze—just staring at each other —our breath mixing. Heartbeats passed. Finally, he stepped away and went to open the door. Alias was standing with Devron in the doorway. *No. No. No.* He was sending me back to Beck.

Devron nearly burst through the door, "Genevieve, thank the Mother you are alive. Beck is losing his mind—"

"I am not going back." I blurted out. Devron stopped at the edge of the kitchen.

You could feel the tension in the room as no one spoke. Alias and Ryett moved into the room. Finally, Ryett broke the silence, "Why don't you want to go back?"

I just glared at Devron. "I had no idea he was capable of that, Genevieve." He whispered.

"Devron?" Ryett's voice was commanding.

"The night Genevieve … went missing," he was choosing his

words carefully, but then he turned back to me, "I saw Beck leave with you and the way he looked, I knew something was wrong. When I felt his power in the house I had to check ... I am so sorry. I knew he could fall fast and be possessive and tended to use females and toss them aside, but I swear I did not know he was capable of *that*." He looked devastated.

"What happened, Devron?" Venom laced Ryett's words.

"He was beating her." I could hear the disgust Devron felt about what he had seen.

Ryett looked murderous. "Beating her?" The question was nearly a growl. Alias stepped into a protective position beside me.

"Devron stopped him and I ran away into the woods, that is where Vossarian ... I am not going back." My voice was barely a whisper. I could feel my palms sweating.

Ryett turned to me, he looked as if he just realized something, "The bruises I saw on your wrists and neck?" He had asked about them in front of the fire in the early morning. I had not answered him then. I thought he had known. I looked at Devron, a horrified and questioning look crossed his face as he realized what he stopped might not have been the only time Beck had hurt me.

"They were from Beck, too." I responded looking back at Ryett. Rage flashed in his eyes. He had known something was wrong, but clearly he had not guessed *that*. I could not go back. I would beg on my knees if I had to. "Please do not make me go back."

Devron cursed under his breath then rubbed his face, "I won't make you. Beck will be pissed, but I won't make you. Where will you go?"

"She will stay with me." Ryett said, authority laced his voice.

"That might not be a good idea for any of us ..." Ryett looked like he would kill Devron right there if he had to. Devron raised his hands in submission and sunk into a chair, "Here me out. There are bigger things at stake here. Beck might back out of helping you if he thinks you refused to return her." *Return her.* I was going to vomit. Like I was a missing cufflink or some other *thing.*

"We tell him she is staying with Sarla then. I will make a visit to smooth things over, to make sure he understands she chose to stay with her friend for now." Ryett replied. I hated the way they were talking about me, like property, but if it meant I did not have to go back then I would get over it.

Devron looked between us. His eyes dipped to my clothes. Ryett's clothes that I was wearing. The room was silent. Waiting. He finally sighed and spoke, "Okay, it is a good plan. It will at least buy us some time. You better come soon."

"I will be there tomorrow." Ryett said tightly.

Devron stood, "I am so sorry, Genevieve. I am glad you are safe now."

Safe? Was I safe? I only knew that I was not safe with Beck. I nodded to Devron. He was a good male and *had* warned me

179

to be careful with Beck even if neither of us thought this is what he was warning me about. "Thank you ... thank you for stopping him."

Ryett showed Devron the door. His voice was still murderous when he spoke, "Devron, you better put up a shield of peace tomorrow or I might fucking kill him."

CHAPTER 22

I sat on a comfy leather couch under a warm knit blanket, a mug of tea in my hands. Sarla had arrived moments after Devron left. Ryett had whispered with Sarla before disappearing with Alias.

I was still wearing a pair of Ryett's clothes. It felt invasive, but I had no other clothes to wear and Sarla assured me that Ryett did not mind. Sarla examined me and gently rubbed an oil on my temples and neck, by tomorrow night I "should be good as new" she had assured me. At least my body would be fully detoxed from the drugs I had been on for weeks.

A small navy gift bag with cream colored tissue paper dropped into my lap. Sarla had finished whatever she had been doing and plopped down into an armchair across from me. "I got you something." She said smiling.

I pulled out the tissue paper and pulled out a black fabric cord from the bag. The black seemed to both shimmer and suck darkness into it.

"So you can rewrap your knife handle ... I sort of bled all over the last one." She said.

"Thank you. That was very thoughtful of you." I replied. It was. I had completely forgotten my knife no longer had the corded handle. It felt like a lifetime ago that I used it as a tourniquet for Sarla's leg.

"You are very welcome, but I should be thanking you for saving my ass." She waved her hand as if dismissing any further thanking. "So! Are we relaxing today or do you want a distraction?" Then her eyes snagged on the huge diamond earrings I found with my other things and had set on the coffee table. "What are you going to do with those?"

"Probably chuck them in a lake." I leaned my head back and yawned. I had not confronted Sarla about the slaves. I couldn't right now. I was not ready to hear what she had to say. "I want to just melt into this couch and do nothing, but that probably means I need a distraction."

"You need sleep. I will put those earrings ... somewhere ... who knows maybe you can buy your next house with them." She smiled at me as if she had some mischievous plan she had already set in motion. "How about you go back to sleep and this afternoon I will make sure you are distracted?"

Fuck Beck's diamonds, but she was right. I needed sleep. So I agreed and found myself crawling back into the huge bed I had been sleeping in.

When I woke again I actually felt rested. I still felt empty inside, but the aches of vomiting and detoxing had left my body. I found Sarla sitting in the same arm chair I left her in, a lunch spread of small sandwiches was on the kitchen counter.

"Eat! And I have a surprise for you." She joined me in the kitchen, "My good friend and favorite clothier is coming with some of my clothes, and I have asked her to help you build your wardrobe. Don't worry, it is a gift from me to you."

"Sarla, that is … thank you." I swallowed my pride. I had no way of paying for clothes and I had none. I would have to accept her offer and find a way to repay her later.

A knock sounded on the door and Sarla jumped to answer it, "Don't you even dare think you need to pay me back!" She flung open the door and a tall blonde female stood smiling on the doorstep.

"Sarla! It is so good to see you! Word is you have had quite the trip!" The two embraced warmly and Sarla led the female into the kitchen. "Balinda at your service." She said to me with a wave.

"Genevieve. Nice to meet you." I responded.

"Genevieve is in need of a *complete* wardrobe, Belinda." Sarla stated as she grabbed herself another small sandwich.

"*Complete?*" Belinda's eyes grew wide, she looked at me and back at Sarla, "Have you just made my wildest dream come true my friend?"

"Yep." Sarla said through a mouthful of food. "She doesn't even have underthings."

Belinda turned to me, thankfully there were no questions or judgment in her eyes, only pure excitement, "This is going to be so much fun!"

Sarla moved us back to the couch, bringing the sandwiches and some water with us. Belinda took my measurements and peppered me with questions about my favorite colors, what I did in my spare time, and if I preferred this various thing to that various thing. None of the questions were too personal, but what they had to do with my clothes I had no idea. Sarla just smiled at me and nodded in encouragement.

Then Belinda—muttering to herself—started pulling racks of clothes from thin air and arranging them around the room. This went on for an hour as she examined the clothes, disappearing some and summoning new choices. Sarla chatted away about Belinda's process and their history as we continued to snack on the food in front of us. Eventually Belinda pointed Sarla to one rack telling her that everything she would need was there. Then she turned to me, "Are you ready to see phase one of your wardrobe?"

Phase one? Each rack was arranged by need: workout and

training, lounging and sleep, casual wear, formal wear, and outerwear and gear. Each type had appropriate underthings and shoes paired with them. There were not too many items, but more than enough to cover any need I had. More clothes than I had in years. I flipped through the pieces, looking at what she curated for me. I had never felt such a variety of fabrics. I loved it all. I had never had clothes that seemed so ... *me*. My throat tightened and I blinked back tears. "Thank you ... this is amazing."

"Come now! This is supposed to be fun!" Sarla popped a bottle of sparkling wine, "Let's have a fashion show!"

Belinda and Sarla made themselves comfy on the couch, rising to help me pick out new outfits or step into clothes when needed. They oohed and ahhed as I tried on various outfits. Belinda kept muttering about how she had never had so much fun and that this might be her best work yet. I had never felt so good trying on clothes. Everything was already tailored to fit and flatter my tall frame perfectly.

Any additional pieces I needed for new seasons or special events I was to call Belinda. She promised me a lifetime of styling and also asked us out to dinner when we were in the city —which city I did not know, but I agreed.

I was sprawled in the armchair wearing a knit lounge set with the most luxurious lace underthings beneath, my face hurt from smiling so much, but I had not thought about Beck or Vossarian or Kieron all afternoon. The cabin filled with the smell of fresh bread and warming soup. Comfort food at its finest. I just might be okay after all of this.

CHAPTER 23

I was on my knees, ass in the air, face and chest pressed into the floor by a broad hand between my shoulder blades. Small whimpers burst from my mouth each time he thrust into me. His cock was pounding into my inner wall sending bursts of pain into my stomach. My hands were useless, clawing into the dirt. I was too weak to push myself up. He pounded into me harder and I screamed. "That's it." Kieron growled.

I was on my hands and knees, sheets tangled around my legs, gasping for breath. The bed was damp from the sweat coating my body. *I am safe. It was a dream.* I had been having a nightmare. Flashbacks. I untangled my legs from the sheets and walked quietly to the bathroom. Nausea hit me and I vomited into the toilet. This nausea had to be left over from the drugs. It was dark out, the stars still bright in the sky. I turned on the shower and sat in the warm stream of water while I cried. Having nightmares was not new to me, but still did not make it any easier.

When the sun came up I asked Sarla if I could just lay low in the cabin for a few days. She agreed, mentioning that Alias and Ryett would stop by in a few days anyway—I assumed she meant after they convinced Beck to let me stay here, but neither of us said it.

We shared stories of our lives from when we were kids. I told her about playing the piano with my mother. She told me about how she and Ryett used to sneak into the kitchen at night to practice making food themselves. It made me smile to think about Sarla and Ryett making a mess of a kitchen when they were children.

We tried our hand at making pastries only to give up and allow the house's magic to serve us some instead. Apparently, the house could summon whatever it needed to serve its occupants. It even acted as its own maid. Sarla explained to me that it was somewhat complex spell work, but many people spent the time to do it because of the convenience later on. It was a luxury I could get used to.

Sarla had next shown me how to throw knives and axes at a wooden target outside. It was beyond satisfying and I could not think of anything that seemed more fitting than axe throwing for mountain people. I had taken to axe throwing quickly, surprising myself with my accuracy.

Three days later we were waiting for pizzas to bake—Sarla had never had or heard of pizza, so with the house's help, we made our own and enough to feed four of us each—when there was a loud knock on the door. "Whatever you are cooking there better be enough for us." Ryett yelled through the door.

Sarla was giddy as Ryett and Alias strode into the cabin, "We made pizza!" She exclaimed excitedly. Both males gave her a look like she had just spoken gibberish.

"Whatever that is, it at least smells good!" Alias plopped down on a stool in the kitchen.

"So did you two kill anyone or are we now officially allies with the Lakes?" Sarla's question would have been funny if the threat of killing had not been so real.

"We are allies. Beck has promised to play nice." Ryett said and he gave me a concerned look.

Thankfully the windup timer buzzed. "Let's eat!" I said, "Good thing you are both here, we made enough food for an army!"

None of them had ever had pizza or heard of it. It was not a food in Savengard. They loved it. Alias and Sarla started planning how we would open a restaurant. All three of them proclaimed I was a food genius. Their enthusiasm had me laughing so hard tears were leaking out of my eyes. *I was laughing again.* Both Ryett and Alias heatedly debated toppings, so much so that we made them make their own pizzas so we could have a blind taste test. Sarla and I were banished to the living room so our votes would not be biased.

Both pizzas were passible. It was obvious who had made which pizza. Alias's had a massive amount of different meats while Ryett's was more reasonable with sausage and small chunks of various vegetables. We put on a show of tasting and critiquing both. Then crowned Ryett the champion after deciding one simply could not stomach more than one slice of Alias's with the amount of meat he had used.

We all lounged in the living room talking late into the night. Finally, Sarla and Alias said goodnight and made their way upstairs to the room Sarla had been staying in. Alias pinched Sarla's ass as they ascended, causing her to squeal. Ryett and I just chuckled to ourselves. "I can only hope for love like that someday." Ryett conceded.

"They do seem perfect for each other." Watching them together made me smile.

"They are soulmates." He responded. I snorted and he looked at me confused. "Why is that funny?"

The seriousness in his face made me pause. Different cultures believed different things, it would make sense if people from different worlds had different beliefs. My cheeks heated at the thought that I might have just been wildly offensive. I swallowed and said cautiously, "Maybe what you mean by 'soulmates' is different from what the word 'soulmates' means to me." He waited for me to continue. "The word 'soulmates' where I am from was just a fluffy word to make love stories seem more romantic. A word to keep young girls daydreaming about finding some handsome male who sweeps them off their feet as if their fates were aligned. It was all just fiction."

"So you do not believe in finding a soulmate then?" The corners of his mouth twitched upwards in a small teasing smile.

"Not that kind. Is a soulmate something different here?" I could feel my relief wash over me like a wave. I had not offended him.

His smile turned genuine, "It is completely different here, but now I know why you laughed. In Savengard, soulmates are something that is very real. There are a few different beliefs on the topic, but what most people here in the Mountains believe is each soul has a pair—a match. An equal partner that completes it. And no, that is not just some belief, people's magic actually changes when their soul and their soulmate reunite. Your magic becomes stronger, there is a deep level of connection and communication and feeling that is tied between them. The legends say that the gods, thinking we were becoming too powerful, split our souls to cut our powers in half, then they scattered the souls across the world.

"To find your soulmate is to become whole again. Unfortunately, it is a rare thing. When our world was fractured and the other worlds created, many believe that some souls were moved into the other worlds. So now there are soulmates that cannot find each other because they are literally worlds apart."

"That is very romantic and also very sad." I studied his face. It was so open. So honest. Hopeful. "So are you just supposed to wait until you find your soulmate?"

It was Ryett's turn to laugh, "No, I think many people would miss out on life if they did that. Maybe it is just up to fate." He winked at me with his last statement. Fate. I did not believe in fate. Believing in fate felt like abandoning responsibility for your life. Giving up all autonomy to some faceless and shapeless *thing*.

"Do you believe in fate?" I asked.

"I live my life like there is no such thing." Ryett's eyes were searching my face. "Sarla told me you had a family?"

"I did. They died before ... before all of this." My heart still ached everyday. I pressed my hand to my chest as if it would heal the pain, fill the hole that was there. Ryett was silent, waiting for me to go on. "My parents died from illnesses when I was entering adulthood. My husband ... partner was my best friend. We were together for ten years and we had a son. He was three when they were killed in an ... accident. That was a little over two years ago."

"I am so sorry," Ryett breathed.

"Me too." Tears threatened to burst from my eyes. We sat quietly for a few moments before I remembered something that had been eating at me, "Why did you insist Vossarian give you my things?"

"Because I thought you might want the few things you still have from your world … from your life before." He was right, it was all there was left. It was a gesture so simple, yet profoundly kind and thoughtful. *This* was the male I thought he was. Not the one buying slaves and killing defenseless people. Ryett was *good.*

I stood suddenly trying to hide the tears that now rolled down my cheeks. "I should go to bed."

Ryett was on his feet and crossed the space between us in a heartbeat. He gently wiped tears from my cheek and wrapped me against his chest. I sunk into his warm arms breathing in his scent. And just like that jagged mountains, bubbling streams, glaciers, and forest fires flashed through my eyes. The same wave erupted from my heart rippling out through my body. I gasped and pulled back.

"I'm sorry!" Ryett's eyes were wide as he abruptly released me, "I … that … I am so sorry." He backed a few steps from me then turned and hurried to his room, leaving me in the living room alone.

The next morning I was staring at the kettle boiling water for coffee, lost in thought when Ryett entered the kitchen. I could feel the tension in the air after last night.

"Well considering you are letting me stay in your residence, please do not make this weird." I was annoyed. I woke up annoyed at Ryett leaving me so quickly last night.

"You are upset. I should not have just touched you like that —" Ryett started.

"I am not upset you touched me. I am upset you ran away without an explanation. What ... tell me why *it* happens?" I turned towards him, crossing my arms.

"I ... now is not the right time." His tone told me the conversation was over.

I ignored it and let my annoyance burst out of me, "Oh, fuck the right time! *Please*, just tell me."

Ryett took a deep breath, considering, "I don't want to scare you or make you feel trapped."

"Should I be scared or feel trapped?"

"No." Ryett was nearly whispering. I could tell he wanted to cross the room to me by the step he took, but he stopped.

Before I could say anything else a cough from the stairs announced Alias's arrival.

"Oh good! Coffee!" He declared too loudly and stepped in to finish making the coffee I had abandoned. Ryett and I stood staring at each other. I finally tore my eyes off of Ryett and accepted the mug Alias was shoving into my hands.

Sarla bounced down the stairs, "Hope you all slept well. We've got shit to discuss today." She took the mug Alias offered her, "Okay ... this is weird." She waved her hand in the air indicating the awkwardness. Alias cleared his throat and shook his head at Sarla urging her to drop it. "Right! I will make breakfast."

Ryett moved past me to set the table, I stopped him with a hand on his arm. His eyes met mine. Fear. He was completely terrified of what I might say. "I am not scared." I said to him, his ice blue eyes locked in mine. I took the silverware from his hands and set the table myself.

CHAPTER 24

Sarla and I were hiking one of the many trails from the cabin. I felt exhausted, I must not have slept well. Ryett and Alias made some excuse to leave quickly after breakfast, letting us know they would be back that evening.

Sarla stopped and turned to me, "What happened with Ryett this morning?"

"I don't know." I tried to catch my breath, "We had a moment, or almost had a moment last night, but he just ran off suddenly. Then I tried to bring it up this morning and he just told me he did not want me to be scared or feel trapped."

"Oh." Sarla started hiking again.

"Oh? That's it?" I followed after her, "Do you know something?"

"No, well maybe, but it is not my place. Also, that explains why he ran off with Alias after breakfast. What happened in your 'almost moment' with him?" She stopped again, probably because my breathing was ridiculously labored.

"He hugged me." She raised her brows as if to ask if that was all, "We almost kissed before they went to the Lakes ... last night he just ... hugged me. I get these visions when I am around him. Mountains, streams, fires. It happened when he hugged me ... and then he ran away."

Sarla smiled at me, "How do you feel about it?"

My cheeks burned, "Please don't judge me. After Beck and everything you must think I am—"

"No one is thinking that and no one is or would judge you for any of this. But speaking of Beck ... Alias told me that Beck had given you those bruises the night you left. Is that why you did not want to go back? What happened?"

"I don't know. Beck was a good distraction from everything. I just ... wanted to feel wanted again. I think he wanted something different than I was willing to give. I rushed into things with him. It was stupid ..." I trailed off. I was about to make excuses for Beck again. After everything I still had a hard time believing I did not do anything wrong.

"You know. Sometimes we all just need a good dicking." Sarla's nonchalant response had me laughing. "Yes, it ended badly, but that had nothing to do with sharing a bed. You have nothing to feel bad about."

I could only nod. I was thankful she did not press me to actually answer her question about what had caused the fight. I was not ready to admit that Beck lost it over me *talking* to Ryett. I should not feel bad, but I did. Sarla continued, "I think Ryett's just trying to give you space after everything. But you did not answer my question, how do you feel about the almost kiss? The hug?"

"It felt good, I wanted it ... but Sarla, he *bought* me and drugged me and took me to a room. I don't know what happened when I was with him. I am mortified by my feelings." I was mortified. I had *wanted* him to touch me, to take me. I didn't care what he did, I had just *needed* him.

"He would never do that to you or any female. He did what he had to in order to trick Voss. He would never hurt someone like that." There was raw conviction in her voice and I believed her. "When you disappeared that night, we looked for you, we all looked for you. And he did not stop looking for you until he found you. He got you away from Voss. He understands that you might need to heal after that and probably does not want to force all of us on you. All of our baggage. He wants you to actually be free and feel free."

It made sense, but a part of me still hated it. And a part of me hated myself that I wanted more from him. I was judging myself. "So basically he is avoiding me right now."

"Yeah he is off being a little baby for sure. He will come around though." Sarla smiled at me.

We walked a little further and crested the edge of the mountain. The trees opened for us and we stood overlooking rolling mountains blanketed in snowy fog. "Do you mind if I stay here for a little bit … alone."

Sarla eyed me carefully, "Are you sure? These are not woods to get lost in."

"I will follow our tracks back and I won't stay long. I just have some thinking to do." I gave her a small smile and silently prayed she would agree. I had to think. Too much was happening and a place like this was the perfect place to clear my head. "Please. I survived two years alone, I will be fine. All of this is just … overwhelming."

She chewed her lip for a moment before replying, "Don't be too long, we are about an hour from the cabin and you really do not want to be out here at night. Stick to the trail and you will be fine. I will come looking for you if you are not back an hour after me. Is that fair?"

"Fair. Thank you." Sarla turned and walked away slowly, she glanced back and I waved.

I sat on a log and stared out into the expanse. I felt small, inconsequential. I closed my eyes and breathed in the crisp air.

Smoke billowed up from the cabin's chimney as I approached. Before I could stomp the snow from my boots on the front porch I heard arguing inside. "We can't risk it. It is not safe." Ryett's voice was lethal.

"You can't just lock her up like Beck did. You can trust her Ryett and we could use the help." Sarla argued back.

"I am not Beck—" My stomach dropped at the anger in Ryett's voice. I was not supposed to overhear this conversation, but I was frozen in place.

Sarla's voice did not falter, "Then let her come with us. Show her what we are doing. She can help us and she would help us if she knew."

"And if something happens to her? She has barely detoxed. Would you risk Alias like that?"

"Ryett, we are not suggesting—" Alias started, but Ryett cut him off.

"Don't we have a warrior or two who wants to move up a rank and we can read them in?" Ryett asked angrily.

"We agreed we would keep them out of it, Ryett." Alias responded strongly.

I had heard enough. I stomped my feet on the porch and banged my boots together to clear the snow from them—and announce my presence. They went silent inside. I opened the door and stepped onto the entry rug to remove my coat and boots. I dropped them in my room on the way down the hall to the kitchen. No one was speaking.

"Hi." I said as I looked from one to the other. "So are you locking me up or do I get to learn what you three were discussing?"

An amused smile crossed Sarla's mouth. Ryett gave her a glare that would have had most people wetting themselves. Alias just leaned back in his seat, content to watch the drama unfold.

"Haven't decided yet?" I asked. No one spoke. Sarla and Ryett just continued staring daggers at each other. I continued, "That is fine. Let me know when you figure it out." I turned on my heels and retreated to my room. I needed a shower anyway.

When I emerged from my room, hair wet and wrapped in a thick sweater, the house was quiet and the lights dim. I found some bread and cheese in the kitchen to eat. As I refilled my glass of water, I noticed there was a fire lit in the fire pit outside. I cracked open the door and found Ryett staring into the fire.

"It is freezing out here." I said in greeting. He did not have a coat on or a blanket over himself. He must have been freezing sitting out in the cold even with the lit fire.

"I was just going to come inside." He responded, tearing his eyes away from the fire. I stayed in the doorway as he stood. The way he moved—it was graceful and powerful. His hand grabbed the door and his other gestured for me to return inside ahead of him.

"Where are Sarla and Alias?" I asked. The house was unusually quiet.

"They went to get supplies." I raised my brows. He sighed,

"We need to go make a delivery and I am wondering if you would like to come?"

"Tell me more."

"The last group of slaves I got from Voss ...I need to move them from the Mountains to somewhere safer. I have a friend who will take them and make sure they are set up with everything they need to live in Savengard until we find out if we are able to return them home." He was fidgeting.

"You don't want me to come." It was not so much a question as it was a challenge.

"I am worried because it is not safe. We have to cross through dangerous territory and Vossarian is already suspicious that something is going on." He looked worried.

I almost laughed. The last decade of my life hadn't been safe. How bad could this be? I crossed my arms, "So why did you ask me to come?"

Ryett took a deep breath, "Because Sarla is right. I do not want to lock you up and we do need all the help we can get. Some of the people are sick and weak and our friends can't risk sending people outside of their territory to help us."

"If you need help, I will gladly help. If you want me to stay here, I will do that and I won't think that you are locking me up. I will respect your decision ..." My voice trailed off. I was leaving the decision up to him and I would be fine with whatever he chose.

"Come with us." He whispered. I raised my eyes and met his

stare. His ice eyes had fear and hope and respect in them. I nodded that I would.

CHAPTER 25

There was no way to jump this many people from one territory to the other, Ryett had explained. The wards the Queen of the Cliffs, Aveline, had in place for her kingdom did not allow for this many strangers to cross into her lands without physically walking through one of the gates—which meant we would need to cross through the Wastelands on foot and enter The Land of the Cliffs through one of the magical gates that created a barrier between the kingdoms and the Wastes.

Once we were in the Wastelands, we could not jump out either. Ancient spells did not allow world walking into, out of, or within the Wastelands' borders. Not only could we not jump into, out of, or within the Wastes, but not all magic worked inside the Wastelands' borders either—and what magic did work was too dangerous to use. There was a subset of beasts who were considered actual monsters—they were creatures, called the Esurimagicae, that fed on magic. The literal translation was 'a hunger for magic' and for short, they were referred to as Esurim. Using any magic in the Wastes would attract the esurim and other unwanted attention.

We now stood in front of a large stone the size of a building. It looked like the surface was swirling and pulsing and the air stretching out from its sides was doing the same. There was a large archway at the bottom of the stone. "Well Genevieve, this is a gate." Alias said simply.

"It is completely safe for us to cross through the archway, but beasts cannot pass through unless the gate is broken." Sarla said as if she was trying to reassure me not to be nervous. She then turned to the group of now freed slaves we were about to escort through the Wastelands, "We will pass through this archway and once on the other side you must stay with the group. I have already explained to you how dangerous the Wastelands are, so stay quiet and let's move as efficiently as we can."

There were some murmurs of acknowledgement and Ryett led the group through the archway. I followed at the rear with Alias. Besides the slight feeling of electricity in the air, I felt nothing as we walked beneath the stone and into the Wastelands.

◆ ◆ ◆

The woods were dark and old. Trees were covered in moss and dead and down trees made travel not only difficult, but slow. We were crossing a narrow sliver of the Wastelands between The Land of the Mountains and The Land of the Cliffs. Once we crossed into The Land of the Cliffs, Aveline's guards would transport the freed slaves to one of the towns in the territory where they would be housed, clothed, and given a chance to live free.

I ushered males and females over a particularly large log, offering my hand as support for them as they jumped down. I recognized some of their faces from Vossarian's throne room the day Ryett had been there. Their faces had been bloodied and bruised and without hope that day. Now their eyes held hope and determination. They also were clean and clothed in new clothing. Alias was on the other side of the log, hoisting people up and over. My orders had been simple: stay with the group, help those who needed help navigating the treacherous terrain, keep my eyes and ears open for threats. The woods were already quiet, but a deeper quiet seemed to fall over them. "Alias, did you hear that change?" I kept my voice steady and offered a hand to an older male as he lowered himself off of the log.

"Yes." Alias's voice was painfully calm, "Only four more people to get over the log."

If the change meant we were in danger, Alias was not

going to broadcast it to the group. Most of them were already trembling and struggling to make the journey. We did not need them to panic. The final few climbed over the log and Alias hopped down behind them. We watched them follow the others along the trail. "I think we have company and not the kind you want to invite in for a drink." Alias said quietly to me. "Keep everyone in the back here moving with the group. No gaps. I am going to run ahead to Ryett and Sarla and let them know we need to find cover."

I nodded and he moved off briskly. The air seemed to thicken as we continued hiking along the trail. Soon enough Alias was back next to me. "There is a cave system not that far ahead. We will move to that and wait it out."

Sarla was moving down the line, urging everyone to move more quickly. Many of the elders were moving as fast as they could already. Some of the stronger males had dropped back with Sarla and were helping to usher the elders along.

A screech broke through the silence and every hair on my body prickled. My heart pounded as another rang out. "Fast as you can go! We have to move to cover!" Sarla called out. "Let's go, let's go!"

People started running as fast as they could. We rounded a bend and I could see the caves ahead. People were already funneling into them, Ryett stood at the entrance guiding them in and shouting at them to keep moving deeper so that everyone could fit. I heard brush and branches snapping. The noise was coming closer. Another screech broke through the air and I whirled around to see where the thing was.

Fifty yards out, through the trees an enormous creature stood on two legs. Its long arms swung and smashed the brush out of its way as it lumbered towards us. It stopped and let out another screech. Alias drew his axe from across his back, then drew a long knife from the sheath strapped to his leg. He held the hilt out to me without taking his eyes off of the creature. I took it.

"Esurim." Alias breathed, "We can't fight with magic. It is going to run at us and we have to create a distraction or it is going straight into the caves after everyone." Alias said carefully and calmly. "There is no way the two of us have time to get to the caves. So we are going to run like hell and loop around. Give Ryett and Sarla time to get everyone safe and to come back and help us fight it."

He was a true general. His voice calmed me. Steadied me. "Got it." I responded.

The esurim started running. Sure enough it headed straight for the line of people hurrying to get into the caves. "Now!" Alias bellowed and he started whooping and hollering at the thing. We jogged at an angle towards where it was coming from, but also away from the caves. Its head snapped to us and I realized it did not have any eyes. Two slits in the middle of its face flickered as it sniffed the air. A thick yellowish liquid dripped from its long pointed teeth and down its pale leathery skin. It was solely hunting us by sound and smell. I started yelling louder and it veered its course towards us. "Run!" Alias shouted and we took off running.

The esurim was gaining on us. We hurtled over fallen logs and skitted across mossy wet rock. My foot slid and I crashed to my knee. Pain shot through my leg as I scrambled to my feet and kept running. Alias grabbed my arm and swung me around as we ducked behind a huge boulder. The creature slowed and stalked close to where we were crouched. It sniffed the air again and let out another screech that echoed through the dense forest. This time, distant screeches echoed back to it. Alias and I looked at each other. Both of our eyes were wide. He lifted a finger to his lips indicating to stay silent.

The esurim's claws scraped along the boulder we were crouched behind. Alias adjusted the grip on his axe. He was going to try and fight it. He pushed me behind him and we waited. Just as the esurim was about to round the boulder, Alias sprung out, slashing his axe across its chest. The creature stumbled back screeching. Black blood oozed from the wound.

A second esurim emerged from the woods from the direction we had been headed. It was larger than the first. I watched in horror as Alias dodged long clawed arms that reached for him. His reach with his axe did not allow him to get close enough to do much damage.

Then one of the creature's claws connected with Alias and sent him tumbling across the ground like a doll being tossed. A scream released from my mouth.

They were going to kill Alias. He was down and not moving and one of the esurim was stalking towards him. I jumped up and moved further away. Shouting at them. They turned to me as I kept yelling.

I weighed the knife Alias had given me in my hand and took a deep breath before throwing it. It stuck into the chest of the larger one exactly where I had aimed. The creature just paused and used its clawed fingers to pluck out the knife as if it was pulling a leaf off of its body.

It screeched again and stepped towards me. I started running, looking over my shoulder, yelling as loud as I could. It worked. The creatures were now following me in big long strides. Their speed picked up, they were coming for me. I stopped looking and ran as fast as I could.

There was screeching behind me as I ran through the trees. I heard the crashing and crunching of trees and brush breaking and being torn away. Another screech seemed to shake the air. I ran faster. The trees were thinning out and I did not know if that was a good thing or if it would just allow the creatures behind me to catch me more easily.

I stumbled over a root and crashed into the dirt on my hands and knees. I didn't even feel pain, my heart was beating so loudly and all I could think was to get up. *Get up!*

"Get up!" A deep voice growled at me and I felt a hand grab the collar of my jacket. I was yanked to my feet and felt a hand grab my arm. I was pulled back into a run before I could even register that I was standing again.

"Faster!" I raised my eyes from the ground we were sprinting over just long enough to realize that it was Kieron who was gripping my arm. I could not even feel my own fear over who was holding on to me before, another blood chilling screech echoed behind us. The creatures were too close. "We have to make it to the cliffs and jump." He panted as he nearly dragged me along.

I followed. If it was between Kieron or the monsters that were behind us, I would pick Kieron every time. I had survived him. I knew I would not and could not survive the esurim. We burst through the trees into an open green and rocky expanse. I could smell the sea breeze. Feel the mist from the water that I could not see. *The Land of the Cliffs.* We were going to jump off of the cliffs and into the water. My legs stopped working. "Run, dammit! Your choice is to run and jump with me or be eaten by those things." Kieron yelled at me as his hand slipped from my arm to my hand.

I turned my concentration back to my burning legs and forced them to keep running. I dared a glance over my shoulder and saw the creatures had already cleared the treeline. Now that we were out in the open they would gain ground on us. "Jump as far out as you can, then pull your arms to your chest and keep your legs together until you hit the water." Kieron bit out between breaths.

The cliff's edge was only a handful of yards away. The dark blue sea and its white crested waves stretched out as far as I could see. "Jump far!" Kieron yelled as we reached the edge. We did not slow down. I leapt with him just as another screech bellowed behind us. Warm air that reeked of death blew past us. The esurim had been too close and now there was nothing but air below us. Kieron let go of my hand and I pulled my arms in tight, crossing them against my chest.

Nothing but air ripped around me as I fell. This was one of my nightmares. Heights. Falling. Water. Deep, wild water. I hoped I would land in water. I did not look to see if there were rocks. There were probably rocks. I squeezed my eyes closed and pinched my nose.

I felt the impact in the entirety of my body. Breath was forced from my lungs. At least I had entered the water feet first. My legs and arms ripped open in the water as I tried to stop the downward plunge. I kicked and flailed my arms trying to get to the surface. It was so far away. I could not breathe. I could not hold my breath much longer. Then my head popped above the surface and I gasped for air. The waves were huge. My body lifted with the crests and dropped with the troughs as I struggled to keep my head above the water.

"Genevieve!" Kieron was yelling for me.

"I'm here!" I yelled back. I didn't know where 'here' was, but I was alive. I had not drowned yet. I turned myself around looking for where he was. As a wave lifted me with it I saw Kieron swimming towards me. "I'm here!" I yelled again and waved an arm above my head.

"Are you okay?" He asked as he swam up to me and we treaded water. I nodded. "Let's get onto shore."

CHAPTER 26

I coughed and spit out sea water onto the narrow rocky beach. I was completely exhausted and nausea was rolling in me again. I did not think I could stand up even if I had to. I rocked back sitting on my heels as I hung my head between my arms and tried to breathe. I felt Kieron's presence as he sat down on the rocks beside me.

After a long while he finally spoke, "Have you been missing me? You seemed to enjoy our time together."

I sat up and looked at him, plastering a questioning look on my face, "Did I? I didn't think you were that memorable." I couldn't hide my smirk as anger rose in Kieron's face. Before he could speak I added, "Thank you. Thank you for saving me." The anger left his face, but he just kept staring at me. "How did you … Why? Why did you help me?"

"Here I thought you might have actually missed me and would want to see me again." It was his turn to smirk as I rolled my eyes at him.

"Considering the alternative was to be eaten, yes, I am happy to see you." I would give him this one. It did not mean I had forgotten what he had done.

"Don't be too happy. I am taking you back to Vossarian." He finally looked away.

"You should have let me be eaten by the monsters." There was no way I was going back. I would force Kieron to kill me on this beach if I had to.

"That seems like it would have been the better choice." He took off his boot and dumped water onto the rocks. "But here we are, so you are coming back to the Deserts with me. Voss is not going to be happy to find out Ryett has been freeing his slaves."

"Why does it matter what Ryett does with his slaves? He paid for them, he can do what he wants with them."

"Does he do what he wants with you?" There was a bite in Kieron's voice.

"Oh let me guess, you are jealous he doesn't have to drug me or beat me in order to fuck me?" Kieron did not respond, but his body tensed. I had struck a nerve. But we were all dead if he told Vossarian. Something bigger than me was at stake if I did not try to do something. Try to convince him to be on our side,

"What do I have to do for you to not tell Vossarian?"

He laughed, "You would have to kill me and we both know you can't do that."

He was right, he was huge and I stood no chance of fighting him and winning. I already tried. I had also put two bullets in him and he didn't die. "I will do anything. Give you anything. Name it."

"Clearly I went too easy on you for you to be offering *anything* to keep this a secret." Kieron's voice was hard.

"Oh please, you are a terrible torturer!" I nearly cackled. His brows bunched in either surprise or confusion. Maybe both. I continued, "I didn't even have to sit in the pain of my injuries for days on end. Do you know how easy it is to manage pain knowing that at the end you will get a magic salve rubbed on you that numbs and heals everything? You definitely fucked that up."

I turned around and sat next to him facing the water. "If you really wanted to torture me you should have brought me flowers and a fancy dinner with too small of portions so I would still be hungry after eating. Add in a private string quartet to play for us while we eat and you have a winning combination for a terrible time. Then to really top it all off, fuck me gently, but only in missionary, and ask if I'm doing okay every five seconds. Bonus points if you can finish in under two minutes." I rolled my shoulders and stretched my neck, "Now *that* would have been torture. Dominated in a dungeon and pounded by that huge cock of yours? That was practically living out a sexual fantasy."

Kieron blinked. Then his head tipped back as he howled with laughter. When he finally stopped laughing he looked straight back into my eyes. A smile was still on his face, "I think I have met my match."

I gave him a wink. He was undeniably handsome with that smile on his face—even with his long hair and beard completely drenched by sea water. My thoughts were interrupted by bile that rose in my throat as another wave of nausea hit me. I turned away from him and vomited onto the rocks.

"Swallow too much sea water?" Kieron asked tauntingly.

I closed my eyes and forced myself to take deep breaths. It was not the sea water. It was not the drugs. "I think I am pregnant." I whispered.

"You think you are what?" He blurted. I didn't look at him.

"Pregnant." It was true. All the nausea, the exhaustion I was feeling. I had felt it before. I did not want to admit it. Especially, because I did not know who the father was—I didn't know who would be worse. "The baby could be Vossarian's or … yours."

"Voss never slept with you." At least I now had that bit of information. I had no memory of what happened to me each night after blacking out from the drugs. The baby was Kieron's. His voice changed. There was a gentleness to his voice I had never heard, "You are pregnant with my child? How far along are you?"

"I don't know. I have not had my cycle at all since coming here. I just started getting symptoms. I do not know how pregnancies work in this world, it is different where I am from." I pushed myself back into a seated position as I spoke. I did not want to think about it. This could not be happening. *Why was I telling him this?* I could not carry a child conceived like that—from him.

Kieron's jaw muscles worked as he stared at me. He finally spoke, "What do you mean you do not know how pregnancies work in this world? You're not from Savengard?"

Shit. I had let that bit of information slip. I shook my head no. Kieron scrambled to his feet and backed away from me cursing. "What world are you from?" He now stood ten paces away from me, his hands balling in and out of fists as if to control the emotions raging through him.

"Does it matter?" I managed to ask.

"Tell me." It was nearly a growl.

"The world you first saw me in, the one you were in when I shot you." His eyes grew wide as I said it. "What does it matter?"

"We have to get you back to Ryett." He looked like he was going to throw up.

"All I had to do was tell you I am not from Savengard and you would return me to Ryett? What aren't you telling me? After beating me, raping me, saving me from some monster, and now finding out I am pregnant, is that all you care about? The fact that I am not from here?" My words had venom to them. This damn temper of mine would eventually get me killed. I didn't care anymore that he had saved me from some demon monster. He was a monster too.

"I am taking you back to Ryett and then none of us are going to breathe a word about me finding all of you out here." He stalked back to me and threw out his hand to help me up.

I took it and he pulled me to my feet. He turned to step away from me, but I did not let go of his hand. "Why the change of heart? What aren't you telling me?"

He faced me and I looked up at him. I had trembled when he stood this close to me before, his powerful body towering over me, but my intuition told me he would not hurt me again. He raised a hand and gently pushed my hair behind my ear, "I am sorry. I am trying to make things right." Then he stepped away from me, "Let's go."

Eventually we found a path up the cliff wall and trudged back into the forest. All I wanted to do was sleep. We stopped yet again for me to take a break and Kieron looked at me with concern written all over his face. I wanted to cry, but I was too embarrassed. "I can't keep going. I'm exhausted."

Before I could protest, Kieron scooped me up in his arms, "Don't you dare say no to me carrying you. Night is falling we both need to get the fuck out of here." I leaned my head against his shoulder and let myself relax. I still didn't know why Kieron was doing this. I had pestered him with questions and he had not answered any of them. We had hardly spoken since leaving the beach. I had been too tired to try to keep talking and I quickly realized I needed to save my energy for walking.

Kieron was setting me down gently. I opened my eyes and realized we were in front of a small cave. The dead forest of the Wastelands was thick and dark around us. "You can step around that boulder and see to your needs." He jerked his chin in the direction he meant. I watched him walk a few paces the other direction before I went to relieve myself.

When I came back he was waiting by the cave. He gestured for me to enter the cave and I stepped into the small opening. I watched as he pulled a bound bunch of branches over the entrance like a door. The moon was bright enough that it leaked in through the gaps and lit the small space. He retrieved a pack that was tucked in the corner and unfastened a bed roll and blanket.

"Here, you can sleep on this, it is not safe to move through these woods at night. Tomorrow we will find Ryett." He lay the bedroll out on the dirt.

"What about you?" I asked as I sat down on the bedroll.

He pulled bread and dried fruit from the pack and tossed

some onto my lap. Then he tossed a canteen with water to me. "I will be fine." He said before swigging from a small flask he pulled out of the pack.

I ate quietly before laying down on the bedroll and wrapping the blanket around myself. The night noises were enough to cause nightmares. Howls and screeches. Branches breaking as creatures moved through the woods and did not try to be quiet. I found myself shivering under the blanket and looked to where Kieron had sat, leaning against the wall. He looked as cold and miserable as I felt.

I wrapped my arms around myself trying to create a pocket of body heat.

"Can't sleep?" Kieron asked, his voice barely a whisper.

"I am freezing." I responded, keeping my voice low. We did not need to be making noise to attract the beasts that were lurking out in the night. I pulled the blanket tighter around myself. "Tell me about yourself ... your parents, your childhood." Anything to distract me from how cold I was.

Kieron snorted, "It's not a great story."

"What happened to your mother?" I pressed tentatively. Rook had made a comment about her.

"My father killed her in front of me and then cut her into pieces and sent her back to her home kingdom." He said flatly, "I was three."

Three. My son had been three when he was killed. Kieron had watched his mother be *murdered* at that age. My throat tightened. "I am so sorry, that is fucking terrible."

"It was centuries ago." He said, as if that made it any better. "Your turn. What was your life like before coming here?"

"I always felt safe and cared for growing up, but around the time I came of age, my parents both died from illness. Then there were wars and I don't know what happened to my brother, we lost touch. Things were good for about ten years … but then my husband and three year old son were murdered. I was on the run for a few years before coming here." I adjusted so I could see him better, "What happened to your father?"

"He died … too quickly." Kieron said. "How old are you?"

"Thirty-three."

"You were already married and had a son?"

It was my turn to snort, "Yes. People only live to maybe eighty years old where I am from, but I am told I will likely get the pleasure of aging the way you all age now that I am here." Kieron only nodded his head. "How old are you?" I asked.

"A lot older than thirty-three." He responded. Then after a long while he spoke again, "What happened to the people who murdered your family?"

I did not respond right away. I shifted under the blanket again and looked away from him. "I killed them. All of them."

He was silent for a while. I just kept shivering. Then Kieron moved closer to where I was laying on the bedroll, his breath clouded in the air. "We can share body heat or you can lay there shivering all night." He paused and looked at me, "Just body heat. I promise."

I swallowed. I was so cold and so tired. Finally I nodded, "Okay. Just body heat." I rolled onto my side giving him space to slip onto the bedroll behind me and pull the blanket over both of us. I felt him settle in, leaving space between us. "Do you have enough space?" I asked.

"Plenty."

We lay listening to the sounds of the night. "Please tell me you don't snore." I whispered.

He chuckled a low warm laugh, "Like you did on the way here?"

"I did not!" I hissed and jabbed my elbow into his stomach.

He gripped my arm, gently, but firmly, pinning it to my side so I could not jab him again. His breath caressed my ear, "Hey now. I will kick you out of this cave to sleep with the beasts."

"You wouldn't." I breathed and I scooted back against his warm body. I felt his breath catch as I pulled his arm over me. His warmth wrapped around me and I stopped shivering.

"Warmer?" He asked.

"Yes." I did not want to breathe too deeply with him against me and I could feel his body was tense. "So if someone wanted to, how could they kill you?" I asked.

His chest shook me with his quiet laugh, "That secret has been kept for centuries." I didn't respond. After a long silence he spoke again, his voice serious, "You would have to cut off my head."

"That is the only way? Anything else you will come back from?" I was whispering too.

"Yep. Or you could blow me into a billion pieces. That would work too. Or those Esurimagicae would probably do the trick. I have not tested that option. Why? Are you making a plan to kill me while I sleep?" His breath was warm on my neck and ear as he responded.

"No. If you were worried about that, why did you tell me?" I asked.

He was quiet for a while, then finally said, "Because at some point I am going to need someone to know how to kill me."

"I guess I will get the honors then." I said and wrapped his arm tighter around me. I tried to adjust myself and my backside brushed against him.

He sucked in a breath. Slowly his fingers splayed out and flattened against my stomach. It was my turn for my breath to catch. He adjusted and pulled me tighter against his body.

I didn't know what it was, but wrapped in his warmth and bathed in moonlight I *wanted him*. Not because I was scared and not for self preservation. I wanted the male he was that was not the murderer, the torturer, or the king's henchman. The one who had roared with laughter on the beach. The one who had realized he was going to be a father. The one who bantered with me and teased me.

I gently ground my ass against him. Testing. His fingers tightened and he groaned softly. "Genevieve. You do not have to …" His body shuddered as I did it again. "Stop taunting me." He ground out between his teeth.

"I'm sorry." My cheeks heated and I inched away, putting space between us. Maybe he didn't want me the way I wanted him. Maybe all the sex had really just been part of his game to break me.

He sighed and pulled me back against his body again. I felt his lips caress my ear before he bit it gently between his teeth. I sucked in a breath at the need that ached through me. Then I felt his hardness press against me, "You said just body heat. So are we doing just body heat or do you want something else?" My skin pebbled and my body arched, pressing my ass against his hardness. "You don't have to … I do not expect this or anything from you." He said gently against my ear.

"Shut up." I breathed rubbed against him again.

His body pressed against mine. His hand slipped under my shirt and he squeezed my breast, "You are sure?" He asked.

My body tingled and ached for him. It was an uncontrollable desire like I had never felt before. "Yes." I whispered.

His hand dipped to my pants and expertly undid the fastenings before sliding down beneath my underthings and between my legs. His hand against my skin caused a gasp to escape my mouth. He let out another groan as I rubbed my ass against him and he buried his face into my neck.

His fingers stroked the bundle of nerves at the apex of my thighs causing me to writhe against him. A whimper slipped

225

from my lips. "Shhhh. Be quiet or you will call in the beasts." He breathed into my neck and his finger teased my entrance. I was soaked for him and his finger plunged into my wetness. I silenced my moan by biting down on my lip.

He held me tightly against his body as his finger stroked pleasure into me. My hand grasped the muscles of his arm. His finger pumped into me and I felt his hardness press against me, "Fuck, Genevieve." He growled quietly. "I love how wet you are for me."

I could not push my pants down fast enough. His hands helped me shove them down around my thighs. I heard his fingers ripping at the fastening on his pants. His length freed from them and I lifted my hips to him. My hand guided him to my entrance.

His tip slipped over my wetness and pressed into me. I rolled slightly and buried my face in the bed roll to stifle the moan that came out of my mouth. He pressed into me further and lifted himself up so I was on my stomach beneath him.

He pulled out slightly then slowly pushed all the way to the hilt filling me with his massive cock. I ground my hips back into him, burying him deeper.

"Fuck!" I gasped and his hand shot to cover my mouth. His hips moved as he pulled out and thrust into me again and again. I whimpered in pleasure, my mouth pressed against his palm.

"Shhh you have to be quiet." He groaned quietly against my

hair as he thrust into me.

I turned my head to look up at him and he leaned his forehead against my temple. My lips parted and I gasped in a silent moan. He pressed his lips against mine. He had never kissed me. Never kissed my body. Never kissed my lips. His lips were full and soft. His kiss was demanding yet gentle and his tongue slipped into my mouth. I met him stroke for stroke as our mouths and tongues tasted each other. His cock pounded into me and his body pressed against mine. A groan escaped his throat.

I had to pull away from his lips as a climax tore through my body. He slid his fingers into my mouth and I sucked them as I climaxed again. "Oh fuck, G." He moaned. My inner muscles were milking him. Begging him to fill me. Our eyes locked and he forced his fingers deeper into my mouth as I whimpered around them.

He slid his fingers out and firmly grasped my face in his large hand as he kissed me again. He groaned as he continued pumping into me. I moaned into his mouth and he bit my lip. Then his body shuddered and his cock thrust deep as he spilled into me.

We were both breathing heavily. His grasp loosened and he gave me a gentle kiss before he slid out of me and onto his side on the bedroll. After a few heartbeats, I pulled my pants up and rolled to face him. His hand brushed my hair back from my face and he kissed my forehead gently before pulling me close into his warmth.

Neither of us said anything as we drifted off to sleep.

I blinked my eyes and swallowed. I was so nauseous. "Hey." Kieron's deep voice whispered, "Did you get some sleep?"

"Yes." I tilted my chin up and looked into his golden hazel eyes. I had never really noticed them before. "You?"

"Yes." His hand stroked my back. "We need to get you back to Ryett. He is probably tearing this forest apart looking for you."

"About last night ..." My voice trailed off.

His thumb caressed my lips, "I am a monster and you should want nothing to do with me."

"You are not a monster. You do not have to be a monster." I searched his eyes. They were soft and looked back at me longingly.

"How could you ever trust me? How could I ever believe you trusted me after what I have done to you? How could I look you in the eyes?"

"Just like you are doing now." I countered gently. I did not know if I would or could trust him, but after last night—how I felt around him—I was willing to try.

"What I did is unforgivable." There was gravel to his voice.

My thumb stroked the back of his hand. I did not care. I needed a fresh start. Maybe he needed one too. "You aren't the one who decides that."

"*I* will never forgive myself." There was pain in his eyes. I brushed my lips against his and he kissed me back. "I will *always* be a monster." He said against my mouth.

I pulled back and looked deep into his eyes. "Maybe I am a monster too." I breathed.

It was his undoing. His hands tore at my clothes as he peeled them off of me before removing his own. My fingers touched the scars I had given him. His eyes burned with desire as he kissed me. Then he buried himself deep inside of me.

Kieron lay with his head on my naked chest and I ran my fingers through his long hair, massaging his scalp. "I am bringing you back to Ryett and you are going to live your life far away from me and far away from Vossarian. It is not a discussion. It's what's best." He said.

"Is that what you want? To be rid of me?" I asked quietly. *Why did it hurt my heart for him to say he wanted me far away from him? What was wrong with me?*

"It does not matter what I want. It matters that you are safe." His hand flattened against my stomach. *It matters that our child is safe.* Were the words he did not say.

"What about your child? Will you come see them?" I asked, my throat burning. He lifted his head to look at me.

He looked completely devastated. Finally his throat bobbed and he whispered, "Yes."

A twig snapped and Kieron pulled me close behind his body to shield me as he threw up a hand in surrender.

"Let her go." Ryett's voice growled.

"I did not hurt her. We have been looking for you." Kieron called out. I saw Alias emerge from the trees to our right, palming his weapon. Ryett stepped out from the trees in front of us a healthy distance away. Kieron slowly pulled me around to the front of him so Ryett could see me. "You are safe now. I am going to let go of your arm and you are going to walk to Ryett." He whispered in my ear.

I looked up at him, "Kieron …" There was so much pain and longing in his eyes as he looked back at me. I didn't know what to say, "Thank you. I—"

"Stay away from Vossarian. I won't tell him anything. Now go." He interrupted me. Then he lifted his eyes back to Ryett and Alias who were moving closer. Both males looked ready to kill him as soon as I was out of danger. Kieron raised both his hands to show he was not a threat and spoke loudly, "I am leaving. I never saw any of you here."

I nodded to him before turning and hurrying through the woods towards Ryett. Ryett ran to me and wrapped me in his arms. He never took his eyes off of Kieron behind me. Ryett was holding me so tightly I could barely turn my head to look and when I did, Kieron was already gone.

CHAPTER 27

Ryett held me at arms length and looked me over. "Are you okay?"

"No permanent damage." I said. The relief on Ryett's face was sobering, "I am fine. How is Alias?" I turned my head to look at Alias. He was fine, his clothes were covered in dirt, but his eyes were clear and I did not see any blood.

"I am fine, thanks to you, Genevieve." Alias said. Giving me a nod of thanks.

Ryett nearly crushed me as he pulled me back into his arms again. "How did you end up with Kieron? What happened? And why did he just bring you back and leave?"

"He saved me from those ... things. We jumped off the cliffs to get away from them." I said.

"He must know about the freed slaves now. He is going to tell Vossarian. Why did he bring you back? A warning? Did he give you a message?" It was Alias's turn to ask questions.

"He knows about the slaves, but he is not going to tell Vossarian. I somehow managed to convince him to not breathe a word of this to anyone." I had not really done that. That was what Kieron had said to me and I completely trusted him. I was not ready to tell them the full story.

"Are you sure?" Ryett looked at me confused.

"Completely. Kieron is not going to tell Vossarian. I am sure of it."

"What did you promise him? Why not?" Ryett asked, his questions coming rapid fire.

"Nothing and I don't know." A partial lie. I did know, but I did not fully understand it.

Ryett and Alias exchanged looks. "We need to get out of here and meet back up with Sarla." Alias said.

Ryett looked at me and I must have looked as weak as I felt, because he hooked his arms under my knees and lifted me off the ground. I started to protest, but he gave me a little squeeze, "You are in no shape to keep walking." I let out a sigh and resigned to let him carry me. My eyes were heavy and the steady beat of Ryett's heart lulled me to sleep as he carried me through the woods.

When I opened my eyes again Ryett was still holding me, but we were in the entryway of the cabin. "Hey, welcome back. You completely passed out." He said gently as he set me down and kept an arm wrapped around me for support.

"I am so sorry. You had to carry me—" I was still trying to get my legs under me. I had never felt so weak.

"It was not a problem." He said. "Come on, let's get you cleaned up and get you some food, it looks like you need it."

Ryett led me to my room and helped me pull off my jacket and boots. He hung my jacket neatly on a hook and set my boots in a boot tray by the door. He disappeared into the bathroom to turn on the bath, but was now loitering in the bathroom doorway.

I sat on the bed, "Did everyone make it? Were you and Sarla able to get them safely to wherever it was we were taking them?"

"Yes," Ryett said tightly, "Everyone made it safely thanks to you being completely insane and luring the esurim away."

"Good." I responded and averted my eyes to the floor.

"I would prefer if you never did that again, but thank you." His voice was soft but not weak.

I chuckled, "Same."

"What aren't you telling me about what happened with Kieron?" I expected his words to be laced with something lethal or to be full of anger, but they were not.

I looked back up at Ryett and I took a deep breath. "Kieron

233

was the one who tortured me when I was in Vossarian's dungeons. I put two bullets in him when I helped Sarla escape and I guess it was his way to get payback for that. I don't know. It became this game. How much of his torture could I withstand? Could he break me into obedience? I eventually became more and more obedient. He thought he had won. *I* thought he had won. Then yesterday happened and after we had gotten away from those creatures ... I don't know why he decided to bring me back or not say anything to Vossarian. He just said, 'I am taking you back to Ryett and then none of us are going to breathe a word about this.' That is all I know. I was not going to argue with him when he said he was going to help me find you."

Ryett only nodded. I had not told him everything, but I was not ready to tell him everything. I might never tell him everything. The silence reminded him that the bath was running and he stepped back into the bathroom to turn it off. I stood from the bed, a warm bath sounded so inviting, but Ryett stopped me in the doorway. His fingers traced down my arm and wrapped around my hand. I looked up into his eyes, he was standing so close to me, "Please do not go taking on any type of beast on your own again. Ever."

"I can't make that promise, but I can promise you that I really would prefer not to." I gave him a small smile. He squeezed my hand then left me in my room to bathe.

◆ ◆ ◆

I wanted to stay in the bath for hours, but I only let myself stay until I knew my bones were warm and I did not smell like the rotting bits of the sea and forest. I could only smile to myself as I selected a beautiful tan sweater set—flowing pants, thin strapped top, and long sweater all made from the same material—to wear from my closet. Belinda was a genius.

Sarla, Alias, and Ryett were all sitting at the large worn wooden table in the kitchen when I came out of my room. Sarla jumped up and gave me a big hug. I hugged her back.

"We need to fill you in on what is going on here and in Savengard." Ryett said. He nodded to a place setting with bread and a bowl of soup, indicating that it was for me. I sat and dug into the food. Then he began, "The Lands of the Mother are a holy place, believed to be the heart of all creation. Savengard is made up of seven kingdoms. These seven kingdoms, ruled by seven kings, keep the balance of our ecosystems and protect the power of life and death that The Lands of the Mother provide. At some point in time, before our written history, there was a great war. The Lands of the Mother almost fell to a dark lord. In order to save Savengard, The Lands of the Mother split our world into twenty-six, or some believe twenty-seven, realms. They also locked themselves off from the rest of Savengard and twenty-six of their top warriors were given a way—a key—to unlock The Lands of the Mother. Those twenty-

235

six warriors fled Savengard and hid in the other realms.

"Throughout history, there have been many who have wanted to disrupt the balance that we have—most wanting more power for themselves. None of them have been successful in overthrowing the seven kingdoms of Savengard or entering The Lands of the Mother. However, some have been successful enslaving other realms, other worlds. We have fought many wars to keep Savengard whole, as well as, to keep other worlds from coming here.

"Vossarian comes from a bloodline of kings who seem to have made it their mission to expand their power. The people in his territory have been taught their whole lives that they are the rightful rulers of all of Savengard and should also rule The Lands of the Mother. His father before him was successful in enslaving six other worlds. His goal was to build an army big enough to remove the other kings of Savengard from his path. With the kings gone, his next step would be to enter The Lands of the Mother and become the one True King of Savengard.

"If a world did not bow to him and agree to help him, he would enslave its people, and in some cases, he completely decimated the world when they tried to fight back. These destroyed worlds became nothing more than ashes and dust. We know of three worlds that he completely obliterated. However, something must have gone wrong in the third world, because Vossarian was the only one of them to return. We think Vossarian destroyed your world after you and Sarla came through the portal."

I listened in silence. Sarla had guessed that my world was gone now—destroyed. Ryett thought it was too.

Ryett continued, "The other five kings of Savengard—well four kings and one queen—have been barely holding on to an alliance since the last war. Their combined strength and disapproval of Vossarian's goals are small threads keeping them together. Only Aveline of the Cliffs sees me as an ally, but it is a secret allyship. I am seen to be just as bad as Vossarian by the other kings."

Ryett paused. The others just sat quietly, "What about the slaves?" I asked. This was a lot to take in, but I needed a distraction from myself and this was a good one.

"Vossarian and his father, and his father before that, have used slaves to build their wealth and armies. He takes slaves from the other worlds and he sells them to other worlds and even some buyers here—" Ryett explained.

"Like you." I interrupted.

I saw the muscle flutter in Ryett's jaw, "Yes, that is why I am not well liked among the other kings. I have been working to get close to Voss for centuries and find out who the players are here in Savengard. I want to take apart his entire operation."

"Do you free all of the slaves that you buy?" I had to know.

"Yes. Every single one. I give them what they need to live free in my kingdom or we move them to the Cliffs and Aveline provides them what they need to live free in her territory. If possible, Sarla returns them to their home worlds. We have held a secret alliance with Aveline for centuries." Ryett's eyes were searching my face, trying to discern if I believed him.

"And the male that I watched you kill in Vossarian's throne room?" I could not unsee the blood of the broken male as it sprayed across the marble floor.

"He had endured days of torture and would endure more. He deserved a quicker death than I was able to give him." Ryett's voice was hard. I could see the pain in his eyes. That it destroyed him. I could see that he had chosen to do far worse things over the centuries, things he would not speak of, and it haunted him.

My heart cracked further. I *was* broken. Not by Vossarian or Kieron, not in the way they wanted me to break, but by the horrors that they inflicted on others. By the rulers in my world and the injustices that they had committed. By every male in a place of power who played with the lives of others. This life was a second life. I should not be here, but since I was, I was going to do something—anything—to right as many of these wrongs that I could. "So how do I help?"

"You help by not getting caught by Vossarian." Ryett said solemnly. "You are likely the last living person from your world and you have significant power, which you have said is not possible because your world did not have magic. This could mean two things: First, you could reset the twenty-sixth world and bring back life to it, keep it from disappearing

238

into nothingness. And second, it is possible that you are a descendant of one of the twenty-six warriors. Which would make you one of the keys that can open the gates to The Lands of the Mother." I looked at all their faces. Sarla and Alias only nodded in confirmation, "If Vossarian finds out you are from the twenty-sixth world and that you might be a key, he will do anything to get to you."

"What do you mean to reset my world or bring back life? Why would that matter?" I was having a hard time speaking. This was a lot of information.

It was Sarla's turn to speak, "Worlds can die and when they do, the magic keeping The Lands of the Mother safe becomes weakened. In theory, if you destroyed all twenty-five other worlds, there would be no gates or borders left to keep The Lands of the Mother safe. Worlds die when there is no remaining life. So Vossarian wipes out all life, then lets the world slowly fade into nothingness on its own. If every single being from a world is wiped out, then that world completely disappears instantly. This rarely happens as Voss has usually taken slaves from a world before he destroys it. With your magic, you could restore life in your world as long as you do it before it fades out. Only someone from a world can restore that world. Which means you might be the only one who can restore the twenty-sixth world."

"Okay, so I need to not get caught by Vossarian and I need to restore my world so that the border to The Lands of the Mother is not weakened. Am I getting that right?" I tucked my hands into my lap as I spoke, trying to keep them from shaking.

"Pretty much." Sarla confirmed.

"We do not think Vossarian has figured out who you are yet, but he definitely has a strong interest in you. We can not let him figure it out." Ryett said.

"What is the plan with Vossarian then?" I asked. *Had Kieron known this? Is this why he brought me back to Ryett?* I would have thought I would be more of a prize to bring back to his king ... unless he did not support Vossarian's plans.

Alias spoke, "We need to kill Vossarian and replace him with a new king. He does not have an heir, so assassinating him might create enough of a disruption in his kingdom to upset their plans for complete domination."

"We have just barely gotten enough information on Vossarian's partners to be able to take down his whole network here in Savengard. Unfortunately, we might need some assistance and that is why we have been trying to work with Beck. We need to act on all fronts at the same time so that no one is able to sneak away into hiding." Sarla explained. "Voss will still be the trickiest to get to. He is difficult if not impossible to get alone."

"Well if Vossarian already has an interest in me and he does not yet know who I am, maybe I should go back to him. He propositioned me to be his queen. I could let him think I have accepted his proposal and kill him while he sleeps." Ryett choked at my response. I continued, "It is a simple way to get him alone and his guard down. I am not proud to admit I have done similar before."

It was Sarla's turn to choke. "That is going to need a more thorough explanation, Genevieve."

I sighed. This was part of me I had kept secret for over a decade. The part I had been running from. The part that I left behind eleven years ago, before my family. The part that had sought me out again after my family had died and the world was going to shit. The part I had kept close to my chest in this new world—it was safer to pretend to be a helpless female. "I was in the military, we all were required to serve three years." They all just stared at me, "I have picked up a few skills and I have killed more than a few people."

"Tell me the knives and axes were not just beginner's luck, please spare my pride and tell me you knew how to throw before." Sarla was laughing. *Laughing.*

"The axes were new and it has been a decade since I have thrown knives, but yes, I have done it before." I shrugged.

"Well boss, looks like we have a plan now." Alias said, his eyes dancing with amusement.

"No." Ryett was the only one not smiling. "It is too risky. It is only a matter of time before Vossarian figures out you are actually from the twenty-sixth world. We can not risk you being near him when he figures it out. Also, if he thinks you might be a key he will try to use you to get into The Lands of the Mother. He is one of the strongest kings and we have to consider his magic. You do not know how to use your magic yet. We can not risk it ... or you." He had not taken his eyes off of me.

I met Ryett's stare, "Then tell me how I can help."

CHAPTER 28

The next day we jumped to the capital city of the Mountains, Montvera. That evening we would be meeting with the rest of the Ryett's circle—The King's Circle. I already knew Alias, his General of the Armies, and Sarla, who did not have an official title that I knew of, it was just Sarla, like everyone knew what that meant. Then there were two other commanders I needed to meet.

Standing on the chateaus gravel courtyard I looked out over the most beautiful lake framed by forested mountains. Small cottages dotted the estate between the lake and the chateau —homes for Ryett's circle. The city was made of rolling cobblestone streets and ancient stone buildings. Two rivers cut the city in thirds.

"What do you think?" Ryett asked quietly from my side.

"Don't tell Beck you have the most beautiful lake, he might throw a hissy fit." Ryett just laughed at my response. Montvera was the most beautiful place I had ever seen. This chateau might be the most beautiful estate I had ever seen.

Ryett led me inside and pointed to a living room, the dining room, and various hallways off of the grand entry. I heard a small clicking noise coming towards us. I had heard that noise before ... A gigantic black wolf stepped into the entryway from the living room. His dark fur glistened in the light and he had warm golden eyes. His nails clicked on the stone as he padded his way towards us and weaved under Ryett's outstretched hand.

Any sensible being would have been completely terrified of the wolf. He was huge. His shoulder was nearly as tall as Ryett's waist. His teeth were long and could easily remove a limb in one quick snap. I somehow was not afraid. His eyes looked at me and I lifted the back of my hand slightly to invite him to sniff. He did and stepped closer. I sank to my knees and cautiously lifted my hands to scratch behind his ears, his snout inches from my face.

"This is Mintaka." Ryett said as the wolf's gentle tongue licked my face. *Mintaka—he had the name as the western most star in The Hunter's Belt.* "Hi Mintaka, it is nice to meet you." I said gently. He turned and offered his butt to be scratched. I obliged.

When I stood back up and looked at Ryett his mouth was open, gaping at me, "What?" I asked.

"He has never done that. Not even with me." Pure wonder crossed into his eyes. I only smiled at him and shrugged my shoulders. He grinned back, "Mintaka came here when he was a pup. Just showed up one day. I was a toddler at the time. We grew up together of sorts. He comes and goes as he pleases and it looks like I do not have to worry about the two of you getting along."

"How long ago was that?" I hadn't asked. I had no idea how old Ryett was.

"Three hundred and sixty-four years ago." He responded. *Three hundred and sixty-four years.* Both Ryett and Mintaka were three hundred and sixty-some years old. I could not even fathom the lifetimes of things that they had seen. "He will probably outlive me too. Great Wolves like him can live for tens of thousands of years."

"He is beautiful." I breathed as Mintaka wandered back into the living room and lay down in a beam of sunlight filtering through the window.

"The legends say that Great Wolves can travel through worlds just like the World Walkers. Some believe them to be the balancers of what is not right between the worlds—removing or killing things that shouldn't be. Some believe them to be the protectors of those who are most needed or most important to the fate of our world. I like to think it is a little of both.

There were once Princes of the Great Wolves too—males who could shift between their wolf form and a form like us. It has been thousands of years since one of the Princes has revealed himself so maybe they are just myth and legend now." Ryett pointed up a set of narrow stairs to our right and indicated that I should follow him.

The hallway at the top contained a few doors. He opened the second door on our left and showed me into a private bedroom. It was made up of a little sitting area with an armchair, writing desk, and a small balcony just big enough for a cafe table and two small chairs. The view looked out towards the lake. The bed was massive with crisp white sheets, pillows, and a fluffy comforter. The bathroom had a separate room for the toilet, two sinks, a soaking tub and a shower, and a cushioned stool set in front of a vanity.

"I hope you will be comfortable here. You will find all your things already in the closet. If there is anything else you need, just let me know." Ryett said from the doorway.

"Thank you, it's perfect." I responded as I stared out the window towards the lake.

I had spent the evening before filling in Ryett, Sarla, and Alias on the relevant details of my training and the history of the end of my world. My world had once been magnificently prosperous, but as time went on, the rulers of the territories grew more and more greedy. The working classes were so caught up in their own lives that they did not see the greed and deception of the rulers until it was almost too late. Until territories were warring against each other and people had barely enough money to put food on the table.

At some point in time the people in my territory stopped volunteering for military service. No one wanted to be sent off to war to be butchered and no one supported the wars that our rulers were waging. So our rulers made it a requirement for all people to serve in the military for three years. As our rulers became richer, there became a bigger divide between the people who had and the people who had none. The people who had none rebelled against the rulers. It was then that the rulers had realized their mistake of military training the majority of their population.

In order to stay in power, they resorted to weapons of mass destruction against their own people. Which were effective, but also destroyed the world that we lived in—turning our skies gray and waterways toxic.

Our local ruler, fearing being overthrown, started murdering anyone and everyone he thought might be a threat to his reign—which amounted to any male of ruling age who had advanced to a leadership position during their time in the military. My husband was one of them. It had been a coincidence that my son and dog had been with him that day. I had lost my entire family in a blink of an eye because of greed and paranoia.

So I changed my hair and with a few tricks of makeup

made myself unrecognizable. I learned the male who carried out the murder frequented a fancy tavern and liked to take home females—I became the last female he took home. Then I systematically assassinated everyone else involved.

I left my town and over the next months I did what I needed to in order to survive. Eventually, I had decided it was not worth living anymore. That is how I found myself near the river, helping Sarla.

I watched the way Ryett's eyes had changed as he looked at me while I had shared some of my story. I did not know if it was pity or sorrow or if he thought I was as big of a monster as I felt I was. There was no turning back now.

I stood staring out towards the city as the sun set. There was a knock on my door and Sarla popped her head in. It was time.

We were the last to arrive. Ryett and Alias sat with two males —the commanders. They all stood when we entered. Mintaka lay in the doorway between the dining room and the hall to the kitchen. The way he lay on the floor with his head raised made him look like he was on watch, but his eyes were closed. His belly rose and fell with his deep breaths.

Sarla had explained that the two commanders were not just commanders over the warriors, but each had specific advisory roles under Ryett. The larger of the two males was named Jax. Like Alias, he had a long beard, and he knew the ins and outs of all of the cities and towns in the kingdom.

The other male, who was clean shaven and wore his hair short, was a liaison to the other kingdoms, making it his business to know the similarities, differences, and who's who outside of the Mountains. He was introduced as Zain.

Ryett, Alias, and Jax all looked like they could tear a person limb from limb with their bare hands, but my gut told me that Zain was the one to watch out for. He had a calm lethal quiet to him.

"You were with Ryett at Vossarian's." I said carefully after Zain was introduced. He had been the male in all black with silver knives across his chest.

"Yes. I was." He responded coolly, holding my gaze.

"Zain gets the unfortunate pleasure of accompanying me when we go do our business deals." Ryett stepped in to provide further context. "Alias and Jax tend to kill first and ask questions later, so I need someone who can play the role needed."

Both Alias and Jax rolled their eyes at Ryett. Alias also gave him a crude gesture.

"How did you all meet?" I asked, pulling my eyes away from Zain.

"Well unfortunately I am Ryett's cousin," Sarla said sarcastically, "And we grew up terrorizing this place together."

"Jax and Alias showed up to study under my father's general and commanders when they were just boys," Ryett cut in, "The three of us grew up training together." I looked to Zain and Ryett continued, "Zain has been serving this kingdom longer than the rest of us have been alive."

"He comes with the house." Jax drawled. Zain just chuckled and shook his head at the joke. He did not look older than the rest of them, but I still had no idea how aging worked in this world.

Sarla poured glasses of wine and started filling in Jax and Zain on what they had learned about me. I clutched the glass she handed me and only pretended to take small sips as I watched them. They were all so comfortable together. They were a family. A family of their own making. I could feel the love they had for each other. The respect they carried. Ryett and Sarla had invited me into this. Into their family. If my shattered heart could begin to mend itself, this was a good place to start.

CHAPTER 29

Ryett had shown me every room, closet, and secret passageway in the chateau. He had even shown me the entrances and map of the unlit and cramped tunnels that connected each cottage to the main building—the tunnels were so creepy they did not get used, but they existed. Just peeking into the tunnels' entrances made my stomach do flips and the hair on my body stand on end. I never wanted to step foot in another tunnel or cave system in my life. I had promised myself that I never would unless there was a damn good reason. As he showed me around I noticed Ryett staring at me. I had even felt his hand raise reaching to touch my back as if to guide me, but it would always lower before he touched me.

The staff for the estate was small. A groundskeeper, a chef—

who insisted everyone call him Chef—and two maids who also serviced the cottages and, according to Sarla, were excellent at hair and makeup for special occasions. They had all been kind and welcoming.

True to what Ryett had said, I noticed Mintaka coming and going as he pleased. The staff all gave him a wide, but respectful berth. No one gave him commands or expected him to listen to them. I often found him at my side and my hand mindlessly stroking his soft fur as he almost silently slid by. Sometimes he would sit close by or follow me room to room. Ryett was completely baffled and one night Alias had also looked on in wonder as Mintaka nuzzled his head into my lap and I scratched behind his ears.

It was one of those nights. Mintaka was curled up on the floor in front of the couch I was tucked into. I had found an almost embarrassingly erotic novel on one of the bookshelves and shamelessly dove into reading it. "I do not think he has ever been so attached to anyone." Ryett said from the doorway. "What are you reading?"

I snapped the book shut. "Did you know you have erotic novels laying around your residence?"

Ryett laughed, "I think Sarla leaves them around to make Jax and Zain feel uncomfortable."

"Well I found one and it is positively delightful." My cheeks heated and I blushed as his eyes lit with amusement. "You really should read it. It is a literary masterpiece." I continued, my words dripping with sarcasm.

"You will have to let me know when you finish it." He replied with a teasing smirk. "Maybe you should be reading it in your room, so you can more thoroughly enjoy it, if you know what I mean."

My cheeks heated more. "I thought right here in the living room would be more exciting." I met his stare as he crossed the room towards me.

Mintaka let out a low growl and we both startled. Ryett stopped and his eyes flicked to Mintaka. Then he laughed, "Mintaka is getting territorial I see. Sorry, buddy."

Mintaka huffed and stood, taking a long while to stretch before giving Ryett a long stare and leaving the room.

"Why do I feel like I just got lectured over my behavior?" Ryett said and I burst out laughing. "Do I need to give you some privacy to … finish?" Ryett teased, his voice low and sultry. I rolled my eyes and chucked the book at him. He caught it and sat down on the couch with me, leaning back and propping his feet onto my lap without even asking. Then he opened it to a random page and began reading aloud, "He took her breast in his mouth and sucked, flicking his tongue on the tip of her nipple. She moaned and gripped his throbbing cock in her hand. The way she squeezed him and pumped his hard steel made his tip drip in anticipation …" His eyes flicked up to me, "You are right, it is a literary masterpiece."

We both burst into laughter. When I finally wiped the tears

from the corners of my eyes, he asked, "Are you actually enjoying this trash?"

"A girl has needs." I responded with a mocking wink. It was garbage, but I was enjoying it. I was enjoying escaping from my thoughts. He tossed the book back to me and I set it on the arm of the couch.

He moved his feet off of me and beckoned to my legs, "Give me your feet." He said and pulled my legs up so that my feet were nestled into his lap. He started rubbing them, "You said you have needs … What else do you need? Name it and I will make sure you get it."

"Ryett, you don't have to …" I started.

He interrupted me, "I want to."

"I have no idea. I already have more than I have had in a long time." I paused and his hands stopped rubbing, "That does not mean I don't *need* this foot rub." I teased. He tickled my foot and I squealed, yanking my foot away. He gently grabbed it, pulling it back into his lap and resumed massaging.

"I actually came out here to see if you wanted some dessert." Ryett finally spoke. I raised my eyebrows at him, "I hope you like chocolate." He continued.

"I love chocolate." I smiled.

He grinned back at me, "Good, but it's in the kitchen. Want me to bring it to you or do you want to come to the kitchen?"

"I will come to the kitchen." I replied. He helped me untangle myself from the blanket I was wrapped in and I followed him down the hall and into the kitchen.

A simple and small cake sat in the middle of the large kitchen prep table. Ryett pulled out two forks, "I am not going to pretend that we aren't going to eat the entire thing." He said as he handed me one.

"A male after my heart I see." We both sunk our forks into the cake and took a bite. It was delicious. Rich and creamy. I almost moaned at the taste of it.

"Maybe I should read that book of yours. Get some new ideas, you know." Ryett said around a mouthful of cake.

I took another fork full and turned my back to the table so I was facing him. "I don't think you need books, Ryett. Just bring this cake with you and you will be fine."

Ryett's eyes burned into mine. Then he looked me up and down as I leaned against the table. He licked his lip. I set my fork down. Ryett slowly wrapped his hand around my waist and pulled me close against his body. Everything in my body thrummed as if it were humming to his touch. My breath shuddered and I drug my fingers down his back slowly.

His hands dropped to my ass and he lifted me onto the table. My legs wrapped around his waist. His fingers caressed my jawline as he lifted my face to his. His hand tangled in my hair behind my head as our breath mixed. His nose lightly brushed my cheek as he breathed me in. I could hear the desire in his breathing. The same desire raced through my body, just like it had that morning in his cabin. His lips grazed the corner of my mouth.

"I can't." I gasped. Ryett froze. I had slept with Beck. Fallen for and fucked Kieron in the Wastelands even after everything he had put me through. And *I was pregnant.* I was a complete disaster. *How could I drag Ryett down with me?* I could not get involved with him further. I could not do it. "I'm sorry. I can't." I said again and pulled away from him. I hopped off of the table and hurried to my room.

CHAPTER 30

"Did you know Beck has a daughter?" I had just sent an axe into the wooden target with a satisfying thunk. It had become Sarla's and my ritual to throw knives and axes each morning. There was something calming and empowering about sinking blades into a wooden target.

"Yes, I am surprised he told you. No offense." Sarla yanked the axes out of the target.

"None taken. It just sort of came up. What happened to her mother? He said they were never joined in union and things did not work out? Did you know her?" I was trying to sound casual, but I had to know what happened to females who were pregnant and not in a union. In my world, it often was not a pretty fate.

She sent a knife deep into the center of the board and let out a long breath, "The law is that a female pregnant out of union becomes the male's property. That is how it has always been and still is in most of the kingdoms. The Deserts and the Giants being the worst—females are considered property there no matter their status. Beck did what he was told and followed that law until he realized she was completely miserable. His parents would not bless a union between them and he actually cared for her enough to help her leave. He set her up in another city with more money than she could ever spend. It was probably the kindest thing Beck has ever done for someone."

"What do you mean when you say 'property'?" Nausea was rolling in me and I did not think it was from the baby.

"It's disgusting, but basically the male gets to decide everything. If you are in a kingdom where you had rights to begin with, you lose your rights. Hopefully, the male actually cares about the female and they join in union or he gives her money to raise the child. But in the case of an unwanted pregnancy, many of the females get thrown out on the streets with nothing." Sarla's face held a rage to it. The injustice really bothered her. "Ryett changed the laws here, but that only applies to females and males from here. He can not enforce it if the male is from another kingdom. The inter-kingdom laws are laced with old magic that enforces them."

I might actually vomit, "That is terrible."

"It is the issue that I used to convince Beck and Ryett to

become allies over. Well the issue that got Ryett in the door. After Beck became king, he changed the laws in the Lakes, just like Ryett did here. With Beck's help we might be able to take out all of the slave trade and Vossarian." An axe split the wooden target as Sarla sent the blade deep into its center.

"Will he still help? After everything with me?" I asked. *What if I had ruined their alliance?* I couldn't stomach it.

"I think so. Things are tense, but I think he will. I think he finally understands what Ryett's been doing all these years." She secured a new wooden target in place and held out the axe to me, "Your turn."

I shook my head, "I think I am done, I am not feeling great this morning. Maybe I didn't sleep well." I already felt exhausted.

Sarla looked at me concerned, "Need me to bring you anything? You detoxed rather quickly, maybe some of that is still lingering."

I thanked her, but declined. I needed to sleep and process what she had just told me. I was Kieron's *property. Why hadn't he kept me when he found out? Why had he brought me back to Ryett?*

I did not feel better when I woke up that afternoon. Hiding a pregnancy was going to be difficult. Kieron had returned me to Ryett after learning about the baby—his baby. *What if he came*

back? What if he changed his mind? Did I want him to change his mind? I was not going to solve this feeling like I was going to vomit. I needed something in my stomach.

I snuck down the halls towards the kitchen praying no one was hanging around the chateau. I did not want to explain myself. I almost let out a sigh of relief as I pushed open the kitchen doors—I had made it here without running into anyone.

"Need a snack?" Ryett was standing at the long work table with various herbs, vegetables, and a huge hunk of meat laid out before him. His sleeves were rolled up and he was chopping a fresh bunch of herbs.

"I can't believe Chef lets you make a mess of his kitchen." It made me smile seeing Ryett so casual and doing something so —*normal*.

His ice eyes sparkled with his smile, "Oh it takes some convincing, but I am the king you know. I just threaten a beheading or some shit and he gives in."

"Do beheadings happen often?" I raised my eyebrows at him.

He chopped an exaggerated vicious chop with his knife and paused. "Not nearly often enough." I could only chuckle, "What brings you to the kitchen?" He asked.

"Looking for food, maybe just some bread." I glanced around, hoping there would be something I could grab and leave with before my nausea came back.

"Sit, I will get something for you." He was washing his hands and drying them on a kitchen towel thrown over his shoulder before I could refuse. I slid onto a stool across from the food he had been preparing. A plate of bread and glass of water was placed in front of me a moment later. "What else? This seems like a pretty lame snack so far."

"No, this is perfect." I tore off a piece of bread and willed it to keep my stomach settled as I ate. "How did you learn to cook?"

"When we were kids, Sarla and I used to sneak into the kitchen at night and try to make food." Ryett said as he went back to chopping vegetables, "One night, Chef caught us. We both thought we would get in so much trouble. We were so terrified, but he just laughed at us and then started to teach us how to cook. I will never forget it, he just looked me right in the eyes and said, 'Someday you will be king, but that does not mean you need to grow up a worthless male that needs a mommy to cook, clean, and wipe his ass for him.'"

I almost choked on my bread as I laughed, "Many males need that lecture while growing up and do not get it!"

"Well I am glad I got it. I do not pretend to be an expert, but I enjoy it and I like being able to sneak off to the cabin and have time alone while still being able to eat well." He said with a smile.

He was so *normal*. Extraordinary, but normal. He had grown up with everything he could need or want or ask for and yet this was how he turned out. Maybe it was through people like Chef, or his parents, or maybe it was just the way he was. "What are you making?" I asked.

"A roast. I thought I would have everyone up to the house for dinner tonight." He said. I watched quietly as he rubbed seasoning on the meat and rolled it up stuffed with the freshly chopped herbs and vegetables. He tied the meat up into a neat bundle before taking a rolling pin and smacking it. He smacked it over and over, pounding the meat, before setting it into a roasting pan and arranging potatoes and the remaining vegetables around it.

"What did the meat do to you?" I had never seen someone beat on meat before—then again we rarely had meat to eat and never a roast.

He slid the pan into one of the ovens and washed his hands again, "It makes the meat more tender. Have you had a roast before?" I shook my head no. He set about cleaning up the mess he had made and I stood to help him wash the dishes. "Well I am honored mine will be your first."

I heard Alias's booming laughter down stairs before I even finished getting dressed for dinner. Seeing Ryett that afternoon had left me feeling like a teenager again. I guess when all my basic needs of food and shelter were met then I regressed into a silly girl again, pining after any handsome male. But Ryett was not just any male—he was *good*. Too good for me. Thankfully he had not brought up the other night when I had rejected his advances. I felt embarrassed and especially embarrassed considering my current state. What I had just done with Kieron.

I took a final look at myself in the mirror. My skin was radiant despite how ill I had felt most of the day. I turned and examined my outfit from each angle—I had chosen tight black pants and a flowing top with a neckline that plunged so deep my lace underthings peaked out. At least I could still fit in my pants. I did not bother with jewelry, I had never become accustomed to wearing anything other than the three rings that represented my marriage and the birth of my son. Two of those rings were hidden safely in a secret pocket in my pack.

I took a deep breath and prayed that I would not get sick during dinner, then I slipped out of my room to find the others.

It was not hard, they were a rowdy bunch. Zain was the most reserved, I could tell he spent lots of time blending in with other groups and cultures. He was a chameleon and, from what I had gathered, his skills led him to have many deep connections across the kingdoms even in spite of Ryett's reputation. Alias's booming laugh echoed through the halls again and I turned to the living room off the entry.

Alias, Sarla, and Jax were sprawled casually on the couches. Jax's face was flushed as if he had been blushing. "We need the full story, Jax." Sarla was saying through her giggles.

"It will have to be over dinner." Ryett poked his head in from the dining room. "I can't wait to hear how you scared off yet another poor female."

I could not help but smile as we all filed into the dining room and took our seats. Alias, Sarla, and Zain, who had somehow quietly slipped in, all sat on one side and Ryett and Jax sat on the other leaving a seat for me between them. The table was already covered with steaming dishes of food and Jax and Alias wasted no time digging into the platters and piling food on their plates. Jax passed dishes in my direction as he heaped more food onto his plate. "Let's hear it Jax, what happened with this one?" Ryett asked as he took a dish of green beans from my hands.

"I did not scare her off, I think we just didn't ... click when it came to ... you know." Jax trailed off and Sarla started giggling again.

"There are tinctures you can take if you need help, Jax, there is nothing wrong with getting some help." Sarla was pointing a serving spoon at the table—no, at Jax's lap.

Jax's face reddened. "I do not have that problem, Sarla! And I try to be respectful. I am kind and gentle—"

"Not all females want 'kind and gentle' in the bedroom, Jax." Alias interrupted, winking at Sarla.

"Not all females are Sarla, Alias!" Jax countered.

"Genevieve you are going to have to weigh in, Sarla's is the only female advice Jax has gotten in years and he does not seem to listen." Alias continued.

"Do not pull me into this!" I said. I could feel my cheeks

redden.

"Oh come on! Jax is having a tough go with the ladies these days and needs a bit of bedroom advice. Help him out." Alias teased.

"Okay. Okay!" I resigned. "I don't know much about your situation, Jax, but it sounds like you would have better luck treating her like a roast." I took a bite of the delicious meat and chewed. The meat nearly melted in my mouth.

"What does that mean?" Jax asked, confused. The table was quiet, waiting for an explanation.

I swallowed my bite and skewered another piece, "Tie her up and pound her until she is tender."

Zain spit his wine across the table and Alias roared with laughter. Jax coughed as he tried to not choke on the bite of food he had just put in his mouth. Ryett's eyes gleamed with amusement and his shoulders shook with his stifled laughter.

"Told ya!" Sarla gave me a wink and sipped her wine looking positively triumphant.

"I am never going to think about roasts the same." Ryett finally choked out. His hand casually slid along the back of my chair as he spoke.

"You are welcome for that." I tried to hide my smile as I caught Ryett's eye. Then I turned back to my plate of food, "Do let us know how it goes, Jax."

Zain, having composed himself and snapped his fingers to make the spilled wine disappear, finally spoke up, "I think you will fit in nicely here, Genevieve." I smiled at the comment, especially coming from Zain.

CHAPTER 31

I stood with a towel wrapped around myself, waiting. He had summoned a bath from thin air and left me to clean up. I lingered in the warm water until it had turned cold. How long would he be gone? How many times could a male climax in a day? I could not take the beatings or him pounding into me anymore—my body was still shaking. At least the nausea from the withdrawals had seemed to pass.

The door opened and his large frame filled the doorway. I unconsciously backed against the wall.

He crossed the room, stopping inches from me, and rested a hand on the wall beside my head. He was waiting. Waiting to see if I was going to fight him. I let the towel drop to the floor. I did not have any fight left in me. His hand stroked my hair and raised my chin so

I was looking at his face.

I slowly reached out my hand and cupped between his legs. I rubbed my palm over his leather pants and along the length of him. These males could fuck for hours and how was he so huge? He gave me an approving nod and I pressed my hand more firmly against him. He hardened more under my touch.

I turned, facing the wall and spread my legs, arching my spine to offer myself to him. I heard him spit and wet fingers slid into me as he leaned over me and pressed his face into my hair. I gasped as his fingers stretched me. I tried to focus on the pleasure of it as they pumped in me. I squeezed my eyes closed and tried to let my mind go blank. I tried to relax. I felt wetness building between my legs. Finally his fingers slowly pulled out.

He took my hand and guided me to the middle of the room where he sat in the chair. I knelt on the dirt floor between his legs. His pants were almost bursting at the strain of his hard cock. I undid the fastenings to release it. My mouth dried at the size of him. I had not actually looked. No wonder I ached between my legs.

He stroked himself with long firm pumps. I could not look away. He directed me to stand. I did. His hands guided my hips as I straddled him. He pressed against my entrance. I had no idea how he would fit inside of me, only that he had already. He firmly pressed my hips down and his broad tip penetrated me. I tensed. "Breathe." He instructed. I did and slid him a few more inches into me.

I whimpered at the stretch and my hands grabbed his muscular *shoulders. "Come on sweetheart, breathe." It was commanding, yet laced with hungry encouragement. I whimpered again as he slid deeper. He still was not fully inside of me. I was panting at the slight pain of it.*

His hand brushed my hair back from my face and rested gently grasping my neck. I cried out as he pressed his full thickness into me. He paused as I tried to catch my breath while straddling his lap. "That's it. Take a deep breath." He coaxed. I did, my breath shuddering.

Both his hands gripped my waist as he lifted me, pulling himself out inches before sliding me back down, burying himself in me. I saw pleasure cross his face as he did it again. My nails dug into his shoulders as I struggled to take breaths.

His hands guided my hips to move as I rode him. My brain was blank. Pain slowly gave way to pleasure as I relaxed around him. A moan parted my lips and my inner muscles tightened, squeezing him. "Yes, baby, that's it." He groaned.

My climax was building in me. Kieron thrust into me again and again. I cried out as his hands gripped my ass, forcing me to take him deep. I was screaming. His cock pulsed and twitched in me. Warmth dripped between my legs as I screamed again.

I kept screaming, gasping for air as hands grabbed my arms. Pain ripped through my abdomen. "It's me, Genevieve. It's okay, I am here. I'm here." My eyes snapped open to see Ryett. He was holding my arms. I was in bed. "You were having a nightmare. It's okay, you are safe." His face was pale.

Pain tore through my abdomen again. I cried out. It was wet and warm between my legs. I fought against his grip and he let me go. I pulled back the covers. Bright red blood stained the sheets between my legs. I grabbed my stomach as pain tore through me again.

Sarla burst into the room and shoved Ryett to the side as she knelt on the bed next to me. Her hands glowed as she pressed them to me. "Genevieve, it's okay. Let me feel what is going on." Her glowing hands moved to another spot on my abdomen. "You are ... you are having a miscarriage." Sarla's eyes lifted to mine brimmed with shock and sadness, "Beck?" She mouthed her question to me.

I shook my head no and gritted my teeth as more pain shot through me. Her sadness turned to horror. Ryett was yelling at her to do something. She turned to him and ordered him out of the room. He did not move and she yelled at him again. He opened his mouth as if ready to argue, but left and closed the door behind himself.

"You are going to be okay." Sarla assured me gently and warm light flowed from her hands into me. "I can't stop this, but I can make sure you will survive it."

Eventually the pain subsided and the bleeding slowed. Sarla ran a warm bath and helped me into it. She left me to soak and I sank up to my chin in the warm water. Leaning my head against the side of the tub.

When she returned she carried a small bundle of clothes in her arms. Underthings designed to catch blood flow from our cycles, postpartum, or miscarriage she explained. She then helped me dress and crawl back into bed. The sheets had been changed and there was a steaming mug of tea on the bedside table. "Do you want me to stay with you?" Sarla asked. I shook my head and pulled the covers up. "Okay, I will come back to check on you in a little bit." She left and quietly closed the door. I heard arguing in the hallway, but did not bother trying to hear what was said. I curled on my side and cried.

The world had a sick sense of humor. It had taken my husband and me years to have a baby, then I got pregnant like this? I had gotten over the initial horror of realizing I was carrying Kieron's baby, only to have the guilt of losing his child shatter my heart even more.

The bed shook and Mintaka's head rested on the side. His golden eyes were soft as they looked over me. He gracefully crawled up onto the white bedding and lay down, resting his large head on my curled legs. I extracted my arm from the sheets and stroked his fur. I let the tears flow. Warmth pulsed gently through my body and I closed my eyes, letting sleep take me away.

I woke up and found that it was still dark. The room was

bathed in moonlight. Mintaka was gone. I pushed myself up in bed. Ryett was in one of the chairs and he jumped to his feet when he saw I was awake. He was at the side of the bed in a heartbeat, "How are you doing? Can I get you anything? It is still early ... you should keep sleeping." I could only shake my head no. I did not want him here. I could not bear the sympathy. The kindness. "Did ... did Beck know?" I could hear the pain in his voice.

"Beck wasn't the father." I whispered. His eyes searched my face in confusion. "Kieron." I conceded. Ryett's eyes widened, then rage filled them as he realized what that meant. He sat on the edge of the bed. I pulled the sheets up and turned away. "Please just go." My voice broke as more tears came.

I felt his hand touch my back, "It is not your fault. None of it is your fault." I cried harder. It was my fault. I had fallen into bed with Beck before I knew anything about him. I thought pushing back with Voss would get me out of a cell faster. It all led me to this. And even though the baby had been unplanned, I could not even do that part right.

"How can you even stand to look at me?" I bit out.

"I can't stand not to." He gently turned me back towards him, "All I care about is you being okay."

"I can't imagine what you think of me." I dropped my chin and averted my eyes.

Calloused hands gently cupped my face and guided me to look back up into his eyes, "I think you are the most wonderful, smart, beautiful female there ever was and you have been through too much horror, but it does not change how amazing you are." Tears spilled down my cheeks. His thumb brushed them away before he climbed further on the bed and cradled me against his chest.

I was too defeated to move away from his embrace. I wanted it—I needed the warmth and safety and comfort. I closed my eyes and cried into his chest. I cried for the baby. I cried for myself. I cried for everything I had lost. I cried until Ryett's steady heartbeat and rising chest lulled me to sleep.

CHAPTER 32

I sat on the stone patio with a blanket wrapped around me staring into the fire pit. The stars were out in a magnificent display. But I was not looking at the stars. I was looking into the flames. I was trying to figure out who I was. I had been in survival mode for so long that I had completely lost myself and completely lost myself again when I no longer was struggling to survive—food and shelter and clothing all provided in excess.

I had made poor choices. Very poor choices and I felt like I had been given yet another chance I did not deserve. I could not fathom why fate would keep teasing death in front of me and then yanking it away again.

Dark thoughts had started invading my mind again. It was

a losing battle. I could not think of a single reason why I was worth any of this. Not the clothes, the food, the shelter, the kindness. Maybe if I knew what I wanted there would be a reason for me to stay ... to stay alive. I could not find a reason.

"It is the storm that everyone fears. It causes them to panic," I raised my eyes. Zain had somehow silently slipped onto the patio, probably heading back to his cottage from the chateau. He was looking out towards the lake and the mountains beyond, "They fear it because it thrashes and screams and beats down on us with rain and snow and wind. But the wisest among our kind know not to fear the storm, but to fear the mountain, for even the storm breaks against the mountain."

I just stared at him until he looked back at me, "You think you are the storm, Genevieve, but you are not the storm. You are the mountain." He nodded his head as if to affirm whatever he just said and strode off into the night.

I am the mountain. I said the words to myself and my skin tingled as if it agreed with the nonsense Zain had just spoken. I did not know what he meant, but it quieted my mind. Suddenly, I felt very tired.

I stood to find my way back to my room only to face Ryett leaning in the doorway, arms crossed and watching me. "I was going to ask if you wanted some company out here." He said, but did not move.

"No, thank you. I am headed to bed." I forced a small smile to my lips and made a gesture indicating I needed to slip by him to get inside. He still did not move.

"Is there anything I can do?" He asked. His kindness made me want to shrink into a ball, I did not deserve it, any of it.

"I am not something to be fixed." Even my own words startled me. He had been nothing but good to me and I was pushing him away. I swallowed, I did not trust my judgment anymore. I needed to put space between myself and Ryett before I fell like an idiot into the arms of another male.

He sighed and turned, giving enough space for me to slip past him. I started to step through the doorway when his hand grabbed my arm. I looked down at his hand. "Do not punish yourself for this." He said. He was so close I could feel his breath. This morning I had been tucked safely in his arms. It had felt *right*, but I had hated myself for it. I was whoring myself to just feel the illusion of safety.

I jerked my arm away and left him standing in the doorway.

It had been a few weeks. Sarla had brought me a bottle of bitter liquid to take each day to balance my body, she had also left me a small bottle of contraceptive tincture. I almost refused the contraceptive, but she left it on the bathroom counter as if it was not even a question. Physically I was feeling back to normal. Mentally and emotionally I was completely numb. I mostly kept to myself and stayed in my room, but I did venture to the patio in the evenings to sit by the fire and get fresh air. Ryett, Alias, and Zain came and went often. Sometimes I would not see any of them for days at a time. Jax kept mostly to himself even though I saw him loitering in the chateau most days—probably keeping an eye on me. Sarla checked in on me daily, but I found myself withdrawing from her too.

The chateau was quiet tonight. Ryett, Alias, and Zain were gone again. I stood at the end of my bed, staring out the window down towards the lake. I had just returned to my room after staring into the fire until my eyes burned. Lights from the town flickered across the water. A loud crack shattered the air and I dropped to the floor out of instinct. Yelling from the chateau's entry hall erupted a heartbeat later. The shouting continued as I scrambled to my feet and ripped open my door. I could not hear words, only yelling. My ears roared and I ran down the narrow staircase.

Blood covered the stone floor of the entry hall. I followed the shouting and the blood smeared across the stone as if in a fog. *Whose blood?* My heart was pounding in my chest. I stood in the kitchen doorway as pans clattered to the floor—Sarla was clearing the large kitchen table. Ryett lay a male across the table. Blood poured from him. Light flowed from Sarla's hands into the male. Alias and Jax were holding Zain in a chair, bloody rags pressed to his shoulder. Zain's face was ashen gray.

I grabbed towels from the cabinet and found myself pressing them to the wounds covering the male who was splayed on the table. He was coughing blood as Ryett held his shoulders down and Sarla's magic worked to close wounds. There was so much blood. Too many wounds. His body shuddered under my hands and I knew he would not live. His eyes looked into mine. Dark brown eyes, already starting to cloud with death. He was saying something as he looked at me. I saw his mouth move and I heard his voice through the roaring in my ears. "The king needs you." He whispered, eyes locked in mine. Then his eyes clouded and he stopped breathing.

I wrapped my hand around the dead male's hand. *The king needs you. The beggar had told me the same thing. The old male I brought food to for months. The one who had slowly lost his mind and babbled nonsense to me. Who had died alone in the streets.* My lips were moving with a prayer of the gods who had long since forgotten us. "May you find comfort in the arms of the Mother. Depart in peace, knowing you are not alone. May the light guide your journey to eternal rest. Rest well in Her warm embrace."

I stepped back from the table until my back pressed against the wall as Jax and Alias removed the dead male. I heard them take Zain from the room and looked up long enough to see that he would be okay. He would live. My eyes fell back to the table soaked in blood. Ryett stood with his back to the room, his blood covered hands grasping the edge of the sink. We stood in the silence.

Ryett finally spoke, his voice rough and gravelly. "They all died. Rook had them all killed. We were too late." Ryett moved suddenly and I heard the dish he threw shatter against the stone wall.

I crossed the room to Ryett. This rage did not frighten me. This rage did not cause the little voice inside of me to tell me to run. This rage pulled me towards Ryett. I was not afraid of his rage. His hands still gripped the edge of the sink. He was shaking and looked away from me. I turned the water on and took one of his hands off of the edge of the sink. Using a clean rag, I gently scrubbed the blood from his skin, then I took his other hand and did the same. I looked up at his face and saw blood splattered across it. I reached up and gently wiped the blood away. His eyes were haunted. Pained at what he had witnessed.

"I should have found a way to save him." He whispered.

I stared up into his beautiful ice blue eyes and I shook my head, "He was too wounded, it was not your fault."

"No. The male in Vossarian's throne room. I slit his throat. I should have found a way to save him." His head dropped. "I should have done more. There were so many times I should have done more."

"Ryett …" I began, but I did not know what to say. He had done so much to help so many people. I squeezed his hand in mine and lifted my other hand to his face. His cheek was warm against my palm. For a heartbeat I felt him lean into my touch —his body move closer to me. Then he stepped away from me and left me standing in the blood soaked kitchen alone.

I filled a bucket with water and began washing the blood down the drain.

Ryett and Alias continued their habit of disappearing for days at a time. Ryett had not spoken to me since the night in the kitchen. I had not sought him out either. It was late in the evening and the others had returned to their cottages. I ventured down the stairs and into the living room. A piano sat in the corner, I had never seen anyone play it. I cringed at the loud scrape of the bench as I pulled it out to sit. I lifted the key lid and looked at the beautiful white and black keys. It had been too long since I had played. I always loved playing the piano, even if music was one of those skills trained into me to make me a more desirable mate.

I pressed a key down and the familiar note rang into the empty room. I pressed the pedals a couple of times and hovered my fingers lightly over the keys. I closed my eyes and let my fingers guide me. I stumbled and slowly found the right notes as a melody started forming under my fingers. The music poured from deep inside of me. A haunting love song. The lyrics told a tale of loving someone with a dangerous and self destructive side and the turmoil of loving them unconditionally.

Of course *that* is the song I would remember. I paused and rolled my shoulders. No one was here. I was going to play it.

I took another deep breath and let my fingers strike the keys. My lips moved and I sang quietly. Barely a whisper. My throat felt raw and tight. My singing was not beautiful, but I could hold the melody well enough. The hair on my body prickled at the haunting notes. I did not know if I was singing about Ryett, or Kieron, or myself. I knew all of us had demons. That it would be hard to love any one of us.

I lifted my eyes and my fingers stumbled. I sucked in a breath. Ryett was leaning against the doorway, his arms crossed, watching me. His shirt and pants were covered in blood splatter, his axes still crossed his back. I had never sung in front of anyone. It was something I had only done when I was alone.

"Don't stop." He said, his voice was gravelly.

"I can't." I whispered. My fingers gently resting on the keys. My heart was pounding in my chest.

"Please?" He responded. There was a sadness in his voice that made me pause. I swallowed and dropped my head, looking at my hands. My mouth was dry, but I started playing again. I raised my head as my fingers found the notes. My eyes locked in his and I started singing again. Tears silently fell from his eyes and I kept playing. Kept singing.

I looked away as I played the final chords. My fingers hovered above the keys that had played the final notes. I balled my hands in fists, squeezing my nails into my palms, before closing the lid to the piano. When I looked up again, Ryett was gone.

CHAPTER 33

I rose before the sun and carefully slid folded clothes into my pack. I packed as light as I could not knowing where I was going or how long I would be out in the elements. I had decided I needed to leave. I did better when I was on my own. Ryett and Alias had disappeared again the day before and I was going to sneak off before they were back or the others were awake.

I took one more look around the room, I would miss it here. This place felt like I could make it my home. It was the only place that had felt like a home in years. I glanced at my clothes still hanging in the closet, then out the window towards the lake and the mountains. I finally turned and opened the door. Ryett stood leaning against the wall opposite my room, his arms crossed. "Planning on sneaking out of here?"

"How did you know?" I did not know if I was surprised or not to see him.

"The chateau is spelled. Major medical events summon Sarla." *So that was how she had come so quickly when I lost the baby*, "Security threats summon Alias or Jax, food needs summon Chef, excetera." He had not moved.

"What is this classified as?" *Was he going to stop me?*

"Ah, something like a general disruption to the normal order of things." He pushed off the wall and took my pack out of my hands. "Before you go, can I at least show you something?"

"I am clearly not sneaking out of here anyway." His lips twitched upwards into a small smile. He leaned my pack against the wall and extended his hand to me. We were going to jump somewhere. I took his hand and let him pull me close as the hallway folded in.

The air was crisp and fresh. We were standing on the edge of a partially frozen lake. Huge ice chunks rose from the water and snow covered the mountain peak around us—it was as if we were in a giant bowl made from carving out the tip of a mountain.

"This is the mountain above the city. If you climb to that peak, you can look down on the lake and the city." Ryett pointed to the peak, the sun was just turning the remaining snow pink in its morning glow. "I used to come up here all the time, to get away from … everything."

He took a deep breath, I saw pain in Ryett's eyes, "I have

not walked between worlds in centuries. I used to go all the time, exploring other worlds, learning what I could, and I fell in love with a female in another world. Her name was Rachel. We were in the middle of planning our union and I was visiting her in her world when ... when my family, my parents and baby brother, were killed by Luther, Vossarian's father. I did not know it had happened for weeks. I was too caught up in myself to check back in. When I finally did, I found Sarla holding down the throne to the kingdom. I never walked between worlds again. I lost almost everyone I loved. So I shut off the Mountains from the other kingdoms. I could not lose anyone else."

"I am so sorry, Ryett." I said. His jaw was set, fighting back emotions that threatened to come out of him.

"I never went back. Never went back to tell Rachel what had happened. And by the time I realized I had made a mistake, Luther and Vossarian had destroyed her world." I covered my mouth with my hand, tears welled up in my eyes and my throat burned as it tightened. I knew that feeling. Losing the ones you loved the most. "That was the trip that Luther did not return from. And with Luther gone, I decided I would do something about Vossarian. I decided I would play his game and find a way to end him and the horrors his kingdom inflicts on others.

"The other kings already saw me as an outsider for closing off my kingdom, so it was easy to convince Voss I wanted to trade with him. That my greed and need for power overshadowed the loss of my family. That the war between our kingdoms was a war of our fathers' and not one we should continue if we both wanted to expand our wealth and influence. He offered to slaughter one thousand of his own warriors as a blood payment for the death of my family. Instead I asked for him to give me ten thousand slaves. He agreed. I freed all of them. Some of them still live here in the Mountains, others moved to the Cliffs, and some eventually found their homes in other kingdoms.

"I then helped Voss build his slave trade with the more unsavory groups across the kingdoms only so I could learn who all the players were. I became as bad as Vossarian to almost everyone outside of this kingdom. I gave Voss so much business I was able to convince him to at least not deal in children, but he broke that agreement and Sarla found out. He was trying to kill her so she could not tell me when you met her."

The pieces were all falling into place. Why Beck hated Ryett. Why Ryett had been doing what he was doing. How he had found me in Vossarian's dungeon. "I am going to end all of it. Collapse the entire slave network and end Vossarian along with his family's claim on the throne. Voss does not have an heir yet so his bloodline ends with his death."

"Why are you telling me all of this?"

Ryett slowly turned to face me. "Because I wanted you to know the *why* behind what I am doing and because I do not want you to leave."

"Why do you care if I leave?"

"May I?" He held his hand up to my chest as if asking if he could touch, I nodded and he placed his hand over my heart. I saw jagged mountains, bubbling streams, glaciers, and forest fires. I saw the soil rejuvenating with new growth among the fire's ashes, mountain meadows covered in wildflowers, light snow catching on evergreen branches. I gasped and Ryett's face came back into focus, "You are one of us, of the Mountains, even if you want to leave, the Mountains will always be a part of you. You *belong* here. You can stay in the chateau. If you want the mountain cabin, it's yours. Or if you want an apartment in the city or a house in the forest, tell me and it is yours."

You are the mountain. Zain had said it the other night, is this what he meant? "I can't." I whispered.

"Why not? Is it that bad to be here? You have shown me again and again you do not want anything to do with me, but that does not mean you have to sneak off on your own." There was a bite to his words.

"It is not that I do not want anything to do with you—" I countered, but my voice faltered.

"What is it then?" He interrupted me.

"After Beck and being stuck in that fucking dungeon and Kieron and the baby ... I just ... You do not need this mess that is me." I said exasperated.

"None of those things were your fault." He responded gently.

286

"They weren't my fault? Ever since coming here I have made bad choice after bad choice! This world gave me a second chance that I didn't even want—" I was imploding. I had not wanted to face any of this reality. I was just going to do what I did best: run away from it.

There was a growl in Ryett's voice as he cut in again, "You do not mean that! *None* of those things were in your control."

"I slept with Kieron in the Wastelands!" I wish I had not said the words as soon as they left my mouth. But that was it. I had given myself to Kieron after everything that he had done to me and how could I ask anything of Ryett after that?

"Is that why he returned you? *That* was the price? To fuck you again?" Ryett's voice was filled with rage.

"No! There was no price. I just … This time it was consensual." My voice broke. "I could not just come back and pretend it didn't happen. Especially knowing I was pregnant. I could not drag you into that mess."

"Consensual?" Ryett was nearly yelling.

"You know what?" Now I was yelling, "If he had asked for it, demanded that be the price, I would have paid it! And I would pay it over and over again to keep *your* secret, to keep *you* safe. What would it matter if it was one, two, ten, or one hundred times more?"

"*Everytime* he hurts you it matters." He seethed. I just glared at him. Ryett's expression turned from anger to terror. "Did Kieron know you were pregnant?"

"Yes and he knows I am not from Savengard." I responded with a defeated sigh. "He was going to take me back to Vossarian and tell him about you freeing slaves, then he learned I was pregnant and not from here and he changed his mind. He would not tell me why, he just insisted I go back to you and we all pretend we never saw each other out there."

"You should have told me! What if he comes back for you? Do you know the laws? Do you realize how much danger you could be in? You lied to me. You shut me out." He said strongly. I didn't know if he was angry or terrified.

"I did not lie to you, I just did not tell you personal information. And now I know the laws and how differently everything could have turned out. But it didn't. It was not just me. You disappeared too. You were gone more than you were here." *Why did I care?* He was right. I shut him out. He had tried and I had shut him out. I hadn't wanted to. I thought it was the right thing to do. Maybe I had wanted him to come after me.

"I was trying to give you space!" Ryett started. He took a deep breath and continued, "I realized how selfish I was being. How much I wanted to be near you regardless of what you needed or wanted. I have wanted you since the moment I saw you. I just want to be around you … however you will let me. But I am afraid. I am afraid that if I do not give you space I won't ever be able to stay away from you. And every sign you gave me was to stay away. Do you know how *hard* it is to stay away from you?"

"I am a fucking disaster, Ryett!" Tears threatened to fall

down my face.

Ryett stepped close to me again, his fingers interlaced with mine as if they were a perfectly fitted puzzle piece. He pulled me close to his body and lifted his other hand to my cheek. "I do not care if you are a disaster. Stay. Stay and we will figure it out." His voice was strong, unwavering. His eyes searched my face. Maybe I could figure things out. "Every piece of my soul is screaming at me to convince you to stay. So what can I do to convince you?"

My blood thrummed in me and I looked down at Ryett's tattooed hand that held mine. I was staying. I had told him everything and he did not run from me. He did not reject me or judge me. He fought for me. "Okay, but I need something from you."

"Okay." He breathed, "Anything."

A wicked smile broke across my lips and I jerked my head towards the nearly frozen water, "I am going to need you to jump in the lake."

He looked over at the lake and then back to my face. His eyes lit with amusement as he dropped my hands and bent over to untie his boots. A moment later he was dramatically dropping his shirt at my feet. He unfastened his pants and dropped them to the ground. I forced my eyes to stay on his face as he gave me a wink and took off running to the lake. With a wild whoop he plunged into the water and disappeared beneath the surface. He shook his head as he emerged, flinging water from his hair,

289

"Are you going to join me?"

"Nope!" I yelled safely from the spot where we had been standing.

"Your loss." He called back before lifting himself out of the lake. I turned and put a hand up to my face, it took everything in me to not look at his naked muscled and tattooed body as he walked across the space between us. He walked right up to me and laughed, "Don't tell me you are afraid of a little nudity."

"I am trying to be polite!" I turned further to stop myself from peeking.

He only laughed again and pulled my hand down, "Don't be polite." Heat rose in my cheeks as I struggled to keep my eyes on his face. He bent and started slipping his clothes back on. "Did I pass? Will you stay now?"

"Yes, I will stay." He was the most beautiful male. Water dripped from his muscular body. Scars and tattoos covered his skin.

He tugged his pants up, leaving them untied, and he wrapped his still wet arms around me, pressing me against his wet chest and planting a kiss on my forehead, "Good, because I do need to admit that we have quite a walk ahead of us. We can jump up here, but we have to walk back."

I pulled away from him, "We have to walk back? What if I wasn't staying?"

"Then I would have had the whole walk back to convince you or you would at least be tired enough that you would have to stay another day." He gave me a big grin and I rolled my eyes at him.

CHAPTER 34

I cupped my hands in the frigid mountain stream and brought the water to my lips. We had been hiking down the mountain for hours, the sun was now directly overhead and it did not seem like we were any closer to the city. Ryett knelt beside me and placed a hand gently on my arm as if to get my attention. I raised my eyes and saw him pointing down the stream. My gaze followed the line of his finger and through the trees—an elk cautiously made its way to the stream. As it reached the water, it paused and looked around. We both held still, barely breathing. It was the most beautiful creature I had ever seen. Large and healthy. Its coat was smooth and full. The animal was not skinny like I expected one to be at the end of winter.

The elk dipped its nose in the water and drank from the stream. Then it looked around again and moved quietly back into the woods. I finally let out my breath and turned back to Ryett. We both were grinning. Slowly we stood, marveling in the beauty we had just witnessed. I was lost in thought as we started hiking down the trail again. This forest was beautiful.

A large branch cracked deep in the forest. Ryett froze and threw up his hand indicating for me to stop moving and be quiet. Another branch cracked. Ryett grabbed my hand and pulled me off of the trail pressing my back into one of the large trees. His body was braced over mine and his finger raised to his lips. A piercing roar shook the forest around us. The hair on the back of my neck prickled. Whatever had made that noise was big.

I no longer heard birds chirping or rustling in branches. Even the leaves and the wind seemed to quiet. "I am not going to let anything happen to you." Ryett whispered, "Just look at me okay." Another piercing roar split through the forest. Whatever it was was significantly closer. The air around us started to shimmer—Ryett had put up a shield around us.

I glanced to my left, where more branches were breaking. A large shape moved through the forest. The beast's head bobbed and swayed in front of its body as it sniffed the air. Two dark eyes turned our direction and I saw the glint of pointed teeth as the beast's lips curled back. I felt Ryett's hand on my cheek and he gently turned my face back to his, "Just look at me. It can't hurt us. With this shield it won't even see us. We just have to wait for it to leave. Keep looking at me." He took an exaggerated deep breath, reminding me to breathe also.

The beast moved closer to us. Ryett kept his hand on my cheek and held my stare. I stared deep into his ice colored eyes. There was calm in them, unflinching calm as branches near us crunched and snapped. I could smell the foul odor from the beast's fur—it was decay and death and blood. It sniffed the air again and with a huff started moving away. I held still, forcing my shaking body to keep breathing and to keep staring into Ryett's eyes.

A smile crossed Ryett's face, "Are you okay?" He asked. I only nodded. "You did good, I was half expecting you to pass out on me."

I rolled my eyes, "I almost wish I had, I am not a fan of these beasts. What was that thing?"

"Not something that should be in these woods." The shimmering shield disappeared and Ryett helped me step away from the tree we had been pressed against. "I know we have been having a leisurely walk back to the city, but now we need to hurry. I need to tell the others that a durgedon has found its way into the mountains. Are you up for a run?"

"A durgedon? A beast from the Wastelands?" I read about some of these beasts while in Beck's library. Beasts of death and horror that were banished to the Wastelands that separated the holy kingdom from the other seven kingdoms.

Ryett gave me a look that could only be interpreted as him being impressed. "What is the difference between beasts and monsters—esurimagicae?"

"Beasts are like animals, just … much more deadly. That durgedon is considered a beast. Esurim are a subset of beasts who are more like us. They have greater communication, higher order thinking, magic, and a desire to rule and eliminate our kind." His voice was serious. I had drawn away an esurim in the Wastes the first time I had gone with them, not a beast. No wonder he had been so worried and insistent that I not do it again.

I took a deep breath. "Yes, I am up for a run."

My thighs burned as I followed Ryett down the mountain trail. I focused on each quick step, my feet dodging the tree roots and rocks that scattered the trail. The forest flew by on either side as we ran. The wind whipped my hair and I felt *alive*.

I glanced ahead of Ryett and saw we were approaching a bridge. We must be getting close. Ryett slowed and gave me a smile, "You can run!"

"I am full of surprises." I had been about to leave all of this behind this morning, leave Ryett. Now half a day later we had faced a beast from the Wastelands and ran down a mountain side. The mountain air had filled my soul. I smiled back at him.

We reached the rickety bridge and made our way across,

"We can jump back to the chateau from here." Ryett said as he offered his hand. I took it and braced for the world to fold, but he only pulled me close. Our chests rose and fell as we both breathed heavily. His eyes met mine. "I am happy you are staying." He whispered.

"Me too." I responded. It was hard to breathe. Not because we had just run down the mountain, but because being this close to Ryett made my body hum with energy. Touching him made my breath catch and every thought leave my head.

The forest folded and we were standing in the chateau's entryway. Alias and Jax were waiting for us, already armed. Alias held out an axe to Ryett as he spoke, "Ready to go hunting?"

CHAPTER 35

Ryett asked us to gather before dinner. When we were all seated, Zain broke the news. Vossarian's army had broken at least one of the gates to the Wastelands and beasts were now able to slip into the kingdoms as they wished. He sent messages to the other kings, but none of them trusted Ryett enough to help push out Vossarian's army and restore the gates.

Beck would have to send forces if there was any chance to win in a battle against Vossarian's army or convince the other kings to trust Ryett. Even though Vossarian had crossed into the Wastes, he still needed to find a way into The Lands of the Mother. His army would just be waiting at the border until then. This gave us some time, but also meant if Vossarian found out I was a key, he was positioned perfectly to enter The

Lands of the Mother before the other kings could stop him.

Alias and Zain would leave in the morning to share what we knew with Beck and Devron—to see if they would help.

As for the rest of the night, Ryett was taking us all out for dinner. After grabbing coats, we walked down the gravel path towards the city. Lights twinkled off the lake and the streets between the small restaurants glowed under tiny lights that seemed to hang from nothing.

The group laughed and chatted through dinner as if we were not planning a potential war. After we had filled our stomachs and drank too much wine. We made our way back to the cobblestone streets and started walking towards the chateau. Ryett fell into stride next to me. "Montvera is my favorite city in all of The Land of the Mountains."

"I can see why." I could and I could see how this city could become my new favorite place too.

He stopped me on one of the bridges, letting the others get further ahead of us. I looked up at him. If Beck's eyes were deep blue lakes to drown in, Ryett's were the snow and ice on the peaks of his mountains. "This is my favorite view." He looked down the river. The lake was smooth like glass and in the moonlight one of the large jagged mountains reflected on its surface. The real mountain towering directly down the river and across the lake from us.

I could not help myself from leaning into his warmth. Beck had been a distraction. But Ryett. Ryett made me want to *live*. I could not explain it—I was just drawn to him. I turned back to him. A smile on my face. His hand wrapped around mine as we started walking back to the chateau.

We could hear Sarla, Alias, Zain, and Jax laughing loudly from the nearby living room as we hung our coats in the entryway. I started walking that way, but Ryett stopped me and stepped close. His face dropped to mine, lips brushing my cheek. I breathed him in, my body warming. Our noses brushed and Ryett's hands raised to my face. Our lips were dangerously close. My breath caught.

"You two joining us?" Jax yelled from the other room. Ryett slowly pulled back. I shook my head no, but he laughed and pulled me to the living room.

I could not think of anything but Ryett's lips so close to mine. Not as a glass of amber liquor was pressed into my hands. Not as Alias and Ryett snuck off to another room, presumably to discuss tomorrow. Not as Jax and Zain bid us goodnight leaving through the living room's glass door and across the patio. Not as Sarla followed them out a few minutes later and I climbed the stairs to my room. I was still thinking of Ryett when I sunk into bed—hoping to hear a knock at my door.

One did not come.

I made sure to wake before dawn and to be downstairs in the breakfast room to see Alias and Zain off. I sipped coffee while they ate their breakfast and finally took their leave. I did not know why I felt it was important to be up. Maybe I was done with being on vacation. I had a reason to get out of bed now.

I stayed in the breakfast room picking at my food even when I heard Ryett and Jax in the study down the hall. Sarla must still be in bed. I had the sinking feeling that something was wrong. Very wrong.

There was a sudden crack and yelling. I jumped from my seat and ran towards the entry hall where the sound had come from. Zain was on the stone floor. Blood everywhere. Jax knelt over him, glowing light streaming from his hands, stopping much of the blood flowing out of Zain. Ryett held Zain's head, Zain was doing his best to speak, "Voss ... ambush at Beck's. Alias ... Voss is going to kill them ... they are trapped in the estate."

Sarla must have just come up from her cottage, she was now in the doorway, "We have to help them!"

"Jax and I will go. Zain needs your healing magic while you wait for the healer." Ryett responded.

"No, we can't leave the kingdom without a commander and Alias ..." Sarla's voice trailed off, I had never seen her with that panic in her eyes, even as she moved to the floor beside Zain and light streamed from her hands as she lay them on Zain.

"I will go." I heard myself say, they all looked at me. "I know the estate, Jax and Sarla are needed here, and Vossarian won't expect you to bring me into danger. He will expect me to be here and for you to leave your kingdom unattended."

"She is right, Ryett." It was Jax, "You two go." Ryett nodded and I sprinted up stairs to grab my things.

I slung my gun harness over my shoulders and secured the gun at my chest—I knew it would not kill Vossarian and his assassins, but maybe it would slow them down if needed. I slipped my knife on my belt and grabbed my leather jacket as I hurled back down the stairs.

Ryett was waiting, two axes crossed his back. He looked worried, but reached out his hand. Zain was stable now and sitting instead of laying on the floor, Sarla supported him. Jax was pacing the room. "Let's go." Ryett said and I took his hand. The room folded in.

We were standing at the edge of the woods that bordered Beck's estate. The air was warm and the grass was already beginning to turn green again.

From here we could see into the dining room through its large glass windows. I scanned the room. The table was overturned. Beck was in a chair, Alias was on both knees, and Devron was face down on the floor—I said a silent prayer that he was still alive. Vossarian paced back and forth in front of them. Two of his assassins were there, one stood by the fireplace looking bored and Rook stood by the glass double doors to the room.

"We have to go through the house." Ryett said quietly, "Can you get us to that room?"

"Absolutely. But what then? Are you just going to walk in there and ask him to let everyone go?" I responded. I knew Ryett was powerful, but I did not know what that meant in a situation like this.

"Well it is not like we can sneak in and break them out. Voss must have a holding shield up to prevent them from jumping … all three of them are powerful enough to have left if he did not. So we have to disable the shield."

"How do we do that?" I asked.

"Either my magic or my magic combined with Beck's might be able to break it. Or we take down Voss. I will go in, if we can not break it outright then I may need you to create a distraction long enough for Beck to help me break it. Can you make that happen?" He looked at me stone faced.

"Yes."

"Good. When the shield is down the priority is to get all of us out. Any one of us will be able to jump you out too. If you have to, hide and I will come back for you."

"Got it. We need to move, we have been here too long and I know the perfect door to slip in undetected." Ryett gave me a questioning look and I only shrugged in response. It was the door I had escaped from. It would put us twenty-three doorways, one set of stairs and another thirty-four yards away from the dining room. Best of all it was out of sight from this entire side of the estate.

We retreated further into the woods, Ryett following me as we skirted the house to the guest wing. Just as I remembered, our path to the door was completely blocked from view from the dining room by another wing of the estate.

The halls were quiet. The air inside felt dead as we methodically worked our way towards the dining room. There was no sign of any of the estate workers, and thankfully no sign of additional warriors with Vossarian.

As the double doors to the dining room came into view I could see the air swirling—magic, lots of magic. Just like what had been in Sarla's room when she was being healed. I mentally prepared myself for the feeling, I could not help anyone if I passed out.

Ryett stopped. I nodded to him that I was ready. Best case he was able to get in and get everyone out, then come back for me. Worst case, Vossarian kills us all.

Ryett rolled his shoulders and stood up straight. He looked lethal with the two axes crossing his back, a knife at his belt. If his magic did not work, he was at least armed. He strode slowly for the doorway in a stride that showed boredom and arrogance.

"Rook." I heard him say in greeting. Rook startled, but didn't look too surprised to see him. Ryett walked right past him and into the room. I could barely hear him, "Vossy, if you wanted us all to get together you could have sent a written invitation."

I moved closer, careful to stay hidden. I had to be able to hear.

"Ryett, nice of you to join us. Obviously you received my present this morning. Was that not a good enough invitation?" Zain. The present had been Zain, barely alive. "Still foolish of you to come. Sarla dearest did not insist on joining you?"

I still did not understand Vossarian's obsession with Sarla. "She was too occupied cleaning up your present. You did not kill poor Devron already did you?" Ryett still sounded calm and bored. To hear them talk about life so nonchalantly made my skin crawl.

"No, he is still alive for the moment." Vossarian chuckled. "Beck here was just about to hand over the keys to his kingdom to spare his general." Light flared from the room followed by a deep cackling laugh. "That was an excellent effort, Ryett, but none of you are jumping out of here!"

I moved again, I needed to see inside that room. Ryett was drawing his axes and lunging at Vossarian. The air moved between them, axe and sword clashed, both males disappeared and reappeared as they moved around the room. Ryett was clearly more skilled than Vossarian at this type of combat. Vossarian's sword went skittering across the floor, but Vossarian disappeared and reappeared across the room. "Careful Ryett, or Alias will lose his head." Voss sneered.

The second assassin now stood behind Alias with a sword pressed to Alias's throat. Ryett froze. Blood trickled from below Alias's beard where the sword was pressed. Vossarian laughed again, "I assume our business arrangement is over after all of this."

"Our arrangement was over when I found out what you did to her." Ryett growled.

Vossarian smirked at him, "How is your newest pet? Kieron worked hard on her."

Ryett's eyes flashed to Alias, then back to Vossarian. He looked murderous, but was still frozen in place, he would not let Alias be killed.

Vossarian continued, "You know I could not figure it out. With how she had helped Sarla, I thought she might be from the Mountains. But then I found her here, clearly sharing a bed with Beck, so I thought maybe she was from the Lakes. Then when you retrieved her from my care, Ryett, I knew she was not from the Mountains or you would have torn me to pieces once you learned I had a member of your kingdom in my possession. But she did not return to the Lakes and yet Beck stopped trying to find her. So you must have told him you had her. Clearly whatever bromance you have going on here transcends female whores."

"Your point." Ryett growled.

"I had the sole remaining person from the twenty-sixth world in my possession and I let her slip right through my fingers." Vossarian replied.

I could see Ryett calculating his next move. Beck was clearly restrained by some sort of magic to that damn chair he was sitting in. Both looked absolutely murderous and frozen in place.

They needed a distraction.

My feet moved before I could be afraid, one hand pulling the gun from my holster and my other hand unsheathing my knife. I did not hesitate. Rook's head snapped to the side as my bullet blew his brains all over the shattering glass door beside him.

How he could live after that I had no idea, but I did not care. It was payback and I just needed him down and out of the game for right now.

My feet kept moving as I stepped into the room turning my gun towards the other assassin. *Save Alias.* But Alias had used the distraction well, the assassin was stumbling backwards as Alias beheaded him with his own sword.

"Go!" Beck's voice broke through the air. He now was on his feet pointing towards Alias and Devron. Alias flung himself next to Devron and they both folded into the floor. Gone. Ryett and Beck had been able to break the holding spell.

I turned towards Vossarian, gun raised, and saw a smirk on his face as he disappeared—only to feel a strong hand wrap around my waist a heartbeat later.

Everything was slow motion. Both Beck and Ryett's eyes grew wide as they looked at me. Air and light rippled off of them as their magic shot towards me. They were both yelling.

"Time to leave." Vossarian whispered in my ear and the room folded in.

CHAPTER 36

The air was thick. The landscape was barren, black and gray dust covered the ground, the shell of a few trees still stood, and gray water flowed nearby. Everything was dead.

Vossarian held me tightly. My legs were weak. It had taken a long time for us to get here, the swirling darkness had pressed tightly on us, squeezing the air from my lungs. I could still hardly catch my breath.

"Mmm, what a fun surprise that you joined us today." I felt his breath on my neck and I jerked my head trying to get away. "I hope you are still considering becoming my queen? What do you think?" He chuckled in my ear.

I sunk my knife into Vossarian's leg. That is what I thought. He grunted and shoved me out of his arms. I stumbled a few paces away. He simply plucked the knife out without even a grimace and chucked it into the water. His eyes were evil. Hate. Death.

"You have a choice now, Genevieve." Vossarian's voice was low and threatening. "Help me enter The Lands of the Mother or I will kill you here."

Shit. He knew I might be a key and I had gone straight to him. "Where are we?" I already knew the answer.

"This is your world, what is left of it. It is slowly fading away as we speak, but if you die while you are here, all of this disappears from existence in an instant." He paused, waiting for my answer.

"Doesn't seem like much of a loss." I said. The place was completely barren, "And what happens after I help you?" I had to delay. Maybe Ryett could find me here. If I did not leave with Vossarian I was stuck here and would die anyway.

"I assume the knife in my leg means you do not accept my proposal. It is a pity, with magic as strong as yours, you would give me a strong heir for my kingdom—one strong enough to rule all of Savengard. However, I will still let you live."

I laughed, he wanted me for *breeding.* "Letting me live sounds like a mistake. Why wouldn't you just kill me?"

"I would give you the opportunity to live. The opportunity to earn your life by helping me get what I need. If you cause too much trouble then yes, I will just kill you. Or maybe I will give you back to Kieron. He seems to have become rather attached to you." Voss was stalking towards me. I backed further away.

Kieron did not know I had lost the baby. *What would he do when he found out?* Not a helpful thought right now. I pushed it from my head.

"I won't help you." This world was dead and gone before Vossarian had destroyed it, it was just a matter of time. I had already been willing to die. If me losing my life meant Vossarian could not get into The Lands of the Mother then it was worth it.

Anger flashed in his eyes. I could not even block the blow as magic smacked across my face. I stumbled, but stayed on my feet, using my momentum to move further from Vossarian.

"Is it worth it? To die?" Another blow sent me sprawling face first into the dirt. I spit dirt and blood and tried to stand. "Is it worth it?" Vossarian bellowed.

The air was forced out of my lungs as my back smashed against something hard. I crumpled into the black dust. My head was ringing. I struggled to my hands and knees.

"This is your last chance, Genevieve." His voice had instantly turned calm, trying to coax me and convince me. Disgusting.

The gun was still clutched in my hand. I had somehow managed to hold on to it. "I will not help you." I gritted out through my teeth.

Pure venom filled Vossarian's voice again, "Then you will die here."

"And you will too." I managed to gasp. My body stung with

pain, nausea welled up inside me. I pushed to my knees, raising the gun and pointing it at him. I only had two bullets left.

He *laughed*, "You can't kill me and even if you could, there is nowhere for you to go."

He was right, but he had given me the answer—take him down long enough to destroy this world with him in it, which meant one bullet for him and one for me. The red laser dot held steady on his face.

I smiled at him, "You made a mistake thinking I care about living."

I squeezed the trigger. Vossarian's face barely registered what I had said before he dropped to his knees and fell forward into the dirt. The back of his head was blown open.

I let out my breath. How much time I had before Vossarian healed I did not know. *Find me, Ryett!* I sat in the dirt next to Vossarian's body trying not to look at the gore that was the back of his head. I would wait as long as possible. *Please find me.*

I closed my eyes and took inventory. I had lost my knife—the only other killing instrument I had was somewhere in the gray river. I checked my gun. One bullet. My head hurt, there was pounding in my ears. My body ached, but nothing felt broken. I had no water, no food. Magic. *I had magic.*

I imagined the feeling my body had when I saw Ryett, when he hugged me, when he placed his hand over my heart and showed me I belonged. He said what I had felt was my magic responding to him. I pictured the images I saw when Ryett touched me. My skin tingled and I felt the wave rising in me. As it crashed against my skin I imagined it erupting past and escaping into the world. I let another wave roll and crash within me. *Let it out.*

Wave after wave rolled. I saw my family, my husband chasing my son, giggling, around the yard as our dog bounced next to them. The waves grew bigger. I saw Ryett's eyes, the ice in them, the feeling of hope they elicited from me. A wave rolled from me, but I did not feel it crash against the wall of my body. Then another rolled through. I opened my eyes to see my hands faintly glowing and the air around me shimmering.

I sent the shimmer further from me on more waves. *Find me.*

It had been hours. My mouth was dry. I was exhausted. The waves I continued to send out were now only small ripples. The sky was getting dark.

Vossarian's body was still on the ground next to me. His head wound had fully closed back up. He could wake at any moment. This was it. *Breathe.* I looked at the gun in my hands. Tears fell down my cheeks. I wrapped my fingers around the grip and lifted the gun from my lap.

"Genevieve!" I shot to my feet. Ryett had found me. "Genevieve, you are alive." He was running towards me and slowed when he saw Vossarian on the ground. "We have to go." *Ryett had come.* He walked closer and extended his hand. His voice was urgent, "Genevieve, we have to go."

Vossarian stirred on the ground next to me. I put my last bullet in his head before dropping my empty gun on his body. I took three strides to Ryett and grabbed his outstretched hand. "You came for me." My voice was hoarse.

He nodded, his face was pained as he looked at me. "Of course I did." Then he pulled me close, wrapping an arm around my waist and one cupped my head to his chest. "Just keep breathing, this is going to be ... uncomfortable." The world of black and gray dust folded in. Everything kept folding. We were moving. Pressure pushing in on all sides. I squeezed my eyes closed, trying to just breathe. "Breathe ... we are almost there." Ryett gritted into my ear. I felt like we were going to be pressed completely together. Smashed into each other's skin.

CHAPTER 37

Beck was pacing the dining room when we appeared. Ryett loosened his arms around me. I felt the world tilting. Beck jumped across the room, appearing beside me. Ryett staggered back as Beck grabbed me into his arms. "Are you hurt? What happened to Vossarian?" He asked.

I pushed away from Beck. Staring at his still outstretched hands. Hands that had hit me.

"Genevieve happened to Vossarian." Ryett said, "Unfortunately, he will live. I could not risk depleting my magic to end him." He sounded frustrated as he stepped back to me, putting himself between me and Beck.

Beck looked between us then glared at Ryett, the muscles in his jaw working. "You should not have brought her, Ryett." He said between his teeth.

I stared at him. He still thought he had some say in my life. The nerve.

"Who else's cock have you shoved down your throat, Genevieve?" His eyes were locked on me. I felt Ryett tense, the air began to ripple around us. I gave Ryett's hand a squeeze. Even with everything that needed to be said between Beck and me, even after his vial comment, now was not the time.

"I will send Jax to help you clean up." Ryett waved idly at the two assassins' bodies still on the floor, the glass shattered and the general disarray of the room. "Let's talk when Vossarian resurfaces." Beck just continued glaring at me.

Before any of us could say anything more, the room folded in. We were suddenly back in Ryett's chateau. Zain was still bloodied, but pacing the room. Sarla and Alias sat on the steps. Jax stood leaning against the wall. Devron was awake and sitting in a chair.

Devron jumped to his feet at our arrival, questions plastered his face. "Beck is in a mood, but he is fine. Jax, take Devron home and help them clean up." Ryett said.

Jax nodded. He and Devron linked hands and disappeared without another word.

"Voss is out of commission at the moment. Let our scouts know to be on the lookout for news of him returning. Meet in my office in the morning, take the rest of the day to yourselves." Ryett ordered. Everyone nodded, their eyes scanning both of us, but no one asked any questions. They left Ryett and me standing in the entry.

I was suddenly aware of the black and gray dust that covered me. I needed to clean up. I was two steps up the stairs when Ryett spoke, "Genevieve, are you okay?"

I turned to him and could not help the tears that fell down my face. "Today was the second time I almost put a bullet in my own head. The first time I wanted to die …" My voice trailed off.

"And this time?" Ryett whispered.

"I was *willing* to. For all this … for all of you. I did not want to, but I was *willing*." All of this was worth dying for.

Ryett was up the steps in a heartbeat, his lips pressed to mine. I parted my lips for him, let his tongue slip into my mouth. The room shifted and we were in a large bathroom—his bathroom. The shower was already on, "Let's get you cleaned up." He said against my mouth.

I let him help me undress. My body hurt and it was hard to move. His hands were tender as they removed my clothes, dropping each item on the floor. I grasped his shoulder as he helped me step out of my leather pants. It was then that I realized he had been the one to help me through detoxing from Vossarian's drugs. He had washed me. He had dressed me in his own clothes. He had held the bowl while I vomited. He had stayed and rubbed my back as I sweat and shivered and wanted to die for days on end. He did not even know me and he had cared for me when I could not care for myself.

I helped him remove his clothes. My hands ran along his hard muscled chest. Tracing his tattoos. We stepped into the warm shower and Ryett kissed me as black water swirled off of me and down the drain.

He washed my hair and soaped my body. His callused hands rubbed gently over my sore muscles. "What happened? Your back is all bruised." He asked.

"Vossarian tossed me into a boulder." It was an effort not to grimace at his touch.

Ryett's hands froze, "Seriously? Shit. What else happened?"

I told him everything.

When the water finally ran clear he pulled three fluffy towels from the shelf, wrapping one around his waist, one around me and the third dried my hair.

He pulled out a jar of salve, "Will you let me put this on your back? It will help you heal." I nodded and let the back of my towel drop so he could access my back. His hands rubbed over my back again, working the oil into my skin.

"I might need a full body massage." I smiled at him in the mirror, his eyes catching mine when he looked up.

He grinned, "I think that can be arranged, but I did have dinner sent up ... I thought you might be hungry."

I was. I was starving and had not even realized. He led me from the bathroom. A small cart with covered plates and a bottle of wine with two glasses sat near a window between two chairs. He lifted one of the lids. Pizza. I let out a laugh.

"I told Chef about it and I think he got carried away. We might be eating pizza for the next month. Or decade." He had a huge grin on his face.

I gingerly sat myself in one of the chairs, my body barking at me in pain. "Pizza is perfect." We didn't even bother getting dressed before diving into our slices. We ate with our towels still wrapped around us.

When we were done eating, Ryett waved his hand and the cart disappeared. I sipped my wine and stared out the window looking across the lake and up to the mountains.

"Would you like to stay here tonight … in my room?" Ryett sounded a bit nervous, "Only if you want … or you can sleep in your room … I mean I would like you to stay …"

I smiled at his blabbering. "I'll stay." His ice colored eyes twinkled and a set of my luxurious pajamas appeared on the bed. I laughed, but did not tell him I preferred not to wear pajamas. That I usually slept naked.

Ryett had to help me into my clothes, my body was stiff and aching. He tucked me in bed and crawled in next to me, sliding one arm under my head. Our faces only inches apart from each other.

"Tell me about your scar?" He asked gently.

"Which one?" I had many, but I knew he meant the one across my abdomen. It was by far the largest.

"The big one. Lower abdomen."

"That is how my son was born." I nearly whispered.

He did not even try to hide the shock, "They cut babies out of females?"

His distress had me smile, "Not all babies, but it is a procedure they do if something is wrong and it is the only way to save the baby or mother or both."

"We do not do that here …" He still looked concerned. "It seems very traumatic."

"It can be, but everything went fine for me … I felt guilty for not being able to deliver normally, but the procedure went well and my son was healthy." I could not stop the tears that welled up in my eyes and started to slide across my face.

Ryett gently wiped one from the bridge of my nose. "You must miss them terribly." He whispered.

Tears were streaming now. I nodded and let Ryett hold me close. Every tear I held back over the years seemed to be flowing out of me. He let me cry. Didn't try to stop it. Didn't tell me I would be okay. Didn't try to make anything better. He just held me close as if he knew I had no one to hold me after they were gone. As if he knew just being there and not shrinking from my grief was everything I needed.

PART 3: A WORLD OF OBSIDIAN

CHAPTER 38

Beck did not want anything to do with us, Zain reported. He would not help. We had been standing in Ryett's office, gathered around a map of Savengard. Vossarian had not resurfaced as far as we knew, but his army had started moving again. Ryett thought we should go on the offense, push them back to their kingdom before Vossarian returned. Restore the gates they had destroyed. Maybe we would have a chance with their king still gone. It was a huge risk. And we were not sure Vossarian was still gone. We would need Beck's help, but he was not willing to give it.

Zain rubbed his face, "I think he is a little hurt about ... you two." He pointed to Ryett and me.

Ryett bristled, his fingers pressing against the wooden table,

"It is none of his damn business."

"But he is making it his business, Ryett." Zain countered.

"I should talk to him." I said. I was not sure if it was a good idea, but it was the only thing I could think of. Someone had to talk him into it and if I was part of the reason he did not want to help then I needed to make it right.

"No." Both Ryett and Zain said in unison.

"Yes, I should. He is upset because I left and we need his help. Maybe I can smooth things over, give him some closure, convince him that I am not worth risking all of this over." I crossed my arms. I was going to convince them to take me to Beck. I had made up my mind.

Ryett sighed and straightened, "What if it does not go well?"

What if it didn't? I could think of a hundred different ways this could go badly, but I was not going to voice them, "Let Zain or Jax or Alias or all of them take me, if it does not go well then we leave immediately."

"Why can't I take you?" Ryett almost looked hurt.

"Because you might literally rip his head off if it doesn't go well, Ryett!" He would too and that would not help anything.

"She is right, Ryett." Zain said carefully, "Maybe she can convince him to get his shit together and help."

"Okay." Ryett conceded. He took a deep breath and scanned my face, "But if he lays a hand on you—"

"I won't let him." Zain cut Ryett off.

I smiled, "Good! Zain, let's leave in ten minutes." I would not give them time to change their minds. Zain nodded and left the room to grab what he needed—weapons probably.

"Genevieve," Ryett stopped me before I could leave. He still looked concerned, "If he so much as looks at you wrong, please just leave. It is not worth him hurting any of you or trying to ... fuck I don't know what he will try to do. Just be careful."

"I will and I will do my best to convince him to help." I gave Ryett what I hoped was a reassuring smile and hurried from the room.

I had chosen all black. Black leather boots and leather pants. A black silky blouse that opened in a deep V between my breasts and had flowing sleeves that ended in five inches of tight fitting cuffs around my wrists. I left my hair down and darkened my eyelids and lashes with makeup. I was not the female Beck thought I was—soft and fragile. He had only seen a glimpse of the real me, but the real me was the female he was getting today.

Zain waited for me in the entryway. He looked lethal in his leather jacket and pants. Two axes crossed his back. "I thought we would go for a 'take no shit' vibe today, I see you got the memo." He grinned at me in approval of my outfit choice.

"Let's go take no shit then." I smiled and grabbed his outstretched hand before I could second guess myself.

We appeared at Beck's front door. Zain knocked and what

seemed like minutes later, Devron opened the door. The residence seemed quiet. I could not see any guards and the fact that Devron was the one opening the door …

"We are here to see Beck." Zain said, giving a nod to Devron.

Devron looked me up and down, "Of course you are. It is good to see you both, but I am not sure he is in the mood to see you." He pushed the door wider and let us in anyway.

"Devron, I am hoping I can talk some sense into him. We need you all if we are going to go to war." I tried to sound calm, confident.

"I know." He pressed his lips together. His shoulders were tense, "Let's give it a try."

We all walked down the empty hallway, our footsteps echoing. Devron led us to the office by the small dining room. The glass doors to the dining room had been replaced already —no sign of broken glass, bullets, or Rook's brains or blood remained.

Beck sat at his desk, leaning back in his chair and clearly doing nothing but drinking. "Beck, Zain and Genevieve are here to see you." Devron said from the doorway. Beck did not even turn to look at us. He just swirled his glass of amber liquor.

"Can you give me a minute with him?" I looked at Zain and Devron. Both males tensed.

Zain scanned my face, then glanced at Beck. I could tell he wanted to come in with me. He had promised Ryett he would have my back and now I was asking him to wait outside. Finally he spoke, "Okay, I will be right here if anything goes wrong."

"You're sure?" Devron asked, his voice hushed so only Zain and I would be able to hear. I nodded and Devron reluctantly shut the doors behind me as I stepped into Beck's office. I had no idea what I was going to say to him.

"Have you finally come back to me? Do you miss my cock in you that much?" Beck drawled as he swirled his glass of liquor.

That was how this was going to go? Okay, Beck. Two can play that game. "Unfortunately for you, I have been getting plenty of cock." Fighting words.

He slammed his glass down on his desk and I flinched. "So I was not wrong that you left me for *him*."

"I left you because you lost your mind. You forced yourself on me, then made up some story about me wanting other people and you *hit* me." I was impressed with myself, I actually sounded confident.

But Beck was suddenly inches from my face, both of his hands wrapped around my wrists, "I was not wrong was I?" He hissed.

Fuck. This was not going well. I fought the urge to freeze up. Fought the urge to completely shrink against his aggression. This was bullshit. I would not let him act this way towards me. "Let go of me." The command in my voice even had Beck blinking. His fingers slowly unwrapped from my wrists. I continued, "If you touch me like that again, you will lose your hands and then your head. Your little melt down led to me

324

spending two months being drugged and beaten and fucked in Vossarian's dungeon. So I do not give two shits if your feelings are hurt."

He took a couple of steps back, "Who are you? It is like I didn't even know you." His voice had softened.

I walked to a chair and plopped down in it. "Beck, I met you at the worst time in my life. Do you know what I was doing when I ran into Sarla? I was planning to end my own life. I was seconds away from going through with it. I was running from everything. You met that broken female." Beck sat in a chair. "When I got here, you were good to me and I did not have to run anymore and … it was nice to not be alone."

"Did you even care about me?" He almost whispered it.

"I did, Beck, but …" I took a deep breath, "You crossed a line."

He ran his hands down his face, then slammed back the contents in the glass he had abandoned on the desk earlier. "They told me what Vossarian did to you, all the drugs … I thought you would come back to me after you had detoxed …"

"The drugs were not the worst thing that happened to me. Did you miss the beaten and fucked part of what I just told you?" His face paled, "And I was running away from *you* when they snatched me up." I did not care if Beck felt guilty, he should. He had attacked me that night. I would not have run off into the woods alone had he not attacked me.

Beck was quiet. I let him sit in the silence. Finally, he spoke again, "What else do I not know about you? Clearly you have had training that you failed to mention." He could not face it, the reality that his actions had caused this.

My eyes searched him. "Yes, it was over a decade ago, and it was not by choice. I am sorry if you feel lied to. That was not my intention."

He just shook his head and stared blankly out the window, "I messed up."

"I will consider that an apology." I replied. He only took a deep breath and leaned forward to refill his glass from the crystal decanter on the desk. I continued, "Please, help us fight Vossarian and his army."

"He will be back for you and I do not think he wants you dead." There was fear in his voice.

I ignored his warning of Vossarian. I had to get him to agree to help us. "Will you help us? We need you."

"Yes." It was all I needed to hear. I stood to leave. "I am sorry, Genevieve." He whispered.

I only nodded and left him holding his glass of liquor.

CHAPTER 39

The air rushed from my lungs as I landed hard on my back. My feet had been swept out from under me. Again. Alias held out his hand to help me up. "Widen your stance. Do not let me get my leg behind you."

We had been at this for an hour already. Just like the other days. My fighting skills were clearly rusty and against a male the size of Alias who had been training for hundreds of years to kill people ... I was getting my ass kicked.

"Okay, let's do it again. Full speed." I said.

Alias nodded. He had been walking me through different moves to protect myself in close combat. The foot work. How to use the momentum of a larger opponent to my advantage.

I set my feet slightly wider and raised my hands. He grabbed my arm and shoulder, just like he had the ten times before. His body moved fast and with force. I struggled to keep my balance and stepped my foot wider. Feeling the flow of his energy move to the right, I shifted from resistance to pulling his weight the direction he was moving. Using my core and legs to twist as I brought him to the ground.

"Yes!" I whooped in victory.

"Good." Alias said as I extended my hand to help him stand back up. "Three more times now."

I smiled. Maybe this was not hopeless. I had thought of myself as a fighter. I learned the skills, but it had been years and what I had learned did not stand a chance against nearly immortal warriors. This felt like the first step in maybe being able to hold my own without the guns I had hidden behind for all those years.

We did the same dance three more times. Each time I brought Alias to the ground with increasing ease. "Good work. Let's end on that." He said and he walked to the table with the water pitcher and glasses on it. He poured two glasses and held one out to me.

We were in what was referred to as the field house. True to its name it was a large field inside of a building. There were large stones shaped with handles of various sizes in one corner. Large ropes and chains in another and mats stacked against one wall. We had pulled mats out onto the field and created our own sparring ring for training.

"Has there been any news of Vossarian?" I asked cautiously. We had left him in the twenty-sixth world with a bullet in his head. I knew he would come back from it and I knew he would come for me. Voss did not seem like someone who would just forgive a few bullets to the brain. The others had danced around the subject, speaking vaguely, anytime it came up.

Alias downed the rest of his water and then eyed me, "There is no news. His army has not moved more and he has not resurfaced. It could be months before Vossarian returns."

"Explain it to me. How that works. Why no one knows when he will be back." I set my glass down. Waited.

Alias let out a sigh, "It depends on his strength after healing. If his strength is low and he tries to world walk, he might not accurately jump the time continuum between worlds or he might mistakenly jump somewhere else entirely. He is good, but it still can be tricky. There are two ways to world walk: First, brute strength and few people have it, and second, portals. Like the portal that you and Sarla came through. Portals are stable ways to travel between the worlds. You always know where you will end up and that it will at least be within a few months' time when you arrive. Again depending on your strength people with world walking skills can make those jumps very accurately. Sarla, with her injuries, did not have enough reserve in her magic to force the time continuum when you came through the portal, so you both arrived months later.

"But there are only a few portals and you first have to know about them and you have to know which portals have not been used recently. Each portal seems to have a waiting period, once it has been used it will not reopen again for a period of time." That's right. Sarla had told me this after we came through. It was why we had been safe after using the portal by the river.

Alias continued, "People like Sarla and Ryett and Voss also have the gift of being able to just brute strength world walk. They train extensively to learn the worlds and navigate them. Not only which world they are going to, but where in that world they are going, and when.

"Do you know how remarkable it was that Ryett found you? Beck told us that Ryett disappeared as soon as Voss took you and returned maybe two hours later. I know you were out there far longer, but he was able to find what world you were in and where and when in that world you were. Then he somehow got back. Many a World Walker has messed up timing or location, leaving them dead, stranded, or arriving at their destination in a completely different decade. There are very few World Walkers who can jump between worlds and even fewer who can do it accurately. Ryett has always been one of the best, but he has not walked between worlds in centuries ..." Alias's voice trailed off.

I swallowed. Ryett had barely found me in time, but he *had* found me. He had risked so much coming after me. He had world walked again to get to me.

Alias looked over towards the wall. I followed his glance and saw Ryett leaning against the wall, lurking in the shadows. "How long has he been here watching us, Alias?" I said loud enough for Ryett to hear.

Ryett just chucked, "I have been here long enough to know you are talking about me." He pushed off the wall and sauntered over to us. He handed me an envelope with my name written on it.

"What's this?" I asked. It was a plain envelope. The writing on it was slightly sloppy.

"I am hoping you can tell me who is sending you location coordinates and cryptic notes." He responded.

I opened the letter and saw numbers written along the top— coordinates, a date, and time.

There are children. Make heads roll. The
world needs fewer monsters.
By the way, I am a dog person.

Kieron had not signed the note. He did not need to.

"It is from Kieron. There is a shipment of slaves with children and he has given us the coordinates, day, and time to intercept them." I said, handing the letter back to Ryett.

He read it over again. "And the rest of what he wrote? 'Make heads roll'?"

"To truly kill Vossarian's assassins you have to cut off their heads or blow them into tiny pieces." I replied.

Ryett gaped at me, "How did you learn that? We have been trying to figure out how to kill them for centuries and no one has come up with a definitive answer."

"Kieron." I stated. He had told me in the Wastes. *Because one day I am going to need someone to know how to kill me.* Kieron's words echoed in my head. Ryett looked at the paper again, I continued, "The rest is so that I knew the message came from him."

"How do you know it is not a trap?" Alias asked, crossing his arms.

"It's not." Ryett said flatly as he looked at me. Kieron did not know about the miscarriage. He was extending a peace offering to the mother of his child. To the kingdom she lived in. And he had no idea. Would he have sent the note if he knew? All of it was written in the look Ryett gave me. "Sounds like we have business to take care of. Zain will stay here, but the rest of us will go. If there really are children, we need to be prepared." Ryett said.

I looked at Ryett with questioning disbelief, "Did I hear you wrong or was I included in that statement?"

"You heard right." He smiled at me, "Unless you do not want to come?"

"Oh I am coming." Of course I was going with them. I did not want to just sit around. I needed to *do* something.

"Good, both of you get cleaned up and meet me in the chateau in two hours. We have a few days, but we need to plan."

Ryett said. He helped Alias and me fold up the mats and put them back in their stack against the wall.

We walked together across the lawn and Alias peeled off towards the cottages. Ryett took my hand and stopped me, "It is going to be dangerous. We have to go into the Wastes again. You do not have to come."

"I want to go. You said you wanted my help. I can not help you if I stay here." I responded. He nodded and resumed walking with me.

We spent the afternoon planning how we would travel to the location Kieron had sent. Really the others planned and I listened. Alias walked me through their protocols and what we needed to watch out for. We would leave in two days and arrive a day and a half before the time that was written in the note. Ryett lectured me about taking on any of the beasts or esurim alone again and I just rolled my eyes at him before promising I would try not to.

The others left the chateau and I headed to my room to relax or read another steamy erotic novel before it was time for dinner.

CHAPTER 40

I could not sit still. I paced my room and tried picking up the book I was reading multiple times. Finally, I decided I would go find myself a glass of wine and sit outside a while. As I made my way down the stairs, Ryett emerged from one of the hallways and crossed the entryway towards me.

"Oh good," he said, "I was just about to come find you. I need you to try something on." He beckoned me to follow and we walked down the hall to the weapons room.

The weapons room was exactly as the name implied—a room filled with weapons. Weapons of every size and shape lined the walls and were stored in drawers and cabinets.

Straps of leather lay on the large metal table in the middle of the room. I raised my eyebrows at him.

"It's a weapons harness. If you are going to keep coming with us you need better equipment." He picked up some of the leather and showed me how to slip it around my shoulders. His hands worked the buckles to fit around my ribs and down my chest around my breasts. "An axe can strap to your back now and we can add various knife sheaths here, here, or across here." He showed me each place they could attach. "How does that feel?"

I moved my arms and twisted my upper body. "Fits good, I can hardly tell it's there."

"Good." He picked up another piece and looped it around my waist, "You can wear either piece separately or if you need to bring an entire armory you can wear both." He knelt down and looped straps around my thighs as he spoke, cinching down the buckles. "How is that?"

I moved my legs and did a few squats. I could feel the leather across my ass, but nothing dug in and I could move well. "Seems to fit." I said.

Ryett looped his fingers through various parts and tugged and wiggled the leather. "Perfect." He said to himself as he inspected each of the metal loops and buckles, moving around my body, sliding his fingers under the straps and adjusting how they lay.

"If you had not said this was a weapons harness I would think it was something else." I teased.

Ryett's fingers paused, "Why can't it be dual purpose?" There was a slight gravel to his voice.

"Mmm." I responded and his calloused hand ran up my arm. His thumb stroked the inside of my wrist. He raised my hand to his face and kissed where his thumb had rubbed. Then he buckled a leather cuff around my wrist.

His hand ran up my other arm, lifting my wrist to his mouth. "To protect your wrists when using a shield or bow." He murmured against my wrist and wrapped it in a leather cuff too. "Also good for other things." There was light in his eyes as he gently tugged on the short strap that dangled from each cuff.

"You are going to have to show me what you mean." I said softly, but not weakly. I could feel my skin starting to tingle.

He stepped close, his nose brushing the side of my face, breathing me in. My skin pebbled and my body warmed. He guided my hands down to my hips then attached the straps to the metal rings on either side of my ass. I tugged my hands slightly—my arms were restrained.

He leaned close, his cheek brushing mine. His nose ran along my cheekbone to my temple. "Tell me to stop and I will stop. Tell me you are done and we will be done. Tell me you don't want this and I will walk away." He whispered into my ear.

"Okay." I breathed. My chest heaving as my breath turned ragged.

Ryett's thumb caressed my jawline and he slanted his mouth against mine, kissing me deeply. I parted my lips and let his tongue slide into my mouth. I met him stroke for stroke as he kissed me, his hands holding my face.

He bit my lip and pulled his mouth away. Then Ryett's body pressed me against the table as he leaned over to pick up a knife behind me. His eyes watched me as if looking for any hint I wanted him to stop. He gently lifted the edge of my shirt and sliced a clean line up the center.

"I liked this shirt." I breathed.

Ryett let out a dark chuckle, "I will buy you another." Then he sliced down each sleeve before tugging the shirt out from under the leather straps.

Then he moved to the waistband of my pants, "I *really* like these pants." I said.

His wrist flicked quickly, shredding the front of my pants into a few pieces. Then he grabbed the pieces and ripped the pants all the way down the legs and tugged them off of me from the back. "I will buy you two." He growled in my ear.

I was standing with my wrists restrained at my waist in nothing but my flimsy lace underthings and the leather weapons harness.

Ryett's hands traced along my skin, burning pleasure into me. I did not need drugs for my body to light on fire under his hands. His mouth dropped to my neck and I felt his teeth scrape up to my ear where he bit and tugged gently.

A small noise released from my lips. I was going to melt right here on the floor. Then he tugged the straps on the harness and turned me around. One of his hands wrapped around the strap at my waist and the other around the strap that ran down between my shoulder blades. He pulled me back against his chest and whispered into my ear, "Shall I keep going?"

My body shuddered and I gasped in a breath. "Mmhmm." I managed to whimper. Then he pressed between my shoulders, guiding me to bend over the metal table. I turned my head to the side as my cheek, chest, and stomach pressed onto the cool metal.

Ryett tugged the ring that lay on my lower back and I heard a clasp click into place. Then I heard another clasp click. He had strapped me to the table.

His hands gripped my ass, squeezing firmly before slicing away my lace underthings.

I was completely at his mercy. Bent over the table. Hands restrained. Strapped down. Exposed to him. And I knew all I had to say was 'stop' and he would stop without a question. He would remove the restraints in a heartbeat. He would not do anything I did not want him to do. And he would ravish me if I let him.

His hands slid down the front of my thighs and his teeth bit my ass. He had dropped to his knees behind me. My reflex was to pull my arms up, but leather cut into my wrists and inner thighs as I only tugged on the straps.

Ryett's tongue flicked over me teasingly. I whimpered as he did it again. Then he slowly licked up my center in one long stroke. He groaned with pleasure and tasted me again. And again. His hands firmly gripped and wandered my legs and ass as he feasted on me.

My body tensed and loosened and shivered in pleasure. I panted as he built up towards my climax in waves—building me up to a near peak before letting me fall into nothing but deep pleasure and bliss.

He built me up again and I did not think I could go any higher. Then his tongue plunged into me. My climax completely obliterated me.

Leather snapped taunt as my arms pulled against the restraints. Jagged mountains, bubbling streams, glaciers, forest fires, the soil rejuvenating with new growth among the fire's ashes, mountain meadows covered in wildflowers, and light snow catching on evergreen branches all crashed through my vision. My blood heated and tingled as it raced through my entire body. I was going to shatter into a billion pieces. A wave of energy pulsed out from my core, ripping through my body and out of my skin only to be met with a stronger wave wrapping around me—holding me together. Stroking me gently and containing my pieces.

Finally my soul settled back into my body and I felt myself trembling on the cold metal table. Ryett's hands moved over my skin as he unhooked each of the restraints. I could not move and just lay there panting and trembling.

Ryett's strong hands slid under my chest and lifted me off of the table. He pulled my back to his body and cradled me against him. Warm kisses caressed my shoulder and neck as I sunk into him.

"I do not have words ..." I breathed. Ryett just chuckled against my neck.

He had completely obliterated everything I thought I knew about pleasure. I turned in his arms and looked up into his eyes, they were filled with light and desire. I lifted my hands to his waist band and pulled his hips against mine as I unfastened his belt. "You don't owe me anything." He said firmly.

"You just completely changed my entire existence and now I don't even get to repay the favor ... I don't even think I am capable of repaying that, but I want to try." I replied.

"What I mean is that I do not expect it to be an exchange. I am not keeping score." He said against my lips before kissing me.

"If we are keeping score, you have definitely won." I kissed him back then lifted his shirt over his head and dropped it to the floor. I turned him so that he was now backed against the table and I dropped to my knees. I unfastened his pants and slowly pulled them down. His cock released from them and my mouth watered at his size. The beauty of it. I needed him in my mouth. Inside of me. I swallowed and looked up at him. His breath was heaving in his chest as he looked down at me. I pulled his pants to the floor and helped him step out of them.

His fingers ran through my hair and I grasped his hard cock

in my hand. I flicked my tongue over his tip and looked up at him again as he let out a breathy groan. His hand firmly pressed on the back of my head and I slid his cock into my mouth. I gently skimmed my tongue along his hardness then licked and sucked and sunk him deep into my throat. I moaned around his thickness as I pumped him into my mouth.

I decided I could suck him for all of eternity. I wanted him deep in my throat. I wanted to taste all of him and never stop tasting him. I felt his body shudder in pleasure and it was my undoing. I pumped him with my hand and mouth in tandem.

I slid my mouth off and gasped for air as my hand continued pumping him. I licked his tip and before I could sink him back into my throat I felt his strong hands under my shoulders. He lifted me to my feet before grabbing my ass and lifting me off of the ground. I wrapped my legs around his waist as he turned and set me on the table. He kissed me thoroughly and desperately. Then he pulled my head back and dropped his head to my breast, nipping it with his teeth before sucking it into his mouth.

His other hand pulled my hips to the edge of the table and I felt him press against my entrance. He paused. I dug my fingers into his back and it was the only invitation he needed as he sheathed himself deep inside of me. A cry of pleasure spilled from my mouth.

The room seemed to disappear as he pumped into me. There was only him. Pleasure flowed through my entire body with every thrust of his cock. Our hands desperately dug into each other's skin. His tongue plunging into my mouth was equally as desperate as mine—desperate to taste and explore.

His forehead pressed against mine as he pounded into me deeply. Our climax broke together and the entire chateau shook. Weapons fell from the wall as my soul left my body and was wrapped in strong warmth that held every exploding piece of me into place.

I clung, panting and sweaty, to Ryett. My legs still wrapped around him and my face pressed into the soft spot between his shoulder and neck. One of Ryett's hands braced us on the table and his other clutched me against his body as he tried to catch his breath.

We finally peeled back from each other and looked at the scattered weapons around the room. Ryett let out a laugh, "Well shit." He said. I could only laugh too. "We should probably get out of here before someone comes looking to see what the commotion is."

I looked at my shredded clothes on the floor and back at Ryett. He only winked and pulled me close as the room folded in. My legs were still wrapped around him and I now sat on the marble counter in his softly lit bathroom. "My bath is bigger." He said against my ear before setting me on the ground. And indeed it was. His bath was big enough for two and was already full of steaming water. Two glasses and sparkling wine sat on a small table next to the bath. "Care to join me or should I take you back to your room?"

"Wine and a bath? I am definitely joining you." I said with a smile. His fingers slowly unbuckled the buckles of the weapons harness and he dropped each piece to the floor. Then he tugged my hand and led me towards the water.

I sat neck deep in the warm tub with my head leaning back on Ryett's shoulder, my back against his chest, and my hands idly stroking his legs. Ryett held his hand above the water, weaving water between his fingers and turning it into shapes. He turned the water into hundreds of tiny droplets and let them rain back down into the tub.

"So you're telling me that *I* have the ability to do *that*?" I asked in disbelief.

"Or something like it." He said and sipped from his wine glass. "Considering you just about brought down the house and I am pretty sure the entire city felt your magic—"

"What?" I interrupted.

"What do you think that was when you climaxed? All the weapons falling from the wall, that was you—your magic releasing." Ryett said amused.

"You're kidding." I breathed.

"Nope."

"I felt like my body was exploding into a billion pieces, but I was wrapped in something warm … like it was containing me —" I started to explain.

"And *that* was my magic." Ryett said.

"Oh great so I almost completely destroy your house when I climax and you have to worry about containing it? That sounds pleasurable for you." My cheeks heated. Thankfully he could not see my face and how mortified I was.

Ryett only laughed. His chest shook me with his laughter. "Don't worry, it's not like that at all." His fingers brushed my hair over one shoulder and he kissed my neck. I only grumbled in response. He continued, "I have seen your magic manifest when you run, the way your body heals, how you sent it out into the world on waves, and now during sex."

I sipped my wine. Then asked, "Can you teach me? Teach me to use it intentionally?"

"I thought you would never ask." Ryett teased.

CHAPTER 41

Ryett and I trudged through the woods. He was carrying a pack with who knows what in it and apparently we were going somewhere where I would not "knock shit off the walls" while I practiced using my magic. "When we have jumped, sometimes it is completely quiet, but other times there has been a loud 'crack' noise. What is the deal with that?" I asked, as I hoisted myself over a log that was laying across the trail.

"World walking and jumping take a lot of power. You can do it quietly, but if it is too forced or you are going really fast because you are in a hurry or you send someone else across space and time without you, then there is that loud cracking noise. It is like the world or place you are stepping into snaps shut, like you closed a book quickly or slammed a door." Ryett replied.

"Hmmm." My brain was running through all the times I had jumped with others or seen someone jump. All of it lined up—every crack had been associated with a quick jump or sending someone else through. "Do you think I am capable of doing it?"

Ryett stopped and looked at me. He smiled, "Of world walking? Yes. Definitely. We are going to start with something a little more basic though." He dropped his pack. I looked around and realized we were in a clearing on a rolling mountainside. The sun was warm and everything smelled so ... *fresh*.

Ryett spread out a large blanket and plopped down on it. Then he pulled out a bottle of wine and two glasses and set them on one side of the blanket. He patted the spot next to him, "Sit. I thought we might start with summoning things. Wine felt like the right choice."

I rolled my eyes at him and sat down, "What does that say about me if you thought wine was the right motivator?"

He laughed, "That you like wine."

"You are not wrong." I chuckled, "So, how does this work?"

"Think about all the times that someone has just summoned something from thin air, maybe it was wine, or a blanket, or food. They did not just create that item out of nothing, they summoned it from somewhere. Here we have a bottle of wine and wine glasses." Ryett said as he pointed to the wine he had set down on the edge of the blanket. He held up his hand and a wine glass with wine appeared in it. "Now look again." The bottle was now open, there was wine missing from the bottle, and only one wine glass remained on the side of the blanket. "I wanted wine so I thought of wine that I had and a glass and that is what I summoned."

"Okay, well that is pretty cool. Here I thought you really just created whatever you wanted out of thin air." I kept looking back and forth between the bottle and the full glass in Ryett's hand.

"Nope. It has to exist somewhere and before you ask, no you can not just summon whatever you want out of the shops —everything has been spelled against people stealing it that way." He teased me.

"I was *not* going to ask that, but it is good information to have." I glared at him. *Who did he think I was?* I was not going to start stealing from shops. I had done a lot of bad shit, but I never stole from people. "So I just think about it and it happens?"

"On a basic level, yes. Start with thinking about it, then release your magic to *do* it." Ryett sipped the wine. "Try."

I would die of starvation and dehydration if there was food and drink one centimeter away from my mouth and all I had to do was use my magic to get it. I lay back on the blanket feeling totally useless. White and gray clouds rolled by. "What the fuck?" I huffed.

Ryett laughed, "It's okay. This is the first time you are trying this. It will take a bit. What worked when you were back in your world and you sent out those pulses of magic?"

"I thought about you and the images I see when you are around ... and I thought about my family ..." my voice trailed off.

"I imagine all of those things bring up emotion." Ryett said carefully, "Sometimes releasing your magic feels similar to bringing up emotions."

I stuck my hand straight up in the air. I was going to summon that glass of wine straight to my hand. Then I closed my eyes and tried to summon the same feelings and images that had worked before. Nothing. Then I thought about Ryett slicing my clothes away. I let out a small snort, laughing at myself for where my mind had wandered. I gasped as wine splashed all over my face.

Ryett exploded with laughter next to me. "Well you summoned wine!" He choked out between laughs.

I laughed with him as I pushed myself back up to sitting and wiped the wine off of my face. A cloth appeared in Ryett's hand and he handed it to me. "Do I at least get to drink some wine since I summoned it?"

"Nope. How is that motivating if I just hand it over? Try again." He chuckled.

I glared at him, then summoned bath water to dump on his

head.

Ryett sucked in a gasp as a tub worth of water poured over him. My hands shot to cover my mouth and my laughter. *I had done it!* He slowly turned to look at me. "You. Did. Not." He hissed. Then he tackled me onto the blanket while laughing and shaking his hair so that I was sprayed with water.

"Did I mess up your hair?" I giggled as we rolled on the ground. He paused on top of me, pinning me on my back.

"You did." He was grinning. "Punishable by death … or a thousand kisses." His lips attacked me. Pecking kisses all over my face and neck. I only giggled harder. Then he pressed a kiss to my lips and pulled me back up so we were both sitting. I was straddling him, my arms loosely wrapped around his neck and my clothes soaking up the water that drenched him. "That was really good, though. You have earned your wine."

He had to summon a new bottle as I had knocked over the one we had with the waterfall of bath water.

"What's next?" I asked as we sipped our glasses of wine and Ryett used his magic to dry both of us off.

A box of throwing knives appeared on the blanket in front of us. "You can already throw well, now let's try adding in your magic."

The sun was setting as we walked back towards the chateau. "Why don't you just jump everywhere? Why walk?" I asked.

Ryett laced his fingers with mine, "When I first learned how, I jumped everywhere all the time, but it drains your magic. And I learned that you miss out on a lot of life if you just jump from destination to destination. I think life is lived in the inbetween … the journey." He raised the back of my hand to his lips.

I stopped him. *How was I so lucky to have found him?* Or maybe he found me. *But how was I so lucky to have found a second person I thought I could spend my life with?* Besides my late-husband, there was not a soul that I had met that I wanted to spend this much time with—until Ryett. I was starting to think I could spend centuries with him. "Thank you. Thank you for not giving up on me."

"Never." He said as he wrapped his arms around me and kissed my forehead, "I will never give up on you."

CHAPTER 42

We were camped near the border of the Wastelands, the last place we would be able to safely use magic. The fire was warm and I was curled up next to Ryett under a blanket. Alias and Sarla sat across the fire from us and Jax lounged to our right, spinning a knife in the dirt.

"How is your love life going, Jax?" Sarla asked. He stopped spinning the blade. "Did you take our advice?"

"I did." Jax said tightly.

"And?" Sarla pressed.

"Well the sex has been incredible, but that female is crazy … no offense, I know you do not like when we call your sex crazy." Jax said with a huff. "She just wants it morning, noon, and night, and middle of the night, and I am *tired*."

We all burst out laughing. "Enjoy it brother!" Alias held up his drink in a salute. Jax rolled his eyes at him.

"How did you two end up getting together?" I asked, gesturing to Alias and Sarla. Jax gave me a relieved look, he seemed happy the conversation was moving away from his love life.

Sarla spoke, "Well we all grew up together of sorts. Nothing happened when we were growing up. We weren't 'like siblings' there was no 'young love'. We just knew each other. Then I went off to World Walker training … and my parents arranged a union for me. It was part of a peace deal. I came back after training and before the union ceremony and one night we were all just hanging out. Ryett went to bed and Alias practically verbally assaulted me about the arrangement."

Alias interrupted, "Verbally assaulted? More like aggressively questioned why you would agree to go along with it, why you were not fighting like hell to get out of it."

"Same thing." Sarla said as she flashed Alias a big grin, "That aggressive questioning led to aggressively tearing each other's clothes off and well, I obviously backed out of the arrangement."

"Vossarian was fucking pissed." Jax chimed in. *Vossarian? Had I just heard that right?*

"I'm sorry, what? Vossarian?" I asked.

"Yep. The plan was that I would marry Vossarian and our kingdoms would stop warring with each other." Sarla sighed.

I could almost hear what she did not say. That the war continued and many more people died because she did not marry Vossarian. That the weight of all of it still sat heavily on her shoulders.

"That explains *a lot*." I breathed. Vossarian was always mentioning Sarla. This was why. She had been betrothed to him as part of a deal between the kingdoms and she almost went along with it. Then she had agreed to help Ryett bring Vossarian and his slave trade down. I could not imagine that burden. I could not imagine the will power it took to set aside her history and play the game. I searched for something to say to lighten the mood, "When did you know you were soulmates?"

"When Sarla brought down the shed we were fucking in around us." Alias laughed. Sarla jabbed him with her elbow and he just looked at her confused and batted her elbow away with his hand before continuing. "I was not ready for the way our magic exploded the first time we were together like that ..." His voice trailed off as if he was reliving it in his mind.

Ryett's body had tensed. It clicked. *The way our magic exploded.* I slowly lifted myself away from the crook of Ryett's shoulder and looked at him. "You are my soulmate?" I breathed.

Ryett's throat bobbed as he swallowed, then he dipped his chin in confirmation.

"How long have you known and not told me?" I pressed him. I heard Sarla hiss something at Alias. I could feel the tension around us.

"From the moment I saw you across the room at Beck's." Ryett said. I just stared at him in disbelief. This is why he fought for me again and again. He *knew*. He continued, "I realized you didn't know ... did not know the signs. I decided that instead of telling you and making you feel forced into anything with me I would let you figure out what you wanted ... *if* you wanted me."

I do not want you to feel scared or trapped. The words Ryett had spoken to me when I had asked him about my magic responding to him. He had known the entire time. "I am not sure if I should be angry with you." I breathed. My mind raced through all of our interactions. How I had been pulled to him.

"You do not have to decide now. You are not stuck with me if you do not want to be." Ryett said quietly.

"And do you want to be stuck with me?" I challenged him. *Had he just stuck around because he knew we were soulmates or would he have chosen me if he had not known?*

"You are the only one I want to be stuck with." His hand wrapped around mine and squeezed.

I wanted to believe him. "Okay." I finally responded and then settled myself back into the crook of his shoulder. *Okay.* This did not have to change anything. I already wanted to be with him and I had not known we were soulmates. What was the difference now? The others were just staring at us. Waiting.

"That's it?" Jax finally blurted out. "Ryett you knew she was your soulmate and didn't tell her? And Genevieve, you just find this out and all you have to say is, 'Okay'? I mean we can go find ourselves another camp spot and you two can work this shit out. How are you both just sitting there like this is not some major moment?"

Both Ryett and I burst out laughing. He was right, this *was* major.

Jax stood up and motioned to Alias and Sarla, "Let's go you two. These idiots need some time to themselves. I can not just sit here with you two after that and pretend like nothing happened. You at least need to fuck under the stars and have a real conversation about it and I am not sticking around to watch." Sarla stared daggers at Alias and Alias averted his eyes, clearly aware that he let slip something he was supposed to keep quiet.

"Jax, you guys do not have to go. Please." I responded. *Please don't leave, I do not want to face this right now.* Is really what I wanted to say, but didn't.

"Nope. Sarla, Alias, let's go. We will see you bright and early." Jax said as he gathered his pack and waved aggressively at Sarla and Alias to follow. They did.

Ryett and I were alone. "You weren't going to say anything? Maybe stop them from leaving?" I turned to Ryett again, nearly glaring at him.

He just chuckled, "And give up an opportunity to fuck you under the stars? Never." I squealed as he pulled me back into his arms and kissed me as we fell into the dirt.

CHAPTER 43

If my heart could shatter more it would have. Children of all ages were chained in a line. The youngest had to be no more than three. They were dirty and bloody and bruised and shaking. I had never felt such anger rise in my body. Ryett's warm hand settled on my arm. A reminder to keep my head. We had to get them out of here and the eight warriors with them would not make it easy.

We watched from the treeline as Sarla sauntered into the clearing, just as we planned. The warriors' heads snapped to her and four started moving towards her. The other four kept the perimeter, just as we expected.

Ryett gave my arm a squeeze then disappeared into the trees, moving to his position. Alias, Jax, Ryett, and I were to take the other four warriors. Get them away from the children. I just had to not die long enough for Ryett to kill his assigned warrior and be back to help with mine. Or get extremely lucky and take down an immortal warrior who has been training for centuries. No big deal. *No big deal.* I took a deep breath. I could do this. I had a knack for not dying.

It was time. The four of us emerged from the forest as one. Sarla engaged the four warriors who approached her and the other warriors were now deciding between helping them and addressing us. I couldn't help but admire the way Sarla utterly kicked ass. The four warriors did not stand a chance against her and they had let her walk nearly all the way to them before they realized their mistake.

I had to focus. My palms were sweaty and the knives in my hands felt heavy. The warrior I had been assigned was indeed coming for me. I ducked and spun and slashed and found myself on the inside of the line, with my back to the children and the warrior pushed to the outside—exactly as we planned.

I dodged him again as he swung his sword for me, but he came again, faster. I blocked and he simply dropped his sword and grabbed my arm and shoulder. The fight went from a fight with blades to literal hand to hand close combat. His body moved right and muscle memory had my feet stepping wider. I shifted my weight and as he moved I pulled. I brought him to the ground exactly the way Alias had been teaching me. The warrior rolled and was back on his feet an instant later. He drew a long knife from his belt, "Nice trick." He snickered at me.

My heart felt like it had stopped beating. *How long would I have to hold him off? Where the hell was Ryett?*

Then the male's body buckled as a hand grabbed his head from behind and an axe separated his head from his body. Blood sprayed and Kieron stepped over the fallen body, dropping the male's head to the ground.

Ryett was beside me a moment later and he took a protective step in front of me. I saw Kieron's eyes look me up and down—pausing on my stomach where I should have been swollen with a child. His child. I saw a flicker of sadness cross his eyes.

"It's okay." I said to Ryett. I had no idea if it would be okay. I had no idea what Kieron would do, but he had just killed one of Vossarian's warriors. I stepped from behind Ryett and took a step towards Kieron. "I'm sorry … I lost the baby." I said.

"I already know. There is nothing to apologize for." He said softly. "That is not why I am here."

"How did you know?" No one outside of Ryett's inner circle knew about the baby. None of them would have said anything to anyone let alone to Kieron.

"A seer told me … long before I even knew you were pregnant. Before I knew it was you." He said, his voice thick.

"You *knew* I would lose the baby and you didn't say anything?" I was trembling. I didn't know if it was anger or sadness or hurt. This was the second time a male had just revealed they knew something critical that affected me and did not tell me.

"I am so sorry. I could not put that fear or stress on you. I hoped it would not come true, that the seer was wrong." I could see in his face that he really did care. That even though he knew it as soon as I had told him I was pregnant, it devastated him. It was why he had looked so devastated when I asked if he would come visit his child. He knew there would not be a child to visit.

I could not speak. I could hardly stand. My head was spinning. *He knew. Was that why he had brought me back to Ryett? Because he knew our child would never live?*

"Why are you here?" Ryett's strong voice broke the silence between us.

Kieron tore his eyes away from me, "Voss is back and he is looking for her. Both of you. He is going on and on about how he is going to kill you, Ryett. He thinks he has something on you that will break you. He is destroying gates knowing that you will come to restore them. I don't know his full plan, but he is trying to trap you."

"Why would you tell us this?" Ryett asked.

Kieron looked back to me, "Because this world needs fewer monsters."

"So you are just switching sides after centuries of working for Vossarian?" I blurted.

Kieron replied calmly, "No. The seer also told me that you would be my salvation. Savengard's salvation. He said I must help you in order for the True King to live." He glanced at Ryett.

The True King. It was the same words the beggar had said to me the night before he died. *Was Ryett the True King?* My skin pebbled and a chill ran down my spine. *Was this fate? Was all of this written in the stars and beyond my control?*

"Be careful." Kieron said as he turned to leave, "Like I said, it is a trap."

"Kieron, wait." I took another step towards him. I didn't know what I was going to say.

"I am not delusional. You are exactly where you are supposed to be and you are with exactly who you are supposed to be with." Kieron said and he ran off into the forest before I could say another word.

CHAPTER 44

"Are you okay?" Ryett asked as I hung my leather jacket on a hook inside Ryett's massive closet and began unfastening each buckle on my weapons harness. I tossed each piece and its attached weapons onto the dressing table in the middle of the room.

It had been a quiet trip back. The others had safely gotten all of the children back to the border and through the gate before jumping them to the city where they would be cleaned, clothed, fed, and sheltered. Ryett and I had not been far behind them, but had not spoken since our exchange with Kieron.

"I am beyond sickened by what Vossarian has been doing. To see those children *chained* … It's my fault, you agreed to him selling children when you bought me." I chucked the final strap of my harness onto the pile. I wanted to scream and vomit. I felt murderous. And to top it all off my head was spinning with the realization that the beggar had not been speaking nonsense to me. That my life was twisted around the fingers of fate.

"Hey." Ryett said as he stepped to me and grasped my face between his hands. "Hey. I know. I know it is beyond awful. It is not your fault at all, Voss was doing it already. Today we saved all of those children. They are all safe. And we will do everything we can to get them home or to ensure that they will continue to be safe."

"I know. I am just so enraged by it." I breathed. Those children would never be the same. They would never forget the horror Vossarian had put them through and the fact that they had to watch us kill eight males. I closed my eyes and took a deep breath.

"Come," Ryett said, "I have just the thing to help you relax, but first we are going to shower."

I finished running the comb through my wet hair and Ryett playfully tugged on my towel. "I seem to remember that you once asked for a full body massage. Care to cash in on that?"

My eyebrows raised. "Yes, absolutely yes."

He led me out to his bedroom and I climbed onto his bed, laying on my stomach. He gently lay a towel down covering my ass and then he climbed on the bed with me, straddling my legs. The oil was warm and soothing. His hands worked methodically and I tried to block out all of my thoughts. Focusing on the feeling of his hands on my sore muscles.

Eventually, he moved down my legs. As he massaged up my hamstrings his fingers dipped under the towel dangerously close to the warmth building between my legs. He paused, realizing his invasion. "Don't stop." I mumbled, my face half pressed into his sheets.

He laughed and his hands resumed. When they moved up to the top of my hamstring again, I lifted my hips slightly, inviting his touch. He kept rubbing. Hands moving higher and higher with each pass until his fingers brushed my wetness. I ached for him.

I tilted my hips again inviting him. With his next pass, his finger dipped into me. I heard him suck in a breath. His finger pulled out and he kept rubbing my legs. But as his hands worked their way up the backs of my legs again his breathing grew heavier. Another finger slid into me. A small moan released from my lips. It was all the invitation he needed as his finger stroked in and out. He slid a second finger in, his other hand continuing to massage my leg.

His fingers slid out, only to be replaced by his thumb sliding deep into me. His fingers curled around and found the bundle of nerves at my front. My hips lifted more as I moaned. The towel slipping up my ass to my lower back. I did not care that I was fully exposed to him, that everything was on display. I could not think of anything other than his hand.

He let out a low groan and bent over me to kiss a trail up my back and along my neck. He slid his hand out of me as he kissed my cheek. I turned over to my back as he kissed my mouth. My lips parted and our tongues met, tasting.

He moved between my legs, pulling his towel off from around his waist and tossing it on the floor. My mouth watered as I looked at the beautiful thick length of him. I lifted my legs around him as he guided his tip to my entrance. It slipped over my wetness and pressed against me.

I moved my hips and let his tip slip inside of me. I gasped at the feeling, he pressed deeper, stretching me, and pulling back slightly before pressing in further.

We were moving together, our breath synced. Our mouths tasted each other. My fingers dug into his back. His fingers tangled in my hair. Sweat mixed between us.

My eyes rolled back as I felt my climax rising. I saw jagged mountains, bubbling streams, glaciers, and forest fires. I saw the soil rejuvenating with new growth among the fire ashes, mountain meadows covered in wildflowers, and light snow catching on evergreen branches. My climax washed over and out of me. Warmth wrapped my skin and held the pieces of me in place. I moaned as another and another flowed through me.

Ryett hungrily tasted my neck. His forehead pressed to mind as I felt his cock twitch deep in me. My inner muscles milked him as he thrusted into me again and again. His body

364

shuddering as he spilled into me.

He collapsed over me, both of us breathing heavily. My body was completely spent, wholly satisfied. He slid his cock slowly out of me with a groan of satisfaction. Between my legs ached for him to fill me again as he wrapped me in his arms. He kissed me gently and brushed a strand of hair out of my eyes.

"That was not my plan ..." he said softly.

I smiled, "As long as you plan to do it again."

Amusement and hunger danced in his eyes, "Is right now too soon?"

I laughed. To my surprise he slid off the bed before pulling my hips to the edge and resting my legs over his shoulders. His cock was rock hard again as he slid it into me. I almost came out of my skin at the pleasure of him back inside of me.

Sex with Ryett was ... everything. He took the lead and seemed to know exactly when I needed it slow or when I wanted him to pound me. He would pull out and feast on me until I climaxed and ached for him inside of me again. His eyes had lit up when I knelt between his legs, taking him in my mouth. The skin on his cock was silky, pulled tight over steel. The way he fucked my mouth, firmly fisting my hair and guiding my head almost made me climax as well.

When I needed him in me again he flipped me onto my stomach, sliding deep into me from behind in one thrust. His body pressed on top of mine, his breath on my ear as his hard cock slid in and out of me, pressing deeper and deeper.

We climaxed together and somehow did not bring down the entire chateau or knock a single painting from the wall. Our magic had played and danced and soothed and ravished each other and we now lay tangled in each other's arms. My body was still shivering in pleasure.

"That was ..." Ryett could not even finish his sentence. I could only kiss his chest in response. I did not deserve something this good—*someone* this good. *How was this real?* Being here with Ryett felt like I had continued living just so I could be with him. Maybe fate would argue that I had.

CHAPTER 45

"We are going back to the Wastes already?" Sarla grumbled.

It had only been two days since our return from the Wastelands. Ryett was standing by the floor to ceiling windows in the living room of the chateau. The rest of us were sitting on the couches and chairs. "Zain just reported that more of the gates are down than we expected. We have to do something and do something soon."

Zain nodded his agreement, "We know some of the smaller gates are down, but we do not know how many. As of now, the four king gates are still working. If we can restore the smaller gates, Voss will not be able to take out the king gates."

"Small gates and king gates? Someone get me up to speed here, please." I asked. This was all new. I had been in the

Wastelands a few times now, but had not been told many details.

"We believe the gates, along with the borders, were created when the world was split. The Lands of the Mother sealed themselves off from the other kingdoms, sacrificing part of their kingdom to become what is now considered the Wastelands. There are twenty-seven gates bordering the seven kingdoms and there are twenty-seven gates surrounding The Lands of the Mother. Unlike the gates surrounding the Wastelands, you need a key to enter The Lands of the Mother and no one has found a key since they closed themselves off. No one has found a way to destroy those gates besides destroying one of the actual worlds. However, even with three destroyed worlds, the borders to The Lands of the Mother are still intact." Zain explained. I nodded my head to let him know I was following.

He continued, "This is different from the border and twenty-seven gates that separate the Wastelands from the seven kingdoms. Of those twenty-seven gates, four are considered king gates—Gates six, thirteen, twenty, and twenty-seven. The other gates are small gates. The king gates are only able to be restored by the magic of one of the seven kings of Savengard. The smaller gates can be restored by anyone or group with enough magic. If a smaller gate is destroyed, then small gaps form in the border where beasts could slip through, but not in any large numbers.

"The smaller gates also stabilize the power of the king gates, protecting them of sorts. If the smaller gates are up, then the king gates cannot fall. If enough smaller gates are destroyed, a king gate is weakened and could be destroyed as well. When one king gate falls, the entire border will fall and beasts and esurim will be able to come and go between the Wastelands and the kingdoms as they please."

I nodded. This was bad. "Kieron told us that Vossarian was destroying gates as a trap, Ryett. We can not go in there alone."

Ryett's shoulders rose with a deep breath, "We will go back in tomorrow. If we are quick and quiet about it no one will even know we are there. We might be able to get most of the border restored before anyone else knows the gates are even down. We can't wait. We do not need more of the Wastelands' residents sneaking out."

"We need to tell Beck and convince him to bring the other kings." Alias countered, "We do not have to do this alone. Genevieve said that Beck agreed to help, this is when we call in that favor."

"He agreed to help if we had a war. Not to help with something like this." Ryett said stiffly.

I looked between them. Alias was tense and he looked worried, but he didn't press the issue. Finally I spoke up, "What is the difference? If the gates are not restored, everyone will be in danger. Vossarian is the one destroying the gates. This *is* war, Ryett. It is worth asking. Especially if we are walking into a trap." I hated the idea of us going at this alone. It was dangerous. Was Beck on my favorites list? No, but he was powerful and he had agreed to help.

Ryett looked back out the window, "We can be discreet. Let's get in there and determine how bad it is before we go calling in favors. I am not about to use up what little goodwill we have if we don't absolutely need it."

"Okay, but if it is bad, we send for Beck right away. We do not need you killing yourself trying to do this all on your own." Sarla said, her arms crossed.

Ryett nodded and that was that. The others got up to leave and prepare for heading back into the Wastelands the next day.

As they quietly left the room I watched Ryett. He continued to stare out the windows. He did not look as relaxed as he normally did. His jaw was tight and his hands were stuffed into his pockets. "You do not have to do this all on your own anymore. Beck will help. I am sure Aveline will help. They might convince others to help too."

"I know." Ryett breathed, but he did not move. He took a deep breath and continued, "What if they don't come? I have spent centuries pushing them away, making them think I am just as bad as Vossarian. I would not blame them if they did not come."

"They will come. Beck will talk to them." I hoped I sounded reassuring even though I was not so sure of it. I wasn't even sure Beck would uphold his offer to help, but the thought of us trying to do this on our own—of Ryett putting himself in that much danger. It was worth hoping for. Worth trying.

Ryett turned and looked at me, "I hope he will. I hope he will come if we need him and I hope he will bring the others. I just am not ready to call on any of them yet."

"Okay. I support you." I responded. If Ryett was not ready to call on the other kings I would respect his decision. He didn't need people questioning him, he needed support, and I would have his back. When the time came, I would do everything I could to help make sure the other kings supported him too.

Ryett gave me a small smile even though his face was grave. I had a sinking feeling that this whole situation was worse than any of them had really let on.

CHAPTER 46

We walked across the border. The border that should have been a solid wall of magic to keep us out.

The air went from light and fresh to dense and rotting. The color of the leaves and grasses changed. There was a stark line in the earth where the border had been. Where the life of Ryett's kingdom met the death of the Wastelands it bordered. Stepping across that line sent a chill shooting down my spine.

Alias sucked in a breath, "This is bad, Ryett."

"I know." Ryett said solemnly. "Genevieve and I will head west to check the gate. You and Sarla and Jax head east to the next gate. We should be able to meet back here by nightfall. If you can restore the gate, do it, but do not draw attention to yourselves."

"One of us should go with you two." Alias countered. Jax and Sarla stood a few paces away, watching the landscape around us for threats.

"No. I can restore a gate on my own, but it might take the three of you to get the other." Ryett responded, placing a solid hand on Alias's shoulder.

"Understood." Alias nodded even as he gave Ryett a concerned look, "We should reach out to Beck."

"Yes, but we are here, let's try to get at least one of these gates back up." Ryett said. He had agreed to send for help if things were bad—*did this not count as bad?*

Alias nodded again. He was not going to question Ryett's order. I had to trust them even though I had a pit growing in my stomach. This felt wrong. This felt bad. The three of them moved off to the east.

I followed Ryett the other direction.

How far this gate was, I did not know, but it felt like we had been hiking for hours. Ryett paused and pressed a finger to his lips. I silenced my breathing and listened.

It was so quiet. Too quiet.

Then Kieron stepped out between the trees in front of us. "You need to see this." He said in greeting.

Ryett eyed him carefully, "I am getting a little tired of you popping up places with ominous messages."

Kieron laughed, "Noted. Next time I will just pop up with some beers and we can shoot the shit. Unfortunately, this time it is worse than an ominous message."

I tried not to smile. Kieron had jokes. "What is it?" I asked.

"It is better if I show you." He said and I took a step to follow him before Ryett could protest.

We followed Kieron through the woods for miles. Then he motioned for us to be quiet and we slowly approached an overlook. From the cover of the treeline we could see down into the valley below.

Thousands of beasts filled the valley floor and they were all moving the same direction. I looked closer and realized there were people among them, riding them, holding leashes, or just walking between the creatures.

"How did Vossarian get them to join him?" Ryett's voice was low. His eyes scanned the herd and the horizon in the direction they were headed.

"He has been using spells to grow his power—by consuming the power of others. Literally sucks the power out of whatever and whomever he pleases and keeps it for himself just like the esurimagicae. He has sucked the power from most of the gates and now he has compelled the beasts of the Wastelands to help him crush the other kingdoms with the promise that he will let them roam free when he is done." Kieron said flatly.

"Where is he going first?" Ryett asked. The two of them spoke with little emotion. With little surprise. As if they were discussing rocks in a garden or some equally boring topic. *How were they so calm about this?*

"Either to Aveline or to Beck's. He has never respected Aveline, it is an ego thing. But, word is Beck has been drunk and sloppy for months now. Vossarian thinks his army will not be ready and he will be able to get Beck's power before taking the other kingdoms." Kieron turned away from the overlook and beckoned us to follow. "You know what will happen if Voss gets Beck's power—any of the other kings' power—he will be unstoppable."

Ryett and I exchanged glances. Beck has been drunk and sloppy. Kieron continued, "The twenty-seventh gate is down. We have to restore it and block his army. I showed you because I am here to help."

"We have to go now. If we can reach the gate before this herd of beasts we can restore it and cut off their path." Ryett said. His face grim and determined.

No. The twenty-seventh gate. That was a king gate. That meant many of the smaller gates were already destroyed.

"Can your army get there in time to hold them if we can not get the gate restored in time?" Kieron asked as he led us further from the overlook and into the forest.

"We have to at least tell Alias, Jax, and Sarla. They can get help and we can head towards the gate." I said. We could not just leave and not tell them what was happening.

"There is no time to go back." Ryett said. His jaw set. He was willing to risk and sacrifice everything.

"I can jump you to them and then to the gate." Kieron said.

"You can't jump in the Wastes." Ryett said, he sounded confused.

Kieron shrugged his shoulders, "Multiple gates are down. We can jump, I have tested it. It might attract unwanted attention, but it might be worth it in favor of speed." He held out his hand as if to offer to jump us.

Ryett ignored it and wrapped his hand around mine instead, "I guess I will give it a try. Come with us." And then the world folded in and we were on the trail just in front of Alias, Jax, and Sarla. Their faces were shocked at our sudden appearance.

Kieron appeared next to us a heartbeat later and the three of them quickly shifted to fighting stances. Ryett waved his hand idly at them, "He is fine. There is no time to explain. There is an army of beasts from the Wastes heading west. The twenty-seventh gate is down. Us three are headed there to restore the gate and you need to get our army to the border incase we fail. They will likely head towards Aveline or Beck. Be prepared for either and send messengers to both."

"Ryett—" Alias started as if he was going to protest, but he stopped and nodded, "It is done."

The grave look on all of their faces told me this was worse than I could even imagine.

"You can jump out of here." Kieron said flatly from behind us. "Enough gates have been destroyed that it works for now."

The three of them stared at Kieron almost in disbelief. Ryett nodded to them to confirm what Kieron had said. Sarla touched a hand to her heart, "Until we meet again." She said and they were gone a moment later.

"Let's go." Ryett said as he looked back at Kieron.

The stone tower before us was stretched high into the clouds. Carvings etched along the stone created patterns and shapes.

"This might completely deplete me." Ryett said solemnly. "Can I trust you to get us out, Kieron?"

"Of course. You do what you have to do to get this gate restored and I will get both of you out of here. I swear it." Kieron responded. Their eyes were locked, assessing each other.

"What can I do?" I cut in.

"I will watch your back until Ryett can restore the gate, you need to be with Ryett and monitor him. There is a good chance he will lose consciousness and if he does, you yell for me and I will come to you to get you both out of here." Kieron responded.

I looked at Ryett in disbelief. He only nodded confirmation back to me. This would nearly kill him and I just was supposed to watch until he passed out? "Ryett, no you can't—"

"We have to. You watch me and as soon as the gate is up or

I pass out you let Kieron know it is time to get out of here. Hopefully those beasts are slow and don't interrupt us." He said gruffly and took a few steps towards the gigantic stone.

Kieron walked the other direction to what I now realized was the edge of a cliff. I went to Kieron's side and looked over. The herd of beasts was too close. "The first of the herd will get here before he is done. I will hold them off, but you need to scream for me as soon as the gate restores so we can get our asses out of here before we are overwhelmed or can not jump out." Kieron whispered. "Do not tell Ryett. He needs to focus. Don't let him kill himself either."

I turned around and saw Ryett squaring himself to the stone. He turned his palms skyward and dark light rippled off of him wrapping around and into the stone. The carved patterns started to illuminate and fill with light as if Ryett was pouring himself into the stone and it was filling like a glass of water. Then I realized that was exactly what he was doing. He had to fill the gate with his own magic in order to restore it.

I pushed down the fear that gripped me. My heart felt like it would crack into pieces again. *What if this did not work? What if Ryett died?* My throat burned. *Not a helpful thought.* I cleared my throat, "How do I make sure he does not die?"

Kieron looked at me, "You can feel his magic in the air right now can't you?" I slowly nodded. It was similar to the other times I had felt magic. The thickness in the air. The swirling. "You will be able to feel it. If he is giving too much you will feel him slipping away. You will feel his magic sputtering out. If you start to feel that—stop him. Punch him in the face if you have to—but stop him."

"Got it." I breathed. I walked back to Ryett and stood near him. Ready to be there for whatever he needed. Even if that was standing here doing nothing but supporting him. Magic poured out of him and the stone carvings filled with more and more light.

CHAPTER 47

I screamed for Kieron. The gate was nearly restored. I could see the final tendrils of magic filling in the carvings near the top. Ryett was barely standing, his face gray and his breathing labored, but I had not felt him slipping away. I could feel his magic was weaker, but he was still holding on. I turned to see where the hell Kieron was.

Beasts and blood littered the dirt near the cliff's edge. Kieron's movements were fluid and lethal. Severed limbs fell. Growls and roars and screeches echoed through the air around us.

The air shimmered around Kieron and blasted outwards. Beasts turned into nothing but a bloody mist around him.

I glanced back to Ryett, he had collapsed in the dirt, but the gate was restored. The stone glowed and pulsed with the dark light of Ryett's magic. It swirled within the carvings of the rock. I started to see and feel the magic rippling out from the stone as the border started to flicker back to life. I rushed to where Ryett was laying on the ground and put my hand in front of his mouth—he was still breathing.

"We have to go, *now*." Kieron bellowed as he ran towards us. I could see the beasts behind him. The dozens he had killed that littered the ground and the dozens more that crawled over the cliff's edge and raced towards us.

I yanked Ryett to his feet and threw his arm around my shoulder. We had to get to Kieron. We had to get out of here. Kieron could jump us out of here and back to safety before the border fully restored. I staggered under Ryett's nearly limp body. His breath was ragged. Kieron was sprinting towards us in that unnaturally fast way of his. Only a few more heartbeats and we would be out of here.

Then a wall of fire erupted between us. My eyes were locked with Kieron's as he disappeared on the other side of the flames. We were trapped. This was not a fire ring you could just run through. These were flames as tall as buildings that melted everything in their path. The earth bubbled beneath the flames, melting.

"I knew you had help but I did not suspect Kieron. If he is smart he will start running now because what I will do to him when I am done with you two is worse than death." Vossarian's dark voice cut through the crackling of the flames.

The sky was darkening in a red haze. I had seen it before. It was Vossarian's power causing the shift. Ryett tried to straighten up next to me. His breathing was labored. He had nearly depleted himself completely working to restore the gates. He had nothing left for a fight.

Storm lashed out at us and Ryett threw up a shield. It buckled under the weight of Voss's power. Then it cracked and dissipated. Another blast hit us and we were knocked to the ground. Invisible hands grabbed my legs and pulled me towards Voss. I clawed at the ground, dirt piling under my nails as I tried to stop myself. I was yanked to my feet and found myself face to face with Vossarian.

Then Ryett was there, Vossarian barely dropped me in time to block Ryett's axe. I rolled away and drew a knife. I had to help. I had to fight. Ryett was barely alive. *How was he standing?* No, Ryett was not standing anymore. Voss had knocked him down. Ryett lay face down in the dirt struggling to rise. I watched as Voss's boot connected with his ribs and Ryett's body jerked to the side with the impact.

Voss stalked a slow circle around him. He twirled a sword in his hand as he glared at Ryett's limp body in the dirt. "You are done, Ryett. You put all your power right into the gate for me. You practically wrapped it up like a present. I have no more need for you. You will never come back from where I am sending you." Voss growled and I saw the magic building in him.

He was going to kill Ryett. I did not think I just moved. I had to stop Vossarian. Everything was slow motion. Ryett trying to raise his head. The magic flowing from Vossarian towards Ryett. I had no time. I threw myself between them and felt the full force of Vossarian's magic rip into my back.

CHAPTER 48

The blast of magic had nearly crushed my lungs and the folding worlds had suffocated me until I thought my eyes would pop out. I was on my hands and knees, spit dripping from my mouth as I gasped for breath. The ground was smooth like glass and covered in a sheen of water. I stared at myself in the obsidian mirror. Ryett was going to die. Vossarian was going to kill him and I could not do a damn thing about it.

Vossarian had blasted me worlds away. I would die here too. But I did not care about that. I only cared that Ryett was going to die.

I screamed. I screamed at my reflection as spit and tears dripped from my face. My chest was breaking open, it had to be splitting down the center with the pain I felt in my heart. Cold tingles flushed every limb as I sobbed. My throat tightened and burned. Everyone I ever loved was dead or about to be.

"Finally you are letting it out." A deep voice echoed around me. I froze. I was not alone. "You have nothing to fear. I am not here to hurt you." The voice continued. "Welcome to the twenty-seventh world. The bridge between this life and the next."

I wiped my nose and face then looked around the darkness. I could only see black shimmering surface. "Who are you?" I called out, my voice shaking.

"We have met. I watched you for many years, before I was sure you were the key." The voice said.

"You did not answer my question." I replied.

I watched the ground around me shimmer then images started to show blurry and distorted in the water. An old man in ratty clothes sat in the dirt against a building. I knew this man. The beggar. "I have had many forms, but this is how you would remember me." The beggar said.

"I thought you died." I whispered.

"Oh I did. In that body. It was the only way to leave and continue on with what I needed to do." I did not respond. My heart was pounding in my chest. He spoke again. "You need to get back and the only way to do that is to face your own pain and emotions. Let them out of your body and your magic will flourish. Don't worry, you can take a little time if you need to. Days in this world are only seconds passed in that world."

"But who are you ... you watched me? So I am really the key?" He was right, I needed to get back, but he had answers.

"Long ago I had a son. I watched him mature and grow. And as he grew so did his greed and the evil inside of him. I was blinded by my own ambition and greed, too blinded to realize what my son was turning into before it was too late. My son was set to be my heir. Heir of the Land of the Deserts." As he spoke, images flashed through the black water.

I watched Vossarian as a teen grow into a young man and the adult he is today. I saw the light in his eyes turn to darkness as he aged. I watched him turn into a tyrant filled with the greed for more wealth and power. *The beggar is Vossarian's father. Luther.* "Then my brother had a child and when I saw him I knew immediately that he was the chosen next king. The land does that, picks the next heir. Often it is through the direct bloodline, but occasionally it veers and picks someone else. This child, not my son, was the chosen heir.

"I knew Vossarian would kill him as soon as he found out. So I hid it. And even though I saw the pure goodness in this child, we turned him into one of the most brutal assassins we ever trained. We raised him to be a monster, for only a monster would be able to beat my son, to survive. To become one of the True Kings."

"You are Vossarian's father ... I thought the True King was the king to rule all of Savengard—" I stammered.

Luther laughed, "A narrative bastardized through centuries

of ambition and egotistic manipulation—clearly I did a good job of it. No, there are True *Kings* of each of the territories. Our world was not designed to be led by one, but to be balanced by many. I can see the error in my plans now. Regardless, my son is not one of those True Kings and he threatens the existence of Savengard. He must be stopped—you must stop him and the True King of the Deserts must be restored."

"Who is supposed to be the king? Who is your nephew?" I asked.

"The True King of the Deserts is Kieron." My stomach dropped. Luther had done this to Kieron. He had turned an innocent child into an assassin—the most feared and brutal assassin in history.

"Why me? You said I am the key. What does that mean?"

"I thought Kieron would have to kill Vossarian, but I was wrong. I saw it here. In these mirrors. This world shows you the truth of who you are and what is to come. *You* must kill Vossarian. You are the key to restoring The Seven True Kings of Savengard and when they are ready, you will be able to open the gates to The Lands of the Mother."

"How can I possibly open the gates?"

"Your ancestor was one of the original queens of The Lands of the Mother. She left Savengard with the warriors and to hide in one of the twenty-six worlds. Her magic passed down to you and only someone with magic from that land may open its gates."

I did not know what to ask. *How was any of this possible?* "So this is just my fate?"

"No. There is no fate. Ever since Vossarian locked me out of Savengard and separated my soul from a body I have been searching for a way to help Kieron. I watched these mirrors like windows into the other worlds, into the potential futures, and I searched and searched for a solution. Your face kept coming back, so I watched you. I saw what you were capable of. I saw that you had magic in you—you have had it all along, but in your world magic was stifled. It woke the day you went through the portal into Savengard. I did what I could to influence both you and Kieron so your paths would cross. Feeding you scraps of the future and guidance to make it so. Everything was to lead to this moment where you would eventually end up here and get to choose. Choose to pass on into the next life, or choose to return to this one and defeat my son."

"How do I defeat him?" I breathed.

The water rippled all around me. "You have to let out your magic. You cannot be afraid to face every feeling you have bottled up. You have bottled up your magic just like you have bottled up your feelings. Release your feelings and letting your magic flow will no longer be scary. Believe in yourself."

"Are you fucking kidding? That is it? Believe in myself?" What a fucking joke. *Everyone was going to die because after all of this story he told me the only guidance Luther had was to let my feelings out? To believe?*

"That is all I can tell you. It is in you. You are the mountain. Vossarian is full of storms and fury, but you are the mountain." Luther continued, "Before you choose, I have one more thing to show you and you may not like it." The water ripple again and images crossed the ground.

Silence filled the shimmering black world of obsidian mirrors. I had a choice. To pass over to the next life, or to return and be a hero. I never wanted to be a hero, but there were people who would die. A whole other world might die if I did not step up.

I would do it. Ryett deserved to live and to be happy. I was his only chance. I would go back even if it ended up killing me … or worse. I would do it.

Now I had to figure out how to get the fuck out of here and back to Vossarian and Ryett and Kieron. *Let out my bottled up feelings.* Great.

I touched the water which had remained smooth since the last images Luther had shown me. He had since disappeared, leaving me utterly alone here. I touched the water again and sent ripples in every direction. Images started to form in the water.

I watched as every horror I had lived through flashed before me. My throat burned and tightened. My chest felt like it was caving in. I was going to be sick. Tears burned my eyes and slid down my cheeks. The images kept coming.

What I saw next took me over the edge. I watched my family be murdered. I watched myself pull their bodies away from the wreckage. Then I saw myself burn their bodies into ash. I screamed. Screamed at the pain of reliving what I hoped I would never relive. I screamed in anger at the loss I had experienced. At the hole it left inside of me.

I screamed again. And again. Waves built in my body and crashed out through my skin. The ache in my chest built and built until with my next scream it felt like my heart was ripping out of my body. I curled my hands into fists and beat them on the glasslike surface. Pain shooting up through my arms. I screamed again. A wild scream. A scream that had once been pain and sadness was now a battle cry.

I opened my eyes and saw my skin glowing a faint and dark light. My body heaved and fell with every deep breath I sucked in through my nose and blew out through my mouth. I could feel the light shining from every pore in my body. Shining from the rims of my eyes. It was flame and ice and jagged peaks. It was solid and strong and unmoving—like a mountain.

I pushed myself to my feet. This world was dark. Wet glassy mirrored ground stretched in every direction from me. Another deep breath sent a wave of magic pulsing from my body. Light into the darkness. My throat was raw and I wiped the tears and snot from my face with my sleeve. *How could anywhere be so quiet?*

But it was no longer quiet. I heard the soft clicks of padded feet with claws approaching. From the darkness eyes glowed at me. I reached up and unclasped the axe that was strapped across my back. A white and gray wolf emerged from the darkness and slowly circled me. Then I saw another set of eyes. And another. And another. Four wolves stood creating a circle around me. The silence returned. I weighed the axe in my hands.

Great Wolves can travel through worlds just like the World Walkers. Some believe them to be the balancers of what is not right between the worlds—removing or killing things that shouldn't be. Some believe them to be the protectors of those who are most needed or most important to the fate of our world. I remembered Ryett telling me about the Great Wolves when I first arrived at the chateau in Montvera.

More clicking approached and golden eyes appeared out of the darkness. I would recognize those eyes anywhere. Mintaka was here. His black coat shimmered almost as reflective as the mirrored expanse around us.

You will run through worlds with the five warriors of the west, as swift as wolves, for the king needs you. Do not be afraid. The old and dirty beggar's lunatic ramblings echoed in my head— Luther's ramblings. He had seen this. He had known. *Of course. How had I forgotten?* The western star was not a single star at all, but a cluster of five stars. The five warriors who had ruled the western territory.

I reached out my hand to pet Mintaka's head as he weaved around my legs. "Let's go get Ryett." I whispered and Mintaka's golden eyes seemed to light with recognition and confirmation. My feet began to move and the wolves ran alongside me. The blackness in front of us ripped open, tearing right down the center as we sprinted into nothingness.

I followed the wolves. Pressing my legs to run faster than I had ever run before. I let everything go. All of my thoughts and emotions spilled from my body as we ran. The pressure was building around us, but I ran faster than the pressure could hold me. It was like running through syrup and sand and yet we ran and ran. Worlds split open before us as we ran.

I gripped my axe as my arms pumped and I willed my knees to drive harder. I could see it. I could see Ryett facedown and bleeding in the dirt. I could see Vossarian standing above him. I could see the fire and storm that raged around them. I pushed my legs harder and saw the wolves press faster too. We were light and air and wind as we ran. The worlds opened before us. My ears registered the crack as we burst through into Savengard. The air was finally no longer pressing into us from all sides. The wolves turned to flame and ash as they disappeared from around me and I hurtled across the dirt ground, barreling straight into Vossarian.

The impact sent the air bursting from my lungs and we tumbled along the dirt. I shot to my feet as Vossarian rolled into a crouch. His soulless dark eyes filled with confusion and rage as he saw me. I did not hesitate as I swung the axe towards him, but he folded into the air and reappeared across the ring of fire to my right. I stood and faced him. Storm swirled around him and he sent it flying in my direction. I stood tall and squared my shoulders.

Every emotion still burned from me. Pain and rage and anger and sadness. The echoes and memories of happiness and joy and *love*. Lightning blasted dirt across my legs as it struck the ground next to me. Thunder shook the earth. The storm lashed out at me, but it ebbed and broke along the dark light I was emitting. I stalked towards Vossarian as he sent more storm blasting towards me. Rain. Wind. Lightning. I spun the axe in my hand. Those storms broke too, like a wave crashing against rock. *I am the mountain and I will not break.* I took two quick steps and with everything I had I sent the axe hurtling at Vossarian's chest.

The storm stopped as the axe embedded with a deep thunk into Vossarian. He stumbled a few steps before falling to the ground. I kept walking towards him. His hands were grasping the axe protruding from his chest. Somehow he was still breathing. I looked down into his dark soulless eyes and stomped my foot next to the blade stuck in him. Reaching down I took the smooth wooden handle in my hand and yanked the axe out. Blood sprayed my boot and pants.

More blood bubbled from Vossarian's mouth as he tried to

speak. I heard the words, but I did not listen. There was nothing he could say that would stop me. His hand clutched at his open chest. I raised the axe over my head and brought it down with sickening force as I cleaved Voss's head from his body.

I dropped the axe on the dead king.

CHAPTER 49

Ryett was facedown on the ground. The world burned around us as I knelt, pressing my fingers to his neck, praying I would feel a pulse. It was there—barely. I gently rolled him over and cradled his head in my lap. "I'm here." I whispered to him.

I was here, but I did not know what to do. I did not know how to get us out of here—out of the burning flames and the ashes that rained down on us. I searched his body for wounds that needed bleeding to stop or injuries I could do something about. I could not find anything. His breathing was shallow. *I had to get him out of here.* "I am here." I whispered again, stroking his cheek. The air felt thick around us and I realized that I was barely hanging on to my own consciousness. My breath was shallow and darkness pressed in against me. *Hold on.* I urged myself to hold on.

Sizzling started around us. Steam billowed up and the flames faltered then sputtered out as water crashed down upon them. Out of the steam stepped Beck. His eyes caught on Vossarian's body on the ground and looked to Ryett and me. A heartbeat later he was kneeling next to me and placed a hand on Ryett's chest.

"Let's get you two out of here." Beck said gently, grabbing Ryett's arm and pulling him up and over his shoulder. His hand reached out to me. *What choice did I have?* Ryett would die. There was no one else here. Beck said he would help and he had come. I grabbed his hand and the world folded in.

I was getting really tired of passing out and waking up in new places. But this was not a new place. I had woken up in this room before. In this bed. Beck was in the same chair, but this time he was not lounging comfortably. No, he was stiff and glaring at another male sitting across from him. Kieron was lounging with his ankle crossed over his knee, an amused smile on his face, glaring right back at Beck.

"I see you two are getting along." I said from the bed. My throat burned.

Beck shot to his feet and crossed the room to me. Kieron lazily stood up and followed. "Ryett's alive. He is still asleep, but he is alive." Kieron said. I let out a sigh of relief. Of course

Kieron would know that was the first thing I would ask.

"Do you need anything?" Beck asked.

"No, I am fine." I pushed myself up and pulled back the covers to get out of bed. That was when I realized I was in nothing but a shirt and underthings. Someone must have removed everything else to make sure I was not injured. I would have been embarrassed, but both of them had already seen every part of me. When I looked up I saw Beck's gaze lingering on my legs. Kieron was politely averting his eyes.

I swung my legs off the side of the bed and tried to stand up. I had never felt so weak.

"You nearly poured out all of your power, you will be weak for a few days. Can you tell us what happened with Vossarian?" Beck said and offered a hand to help me stand. I took it and slowly got to my feet.

"Kieron, will you help me get to the bathroom? Beck, do you know where my clothes ended up so I do not have to have this conversation in my underthings?" Kieron gave Beck a smirk as Beck stepped back, his mouth pressed into a thin line. Kieron scooped me up easily into his large arms.

"I will get you something to wear." Beck mumbled as he walked to the door.

Kieron set me down in the bathroom and, while holding on to me so that I did not fall over, he reached into the shower to turn it on. "Are you doing okay?" He asked.

I sighed, "Just really fucking tired and weak."

"Using up all your magic will do that." Kieron responded, his face was neutral.

"Kieron," I took a deep breath. "I need you to do something."

His eyes scanned my face, "Of course, what is it?"

Beck, Kieron, and I sat in the chairs in the room that was once mine at Beck's residence. The gates were restored. Messengers had made it to both Beck and Aveline. Aveline had overseen that the gates were restored while Beck and Ryett's armies, led by Devron and Alias, had held back the herd of beasts and Vossarian's warriors. Beck was intercepted by Kieron, who had somehow convinced him to come rescue Ryett and me.

I had told them what had happened and both of them were looking at me like I was crazy.

"The True King isn't just one king?" Beck asked, confused.

"No, he told me that there was a True King for each kingdom. There was never meant to be one king to rule over all. He said Savengard would only survive with the balance of the *seven True Kings*. Kieron has always been the True King of the Deserts." I explained again.

"That would explain a few things." Kieron said stiffly.

"You are the True King of the Deserts and you need to take control of your kingdom. You are the most notorious assassin, you were Vossarian's right hand, and you were related. No one will think twice about the power being passed to you." I said. Kieron rubbed his hand down his face.

"As much as it pains me to say it, but she is right, Kieron." Beck said. "It is fucked up what happened to you and your kingdom, but we can help you make it right. You obviously did not approve of the way Vossarian ran your kingdom—maybe a kingdom under your rule could be much different. I am offering an alliance and whatever help you need."

That was shocking. Beck had been trying to kill Kieron with his glaring ever since I woke up and now he was offering an alliance and help?

Kieron looked just as shocked as I felt, "Okay. Thank you. The Deserts have a lot of changes to make and an alliance with you is welcomed." He rubbed his hands on his pants, "I need to return to the Deserts anyway and while I am there I will get a pulse on what help I might need. I have a feeling taking over the throne may have a few hurdles after my betrayal to Voss. I will leave today and be back tomorrow."

I met Kieron's eyes and just nodded to him. "I am going to go be with Ryett. Thank you both." I said as I stood to leave.

Ryett looked so peaceful sleeping in the big bed a few rooms down from the one I had woken up in. I crawled onto the bed next to him and curled up, interlacing my fingers with his and planting a kiss on his shoulder as I breathed him in.

"Hey," his voice was hoarse.

"Hey," I whispered back, "I didn't mean to wake you, you need to rest."

He rolled on his side to face me and his hand brushed my hair behind my ear. Tears silently fell down my face. He was *alive*. He brushed away a tear and kissed me. I crawled under the covers with him and snuggled in close.

We both needed rest. I could tell him what happened tomorrow. Beck had told me that Savengard was stable. There were no immediate threats. We could breathe.

Tonight there would just be the two of us. We would deal with everything else tomorrow. I listened to his heartbeat and deep breaths as I closed my eyes. I breathed in his scent and I drifted off to sleep.

THE SEVENTH
KING SERIES
CONTINUES IN

CROWN OF SHADOWS

Read on for a sneak peak!

CHAPTER 1

The sun was setting against the red cliffs. I stood on the red stone patio looking out across a pool of water whose edge disappeared against the desert. My magic did not hum under my skin anymore, it only seemed to sputter and flicker like a flame that was running out of fuel.

I walked towards the edge of the pool and without dropping my clothes or even stepping out of my shoes, I stepped into the water. It was cool, but not cold. The perfect temperature to keep you comfortable on a scorching hot day. I took another step into the water and felt it soak my pants up to my knees.

I took another step and another. The calm water rippled as it lapped against my waist. Then my chest. The pool of water did not get any deeper. I took one last slow blink. Soaking in the sunset. Then I dunked my head below the surface.

I felt my hair become weightless and flow around me. I let bubbles of air release from my lips and float up to the surface. I opened my eyes to stare into the nothingness and the salt water stung. A last bubble of air floated up.

My lungs fought me. *Breathe. Don't breathe. Breathe.* My muscles involuntarily flexed and twitched, begging for air. All I had to do was put my feet down and stand up. But I wouldn't. There was nothing in my mind but the silent command to suck in a breath.

The water rushed around me and strong hands yanked me above the water. I fought against them crying and screaming. Hands planted firmly on either side of my face.

"What the fuck? I am not letting you die here. Especially not on your first day, maybe your second, but not today." Kieron's voice was gruff and nearly yelling, his face was inches from mine. "Do you hear me? Not today!"

My body shook with my sobbing and he pulled me against his chest. Cradling my head and body against him and safely above the waterline.

Hours earlier.

I slipped quietly from the bed Ryett and I were in. His deep breaths told me he was still sound asleep. *Good.* He needed to rest. I closed the door to his room with a soft click behind me.

The halls of Beck's residence were quiet, but I could see a guard standing alertly at the end of the hall. As I approached he spoke, "Beck is in the dining room. Kieron has not returned yet."

"Thank you." I replied softly and headed down the stairs to find Beck.

Just as the guard said, I found him in the dining room, sitting at the head of the table with untouched food in front of him.

"Thank you, Beck. Thank you for helping us and letting us stay here." I said in greeting.

"Of course," he replied with an idle hand wave. "I assume Ryett is still asleep."

"Yes." I sat down in one of the chairs and took a deep breath, bracing myself for what I was about to tell Beck. "Kieron is bringing someone back with him. Or at least he should be. She has been kept captive under Vossarian and his father, Luther, for somewhere in the ballpark of two hundred years."

Beck stiffened and his eyes were sharp, "Go on."

"Her name is Rachel. She is Ryett's lover from early in his life. He thought she was dead all this time." My chest tightened at the words. It was hard to swallow. Hard to breathe. I continued, "Luther told me about her when I was in the twenty-seventh world. He had found her and kept her captive as an eventual bargaining chip with Ryett. When Ryett started business with

Vossarian he continued to keep her a secret in case Ryett ever turned on him. Voss tried to play that card before I killed him, but I already knew where she was. Kieron is bringing her here."

To Beck's credit his face was calm and neutral, "I will send for Esmay." Esmay was Beck's healer of choice. She had seen to Sarla and me when we had tumbled through a portal from my world, the twenty-sixth world, and into Beck's kingdom. She was the best of the best.

"Thank you." I said and reached for the small carafe of coffee. I poured myself a cup and cradled it in my hands as I stared blankly at the food on the table.

Kieron strode through the glass double doors into the dining room. The female that trailed him was beautiful. She was thin, but had curves in all the right places. Her skin was creamy white and her lips full. Her eyes a piercing emerald green that scanned the room as she followed Kieron. Her red hair hung in gentle waving curls just past her generous breasts. She tucked her hair behind an ear—a nervous twitch I noted—and I saw the slight point to the tip of her ear. She was indeed not from Savengard.

She was all the things I was not—delicate, gentle, ethereal. My body tingled as I forced down every emotion that welled up within me.

"You must be Rachel." Beck stood as he greeted them. "Come.

Sit and enjoy some food."

She nodded gracefully to him and Kieron pulled out a chair for her to sit.

"Rachel, meet Beck, the King of the Lakes. This is his residence. Also, meet Genevieve, you can thank her for your liberation from captivity." Kieron introduced us, his voice calm and even.

"It is nice to meet you." I said as calmly as I could and forced a smile. "Kieron, can I have a word?"

I stood and followed Kieron into the hall. "I did as you asked and did not tell her about Ryett. She claims she has not been harmed and the servants where she was kept also said she was well taken care of." He explained.

"Good. Thank you. Beck will send for Esmay to have her checked out anyway." I took a deep breath and ran my hands down my face. I was going to throw up. Or explode into a million pieces. "I need to go tell Ryett."

"Are you sure? You don't have to. You certainly do not have to do it yet." Kieron pressed me. His voice was gentle—concerned. "I can keep her safe until you are ready."

"No. Waiting will not make it easier." I countered. It would not. And I could not look Ryett in the eye knowing I was hiding his long lost and thought to be dead lover from him. "I will tell him when he wakes up and he can decide if and when he wants to see her."

"And what about you?" Kieron asked, his voice suddenly

hard.

"What about me?" I said dismissively and turned to go to Ryett's room. Kieron did not say anything more as I left him standing in the entryway. I walked down the guest wing and it never felt so long. Never felt like the wide hall or tall ceilings were closing in on me like they were now.

I quietly entered Ryett's room and found him awake and sitting in one of the chairs. The color had returned to his face and he looked surprisingly well. He stood and crossed the room to me in a few strides. His lips met mine as he wrapped his arms around me. My legs were weak.

"What's wrong?" Ryett whispered, "Is everyone okay?"

"Everyone is okay." I murmured, "But Ryett—" He kissed me again. "We found Rachel."

He pulled back from me, "What are you talking about?"

"Rachel is alive. She is here." Confusion and pain and guilt all crossed Ryett's face. I continued, "When we were fighting Voss, he sent me to the twenty-seventh world. His father was there. Luther was there. He told me many things, one of them being that he had kidnapped Rachel to use as leverage against you. He also told me where they kept her. Kieron brought her here this morning."

"But she is dead." Ryett breathed.

"Red hair, green eyes, pointed ears?" Ryett's eyes grew wide as I spoke, "She is alive and in one piece. We have not told her about you. I wanted to tell you first."

409

"She is alive? She is here?" Ryett asked slowly, his face had started paling again.

"Esmay, Beck's healer is coming to examine her and make sure she is unharmed, but I can bring her here first if you want to see her. If you are ready ..." Pieces of me felt like they were flaking off and floating away as I spoke. Ryett seemed to be pulling further and further away with every heartbeat.

"Yes, I would like to see her." He finally said. I could see tears building in his eyes.

"Of course." I breathed. "I will go get her."

This fucking hallway was too long. I did not know what to say to Rachel as I led her down towards the room I had left Ryett in. I had only told her someone wanted to see her. We stopped outside the room and I swallowed, my mouth was dry. My throat was tight and burning. I reached out and turned the door handle, pushing the door in as I entered the room and held it open for Rachel to follow in after me.

My head went completely silent as I watched Rachel run for Ryett. As Ryett wrapped her in his arms and held her. As he pushed back her hair and stared into her eyes. I stepped back into the hall and closed the door behind me. I did not need to witness this. I had seen enough.

Somehow my feet took me back to the dining room where Kieron and Beck still sat, food untouched.

"So it is really her?" Kieron asked.

I gave a quick nod of confirmation as I walked past them to the small sitting area near the fireplace and sat down. I stared at the low table in front of me and into nothingness.

I did not know how much time had passed, but Ryett's voice jerked me from my numbness.

"Esmay is with her now." Ryett said as he entered the room, "Thank you, Kieron."

"Don't thank me. My vote was to kill her for good, but your soulmate convinced me otherwise. I am still not sure I agree." Kieron's voice had a bite to it.

Beck's head snapped up to look at Ryett, then me. "You two are soulmates?" He blurted out.

Ryett ignored him, "Genevieve—"

"Let me guess, you failed to mention that significant detail to Rachel, didn't you?" Kieron cut in.

"Kieron, don't." I said flatly. It did not matter. I stood and looked at Ryett. I fished inside of myself for the humming in my magic. The electricity that Ryett always brought out in me. There was nothing. I grasped for the invisible bond that tied us together, like a rope always pulling me towards him. I only found a slack line and when I pulled it, a cut end wound up in my hands. I had my answer. I had let myself open up to the potential and possibility with Ryett—of a new life here in Savengard. An opportunity to move forward. To be happy. I felt my heart ache. Felt my chest cave in as that possibility was ripped from me.

Ryett's face was pained as he spoke, "Genevieve, I can't just abandon her—"

"I know, Ryett. I understand. I just can't stay." I responded, my voice soft, but surprisingly steady.

"What do you mean?" He breathed, his eyes growing wide.

Kieron cut in, "Okay, now that *that* is settled, G and I need to get back to the Deserts. I have a kingdom to get under control."

"Genevieve is not going with you, Kieron, what are you talking about?" Beck said sharply.

"Oh, she is. You asked what I needed and I need someone to ensure you two do not stab me in the back once I leave here. Plus you two need someone you trust to report on me. Genevieve fits both." Kieron explained casually.

"Take anyone else." Beck gritted out.

"My mind is made up." Kieron crossed the room to me and put an arm around my shoulders.

"You can't." Beck was stepping towards us, the air flowing around him as his magic built.

Kieron threw up a shield around us, the air rippling like heat above the desert sand.

"He can." Ryett breathed.

"What?" Beck snapped.

"That's right, Ryett, I can. By law Genevieve is still my possession. Do not make me call in on that inter-kingdom law." Kieron said, almost sounding bored. Beck was fuming, "To bring you up to speed, Beck, since clearly you missed out on the gossip, Genevieve here was carrying my child. Obviously it didn't work out, but by law she is still mine."

Beck's face paled. Ryett looked like he might throw up, "If you hurt her—" Beck gritted between his teeth.

"I know, I know. If I hurt her then our alliance is over and you come and rip me and my kingdom to shreds. But don't worry, I won't even touch her … unless she wants me to." Kieron said mockingly. Then the room disappeared around us.

I was dressed too warm for the heat of the desert, but I did not care. I just stared at the pool that stretched into infinity in front of us. Kieron was saying something, but I could not hear him over the roaring in my ears. He had done everything I had asked him to. I did not think it would feel like this though. That every reason I had come up with to fight for this life would slip away like sand through my fingers. I stepped towards the pool.

CHAPTER 2

Kieron - Months earlier.

"You two will not believe who I stumbled upon in Beck's woods." Vossarian sat lounging on his plush velvet couch. Why Voss had summoned Rook and him, Kieron did not know. Vossarian chuckled darkly, "No guesses? I will give you a clue: Both of you died the last time you saw her."

Kieron's eyes flashed, but he quickly schooled his features to be neutral. After over four hundred years of dealing with Vossarian's bullshit he was a master of deception and lies—and pretending like not a damn thing irked him.

"Which bitch, Voss?" Rook looked almost ravenous. His

414

need for revenge and to mend his wounded ego after their unfortunate failed assassination of Sarla months ago had turned him into an even bigger prick than usual.

Vossarian let out a dark chuckle, "Her name is Genevieve."

"And what was Beck's female doing out in his woods alone?" Kieron leveled the question at him, faking boredom. Inside, Kieron was screaming. *Genevieve*. Her name was Genevieve.

She had been unexpected and the only reason he had failed killing Sarla was because he had lost his fucking mind when he looked into Genevieve's eyes that day by the river. Afterwards, he had dreamt about her for months before his spies reported that Aada, Sarla, and an unknown female were spotted out to dinner in Beck's kingdom. He knew it was dangerous— careless even—but he had immediately gone to see for himself. He had hid in the shadows and watched as the females left the restaurant. Sure enough, it was her. She was even more beautiful than he had remembered.

"Frankly, I don't care." Voss replied, "But the game has changed. Beck will bow before me to get her back. Now I just need to break her."

Rook was practically drooling, Kieron noticed. He could not let Rook get his hands on her. The two of them were the deadliest assassins in the history of Savengard—or any world —and their skill sets also included various forms of torture. Rook's brand tended to lean towards permanent damage or death—he was hot headed and not well practiced at containing his emotions.

Kieron was doing everything in his power to not speak first. This was a game of patience and intelligence—two things Rook lacked.

"You both know the drill. So who wants her?" Voss tossed out the opportunity.

Just as Kieron expected, Rook nearly fell over himself, "I'll break her in no time."

Vossarian nodded at Rook's enthusiasm with a dark smile on his face.

"No. She's mine." Kieron growled. He would not let Rook touch her. He had felt her magic even as the bullets she had shot him with had entered his body and killed him—temporarily, but she had still killed him. "Sarla took you down, she took me down. She is mine."

Kieron noticed the change in Voss, he looked intrigued. Kieron had never demanded to be involved in breaking prisoners or slaves, he had only ever been ordered to—and did it with unmatched expertise—but he had never volunteered. Then again he had not lost a fight in nearly four hundred years either.

"You make a good point. She is yours, Kieron." Voss said with a glint in his eye. Rook started to object, but Voss raised a hand sharply. Rook bit his tongue. Voss continued, "Let's go see if she is awake."

Kieron was going to lose it. He stood just inside the doorway and watched as the two female servants dressed Genevieve—wrapped her up like a fucking present. His cock pulsed and he shifted on his feet to relieve the pressure in his pants.

He had to get her out of here. He had an overwhelming urge to fuck her, yes, but that was not the only reason. He had to get her out of here because she did not belong as a prisoner. The magic he felt emitting from her—she was a queen. And not Beck's queen either.

Those golden brown eyes rimmed in a ring of blue gray steel met his briefly as she was brought to the cage. *Fuck she was already so high, what dose of drugs had Voss given her?* It did not matter. There was nothing Kieron could do about it as he lifted her into the cage and secured her in.

Genevieve had blacked out minutes ago, Kieron noted as he stood against the wall watching the crowd dance and Voss lounge on his throne. At some point Voss would notice too and signal Kieron to take her back to her cell. He would get his chance to at least get her away from the groping hands. He had never cared before, never cared with the hundreds of other females he had done this same game with. Sure he hated it, but he had never *cared*. He had also never met another being with powers that matched his and *that* was what this was about.

He had heard the other assassins and warriors talk about the primal and animalistic pull they got when they had found their match, but of all the females he had fucked he had never felt it himself. Until now. And she was a prisoner in the lethal game Voss was playing. That he was playing.

Holy fuck. She just spat at him. Kieron was lurking outside the door to Genevieve's cell, waiting to see if she would continue to comply or eventually tell Voss to fuck off. Tonight it was the latter. Voss did not take disrespect well, but his response had been surprisingly reserved tonight.

"I do not care if you beat her or fuck her or both. Just break her. Oh and I guess leave her in one piece. I would not want any permanent damage on that pretty body or face of hers." Voss seethed to Kieron as he stalked out of the cell. Kieron could do that and it was exactly why he had demanded that she was his. Except now he would have to do something beyond his wildest nightmare. He took a deep breath. He was her only chance at surviving this and even if she never forgave him, he would do this so she could live. He was going to have to torture his soulmate.

ACKNOWLEDGMENTS

I am incredibly grateful to my husband, Taylor Forbush, for his support and enthusiasm from the moment I shared my book-writing aspirations. His words of encouragement, "Hell yes, why the fuck not!" were the fuel that kept me going. Thank you for enduring endless conversations about the book and showing patience when my mind wandered off into the realm of writing. Your belief in me never wavered, and for that, I am truly thankful.

A special acknowledgment goes to Kari Francisco, without whom this book would not have become what it is today. Kari, thank you for introducing me to new book genres. Thank you for dedicating countless hours to reading, rereading, analyzing, and discussing with me the book's content. Your enthusiasm and encouragement propelled me to dream big and aim high. The entire series is better because of you.

Lastly, a heartfelt thank you to my family and friends. Despite your bewilderment at my unconventional choices, your unwavering encouragement has meant the world to me. Your surprise may be evident, yet you have always been wildly supportive. Thank you for being there.

ABOUT THE AUTHOR

Maggie Forbush

Maggie Forbush, a resident of Montana, finds solace and inspiration amidst the rugged wilderness of her home state. When not immersed in the enchanting landscapes of Montana, she can be found nestled in her cozy home with her family, channeling her passion for creativity into various endeavors. Whether venturing into the untamed beauty of nature or delving into the realms of imagination through writing, Maggie embraces each moment as an opportunity for exploration and self-discovery.

BOOKS IN THIS SERIES

The Seventh King Series

The Seventh King

Crown Of Shadows

Made in United States
Troutdale, OR
06/06/2024

20384606R00268